Temptation

Sandy Loyd

Published by Sandy Loyd
Copyright 2013 Sandy Loyd
Cover design by Kelli Ann Morgan at Inspire Creative Services
Edited by Pam Berehulke at Bulletproof Editing

For more information on the author and her works, please see
www.SandyLoyd.com

This book is also available in print from some online retailers.

DEDICATION

As with most of my books, I want to dedicate this story to my husband. He's taught me so much in the years we've been married. He inspires me to write loving men who provide for their families.

Other Books by Sandy Loyd
Contemporary Romance
The California Series
Winter Interlude – Book One
Promises, Promises – Book Two
James – Book Three

Second Chances Series
Tropical Spice – Book One

Timeless Series
Time Will Tell - Time Travel Romance – Book One
Games – Historical Romance – Book Two
Temptation – Historical Romance – Book Three

Romantic Suspense
D.C. Bad Boys Series
The Sin Factor – Book One

Running Series
Running Out Of Fear – Book One

New Releases
Deadly Misconceptions
A Matter Of Trust

Chapter 1

Late August, 1875

"Hurry, milady."

Lady Penelope Lytton darted for the bed. She yanked a satchel from underneath and hurriedly began filling a bag large enough to hold all she needed, yet light enough to manage on horseback. Heaven above had provided a perfect opportunity to escape and she wasn't about to botch it by dawdling. "How much time to you think we have?"

Mindy didn't answer right away. Instead, her childhood friend stood sentinel at the door and listened. Finally she turned back. "Ferguson figures Gervayse will be gone at least an hour, longer if the rain detains him."

Thank God the earl's butler was an ally, rather than a spy like too many other servants in the earl's employ.

She continued packing as Mindy added, "The sooner we are on the road, the safer we will be. The weather will likely slow us as well."

Penelope slanted a quick glance at the window. "Just our luck it's raining."

Torrential rain pounded outside. Wind rattled the glass panes. A flash of lightning lit the night, casting shadows of grays and blacks over the drenched landscape. Rolling thunder crashed in a roar so loud Penelope flinched at the menacing sound.

"Traveling on rain-rutted roads won't be easy." She stuffed the last item into the bag, pulled it closed, and set it on the bed. Then she bent to fluff the down comforter over the padding she used to make it appear as if a body slept underneath.

No doubt Gervayse would take a peek on his return. The earl's minion watched her every move with the precision of a hawk searching for prey, but he wouldn't actually breach her threshold. Only the earl took such liberties, and soon he would push for more. She'd glimpsed the truth in his cold, dark eyes. Her hands shook in terror at the memory of their last encounter.

Inhaling a steadying breath, Penelope shoved the disgusting images away. "I wish we had more time to come up with a better plan." She would not surrender to fear. Not now.

Mindy secured her own packed bag over the sturdy slicker she wore. "Rain or not, you most likely won't get a better opportunity."

How true, Penelope thought, nodding. The earl would return on the morrow. Her year of mourning was almost over. Either she fled tonight or she might as well submit to her fate.

If only her parents hadn't died in that carriage accident. Loneliness engulfed her and raw pain hit with the same force it always did when she remembered her loss. She wiped away an escaping tear. Crying did little good. It certainly wouldn't change her overall outcome.

Her parents had chosen the Earl of Kentworth. Had they lived, she'd already be sealed in matrimony as Gerald Knightbridge's countess, and with a signed betrothal agreement in his possession, as well as guardianship granting him complete control, the earl considered her and everything she had inherited his property. Flight was the only option. Yet she hadn't expected to flee on a night when no one, not even beasts, dared venture out.

Penelope glanced at the pale blue pelisse hanging in the armoire and wondered how a garment created more for fashion than serviceability would keep her warm. And dry. Well, it was all she had and comfort wasn't her main concern. She donned the finely woven wool cape, then grabbed her bag and positioned the satchel's strap over her shoulder. "I'm ready."

"Ferguson said Geoff is waiting in the stable." Mindy motioned and tiptoed out of the room.

"Thank God for Geoff." Thank God her childhood love hadn't forgotten his long-ago promise. Filled with hope, Penelope stayed right behind Mindy as the two raced down the rear servants' stairs. Once outside, rain pelted them. The whipping wind knocked both women back one step for every two. Penelope was thoroughly soaked by the time they reached Geoffrey Collingswood, the man she meant to marry.

A jagged bolt of lightning rent the air. The flash highlighted Geoff's striking golden features as a crack of thunder hit. "I procured my brother's fastest horses, but we need to be careful of the ruts and debris in the road. Markham will kill me if one goes lame in this mess."

She nodded. The Duke of Wyndham would be more than livid if his expensive horseflesh became useless due to their midnight activities, and it would not matter one whit that Geoff was his youngest brother. Of course, if the duke discovered Geoff's plans of marriage to her, he would quash them in a heartbeat. Penelope abhorred deceit, but the earl's threats loomed. Drew closer with every ticking minute. Her life and escaping a monster depended on lies.

Geoff eyed her cape and shook his head. "You can't wear that. The pelisse shouts money and will cause notice. We need to travel as unobtrusively as possible." He turned to Quincy. "Can she wear your slicker?"

"Aye, m'lord." The earl's head groom nodded. "It's been freshly oiled. It'll keep her dryer 'an the bit o' wool she's got on."

Penelope shook off her sodden cape and traded with Quincy. She shrugged into the oversized garment, rolling the long sleeves several times. The heavy canvas swallowed her small frame—its weight adding to her already overwhelming sense of helplessness. "I have no money to pay him." Her guardian, the earl, controlled every shilling bequeathed to her. She'd inherited her father's lands and money due to an ancient codicil, but she couldn't actually inherit until her twenty-fifth year. Oh, how she hated being under such a vile man's control.

"Don't worry about it." Geoff held out a five-pound note. "That should cover it, along with any inconvenience her disappearance might bring."

"Thank you, m'lord, but yer blunt's not necessary. We love the young miss."

"Take it anyway," Geoff urged, placing the note in his hands before helping first Penelope, then Mindy mount.

Disguised as boys, both women wore trousers and muslin shirts, making riding astride easier.

"You take good care of her, mind you," Quincy said, his expression grim.

Mounting, Geoff nodded. "With my life." He slanted her a brief glance. "Ready?"

"Yes." Penelope clicked her heels into the horse's flank to get the mare moving. Mindy and Geoff followed in single file. When they reached the street, they set off, traveling as fast as they dared. Eventually the three riders galloped across the bridge and headed north out of London.

∞

Parker Davis pushed his mount relentlessly, leaning low and guiding the stallion around any obstacles in the rain-ravaged road. He still had another day, maybe two, if this weather kept up before he made it to his brother's ship docked in the port town of Tynemouth. As a US marshal taking on special assignments for President Grant, he'd finally concluded his latest case. He sent up a silent prayer of thanks that he'd connected with Lucas his first week in London and had had the foresight to send his trunks earlier, along with word he'd join his brother on the Tempest for the return trip home. Otherwise the ship would sail without him.

Parker swallowed his impatience and continued on, allowing the horse to set the pace.

Did it ever stop raining in this godforsaken country? For three days he'd trudged forth, accompanied with nothing but drizzly weather, downpours at times and fine mist at others. During his three months spent in England's capital city, he'd seen very little sunshine.

Around the bend, he yanked on the reins, hard, to avoid a collision with a fallen tree blocking the road. "Damn!" This was all he needed to make his miserable journey more miserable.

If he never saw this dismal part of the world for another million years, it would be too soon, he thought, dismounting to walk the horse into the woods. When he veered around another tree, just as he neared the road on the opposite side of the fallen tree, movement through the dense brush grabbed his attention. He stopped, refocusing on the scene a hundred yards away.

Something dreadful had happened, given all the commotion.

TEMPTATION

Though no one could hear their shouts with the wind howling and the rain drumming, the men's body language radiated tension—tension born of fear, anguish, and enormous mental pain—the kind Parker recognized.

Since he traveled through Northumberland, he had a good idea what caused such emotions. Coal reigned in this part of England and mining was the livelihood of the masses. The closer he got to the crowd, the more the idea solidified, its truth mirrored in their faces.

Spying a lone boy standing under a tree, he nodded. "What's going on?"

"A mine accident," the child yelled, affirming his conclusion. "Ten men are buried."

Parker offered a quick prayer for the poor souls who suffered such a cruel fate, as well as one for those left aboveground to mourn. Though rain-drenched, the two dozen or so working didn't seem to notice the discomfort, most likely more concerned with loved ones trapped beneath the earth. He fully grasped their distress. And their hope. The scene was all too familiar.

Sadly, all too soon, they'd realize the brutal truth. Those buried were in their final graves.

A flash of pain stabbed his heart as the moment his world had crumbled in similar circumstances filled his thoughts. Even after the passage of years, the vivid image of his father rushing toward him, shouting to get out as the rumble grew louder, never dimmed.

In the blink of an eye his life had altered. Despite his loss, he'd been lucky. The earth-swallowing explosion that had killed his brothers and father, while also thrusting the responsibility of his then destitute mother and siblings onto his shoulders at the age of fifteen, had given him the drive to get out of such dangerous work. Spying for the Union Army in America's War between the States had provided the lucrative means to fulfill his new role. Yet, the poor souls in front of him appeared as if they barely eked out a living, and without their own Union Army to provide some other means of survival, they had little choice but to keep eking.

Parker tied his horse to a branch and looked at the person he'd determined to be in charge. Then he introduced himself and shook hands with John Cummings.

Even after discovering the mine had caved in two days ago and hope of finding anyone alive seemed miniscule in his opinion, he rolled up his wet sleeves. "What can I do to help?" His past wouldn't let him continue on his way without at least offering.

Parker spent the next sixteen hours digging with the others, clawing at the mess and uncovering only one dead man for their efforts. Not long after, the search and rescue mission was called off. The sodden ground rendered the task too dangerous. The tunnels had to be shored up before anyone else could venture safely below, and that included rescuers.

"Thank you for yer 'elp." Cummings's shoulders slumped in fatigue. His bearded face was haggard from lack of sleep. "Yer generous donation'll ease some o' their plight."

"I'm sorry I couldn't do more." His heart heavy, Parker prepared to leave the group of townspeople with whom he'd found an instant rapport. No amount of money or digging would bring their loved ones back. And for what? So an English earl and his family could continue stripping the land while exploiting those unfortunate enough to be born without options? A miner's life was an arduous one. No one understood that fact better than him.

"Simply by carin', you've done more 'an you know."

Parker nodded, then mounted and turned his horse east toward Tynemouth. His new comrades had imparted much information in the snippets of gossip he'd caught during his short stay. He held the Earl of Lytherton's heir accountable for the horrendous accident. Though underage and living in London with a guardian, the heir now owned the mine, had reaped the benefits of subjugating humans to such horrors for years and, in turn, had inherited responsibility. No one would convince him otherwise.

Just as his young brothers shouldn't have been doing Henry Sterling's dirty work, of lighting dynamite in tunnels barely big enough for children to squeeze through, these miners shouldn't have been underground. Not in such perilous conditions the rain-soaked earth provided. Of course, either scenario was like a double-edged sword, cutting off a miner's livelihood. If he and his children didn't work, his family didn't eat. Hunger forced too many to take dangerous chances, ending too many times in an identical outcome. Tragedy.

Parker spurred his horse faster, wanting nothing but to make it to his brother's ship, if only to escape this godforsaken country and the soul-eating reminders of his past.

CB

"Nasty weather." Arms bent, Parker placed them against the railing of the *Tempest* and looked out into the wet night. The torrential rain had finally abated, leaving a breezy drizzle in its wake. He leaned forward. For once he welcomed the warm mist hitting his face. "I never thought I'd arrive." No amount of hard riding could extinguish the painful memories of the worst day of his life that his ordeal with the miners had conjured forth.

"Hopefully, the storm'll keep up so the winds'll be strong for our departure in the early morn," his brother replied.

Parker frowned. "You aren't pulling anchor and heading out with the tide?"

"Plans changed. Tide's already coming back in." Lucas Davis puffed on a pipe and leaned his hip against the railing. He eyed Parker and grunted, clearly noting his agitated state, then offered, "I'm waiting on two passengers delayed by the rain."

"Passengers?" His eyebrows shot up. "You've always said they're too much trouble."

"Aye." He grumbled the assent. "Passengers usually are, but these two have paid a hefty price, which makes me bend my own rules. Besides, I'm doing this as a favor for a friend."

Parker sighed, impatience seeping out in his exhale. "I'm just eager to get home—to reach the shores of the United States." He focused on his brother's blue-gray eyes, so like his own. "I hate working in England." A god-awful damp and crowded country, in his opinion. "It's rained continuously since I headed north and London's no better. Always gloomy and foggy." He fastened his gaze back on the water. "So, tell me about our passengers."

"Don't know much, as my friend didn't elaborate. When someone flashes the gold, why ask questions when I care little for the answers? My only requirement is that they don't impede my journey."

Parker grunted. If Lucas could make money on the transaction, he would. "Aren't you even curious? I mean, your ship's a decent size, but it's still close quarters."

Lucas offered a careless shrug. "Two women traveling together won't take up much room. I expect them anytime now. And if they're easy on the eye, the scenery will improve a bit."

"Aside from having money to spend, what else do you know about them? They're not stuffy aristocrats, are they?"

"No." Lucas chuckled. "I know enough to keep my business acquaintances far away from you. I'm trying to strengthen my connections, not sever them." He emptied his dark cherrywood pipe, tapping it upside down on the rail before filling it with fresh tobacco. "Instead of despising the aristocracy as you do, I find it much more expedient to use powerful men for gain and provide what they need because they're willing to pay good coin for it."

He lit his pipe. Once lit, he inhaled and added, blowing smoke out with his words, "But rest assured, I have it on good word the ladies are merely immigrants looking for opportunity in a land that boasts of providing such. I gather they are running from something, but then aren't we all." He shrugged. "My friend vouched for them, which is enough. Hopefully, the winds'll be favorable to ensure a quick journey without trouble. Two women on board are definitely a temptation and why I required a hefty fee." He paused a moment, then added with a sly smile, "In advance."

"Attractive females could be a nice diversion." Parker rubbed his neck and heaved a long sigh. "As long as they're not—"

Abrupt laughter cut off the rest of his sentence. "I know. As long as they're not wealthy, spoiled lasses from the upper classes, you'll be happy. Don't you think you're taking this animosity a little too far?"

"I have no use for simpering pampered women, who believe they're so superior to us unsophisticated underlings with no title or backing of big business to validate us."

"Like anyone would consider you inferior." Lucas puffed on his pipe. The clean scent of tobacco rose, blended with those more foul, masking human sweat and the harbor's stench.

A moment later his gaze lowered to the activity below. Parker's followed. Though angry, dark clouds hampered visibility, the gaslights on deck made it possible to discern several seamen loading cargo during the break in the weather to ready the ship for departure.

Shaking his head, Lucas's attention returned to Parker and he grinned. "How you can be so cynical when you're a force to be reckoned with is beyond me. Not all are cast in the same mold, Parker. You're lumping all men and women of means together and few are like Sterling or Lady Margaret."

Parker's back stiffened. His jaw tightened and his fingers curled into a fist. He refocused on the cargo hold and took deep breaths. While two burly men lifted a huge crate with the aid of a hoist, the fury that always engulfed him at the mere mention of either name faded. There was no one on this earth he hated more than Henry Sterling. And he had little use for women like Lady Margaret.

"I haven't forgotten my roots." He inhaled, holding his anger at bay, and purposefully lowered his voice. "I'll never forget how those who have so much take advantage of those who have nothing. You know damn well Sterling reaped the benefits of human sacrifice with his unsafe mines." The man's greed had killed his father and brothers.

"You need to let go of the past. We're not those unfortunate boys any longer."

"My logical mind knows you're right." He closed his eyes, reliving his loss all over again for the hundredth time in the last thirty-six hours. "You were too young to remember, but the images from our youth are embedded in my soul."

"That was a long time ago. We've changed," Lucas whispered fervently.

"What about all those still there without the skills, the brains, or the drive to get out?" In the aftermath of destruction and through sheer determination, Parker hadn't allowed the earth to swallow another of his loved ones. Yet the mental picture of those coal miners' relatives, who had waited for word of buried loved ones, knowing that with their deaths, their problems were now magnified, compounded his emotional burden. "To interact with so many held hostage due to their situation is bad enough." He unclenched and clenched his fist, then pounded the railing. "But three children died. And for what? So some goddamned aristocrat can live in luxury?"

"You have every reason to be angry. I didn't see Dad, Charlie, or Mikey die, so I can't know how that feels. You provided me with a buffer to the cruelties of the world. One you never had." Lucas grinned, that same mischievous smile he'd always offered when hoping to evade punishment for some childish prank. His wink added to the effect. "I just hate to see the past interfere with the future, is all. Nothing good comes from being angry. 'Tis wasted energy."

Parker forced out a laugh to derail his black thoughts. Though he identified too well with the miners' misery, no good would come of fretting over something he couldn't control. Clapping Lucas on the back, he tendered his own genuine smile. "God knows you don't expend any more energy than necessary to get the job done."

"Of course." Another sly smile slid across Lucas's face. "Why waste what can be better used elsewhere?"

"Or on someone else, you mean, specifically if she's feminine." Parker's spreading grin completely expelled the rest of his melancholy. Lucas could always do that—cause his mood to shift with just a few words and that smile. He admired that happy-go-lucky manner, so different from his own brooding demeanor.

"Well, wooing the ladies does require a fair amount of energy to do the job properly," Lucas teased, nodding.

Parker chuckled, only too glad to have spared his younger brother some of the harsh realities he'd faced at an early age. "I gather you're planning on wooing one of the ladies. Is that why you agreed to provide transport?" He raised an eyebrow, meeting his brother's gaze.

"No." Grin fading, Lucas's head moved slowly from side to side. "I gave my word the two would remain untouched while on my ship." He sucked another puff off his pipe, blowing the smoke out in a sigh. "After the fiasco with Gwendolyn, I try to keep away from any and all marriage traps. I've no desire to see myself leg-shackled. My life's the sea. No woman's worth giving up my life."

"At least she was looking for marriage," Parker retorted, remembering Lucas's near miss with the conniving aristocratic girl. The memory elicited others, namely one, as the image of his own English heiress resurfaced for the second time within minutes—and this after

TEMPTATION

having been evicted from his thoughts for years. He snorted. Lady Margaret wasn't worth remembering.

Lucas must have been thinking the same thing, because he said apologetically, "I tried to warn you about her, only you would have none of it. I had no choice but to lead her into that garden and show you her true nature."

"I just wish I hadn't asked her to marry me." Oh, the follies of youthful stupidity. And lust. He and Lucas had worked out their differences with fists too long ago for him to hold a grudge, not when his brother's actions had caused him to propose, which saved him from more heartache in the end. Seems Parker could forgive her for falling into his brother's arms, but the bitch couldn't forgive him for being born common. She'd scoffed at his proposal. Little had he known she'd already accepted a better one. Lady Margaret had even had the gall to suggest they continue as before after she married her earl. Parker laughed bitterly and added sardonically, "God, I hate the aristocracy. They all deserve each other and they all deserve to live in England."

A flurry of activity on the docks drew their attention.

"Capt'n." One of the shipmates rushed up to Lucas. "Passengers 'ave arrived. Where should I stow their trunks?"

"The guest quarters, Johnson. Though not dignitaries, their coin has earned them the right to full amenities. Their chastity should be safe in there." Recapturing Parker's gaze, he shrugged. "Sorry, old boy. I know you usually use that cabin when you sail, but it's the only one with a lock on it. I had your things stowed in the first mate's cabin. Hillman can bunk with Jacques."

Parker nodded and watched his brother saunter off toward the commotion. It made no difference to him where he bunked as long as he got home. His eyes were then drawn to the gangplank. In the gloomy, wet darkness he barely made out three shapes. An obvious escort delivered two females into the safety of Lucas's men, then turned to leave.

"Thank you, Captain, for your kindness," one of the women said. The gentle, melodious tone drifted and swirled around his ears, stirring something deep inside of Parker. Even her clipped, proper English accent didn't deter him from leaning into the railing to capture more of the soft sound as she gripped Lucas's outstretched hand to step onto the gangplank. "And thank you for allowing us safe passage on board your ship."

Smiling, Parker let the cadence of her words roll over him. A heavy coat partially covered her face and hid her figure beneath its thick folds. Didn't matter that he couldn't fully see her, his imagination worked fine. His brother's gushing reply floated up and his grin widened. Seems Lucas was no more immune to the feminine sound than he. He waited while introductions flew back and forth. Then he headed in their direction.

Chapter 2

"I do not want excuses. I want action," Gerald Knightsbridge, the eighth Earl of Kentworth, bellowed to the Bow Street runner spewing feeble explanations. "How bloody hard can it be to find one naive girl wandering the streets of London? You are not looking hard enough."

How had Gervayse let her slip from his control? Even more puzzling, how had his betrothed, Lady Penelope Lytton, simply vanished without a trace?

"I understand you're upset, m'lord. I'm confident we'll find 'er." Terrance Winters, head of his division of runners, stood wringing his hands while sweat beaded on his forehead.

"You're confident? Incompetent is more like it," Lord Knightsbridge snapped, barely able to keep his features from distorting in rage. Her disappearance worried him and meant another flaw in his plans—plans that had seemed so perfect.

He certainly never thought she would defy her parents' last wishes and run away during his trip north. He was Lady Penelope's guardian and her betrothed.

Eager for their union, the Lyttons died believing they'd made a great match for their daughter with another imposing name in England. Little did the couple know that at the time of their agreement, Gerald's need for funds far outweighed the lady's need for his title. But the Northumberland property his betrothed inherited was what he really coveted. Some of the richest minerals sat beneath those lands and, by damn, he would have them. His fingers curled into a fist. He pounded it into the palm of his other hand, restraining himself. Pummeling the runner would solve nothing, would in fact alienate his only avenue of remedying his dilemma.

"We'll find 'er," Winters said. "I have my best men on it."

"Then your best is surely lacking when a week has passed." Gerald clenched his jaw and bit down on his fury with an iron will. He raked a hand through his hair, squelching another urge to slam a fist into Winters. Blast the Duke of Wyndham for his interference. If not for the man's insistence in allowing the lady her period of mourning, they'd already be wed and he would not be in this mess.

Still, Gerald was positive she could not get far. He would find her and correct the problem once and for all. These nine months had seemed like forever around her. With his special license and a bishop waiting for his word, a wedding would take place the minute he had her under his control again. Mourning her dead parents would no longer be an impediment. He'd simply figure out a way to keep the marriage secret from the duke for the next three months.

If perchance Wyndham found out? He swallowed a smile. The man would never risk a scandal, not if it involved his precious friend's daughter or her reputation. Unable to vent his wrath against the deserving peer of the realm, Gerald's control snapped. He ordered tersely, "You have one week to find her or you'll not see another shilling. If you find her before the week is out, I'll double the agreed-upon amount." He pointed to the door and lowered his voice to a growl. "Now get the bloody hell out before I change my mind and hire someone else."

"Yes, m'lord." Winters bowed and almost ran for the door.

Shaking his head, Gerald watched him flee. Some men were so easily manipulated. Then he flashed a satisfied smile and rubbed his hands together. He'd met his objective for the night. No doubt Winters would find his missing heiress now. In no time, Lady Penelope would be back where she belonged—under his control. After all, she was but a woman, an untouched and helpless aristocrat at that. How hard could it be to find such a morsel wandering the streets of London? She'd stick out like a fully bloomed rose in a garden of dead weeds.

CஐB

"Capt'n, Jenkins needs ta know where y'want th' extra barrels o' fresh water stored," someone from the front of the ship shouted.

"Excuse me, ladies." Captain Davis bowed, then headed in the direction of the voice.

TEMPTATION

"Since the captain is detained, allow me to take his place and show you ladies to your quarters. 'Tis best to get inside and out of this weather before it turns nasty again."

Penny glanced toward the deep voice, spotting a man who closely resembled the captain in both his fair good looks and tall, muscular stature. "Watch your step." He held out his elbows and presented a disarming smile. "The deck is slippery."

His dark reddish-blonde hair plastered to his scalp gave him a dangerous appearance, one she could not dismiss. Not when his considering perusal traveled over her body, stealing her air and sending shivers throughout that she wasn't entirely sure had anything to do with being soaked and windblown. She resisted the urge to pull her cloak tighter, thankful for its protection. His fiery glance made her feel naked, as if he could see underneath the heavy slicker she still wore.

"You must be related to Captain Davis." She prayed her voice held nothing of her musings. Why was she having such thoughts about a stranger anyway? It had to be nerves.

"Yes, ma'am." His grin grew an inch. "I'm Parker Davis, the captain's brother."

Penny inhaled a steadying breath to control her racing heart, willing away the unease of being under this man's scrutiny. Surely she wasn't afraid of him? Her spine stiffened at the thought. Of course she wasn't. "I'm Penny Layton. How very nice to meet you."

Mr. Davis was obviously a charmer—a charmer easily dealt with. After all, she had dealt with worse these past months. Besides, she was free now and finally on her way. She smiled and placed her hand in the crook of his bent arm. "And this is my companion, Melinda Bowers."

Mindy gracefully curtsied and took the other elbow, remaining silent.

"Miss Layton. Miss Bowers." He offered a brief nod and held eye contact a moment too long, also holding on to his grin. "I am honored. One could not ask for more beautiful companions to ease our boredom."

Penny's fingertips rested on his damp sleeve, but even through her glove, she couldn't mistake the muscles. There was strength in his arm when it flexed. Keeping her hand in place, she restrained a sudden urge to flee as he then turned to guide them below, talking about the journey to come along the way.

His movements were smooth and his words flowed too effortlessly from his mouth. Heat emanated from his imposing form whenever he brushed against her in the ship's close quarters. Unavoidable or not, the contact sent a shiver of excitement racing through her. That such contact affected her was unnerving enough, but that his presence should affect her at all was unbearable.

Fighting to ignore the sensations, and him, Penny purposefully looked around at the teakwood interior walls they passed. Unfortunately, ignoring the daunting mass of male superiority striding beside her was next to impossible. Nor would her senses shut down, in fact seemed heightened after catching a whiff of his masculine scent, an earthy one of sweat, horses, and wet leather.

Crewmen's shouts and scuffles from above filled her ears. The warm, humid air condensed. She tasted salt from the moisture now drying on her face when she consciously licked her lips and kept her attention on the beauty of the polished brass fixtures rather than on *him*.

Walking next to Geoff had never caused her pulse to race like this. That's because you haven't had a chance to be alone with him in over five years, she reasoned, tossing out the thought. She exhaled on a deep sigh and continued walking, wishing her love could have joined her on this voyage. Without him, this would be a long, long journey.

CR

"Here we are, ladies." Parker stopped at a cabin door, opened it, and stepped aside to allow the two women to go ahead.

Once inside the gaslit room, Penny Layton shrugged out of her cloak and shook off the water. Parker stood near the door, too stunned to move more than his eyes.

His gaze, traveling from head to toe and back up again, didn't miss any part of the petite blonde angel with a lush figure and flawless skin. Such perfection! Despite her travel-worn clothes and obvious exhaustion, she was the most beautiful woman he'd ever seen.

Her mouth curved into a slight smile, drawing his gaze. He could not look away. My God, they were the fullest lips he'd ever seen—just perfect for kissing. When her tongue skimmed first the top lip then the bottom in a nervous gesture, liquid heat shot straight to his groin.

"I see my brother has taken care of you ladies." Lucas's words interrupted Parker's unwanted musings and yanked his thoughts back to less dangerous territory.

"We dine in an hour. That should give you plenty of time to change out of your wet clothes. The crew stowed your trunks inside." Lucas then snared his focus with eyebrows raised. "You should get out of your wet things too. I'll escort you to your cabin." The command in Lucas's voice left Parker no choice but to follow. "She's under my protection and off limits, Parker," he added, once the door to the ladies' cabin shut. "I never thought I'd have to worry about you."

"What?" Parker asked, throwing out an affronted chest.

Near another cabin door Lucas turned and caught his brother's gaze again, his tone deadly serious. "I've eyes. I saw your expression and while I tend to see what you see, she's not for your pleasure. Are we clear?"

"I don't make it a habit of seducing women," he said, becoming annoyed at his brother's assumption. He moved past Lucas toward the cabin and grabbed the latch.

"Maybe not, but she's a temptation for any man, especially when there's a spark. I didn't miss the sizzle of attraction between you. 'Tis obvious she's untried, so leave her be."

Parker snorted. "You saw all that in such a brief time?"

He opened the portal to enter, but stopped at Lucas's warning. "I'm trying to avoid trouble, so just watch yourself."

Pivoting, he flashed irritation in his nod. "I can't believe you're chastising me when you know me better than that. I'm not one to dally with any woman, innocent or otherwise, and I don't plan on starting now. But to ease your mind, you have my promise."

"Good. We're in agreement." Lucas grinned, clapping him on the back. "I look forward to spending time with you once we're at sea. I'll see you at dinner. Jacques has arranged a feast in your honor." Just before Parker closed the door, he added, "Seems he thinks you hang the moon with all your exploits, so I'm sure he'll be plying you with questions as well as good food."

Away from his brother's prying eyes, Parker leaned against the cool wood, unable to totally excise the blonde vision from his brain, even as a strong urge to ignore his promise possessed him for more than a heartbeat.

What was wrong with him? Honor meant everything to him.

That alone told him how potent this attraction was. He wiped his face to expel all ideas of kissing those soft lips. It took several moments before logic and common sense returned. Not a good sign. He yanked his shirt out of his trousers and turned toward his trunk. Since Lucas's observations held some merit and her warm smile affected him much more than he cared to admit, he'd just steer clear of Miss Penny Layton to avoid any and all temptation.

Chapter 3

As soon as the door closed, Penny hurried to one of the beds and sat, exhaling a breath she hadn't realized she'd been holding. She glanced around at the cramped, though richly furnished cabin. Two narrow beds flanked a small night table. An undersized armoire and a table, just inches from the beds, filled the rest of the space.

Her gaze settled on her friend and traveling companion. "I thought we'd never make it."

"You're safe now, milady. When we stopped outside of Newcastle upon Tyne to collect the trunks my mother packed, everything was quiet." Mindy's entire family had helped Penny escape. One brother had met them on the road to escort them the rest of the way in an enclosed carriage, while the other had roamed the inns close to Lytton Hall for word of the earl.

Geoff, her truelove, had arranged everything, in secret of course, but he couldn't be gone from London long, otherwise he'd raise his brother's suspicions. The Duke of Wyndham was determined to fulfill her parents' last wishes and see her married to the earl.

"You've eluded him." Mindy busied herself with their trunks.

"I'll be glad when we sail. Until then, I won't feel absolutely safe. The earl has tentacles everywhere." So did the duke. Goose bumps rose along her spine. Penny hugged herself, warding off unease and forcing herself to remember she was safe. "I just thank God the earl never knew of my connection to Geoff, or else he'd be on the duke's doorstep harassing the man into action of some sort." She was still afraid Wyndham might catch wind of her escape, and if so, she prayed Geoff could hold him off until it was too late.

"It's hard enough to believe your parents betrothed you to that monster." Mindy began unpacking, hanging up several gowns and placing toiletries on the small bureau. "But to make him your guardian? How could they not know his true nature?"

"Easy. The man is a clever chameleon." Tears welled in Penny's

19

eyes. "My reprieve has been my mourning. I thank my lucky stars for the duke. He gave me that time."

"I'm sorry." Mindy's gaze filled with compassion. "I shouldn't speak so freely when you're still grieving."

"Thanks to Lord Knightsbridge, I've dealt with more than grieving these past nine months." She blinked to clear her blurry eyes and offered a sad smile. "If not for Wyndham, I'd be married to the beast by now and you'd be gone. Then I'd have no one."

"It's in the past. The earl can no longer harm you."

"No." He'd never figure out that his servants helped her. Penny's smile became genuine. Her father had taught her all people deserved respect, especially those who serve. The earl didn't share her view, much to her good fortune. Her kindness had paid off. When Ferguson, his butler, overheard them asking for Geoff's help, he offered his.

"I wish we'd left earlier." Mindy's audible sigh came out in one long breath. "You suffered so much."

Penny closed her eyes, wishing the ugly memories weren't so fresh. "His sick cruelty was suffocating me. I was dying inside little by little under his control. That's when I knew I had to do something." More tears formed. This time Penny didn't stop them from rolling down her cheeks. No one except Mindy knew about those nights and his disgusting attempts to scare her into submission.

Mindy handed her a fresh handkerchief. While taking it, her tears increased. "He's demented. I saw it in his eyes. Promise me you will never tell another living soul what you know? I'd die of shame if anyone else found out."

"You swore me to secrecy. I'd never utter a word."

"As God is my witness, I'll never go back," Penny whispered, pushing out the unwanted thoughts and replacing them with thoughts of how in six months, she'd be living a carefree life again as Geoff's wife. "I'll never submit to that vile man! I'll take my own life first."

Mindy sat and pulled her into an embrace, stroking her hair as she would a child's. Nestled in such comforting arms, Penny gave in to indulgence and let the tears flow, something she hadn't done in almost eight months when the earl had packed her off to London and had held her as a virtual prisoner.

TEMPTATION

"Shush, love," Mindy soothed. "Geoff assured us we'd be safe on board, and the captain and his brother appear to be honorable men. You still have your spirit." Mindy gave her another reassuring squeeze, then unwound her arms and stood. "You're not about to give up and let the earl win with such a good plan. There's no way he'll trace you to America."

"You're right." Penny smiled and wiped her eyes. "He won't destroy my happiness."

"Geoffrey's money will ensure you won't starve or have to work." Returning to her unpacking, she hung up several gowns. "You'll be fine until you meet up with him."

"I owe Geoff my life. Becoming his wife will be an honor." And of course she loved him. She'd always loved Geoffrey, her handsome, golden-haired, blue-eyed champion. He'd never control her. Not like the earl had. Penny rubbed her arms and stared at the door, suddenly remembering her reaction to Mr. Davis. Not even eight months under the thumb of the Earl of Kentworth had prepared her for the way she felt when he'd looked at her but a few minutes ago. Warmth stole up her face at the memory. If his eyes had been teeth they'd have chewed her up, and all she'd done was act like a simpering fool without a single word to set him in his place.

Before her parents' deaths, Penny had lived a sheltered life and had known few men outside of her father and the commoners in the Northumberland village not far from her home. Geoffrey was one those few, yet if she compared him to the captain's brother, he was still more the boy she remembered than the man he'd become. Geoff never drew the air from her lungs like Mr. Davis had with just a stare. Maybe that was a good thing.

"Why couldn't your parents understand how much you and Geoff love each other?"

"You know why." Penny sighed and pushed an escaping strand of hair behind her ear. "They thought him too young and not the right husband for me." She was nearly four years older.

Mindy poured water into a bowl and set the pitcher down. "Come and wash up, milady. The water's still warm and you'll feel better."

She stood. "You have to cease calling me milady," Penny

admonished mildly, moving to the bowl Mindy had indicated. "You can't let it slip that I'm of noble birth. Geoff gained our passage sticking to the truth as much as he could without giving our plans away. We can trust no one, so it's best to act the part and be who we say we are, even in private. Call me Penny. I'm a maid, just like you, traveling to America for opportunity."

"It's so hard to call you Penny when I've known you as milady or Lady Penelope for the last five years and have finally gotten used to the names. My mother would throttle me if she heard me be so familiar. The earl would fire me in a heartbeat."

Melinda Bowers was the Lytton housekeeper's daughter. "Your mom is no longer here to disapprove and neither is the earl." Because of their close ages, Penny's father allowed their friendship, even encouraged them to study together. The three of them, Geoff, Mindy, and Penny were always together until Geoff left for Eton. At that point, Mindy's mother decided she must earn her keep, fearful her daughter had risen above her station too much already. Unfortunately, servitude never suited Mindy, who had a hard time following her mother's edict. "Besides, things are different in America," Penny added.

As a compromise, Mindy had become Penny's personal maid, which really meant her personal friend, not servant, when in private. Once Penny was removed to London into the earl's household, the Duke of Wyndham insisted on her maid joining her for propriety.

"From this moment on, we really are equal. I'm no longer Lady Penelope Lytton, just plain Penny Layton. It sounds much more American." She finished with washing and strode over to Mindy. Spinning around, she asked, "Here, help me undress."

"I'll try to remember, Penny." Mindy undid the buttons. "It's sad you have to leave your beloved home. I've nothing keeping me here and everything waiting for me. You have everything here and nothing waiting."

Mindy was joining her sister in Maryland, a decision made after the earl had told Penny her maid would not be welcome once they were man and wife.

"That's not true." Penny tossed her sodden gown aside, shrugged out of her damp chemise, and donned the dressing gown Mindy had just laid on the bed. "I have much to gain by going to America." Mindy's plans had given Penny the idea of tagging along. "Geoffrey is joining me in six months. By then he'll be twenty-one and receive his inheritance and no longer have to live off his small allowance the duke provides." He'd agreed to wait to marry in California because the earl would never think to trace her there. Neither would the duke.

"San Francisco is reputed to be a rugged place, full of adventure and gold-paved streets." She sighed as thoughts of all she'd read filled her mind's eye. Her father had always encouraged her to use her brain, treating her more as a son than a daughter, going head-to-head with Penny's mother over her behavior and his indulgence. Oh, how she missed him. He'd always allowed her the freedom other young ladies never had, teaching her to shoot and ride, encouraging her streak for adventure. Though she'd already discovered firsthand how some adventures held horrors, others were worth a bit of risk.

"I'll miss home, but by then I'll have Geoff as a husband as well as my own fortune." On her twenty-fifth birthday in seven months, she'd gain her own majority. "The earl will have no more say in anything I do." Her plan *was* perfect. Geoff wasn't like Lord Knightsbridge. He loved her. They'd make a good marriage. He'd never intimidate others with cruelty, nor would he ever try to control her.

Penny moved to sit on the bed and watched Mindy wash her face, vowing to keep to her secret plans. If she stayed in England, she'd have little or no recourse but marriage to a vile man. Even the duke was starting to see Gerald Knightsbridge as a good match, calling her shrewish and unappreciative of all the earl had supposedly done for her during the last eight months. It was why she was now willing to risk all by traveling to a new continent, one that offered not only adventure but more opportunity.

"We should dress for dinner," Mindy said after wringing out the cloth and placing it on a hook. She then padded over to Penny, presenting her back. "Could you?"

Anticipation for the journey ahead spread through her as she stood to undo buttons. Traveling on a ship this size definitely afforded a new adventure.

Thirty minutes later, she and Mindy advanced toward the dining hall via sparsely lit, narrow passageways. The understated, luxurious interior she noted, so different from the earl's garish taste, gave her a sense of security. Though diminutive in comparison, this ship reminded her of her parents' estate. She took a deep breath, and the rest of her inner tensions ebbed in her exhale. The more that time and distance separated her horrendous experiences from the present, the less they bothered her. Mindy's earlier comments resurfaced and Penny's resolve stiffened. The earl simply would not win.

Her smile stayed in place as the two entered the dining room.

Captain Davis stood at the sideboard pouring a glass of what looked to be bourbon. "Ah, I see our table will be graced with elegance tonight." He offered a disarming smile. Impeccably dressed in the latest fashion, he appeared the epitome of an English lord. His jacket and waistcoat were cut to fit broad shoulders, and formfitting britches showcased firm, muscled thighs. "Makes waiting for the next tide change worth the inconvenience."

"We appreciate your patience, Captain. And apologize for the delay," Penny replied softly, while noticing how much more attractive he appeared without rain-soaked hair plastered to his scalp. The roguish smile emanating from this charming man had her own smile reaching her eyes. The captain was simply too handsome for his own good. Her attention then roamed to the table. Her breath stuck in her throat when a steely blue-gray stare caught her gaze and held on tight.

"Captain Davis is right." Mr. Davis stood immediately and pulled out two chairs.

Without breaking eye contact, Penny lifted her head higher. His impolite gawking would not affect her. Holding the connection, she moved gracefully toward the offered chair.

His smile was full of appreciation. "Any delay is worth the delightful company of two lovely ladies, Miss Layton. You're both visions to behold." He paused a beat. "Simply stunning."

She could say the same about him. Dressed much like the captain, the attractive man's admiring perusal didn't falter. A flush of warmth crept up her face. She had to look away from those intense eyes and squelched the urge to cover her bosom, as well as the desire to look down to make sure she wasn't naked. Not wanting to appear a simpering fool, she schooled her emotions to show nothing of her inner turmoil. She cleared her throat and said with more serenity than she possessed, "You are both proficient flatterers. I'll give you that."

"You wound us, kind lady. 'Tisn't flattery. 'Tis the truth," Lucas replied, setting Parker's drink in front of him. His nod indicated the other gentleman, who'd also stood when they entered the room. "Miss Layton, Miss Bowers. May I present my first officer, Mr. Todd Hillman."

Hillman nodded. "'Tis a pleasure."

Thankful for the diversion, Penny's gaze moved to the first officer.

"Would either of you like a drink before dinner? Besides bourbon, I have sherry and red wine," Lucas offered, walking back to the sideboard.

Penny shifted her attention to the captain and caught *him* staring at her. Inhaling a deep breath, she lowered her eyes, noting the beautifully set table, including silver place settings, fine china, and linen napkins placed under every fork. She focused on the lit candles in sterling holders, trying to clear her mind of the confusing thoughts the captain's brother evoked. It took a moment before she could answer the question about drinks, and then, her voice was just above a whisper. "I'd love a glass of sherry, please."

"I'd love one too," Mindy said. Unaware of the undertones around her, she continued with, "We're so happy you waited for us, Captain Davis, but sorry you had to delay your trip." The words spilled from her lips faster than melting snow runs to the sea in spring. "The rain hindered our journey here. I hope our delay won't cause problems."

Lucas chuckled and poured two glasses of sherry. "'Tis not often we're allowed the luxury of two beautiful ladies on our voyages. So please, no more talk of problems or inconveniences." He placed their drinks in front of them, retrieved his own, and then sat at the head of the table. "We'll set sail soon enough."

Penny was saved from further discomfort when a commotion from the galley caught everyone's attention. A handsome man with dark European features bustled out bearing a tray laden with food he immediately began serving. Succulent aromas of beef, gravy, potatoes, onions, and spices wafted up and filled the room.

After a dish was placed in front of Lucas, he chuckled. "Jacques, you've outdone yourself. Parker should sail with me more often. Meals never look this good when it's just the crew."

Jacques snorted. "Monsieur Parker is better looking than you."

Penny swallowed a laugh. Almost identical, anyone comparing the two brothers would find it a draw as to who was more attractive.

"You're also not so pretty as the two mademoiselles," he added with his thick French accent.

"I can always throw you overboard for such insubordination once we sail, you know," the captain said.

"*Non.* I have no fear of your threats." Jacques grinned, displaying perfectly straight teeth. He looked at the two women and winked conspiratorially. "The man likes my cooking too much."

Lucas laughed along with everyone else. "Come join us when you're done dishing everything out. You work too hard."

"Aye, aye, *mon capitaine.*" Jacques snapped to attention and said while saluting, "I never disobey the orders, especially when I can sit with the two ladies."

As his chef headed for the galley, Lucas shook his head. "I know I shouldn't encourage him. He already thinks too highly of his culinary skills. He also thinks I can't live without them."

"That is because it is true," Jacques said on his way back into the room, obviously overhearing the comment. "I know my worth, so your insults, um…how do you say?…hold no weight."

"See what I mean?" Lucas picked up his napkin and placed it on his lap.

Jacques stood smiling, then his glance roamed around the table. When no one said a word after eating for several minutes, Jacques's perturbed voice burst forth. "Well?"

"It's palatable. What is it?" Lucas asked in a goading tone.

A flurry of French followed in his wake on his way out of the room.

Lucas laughed. "Man can cook, but he can't take a joke."

Jacques returned through the doorway, still frowning and speaking sharply in rapid-fire French.

"Jacques, sit. Enjoy your fine cuisine." Lucas motioned with his fork at an empty chair. "It's delicious as always. I was merely jesting."

"Some things should not be joked about. Remember," he said as he wagged a finger, "I can always put something in the food to give you the stomach ache."

"You won't," Lucas countered confidently, going back to his meal.

"You insult me and it will be considered," Jacques threatened with head held high and haughty disdain crossing his face.

"No, Jacques, I know you." Grinning, Lucas took a sip of bourbon, then said more seriously, "You'd never ruin your creations. I promise not to jest any more about your cooking. Now, go and get a plate for yourself and sit. I'm sure Parker's dying to enlighten you with his latest exploits, just as I'm sure you're dying to hear about them."

Jacques's frown disappeared. "But only because I like the company of mademoiselles who are so *très jolies*." He left and returned with a full plate of food minutes later.

☙

"So, Parker, how come you to England?" Jacques asked, yanking Parker out of his musings.

"Work." He glanced at the chef and added, "My latest case involved a murdered American dignitary who'd been stationed in London." Parker sighed. "Took me months of painstaking work to unravel the mystery."

"Really? How interesting," Mindy said. "Was he killed by a spy?"

"Nothing quite so treasonous." Parker chuckled, noting her wide-eyed stare. "His jealous lover killed him in a fit of anger over an infidelity and then left the city. Once I figure that out, it was an open-and-shut case, easily solved."

Having already divulged too much information for the ladies' delicate ears, Parker wasn't about to elaborate on the fact that the jealous lover with the penchant for killing was another male, when President Grant preferred to keep the particulars under wraps to avoid a scandal for America. Instead, he regaled them with a few details of the chase, making the story interesting without revealing too much. "Usually most crimes can be attributed to basic motives like greed, jealousy, or anger."

"Sounds so exciting," Mindy said, sighing. "Tell us more."

"There were two cases last year where my partner almost lost his life because he didn't wait for my backup." He then told two stories of his previous partner's impatience to go in without him—one ending in a bullet wound from a gunfight and the other ending in a near fiery death.

"He is still alive?" Jacques asked.

"He's alive and well. Got married and took a desk job, so I came over to England without a partner this trip," Parker replied, bringing Jacques up-to-date on his ex-partner.

"Your work sounds treacherous. I can't believe we're sitting at the same table with someone such as you." Mindy glanced at Penny. "Remember when we used to play highwayman and magistrate with Geoff? Our games seemed so perilous because you always played such a terrifying criminal." Mindy grinned. "Penny has a cunning mind, and her imagination usually led us into trouble. She always went beyond the pale. Still, we thought it a great game, but I never realized how dangerous real criminals could be."

Mindy's words caught Lucas's attention and his eyebrows rose. "So you were playmates with Geoff? What's your connection to him?"

Penny put her hand on Mindy's under the table and squeezed, giving her friend a warning shake of her head.

Parker caught both signals.

"We were both employed as maids in his estate in Northumberland until just recently," Penny said. "When we were little, before Geoff went to Eton, we were great friends."

His gaze stayed on Penny for several minutes. Neither woman looked like any maid he'd seen in London. "Who's Geoff?" he finally asked.

"No need for your hackles to go up, Parker. He's the friend I was doing the favor for, the younger brother of one of my biggest clients," Lucas admitted. "The Duke of Wyndham is one of the dreaded aristocracy you hate, hence I didn't feel the need to expound earlier. Geoff procured their passage, and he was quite explicit about their treatment. I just couldn't figure out why." He turned to the ladies and added with a roguish smile, "At first I figured he was buying you off after a brief liaison to be rid of you, as sometimes happens. 'Twas apparent from the moment I saw both of you that wasn't the case— not with such obvious ladies. I admit I was a bit puzzled. Now that I know you were childhood friends, I fully understand his motives. Geoff has a big heart."

"Yes, he does. Geoff is very generous." Penny lifted her chin. "But it was only a loan. One I have every intention of repaying."

"Oh?" Parker chuckled. "Are you aware of the amount the captain charges for such a voyage?" On a maid's meager salary, she'd have to work ten years to accumulate so much.

"I'm aware it was a daunting amount. Rest assured it will be repaid," Penny stated through clenched teeth.

Her fervency, along with her snooty English accent, intrigued Parker. He'd secretly watched her during their meal. Besides being easy to look at, she incited his curiosity. Intuition told him something about her story didn't ring true. Oh no. This impassioned, enticing woman was no simple household maid. He'd give his right arm if this proved to be the case. Though plain in design, the cut and quality of her gown told him she had money. The fact that she ran wild through the countryside with a duke's brother and another playmate meant she probably wasn't of noble birth. The nobility he'd come into contact with trained their daughters from the nursery to be simpering fools, not hoydens intent on such youthful activities. Yet she'd come from wealth. Her manners and bearing were too polished to let him believe otherwise.

"No need to reassure us," Lucas said. "Parker's suspicious of everyone. It comes from having to deal with the worst in society. Plus, he's always had a hard time trusting people, especially those with wealth and power."

For long seconds Parker's narrowed gaze remained on Penny, causing her to blush again. Oh yes! The lady was hiding something. Of that he was sure.

"So tell us, what takes such lovely women off in search of opportunity in America?" Lucas's words broke into his thoughts.

His gaze returned to his brother before landing once again on Miss

Layton.

"Why all the questions?" Penny asked, chewing on her bottom lip apprehensively.

"You've piqued our interest, is all. Geoffrey wouldn't elaborate, yet was intent on your safety. And since he did place you in my care, I need to make sure I'm not throwing you to the wolves."

Penny's soft laughter filled the air. "Your concern is unfounded," she countered. "You have no need to worry about us. We'll manage quite well."

"I disagree." Lucas presented an engaging smile. "The world is a harsh place, even in America. I'd be remiss in my duty if I didn't make sure two lovely ladies who are under my protection weren't taken care of."

Mindy looked to Penny for direction. She nodded.

"Geoff didn't pay my way. My mother did with her life savings. Like Penny, I intend to pay back every shilling," Mindy said, obeying the silent communication, turning the attention away from Penny, something Parker suspected had been her main intention.

"I'm meeting my sister in Baltimore." As Mindy prattled on, Parker studied Penny unobtrusively. "She's been there for two years, since marrying a gentleman farmer. Mary's been begging me to come, telling me of the opportunities. Of course, Mama was heartsick to let me go, but she's always said I've risen above my station in life too much already to stay in England. Since my sister did so well, she says I now have the chance at a better life. That's all she wants for her daughters."

"Are you going to Baltimore too, Miss Layton?" Parker asked, his focus now fully resting on her as he lifted an eyebrow in question. His penetrating gaze earned another blush and she appeared tongue-tied and flustered. Both reactions evoked a sudden lurch of awareness, and considering his promise to Lucas, along with her connection to this Geoff, he had no intention of acting on it. But that didn't mean he'd leave her be either. No, there was definitely more to the young miss than met the eye and he meant to unravel exactly what that entailed.

"She's going to California," Mindy exclaimed, jumping back in as if trying to help.

TEMPTATION

"California?" The word hung in the air and a skeptical mien replaced Parker's questioning one. Even Lucas glanced up, his gaze wide and full of doubt.

"Yes. California. Why is that so hard to believe?" Penny replied, finally finding her voice.

"That's about as far from Northumberland as you can get." Parker eyed her thoughtfully, his expression challenging, and waited.

"For your information, and despite the fact that this is no business of yours, I'm meeting my fiancé there. We're to be married as soon as I join him," Penny shot back. "So you have no need to worry."

"Ah! A runaway heiress. Now it makes sense and I finally understand," Parker said, grinning openly, unable to hide his amusement.

"You understand nothing," Penny hissed. A volcanic eruption came to mind as her face turned a darker red and her eyes snapped fire. "If I were a man, I'd run from no one."

Which solidified Parker's belief. She was running from someone. Maybe her father had sold her to the highest bidder. The English were a mite funny about their titles. Those who held them usually needed money, and those who had money usually didn't have titles, but wanted them. Bartering with sons and daughters was one way of solving both problems.

He wondered about Geoff's role. Why had he allowed a woman such as her to travel alone? To California of all places? Definitely a mystery. He smiled, watching her expression harden, becoming as challenging as his had been. He couldn't help goading, "So this Geoff just let you go off by yourself, halfway across the world?"

"Geoff would never try to stop me." Her gaze pierced his, one that said she meant every word. "I chose my destiny and fully intend to follow it." She pounded the table with so much force, the silverware bounced. As if sensing she'd gone a little overboard, judging by the stunned reactions of those around her, she inhaled a deep breath. It took a moment, but once she achieved control, she smiled sweetly. "As thoughtful as your concern is, neither of us need it. We both have plans and we mean to follow them."

"I, for one, love the independent women who know their own

minds. They are so, um, how you say? Refreshing? *Oui*, that is it, refreshing, eh, *mon capitaine?*"

"I totally agree." Lucas nodded, chuckling. "Refreshing. Like a new voyage, you never know what to expect." Turning to the ladies, he added, "We'll be pulling anchor in the middle of the night, so don't be alarmed if you feel movement."

Parker's focus remained on Penny, sensing that his scrutiny somehow irritated her.

"How long will we be at sea?" she asked the captain, ignoring him, appearing quite content with his brother's and the chef's timely diversion to move the conversation away from her plans.

"Several weeks, depending on the weather. Hopefully we won't run into any tropical storms. This is a fairly modern ship and I've a steam engine on board, which helps when the winds are light."

Hillman, who'd been quiet throughout most of the meal, chimed in. "You're lucky to be on board this ship. The captain has several others that haven't been modified and are much slower."

"Yes, this ship is definitely my fastest, which is why I'm on it." Lucas stood, picking up his empty glass. He walked to the sideboard. "Would anyone care for another drink before Jacques serves dessert?"

"It's time I took my leave." Hillman scooted back his chair and stood. "I have first watch and I need a clear head." He turned and bowed. "Ladies, it's been a pleasure. If there is anything I can do to make your voyage more comfortable, please don't hesitate to ask."

Lucas waved him off amid the ladies' good-byes, then glanced at his brother. "How 'bout you, Parker? Need a refill?"

Parker stood and sauntered to the sideboard. "I'm weary to the bone. It's been a long forty-eight hours. I think I'll pass on dessert and take a drink to my cabin." Turning back to the chef, he smiled ruefully. "Sorry, Jacques. I mean no disrespect."

Jacques also stood, shaking his head. "No need for excuses, *mon ami*. For tomorrow, I promise a tantalizing breakfast, one the taste buds will appreciate."

"Ah, something to look forward to," Parker answered, chuckling. "Knowing I'll awaken to a feast, I'll be asleep before my head hits the pillow. I'm also looking forward to waking up and being closer to home, far away from English soil."

Lucas poured Parker a liberal drink and handed it to him while Jacques replied, before heading toward the galley, "*Oui*, Parker. I'm not crazy about the English soil either."

Parker glanced at the ladies and nodded. "Miss Layton, Miss Bowers. It's been a pleasure."

☉

Lucas held up a bottle of sherry, eyebrows raised high. "Ladies? More sherry?"

With her attention on Parker's departing back, Miss Layton nodded. "I'd like another glass."

"So will I," Miss Bowers said.

Once they had their drinks, Jacques served dessert. Not fifteen minutes later, Miss Layton rose with praise for the meal gushing from her lips. "It's been a long day and I'm also tired," she added. The moment she got up, Miss Bowers followed.

As the two fled, Lucas grinned at his French chef, raising a brow. "Well, 'tis just you and me again. Care for a game of poker?"

"*Non*," Jacques said. "You cheat."

"I do not," Lucas denied, not at all put off with his claim. His tumultuous nature never ceased to amuse him. Despite his small stature, Jacques Moreau was a tempestuous man who loved the ladies. He was also one of the few men on board with which he shared such a familiarity.

The two had been together too many years now for Jacques to worry about curbing his tongue. The fact that he knew his way around a ship's galley made him indispensable because Lucas liked the finer things in life, enjoying not only good food while sailing, but good spirits as well. Jacques's connections with French wineries provided his chef with even more job security.

"I'm just a better bluffer than you and that makes you mad."

"*Oui*, but I prefer to think of it as cheating, not bluffing. It is much easier on my, how you say, ego? *N'est-ce pas?*"

"All right, if not poker, how 'bout chess? You seem to beat me at that more than I beat you."

"Oui, I could be persuaded to play chess. You cannot cheat at chess."

Chuckling, he stood to get the chessboard and pieces. "Good. I'm too energized to relax and turn in early."

"We have an interesting journey this voyage, eh, *mon capitaine?*" Jacques said after several minutes of play.

Lucas puffed on his pipe without answering for several minutes, keeping his attention on the board while deciding his next move. Once his hand left the chess piece, he stretched his legs out in front of him. Finally he nodded. "Very interesting. Two ladies on board always make for an interesting journey."

"I was talking about the look in Parker's eyes when he spies the pretty lady," Jacques replied, making his move.

"Yes, I noticed his interest earlier." He broke off, concentrating on the board again. "You're not making this easy, are you?"

Jacques grinned, obviously pleased with stumping his captain. "If it was easy, I would not wish to play."

Grinning back, Lucas slid his bishop into place. Then he said nonchalantly, "I've already warned him away, but it may not be enough."

"Parker, he is honorable? The mademoiselles seem so naive. I don't see the problem."

"Normally I'd agree, but those two together seem combustible." Lucas sighed, watching Jacques take his turn. He spent another long moment in thought before advancing his rook. "I want to avoid problems with Markham Collingswood. Wouldn't do for his brother's charge to be seduced under my watch. In close quarters, emotions have a way of veering out of hand."

"I will focus on the pretty mademoiselle and keep her out of the way. That is an easy task."

Lucas laughed. "You do that, Jacques. And I'll work on keeping Parker occupied. Maybe between the two of us we can avert trouble."

Chapter 4

Parker strode onto the higher deck. Lucas stood at the helm as he advanced to the railing where he focused on the wonderful sight of blue on all sides. The brisk wind whipped his reddish-blond hair about and felt invigorating on his face. Waves hit the bow. The sound, along with the gentle rocking motion of the ship slicing through water, filled him with a calming sense of peace.

"You're up early."

Parker glanced up to see Lucas eyeing him speculatively. He nodded. "I love the sunrise, especially after storms have passed."

"Aye. My sentiments exactly. 'Tis a beautiful morning. After a cleansing rain, sunrise does seem to be more vivid, the air more clear."

"It's been too long since I've seen one off the water." Parker's gaze returned to the seas.

"If I didn't sail, I'd have a home such as yours above the bluffs of the Chesapeake."

"I spend far too long away from that home."

Lucas gave a disbelieving grunt.

"You doubt my claim?"

"Aye." Lucas chuckled. "I know you too well."

When Parker started to disagree, he put up a hand. "You're a nomad like me, Parker. You've a beautiful home that you let our mother run and you're never there. Face it. Neither of us is happy unless we're off finding adventure."

"Perhaps you're right." Parker sighed and rubbed the back of his neck. "Lately I feel as if I need home." Since boarding, he hadn't been able to dismiss thoughts of those poor townsfolk in such dire need after the mine cave-in. He felt almost guilty for surviving and thriving after a similar fate when so many others had nothing. In less than twenty-four hours, he'd begun to crave more purpose. To do something to help the downtrodden and better their lot in life, but he had no idea of how to go about it, or what he could do to make a real difference.

"Have you ever thought about settling down and having a family?"

He laughed. "About as often as you do, I'm sure. After Lady Margaret, I've sworn off marriage. It isn't in my future any more than yours."

"I'm not the one wishing for home," his brother said, grinning back.

"That's because you have no home to wish for."

"I'm always home on the sea." Lucas's grin died and he silently eyed him. When he didn't say anything further, Parker's eyebrows rose, as if to say "What?" In answer, he said, "I noticed your reaction to the lovely Miss Layton during dinner. Has me worried."

"You've already warned me off, so why would you worry?"

"I don't know. You tell me."

Parker placed his hand over his heart, adding an innocent air to his manner. "You wound me with your lack of faith."

Lucas's expression didn't change as he held Parker's gaze, causing him to squirm a bit.

"I need no conscience, Lucas," he finally said with a self-deprecating laugh. "I'll not deny my attraction." His gaze roamed over the water. "But I'm not some green boy without control who can't hold the lure at bay. I'll keep my needs in check. You have my word."

"Good. Then you agree it's best to avoid contact as much as possible."

"Avoidance might be a little difficult, given such close quarters. I refuse to hole up in my cabin because you chose to take on passengers."

"When you put it like that, it does sound unreasonable. Just don't be alone with her. Use either Jacques or me as a buffer."

"I don't believe this." Parker's amused laughter carried in the steady breeze. "I'm a grown man, Lucas. I have no need of chaperones."

"Why do you think mothers are so intent on them? They know more than their daughters."

"Is my word not enough?"

TEMPTATION

Lucas heaved a heavy sigh. "I mean no insult."

"Then why do I feel insulted?" Parker's chin inched higher. He couldn't expel the indignation from his voice. "Have a little faith in my honor."

"I do have faith, but I have a feeling there's more to this than meets the eye."

"You'd take me to task for a simple attraction?" Now his tone was curious.

"You didn't watch the two of you together last night. The best way to describe the situation is an explosion about to happen. I intend to keep the fuse from being lit is all."

"You're worrying over nothing." Dismissing his brother's concerns with the wave of his hand, Parker scoffed, "You put too much meaning into a mere attraction, one easily kept in check. She's simply a female, and though lovely, she's nothing I can't handle."

"That puts my mind at ease." Lucas's expression belied his comment.

Parker chuckled. "Why all this concern over a passenger?"

"Geoffrey Collingswood placed the two women into my care. His brother is one of my biggest clients and wields power in shipping. I've spent years building a good relationship with the duke and I have no intention of insulting him by not taking care of his brother's charge."

"Now you see why I dislike men of power. They use it to make others' lives uncomfortable."

"In this instance you are wrong."

"I doubt that." Parker shook his head. Lucas was too trusting and didn't understand about such men as he'd dealt with for years. "They're all users. Men like Sterling, men without honor."

"Markham Collingswood is an honorable man, which is exactly the distinction that makes me want to please him."

"I've yet to meet an honorable man of wealth," Parker exclaimed sardonically.

"You're wealthy," Lucas shot back, his back going ramrod. "By your own admission, are you telling me you aren't honorable—that I can't trust your promise?" He reached for his pipe.

Parker's lips curled into a snarl. "No, you twist my meaning."

"Men should be judged by their actions, not their titles or wealth, or for that matter, their lack of them." He lit his pipe. "Which is how I judge Markham." He blew the words out in a puff. "Although an aristocrat with means, he's never treated me with anything other than respect and dignity. I enjoy our working relationship and have no intention of letting anything destroy it."

"You think something happening between Miss Layton and myself would cause a rift?"

"Don't you? Tell me you wouldn't feel put out with someone who would seduce Catherine?"

Parker raked a hand through his hair and sighed. "Point taken." He'd kill anyone who took advantage of his baby sister. Despite the fact she was no longer a "baby," but a woman reaching her twenty-fourth year, both he and Lucas were still protective of her. A sheepish grin spread across his face. "I'll steer clear of the lady while on this ship. I give you my word."

"I'm counting on it."

"So when's breakfast?" Parker asked, changing the subject. "I'm starved."

Lucas grunted. "Jacques is below. Go down and ask him."

"You're not coming?" He pivoted, searching his brother's face.

"Not yet. Hillman doesn't relieve me for another hour, but I'm ready for a cup of coffee."

Parker left to find Jacques, who was busy cooking when he poked his head in the galley.

A ready smile lit the chef's face. "*Bonjour*, Parker. Your breakfast is almost ready. Go! Sit! I bring it to you."

"Is coffee ready? I'd like a cup. Also, I'll take one to Lucas."

Jacques pulled out two tin mugs, nodding to a pot on the stove. "*Merci*. Tell Lucas I did not forget him, I just got a little behind. Twenty men all hungry at the same time makes me late."

"If it tastes as good as it smells, the wait will be worth it." Parker poured two cups and then headed back out. After delivering the coffee to Lucas, he entered the officers' dining room.

Movement at the table caught his attention. He stopped short and then grinned. The sight of the prim and proper Miss Layton eating her breakfast like a lady to the manor born evoked more than an urge to smile. The petite blonde, dressed in a blue and green muslin gown, had the appearance of a wild, uncultivated garden on a summer's day, not a complete contradiction to the hoyden so vehemently decrying her intentions last night. Yet this lovely creature was like a breath of fresh spring air and watching her thus, a sliver of attraction slid into his consciousness.

Damn if the little minx didn't unsettle him. He stood silently eyeing her unobserved for a moment, trying to decipher why such lustful thoughts had run amuck in his brain ever since he'd first spotted her. Pushing the thoughts aside, he strode into the room. "Good morning. You're up early."

Startled from her daydreams, Penny glanced up. "Good morning."

"I trust you slept well?"

"I slept wonderfully well." She smiled brightly. "Thank you."

"So I see." Both her melodious voice and engaging, shy smile grabbed at his insides, twisted his gut, and sent another zing of heat through his blood. Taking a deep breath, he willfully banished the need she so easily elicited and walked steadfastly toward her. He pulled out a chair and sat across from her, bound and determined not to let this bit of fluff get under his skin. "You look well rested."

"You're too kind. And you?" When his eyebrows shot up in question, she bestowed on him another beautiful smile. "Did you sleep well?"

"Oh, er yes—" He cleared his throat. "Very well." The soft, accented words, along with her animated smile tugged harder on his willpower. Unable to stop himself from responding to both, he added, grinning like a fool, "Sailing does appear to agree with you."

"Yes, it does." She nodded.

"Ah, a seasoned sailor. How refreshing. Most young ladies hate being out on the water." Another jolt of lust hit him as her grin turned impish, almost playful, right before his eyes.

"Not me. I love sailing. So far, this trip has been an adventure."

Parker had purposely looked away, but he couldn't keep his gaze from returning to her face. Not after that statement. "So, you've an adventurous nature?" The question just spilled out, as if his mouth had a will of its own.

"Of course." Penny chuckled, clearly enjoying the exchange, her manner becoming more mischievous. "Weren't you listening last night?"

"Yes, but then you were talking about childhood games, not adult adventures," Parker teased, lacking the desire to stop the conversation from leading into more dangerous territory.

"My adventures do tend to get me into trouble, especially lately."

"Do they?"

She nodded, not seeming to realize the sexual implications her words wielded. "I've always loved adventure. It's why I'm traveling to America. The fact that I'm older hasn't changed what I love."

"I see. So now you love adult adventures?" His eyebrows rose as he awaited her reply.

Suddenly her confidence disappeared. With eyes narrowed and lips pursed, she studied him. Her wary expression amused him. She'd obviously caught the seductive quality in his voice and somehow understood she now broached uncharted territory.

"Of course," Penny said with renewed certainty a moment later, surprising him. "This entire voyage is an adventure I mean to savor." Her chin edged a notch higher. "You doubt me?"

"No." Parker sucked in a gulp of air, impressed she hadn't backed away from the challenge he'd thrown out, in fact threw out one of her own. He coughed and hastily wiped the incredulous expression off his face. The enticing lady naively spouting off about adult adventures was intoxicating enough, but when he spied the daring gleam in her eyes accompanied with a smile that had suddenly become too dangerous, he almost spilled his coffee.

"Not when they're spoken with such fervency," he said, backing away from temptation. He shook his head to extricate other reckless thoughts that wouldn't budge. Maybe his brother's idea of providing a buffer wasn't such a bad one. Retreating further, he asked, "So, where is your lovely companion this morning?"

"Mindy's not so adventuresome. She's suffering from a bout of *mal de mer*."

"She's not coming to breakfast?"

"Oh, you needn't worry. Once she finds her sea legs, she won't hate sailing as much."

"Too bad she won't be joining us." Parker sighed. Would his mind ever shut off? Looking at Miss Layton now, his most prominent thought wasn't about poor Miss Bowers, but about how quickly he could wipe that elfin smile off her face with kisses.

He closed his eyes, praying for restraint. He hadn't been attracted to a female in a long while. Had never felt an attraction this strong after such a short time, and here he sat across from the one person he now wanted and couldn't have. He stifled a laugh. What irony!

Jacques burst into the room just then carrying two hefty plates of food. He placed one in front of Parker and took the other to the empty spot next to Penny and sat.

"Busy morning. Now I eat." He picked up his fork. After a few minutes, he stopped eating. "Is something wrong?"

"Hmmm?" Parker met his questioning gaze.

Jacques pointed to his food with his fork. "Eat. If you do not, I will be insulted."

"Don't want that. I love your cooking and would never jest about it like Lucas does."

"That is precisely why I will feel insulted."

"Sorry," he said. "I was lost in thought."

"Ah! Thinking about the pretty lady." Turning to Penny, he presented a dazzling smile. "I shall eat at the table every morning if I have such *charmante* company."

Penny's blush slid up her face, clearly not immune to the charming man. Then she flashed a warm smile and replied in fluent French, "And I could get used to such charming company."

"*Vous parlez français?*" Jacques's delight came out in every word.

"Oui, monsieur."

The two then carried on a lively conversation in French, excluding Parker, even though he spoke the language well enough to catch on. At first, he was relieved. But after watching the beguiling minx so obviously enjoying Jacques's flirting, he swallowed annoyance with a big gulp of coffee. Did they have to appear so wrapped up in each other? For the rest of the meal, he surreptitiously kept his attention on the two, silently fuming while tamping down the desire to smash a fist into Jacques's face. And because too many of the same unwanted ideas ran amuck in his brain, he quickly finished his meal.

"If you will excuse me," he said, rising. "I think I'll go and keep Lucas company."

"You aren't leaving?" Her question had a disappointed note to it.

"I'm surprised you even noticed," he said more abruptly than he'd meant.

Jacques chuckled. "*Est-il jaloux*? Ah, he is jealous. Because you find me so *charmant*."

Parker snorted. "'Tis obvious she has no discriminating taste if she finds you charming."

☃

"Mademoiselle?" Jacques asked, pulling Penny's attention from Mr. Davis's swift departure.

"Sorry," she murmured. "He seemed annoyed."

"Bah! Do not worry about Parker. It is true. He is jealous, and I am quite charming."

The Frenchman was teasing her. Penny smiled and sighed. This trip was turning into something she hadn't expected. A grand adventure. The captain's fascinating brother was the catalyst. He intrigued her, especially now, after this breakfast. A look that had accompanied the man's quick grin in the brief moment just after he'd sat down flashed inside her mind. She'd detected a moment of uncertainty in his arresting blue-gray eyes. That small glimpse of doubt was enough to make her feel comfortable in his presence. She had no reason to believe she couldn't deal easily enough with Mr. Davis, despite her inexperience with such dashing men. After all, she'd been dealing with Gerald Knightsbridge's unwanted attention for the last eight months.

She shuddered, remembering that last night, before the earl had been called away, noting a definite distinction. Lord Knightsbridge scared her, was always finding ways to caress her, and such attention never failed to make her skin crawl. There was nothing scary in Mr. Davis, or his attention. In fact, quite the opposite. At dinner, and then again this morning, his attentions stirred a heat she'd never before encountered. No, the only frightening element in his fiery gaze was her reaction, making her feel anything but afraid. Truth be told, she felt more alive around him, tingly all over, giddy even, and she had every intention of enjoying these new sensations.

It had been much too long since she'd actually felt anything other than fear. In six months she'd be a married woman. Why not flirt and enjoy her freedom while she waited for Geoff? Though Mr. Davis was too handsome for words, nothing would come from a little flirting. He wasn't her beloved Geoff, and she was no simpering fool. She could handle him. In the last year she'd discovered she could handle just about anything.

❀

Jacques's mocking laughter followed Parker as he made his way to the wheelhouse on the top deck. The sound didn't ease his frame of mind. If anything, it added fuel to his ire.

"What cat scratched your back?" Lucas asked, eyeing him thoughtfully.

"Instead of warning me off, you should've saved your warning for Jacques," Parker snapped.

"He'll behave."

"Oh? You warn me but not him?" His mouth tightened.

"If it makes you happy, I'll warn him off too." Lucas puffed on his pipe as his gaze returned to the water. "But like I said, there's no need."

"No need?" He rolled his eyes and snorted. "He's down below flirting outrageously with a naive girl. He'll have her eating out of his hand in no time."

Lucas chuckled and lifted a brow. "What's the matter, Parker? Jealous? If I didn't know better, I'd say the woman has you twisted up inside and my warning was justified."

"That's not it." His spine straightened.

"Oh? Then what is it?"

"I just don't want that Frenchman getting fresh. She *does* need protecting."

Lucas threw back his head and laughed. "Now you see why I avoid passengers. They're too much trouble and definitely not worth the money."

Parker fisted his hand and glared, resisting the urge to plow one into him.

"All right." Still grinning, Lucas nodded. "I'll protect her from Jacques and he'll protect her from you. How's that?"

"This is not a joke," he said, almost growling. "I'll even concede you were right to worry about my intentions, as the attraction she stirs is a strong one, but I'm not about to let another take liberties either."

Lucas's smile faded on a sigh. "I can't believe we're having this conversation. Jacques is toying with you. We agreed last night. He's to keep her occupied and out of your way. If you feel there's impropriety, then I'll speak to him. But I must confess, he'll only be more amused."

"That bastard," Parker hissed as his brother's words sank in. His grin was quick. "I should've known."

"Aye, you should have. And if she didn't consume you so, I'm sure you would have."

Parker shot his brother a contrite look. "You've made your point. I'll keep my distance."

"Good. Finally I can relax. And since I see Hillman heading this way, I think I'll do just that. I need a little shut-eye and I don't have time to worry about you and your fixation."

"Go and sleep. You'll have no need to worry anymore over me or *my fixation.*"

ભ

Days turned into a week. The weather cooperated and graced them with clear blue skies and steady winds. The ship progressed, but not quickly enough for Parker.

True to his word, he'd stayed away from the enchanting Miss Layton as much as he could. The only time he allowed himself in her presence was during meals or when on deck with the distraction of activity or seamen surrounding them. Those times proved the hardest to endure, because the fascinating woman would hold them all spellbound with stories of her adventures with her two friends in their younger years. She'd have them laughing and jesting in no time. Most of the men, including him, were half in love with her, yet all stayed within the bounds of propriety. If someone said or did something she disapproved of, she had a way of cutting him to the quick with a word or a look.

Parker was no more immune to Miss Layton now than that first night and went to great lengths to avoid her. If he happened to find himself alone with her, he'd offer an excuse and leave. He'd long grown accustomed to the steady arousal he felt around the lovely lady, easily hiding the desire ever present and humming through his system. Still, every now and again, a yearning would overtake him and he'd have to fight harder to ignore the stirrings, especially if she happened to catch him secretly watching her.

She'd then bestow on him a knowing smile, as if speaking directly to him, telling him she knew his thoughts and was amused by them. More and more, the desire to wipe that siren's grin from her face to replace it with one of pure pleasure pervaded his senses. He could barely eat, could barely think, and when he slept, his dreams were erotically disturbing. Dreams in which she would come to him and yield all that he wanted. He'd wake up in a cold sweat, fully aroused, and with urgent need—one that would never be filled.

It was this need that had him standing on deck at the stern of the ship, seeking solace in the middle of the night. Staring into the black waters and seeing nothing but darkness because billowy clouds covered the light of the moon, Parker wished for home. The journey was more than half over, yet every day spent on board the ship was agony.

He turned at a noise and spotted the only thing that could make his nightmare worse step onto the deck. He bit back a curse as the object of his desire floated toward him.

"You shouldn't be out here," he snarled, in no mood to confront her. Raging desire coiled in his gut, waiting to spring forth at the slightest provocation. He was tired of fighting it.

"I couldn't sleep and came out for a breath of fresh air. My cabin was too stuffy."

Her soft, melodious voice filled the space around them, wafted unseen through the air forming invisible tentacles that reached out and wrapped around his soul. Ignoring the siren's pull, his tone became more vicious. "I'm warning you, 'tis a bad idea to be out here alone like this."

She paid no heed to his warning, walked serenely to the railing instead and flashed a smile.

"Well?" He didn't bother to keep the harshness out of the word.

"Well what?" She lifted her chin at a stubborn tilt and met his gaze.

"Why aren't you leaving? Are you goading me?"

"Maybe." Her soft chuckle knotted his insides. Mocked him. "I'm not afraid of you, Parker Davis."

"Then you're a foolish woman. I'd be more than afraid, were I you."

She moved to stand beside him, so close he felt her shrug. His hand clenched into a fist to keep from reaching out and touching her. He could barely make out her features in the moon-hidden night, but he didn't have to see her to know she looked like an angel who'd come to earth to make his life a living hell. The darkness that dulled his vision sharpened his other senses. He caught a whiff of her essence, flowery with a hint of muskiness. The scent more than made up for his lack of sight.

"Then foolish I'll be, for I find I like being in your company and you're always avoiding mine." Her clipped English accent invaded his senses further and sent more signals to his groin.

"There's a reason for that," he hissed. "You pretend innocence, but you have to know this is not a good idea."

"I feel safe enough with you," Penny said, offering another shrug, her gaze remaining on the black waters. "I've never been one to run from mischief, and I know I'm skirting convention, that I shouldn't be here with you, but here I am."

Parker closed his eyes, sending up a silent prayer. He should just walk away. As much as he knew he should leave, he truly didn't want to. She held him spellbound as usual, the urge to find out more about her—to see what was deep inside of her—too great to subdue. Instead of leaving, he opted to satisfy his curiosity and asked about the subject that interested him the most, her fiancé. "So, you're to be married?"

"Yes. I am," she replied in a voice filled with relief.

"Tell me about your intended."

"What would you like to know?"

"Whatever you wish to tell me."

Penny thought for a moment. "Well, he's handsome and funny and we get on well."

"I should hope so," Parker said, grinning at how unenthusiastic she sounded.

"Why's that?"

"I would hope you get on well if you're getting married." When she shrugged and didn't add any more to the conversation, he prodded, "That's it? That's all you have to say about him?"

"He'll be a faithful husband?" At his bark of laughter, she grinned and asked impishly, "What more would you have me say?"

"That you're madly in love with him and can't wait 'til you're together."

"Of course I'm madly in love with him and I can't wait until we're married."

Amused, he chuckled softly, remaining silent. The clouds shifted. A sliver of moonlight escaped, illuminating the deck. He kept his focus on her before hers returned to the water. In the added moonlight, he'd caught a glimpse of ambiguity. He sensed something else. Annoyance. She obviously didn't like that he saw more than she wanted him to see. At this point, he doubted she had such a fiancé waiting.

After several uncomfortable moments, she lifted her chin higher, purposefully seeking his eyes, her glare turning defiant. "What?"

His smile deepened. If the lovely Miss Layton had any idea of the vision she presented to him, with her hair flowing freely and her night clothing covering but not hiding her luscious curves, she'd run from him. The thought of nothing impeding what he craved underneath her night rail and dressing gown was too heady to imagine. His calm restraint amazed him. Schooling his errant thoughts, his gaze roamed over her features.

"He's not the love of your life," he taunted, if only to wipe that sudden appearance of overconfidence from her face. "I realize that now."

"Oh?" Like quicksilver, her expression changed to one of vast amusement. Still, she quickly lowered her eyelids, clearly uncomfortable with his scrutiny.

Parker bit his cheek to keep from laughing outright. "Yes. I'm certain of it."

"What makes you so certain?"

"Your eyes tell me so every time I gaze into their fiery depths."

"That's preposterous. My eyes say no such thing," she said, dismissing the idea with the wave of her hand.

"Liar," he whispered, leaning closer. "I bet if I could see them now, they'd be shouting."

"No." Shaking her head, Penny took a step away. "You speak in riddles."

To stop further retreat, Parker gripped her chin with a thumb and forefinger, forcing her to look at him. He smiled, noting in those oceanic liquid pools what she couldn't hide. Attraction. "Then, how about what this tells me?" he murmured softly, just before his lips descended, covering hers.

He tamped down a raging hunger and kept his pace unhurried for one simple reason, to quell her concerns. When Penny narrowed their distance, Parker swallowed triumph. Need, want, and desire exploded inside him when her hesitant hands reached around his neck.

She kissed like an innocent angel, and God help him, he wanted more. Softening his lips, enticing her to yield all to him, his tongue slid inside her mouth. Her moan floated somewhere above him, unleashing more yearning. By their own volition, his hands found her breasts, cupping their unbound fullness. His fingers stroked and circled. Her nipples hardened into nubs and another soft moan sent a shot of lust straight through him. He groaned in pure delight.

Desperately, he fought to keep his rampant yearning in check, for he had no intention of letting her bolt. Not now when she was exactly where he'd dreamed of having her since the moment he'd spied her that first night on board ship.

He continued, leisurely stroking with his hands, and using his lips, mouth, and tongue as expertly as he could in efforts to mark her with this kiss. Branding her, so that she'd somehow remember him. Finally, before he lost all reason, he tore his mouth away. He glanced at her face and what he could see in the darkness had him closing his eyes, reaching deeper for control.

Disappointment and confusion were evident in her passion-filled gaze. The innocent look laced with the heat of desire sent another jolt of need pulsing through him. Ignoring the longing to lay her down on the deck and have his way with her, he wrapped his arms around her and held her close, gaining more control.

"Now I know so," he whispered seconds later. His chin rested on her head; her dainty body nestled in the circle of his arms. "You'd never kiss like that if you loved another as you claim."

She stiffened and tried to pull away, but he held her steadfastly in place.

"Please release me," she begged, her voice barely loud enough to carry over the splash of the water hitting the boat.

Parker heard self-loathing in her tone. Recognized it because it's what he felt for himself at that very moment. He'd promised Lucas and for one crazy moment he'd almost given in to his need to have her. For one crazy moment he'd lost all honor.

"I'll let you go, but not before imparting my warning. I gave my word you'd be safe from me, and I've no intention of going back on my promise. Be wary, Miss Penny Layton, for I only have so much restraint and your taunts have already pushed me beyond those restraints."

"You lay the blame for this on me?"

"No. I took what I wanted just now, and I know I'm more at fault. But I only finished what you started. Leave it alone. Don't keep pulling the tail of the tiger unless you're willing to ride because if you don't stop, I can assure you, you will receive the ride of a lifetime." When she didn't move and stood silently staring at him as if he'd grown a second head, he nodded toward the stairs. "I suggest you go back to bed. Leave me be and I'll return the favor."

Finally, she found her wits and scurried off as if the devil were after her. Perhaps she was wise to run, he reasoned. At that moment, he did feel much like Satan wanting to seduce an angel of God.

He turned his gaze back to the water and sighed.
It would be a long, lonely night.

Chapter 5

"Have you found her? Is that why you called this meeting?" Gerald Knightsbridge's voice reflected his excitement at seeing Winters again, within days of their last unsatisfying meeting.

Lady Penelope's disappearance had grown his concern into all-out panic. Time was of the essence. Guardian or not, in less than seven months she'd reach the age dictated in her parents' will, giving her control of her assets and greatly diminishing his power over her. He couldn't let that happen.

Apparently his meek charge had a backbone. Surely the stupid girl would see reason. Marriage to him was an honor. Where the bloody hell was she?

"No, milord, but I've news," the runner said, interrupting his thoughts.

"I don't want news, I want the lady," Gerald bellowed, pounding the desk, his scowl forming.

"We are making 'eadway," Winters said hesitantly. "She may have had help."

"She had help?" The news stunned him. How? He'd kept her sequestered. She had no friends other than her servant.

"Yes, milord. I'm fairly confident he left some trail and if followed, it will lead me to 'er."

"It's about bloody time. She disappeared weeks ago. I'd begun to think I'd made a mistake in extending your deadline." The earl eyed the man, waiting for the name. When the runner stayed silent, Gerald prodded with eyebrows raised, "I haven't all day. Out with it."

Winters cleared his throat. "It seems she 'ad a childhood friend. His family's estates in Northumberland border hers."

"Yes, I'm well aware of her estates up north." The mine accident had detained him and allowed her escape in the first place. "No one offhand fits your description except the Duke of Wyndham, and I can't imagine the man flitting about with a child."

"Not the duke, milord, but a brother, some twelve years younger and the baby of the family."

"Bloody hell. Not a Collingswood?" Just mentioning the name filled him with rage.

"Yes, milord." Winters nodded. "The information checks out. Geoffrey Collingswood and the young lady are longtime childhood friends."

"I should've known." Gerald rubbed his temples, absorbing the news. "The Collingswoods are the scourge of my existence. Have you questioned him?"

"No, milord. I only learned of this recently. The servant who spied the two meeting in the park was greedy and easily enticed with a little more coin. Within days he provided a name."

Gerald sighed. "The bloody servants' network of intelligence. Seems they know everything that goes on in the ton."

"Servants always see more than they let on. Certainly worth following up on," the runner said. "I kept after yours, knowing it'd pay off. Someone 'ad to know more than he was saying."

"Good work. But if you expect payment, find her. You won't see another shilling until I see my betrothed."

"I understand, milord. My men are working around the clock. I've dispatched several along the roads north. If anyone saw Geoffrey Collingswood with the lady, I'll know about it in a matter of days."

"I underestimated her. Didn't know she knew anyone in London other than the duke."

"Would you like me to interrogate him, milord, or his brother?"

"No. I'll make a personal call tomorrow morning. After my visit, Wyndham won't sit idly by awaiting information if he's not involved. And if he is, then my visit will spur him into action."

"What would you 'ave me do?"

Thinking, Gerald eyed the runner. "You position yourself outside his residence during my visit. Once I leave, wait for movement and follow. One of them will take us to her."

"Yes, milord." Winters bowed, bade his good-byes, and left.

Gerald heaved a sigh of relief. Finally he had some answers. He stood at the window staring with unseeing eyes as the runner walked down the street and climbed into a waiting hackney. Wyndham had overstepped his bounds. If he'd helped Lady Penelope escape in any manner, he'd pay. Even dukes were not above the reach of the law if found to be guilty of a crime.

Gerald's confidence increased. He was her legal guardian after all. Her foolish parents had given him sole custody of the girl, much to the duke's dismay. He also possessed a betrothal agreement, guaranteeing her parents' support in their union. The willful chit had no choice in this.

Remembering the Duke of Wyndham's reaction during their first confrontation after learning all of that, he chuckled softly. Gerald was certain few men made Markham Collingswood squirm and apologize so effusively or so quickly upon reading the documents that gave him lawful rights to his good friend's daughter. Still, the man had the gall to demand certain concessions.

How those concessions chafed! Without the duke's interference, Lady Penelope Lytton would be his wife now, her lands and title his.

He would have them. Oh yes, and he'd have her. Soon.

 timelinetimeline

Markham Collingswood, the sixth Duke of Wyndham, nodded to his butler. "Find my brother. Pull him out of bed if necessary. I want him here in fifteen minutes," he said with the air of a man used to getting what he demanded, having been taught from an early age to assume the leadership of his family's name and assets. The duke didn't tolerate fools easily and had little patience for incompetence.

"Yes, Your Grace." Putnam bowed. "Lord Geoffrey will be here forthwith."

After Putnam left, Markham glanced back at the note in his hand. What did the earl want? He prayed his brother had gotten over his infatuation with the earl's ward. Yet given Geoff's moody guardedness lately, he had an idea this missive might involve Lady Penelope. After all, the two used to work up all kinds of mischief years ago, and Geoff had been in a dither for months after learning of her betrothal when her parents died.

He tapped the note impatiently. Damn, he didn't have time for this. He was due to meet with his estate manager and this meeting would put him behind.

Twenty minutes passed before his sleepy-eyed brother appeared at the door, barely dressed and out of sorts.

Glancing at Geoff as he made his way into the room, Markham smiled inwardly. He'd interrupted his slumber.

Though very similar in build, both being tall and muscular, the two brothers were as different as night and day in coloring and personalities. Markham had the dark good looks of their deceased father, also inheriting his dynamic and bold personality. His coal-black hair, expertly cut, along with a firm jaw, high cheekbones, and prominent nose, aided his regal bearing. In contrast, Geoff's coloring was fair, the same blue eyes and golden blond hair of their mother. He also shared her fair disposition. Nothing seemed to rile his younger brother.

"What the blazes has you so hell-bent on getting me out of bed this early?" Geoff said in a surly voice.

Or rather nothing used to rile him, Markham amended silently. Geoff had gone through a bit of rebellion since hearing of Lady Penelope's plight.

He sighed. "Sit." Markham pointed to the chair in front of his desk.

Noting Geoff's defiant stance at the one-word command, he shrugged off his annoyance. His baby brother was the only person he couldn't intimidate with simply a look or a few words and lately Geoff constantly rebelled. Although in truth, the two seemed to be more at odds since their father's death two years ago when Markham took over the role of "parent," something he hated. "I've some questions to ask before I meet with Gerald Knightsbridge."

Surprise flitted over Geoff's face.

Catching it, Markham sported his usual aloof, almost bored expression, which tended to be a bit misleading. Intentionally, of course. His dark brown eyes, appearing almost ebony at times, just like his father's, never missed much. "Ah, I see the name has sparked a reaction."

"I don't know what you're getting at."

TEMPTATION

Markham wasn't fooled one whit with Geoff's mannerisms all but shouting. Something churned in his brain. Somehow, his brother was behind Lord Knightsbridge's note.

"Just what have you done to irritate the man into demanding a meeting?"

"Why is it you assume I'm responsible?" Geoff asked, not bothering to hide his irritation. Being the baby of the family, the favored son, simply because of his engaging personality, he'd learned at an early age to get what he wanted out of people by using his boyish appeal to charm and cajole. No one, his father included when he'd been alive, could stay angry with him for long, except for Markham. That his older brother was the only one in his family who was immune to his ploys aggravated Geoff no end.

Markham chuckled, now convinced his brother played a part. "I'm going to find out once the man arrives, so you might as well tell me what's what. That way I'll have some time to come up with a strategy for dealing with him."

"I've nothing to confess."

"Don't take me for a fool, and I'll return the favor," the duke stated, containing his annoyance.

"I have no idea why the earl wants to see you." Geoff raised his chin.

"Now why don't I believe that?" With eyebrows raised, the duke kept his eye on Geoff, causing the younger man to flinch under such close scrutiny. After a moment of silence, he asked, "Geoff, what've you done?"

"Nothing. You pull me out of bed at the crack of dawn to ask such questions? Really, Markham? Have you nothing better to do with your time?"

"That's just it; I've too much to do and no time to waste on your silly games. If you've done something to have that man on my doorstep, I'll know within the hour."

Geoff remained mute, his expression insolent and uncooperative.

"Has this anything to do with Lady Penelope?"

Noting the pink slowly working its way from his brother's chin to his forehead, Markham sighed. "I know she means something to you, that you used to be thick as thieves, but times change. You've got to let her go. She doesn't concern you now."

Geoff didn't say anything for quite a while. When he spoke his voice was just above a whisper. "You're so sure?"

"It's out of our control. I can't go against her parents' last wishes. Please, Geoff, what've you done? Just tell me, and I'll do what I can to help."

Geoff's expression was torn. His sullen silence prevailed until he finally relented. "I haven't done anything but meet with her."

"That's it?" Markham prodded. "Why would the earl be up in arms over her meeting an old friend? It doesn't make sense. There has to be more to it."

"I may have given her a few pounds."

"You gave her money?"

"The man was holding her prisoner and I had to do something to help. You weren't doing anything."

"He wasn't holding her prisoner. The earl is her legal guardian. It's his duty to protect her."

"And who's to protect her from him?"

Markham's exhale came out in a frustrated huff. His younger brother had a point. He'd felt much the same way, but his hands were tied. Robert Lytton, the Earl of Lytherton, hadn't been an idiot. His friend and neighbor would not place his precious daughter under the earl's control without having just cause. Markham had to trust Robert's judgment on this.

From all outward appearances, their match did seem like a good one. Still, Markham had done what he could to give Lady Penelope time to get used to having the man as her husband, because from the first moment he'd met the earl, his intuition told him something wasn't right. It galled him now that over the course of these past months, his concerns had only grown, rather than abated. Oh, the earl appeared proper enough on the outside, but something in his eyes made him wonder. And now this.

Glancing at Geoff, whose expression was now blank, he figured his brother hid much more, but he'd get nothing further from him than he was willing to tell. With this in mind, he asked, "When did you meet her?"

"A couple of months ago. I can't see how an innocent meeting would cause any problems. We met purely by chance."

Markham chuckled. "Good story. Is that how you want me to relay the information?"

"I'm telling you the truth. I had no idea she was in London until I happened to see her riding in the park."

That much was probably true. Markham had kept the news of the lady living in London to himself, fearing Geoff's knee-jerk reaction.

"We met again a week later and that's when she asked me for help. I gave her what I could at that time and I've not seen her since."

"How much money are we talking about?"

"Two hundred pounds. 'Twas a loan."

"Good God, man." Markham shot out of the chair. He began pacing. "That's enough to disappear on." He stopped and nailed his brother with a hard gaze. "Where'd you get all that at one time?"

"I was lucky at cards, and happened to have it on me." When Markham's focus didn't falter, Geoff's face darkened with red once more. His tone turned accusing. "I knew she was planning on escaping, but I've no idea where she went."

"That's it? You know she was planning on escaping, and you've no idea where she went?" he asked incredulously.

"No, I don't." Geoff remained silent, his gaze steady, his chin inching higher. "That's all I know."

"I'm willing to bet there's plenty more, but that's all you're giving me." Markham broke eye contact and sat back down, realizing the futility of his actions. Moving his attention to the floor, he studied the designs in the rug. When he spoke, his voice held contemplation. "All right. I see nothing illegal in what you've done, provided that's the extent of your help. Meeting a childhood friend and loaning money isn't against the law. You have to know that because of your part in this, I'm honor bound now to help him find her, don't you?"

"I understand. There's no way the earl can connect me to Lady Penelope's disappearance. Besides, if I did know something I wouldn't tell you, only to have you track her down and force her to marry the vile man." Geoff met his gaze and asked belligerently, "Are we through?"

"For the moment. But stay close at hand in case I have questions after I've met with the man. I'm already behind schedule. I won't be pleased if I have to waste more time searching your favorite haunts if you're not available."

The air of command in Markham's voice was unmistakable, and Markham's amusement grew as Geoff relied on a tactic he'd used in the past two years to irk him. Straightening, Geoff gave a perfect bow and said in a subservient, mocking manner Markham hated, "As you wish, Your Grace." Then he turned and sauntered out of the room.

Markham shook his head and smiled. Insolent pup, he thought, wondering if his attitude would be so impertinent if his allowance was cut.

His thoughts shifted to Lady Penelope Lytton and the problem at hand. If she did indeed disappear as Geoff had intimated—and he had a pretty good suspicion that's why the earl was pounding on his door—his biggest question was, why? And what was he to do about it? Then he shrugged. Nothing could be done until he met with Kentworth.

At nine thirty sharp, there was a knock on Markham's study door.

"Yes?"

The door opened and Putnam announced, "The Earl of Kentworth has arrived, Your Grace."

"Very good, Putnam. Escort him in."

A moment later, Gerald Knightsbridge stormed into his office, not bothering to hide his fury or offer civil greetings. "What have you done with my ward, Wyndham?"

Markham stood and walked negligently around from behind his desk. Leaning against it while crossing both arms and legs, appearing relaxed and wearing his usual aloof, bored expression, he asked, "Why? Has she gone missing?"

"Don't pretend you don't know."

"So I take it from your response, the lady is truly missing?" He flashed a smile.

"You know damn well she's missing," he hissed.

"My, Kentworth, you do seem to have a problem on your hands—

a missing heiress. Still, why come here and accost me?" The duke kept his bored expression intact.

"Because you're involved somehow. I know so."

"Why would you assume I'm involved with Lady Penelope's disappearance?"

"You've been interfering for months. And then I find out your brother met with her."

"Oh?" He glanced at an imagined object on his hand before returning his gaze to the earl's angry countenance. "Exactly what has that do with me?"

"He was probably doing your bidding," he said, his tone accusing.

Markham chuckled. "My brother doesn't do my bidding, much to my dismay."

"So you say. But I know he aided her in escaping."

"Escaping? Sounds like you were holding her against her will."

"Of course not," the earl denied too quickly. "She's just a bit unruly, still being willful is all. She is free to come and go."

"Really?" Markham caught Kentworth's gaze and held it.

The earl fidgeted under such close scrutiny. He straightened and cleared his throat. "Yes. There's nothing untoward in my behavior if that's what you're implying."

"I merely made an observation of your words."

"Quit twisting this around," he ground out. "My ward's gone missing, I'm worried about her. I want her returned posthaste. Do you understand me?"

"I do understand. The lady is gone and because of that, you have no heiress to marry. But like I said, I can't help you. I don't know where she is."

"I'll bet your brother does and that he's responsible for her disappearance," he sneered. "He's involved. So deep, it's up to his neck. I can feel it."

"That's purely conjecture." Markham shook his head.

"I know he had contact. They were seen together in the park."

"A chance meeting between childhood friends. If Geoff saw her, he'd never ignore her, nor would she him. You're making something out of nothing."

"She just happens to disappear after this chance meeting."

"Mere coincidence." He rejected the notion with the wave of his hand. "You've no proof Geoff acted inappropriately."

"Her trail leads to your brother and I don't mean to stop until I find her."

"I understand. You need your heiress back," Markham mocked in a scornful tone with a derisive smile on his face.

"If you're involved, Wyndham, I'll bring you up on charges and make you rue the day you interfered in my life," he lashed out angrily. "You've done so for the last time."

"If you're through making veiled threats, I believe we've nothing further to discuss." Markham sat behind his desk and nodded toward the door. "I'm a very busy man, Kentworth. Continue to harass me, and I'll be forced to take action." He returned to his correspondence, totally ignoring the man.

"Your Grace." The earl bowed his head briefly, his demeanor becoming more polite and deferential, as if realizing he may have pushed too far. "If you hear of anything, I'd appreciate it if you'd pass on the information." He then turned and walked out.

Markham's gaze stayed on the empty doorway. The man wasn't bluffing. If Geoff had offered more help than what he'd admitted, Kentworth would cause trouble. He waited until he heard the front door open and shut before he quickly turned and yanked on the bell cord, summoning his butler.

When Putnam appeared at the door, he barked, "Get Geoff down here. Now."

Chapter 6

The ship lurched and yawed. As Penny made her way to the officers' dining room, she grabbed on to the polished wood beams for support. After a fitful sleep, memories of her actions the night before continued to plague her. She'd fled from Parker Davis as fast as her legs could carried her, with full knowledge she'd run not only from him, but from herself as well.

How had she willingly allowed him such liberties? Even more mortifying—she hadn't wanted his kisses to stop. The tingling sensations she'd come to associate only with him still coursed through her system.

Warmth engulfed her face. She closed her eyes, working to forget her stupidity, only her mind wouldn't cooperate.

She touched her lips, remembering the pleasure. For too many days, she'd wondered what it would be like to kiss him. The reality of it had been so much nicer than conjecture. His mouth had been tender and gentle. Geoff's kiss never affected her in such a way.

His golden image came into her mind just then and self-revulsion roiled in her belly. She'd wantonly and knowingly kissed another man! He'd not forced her to endure his touch, as she'd had to suffer Gerald's. She'd been instructed numerous times to call the vile man by his given name and that's how she thought of him. Yet the captain's brother wasn't Gerald, an indisputable fact considering she'd loved his touch.

Heavens above! She didn't want to think about Mr. Davis anymore. It was bad enough to find him attractive. And now she'd done the unthinkable. She pounded her fist with more resolve. Geoff was her beloved and she meant to make him a good wife.

When she entered the dining room she felt Parker's gaze, but didn't make eye contact. Shameful heat suddenly washed over her as renewed thoughts of the minutes in his arms flashed through her mind.

She pushed out her musings and sat next to Mindy, eyes straight ahead, seeing only the table with different, less formal utensils and place settings than those used their first night.

The more durable metal plates and wooden cups weren't as pretty, but still held expensive details. Even when calm, like now, the ship pitched and rolled and the dishes and silverware tended to slide from side to side. In rough weather it was next to impossible to sit at the table without holding on to the plate. As they sailed closer to their destination, the seas did seem a little choppier.

"Miss Layton, you're later than usual today," Lucas said. "I thought maybe you'd been overcome with seasickness."

Penny glanced at the captain and smiled, praying conversation might divert her disturbing thoughts. "No, I had a bit of trouble sleeping last night and overslept. Hopefully it's not a problem." Yet no matter how she tried, thoughts of the man and the kiss wouldn't budge from her brain. In the light of day and with him sitting so close, the images grew.

Since that first morning, he'd sidestepped her every attempt to be alone with him, avoiding her like the plague. She sensed his avoidance wasn't born of disinterest. Not when she'd looked up too many times to catch him staring, his bold gaze moving over her like a caress, touching her everywhere, leaving her breathless and also leaving her with no doubts about his thoughts. She'd always sent a knowing smile in return, instinctively understanding what he wanted and that he was denying himself.

Penny had no illusions as to her motives. She'd played with a fire. Heavens, at times she'd felt like a pyromaniac wanting to stir the flames. Without a doubt, the man sitting across from her held on to unleashed power. Power that could burn and still his fire drew her. More than anything, the adventurer inside of her had wondered what would happen if his fire ever fully erupted. Penny mentally snorted. She'd gotten a pretty good dose of flames last night.

"Of course 'tis not a problem. We're not so strict with our schedules that we can't accommodate a little tardiness," Lucas teased, pulling Penny back to their conversation. "I'm only happy you haven't succumbed to the *mal de mer*."

TEMPTATION

The thought of her being seasick had her grinning. "I can't imagine why I couldn't sleep, but seasickness definitely isn't the reason."

Parker grunted, which drew her gaze. His challenging stare caught and held hers.

When he flashed a sardonic grin, his expression clearly indicating he knew why she couldn't sleep, her smile died and more heat rose up her face. Unable to withstand his mocking perusal, her gaze sought her hands and she remained silent.

If anything unseemly had happened and others found out, her reputation would be in shreds, along with her plans. Geoff wouldn't want her. Parker might even have felt honor bound to marry her once he discovered her status, and she had no intentions of marrying a man such as he. Not a man with so much power and virility stored inside him. She sensed he was like a keg of powder waiting to blow. The thought of it blowing in front of her might have sounded exciting to begin with, yet in truth, she'd come to realize she had no control over it.

Penny needed control in her life much more than fire.

No, Geoff was perfect for her. She'd known him forever, and they loved each other.

Completely oblivious to the battle taking place in her mind, Lucas stood. "Well, I'm sure Jacques has no problem with your tardiness. He's always happy to have company when he eats."

Thankful for another distraction, Penny's attention wandered to the captain's back as he left the dining room. Still, her brain wouldn't shut off.

Since beginning her journey, concern over the earl finding her had diminished. The hundreds of miles the ship had sailed provided safety. However, ebbing fear was only part of her inner transformation. She truly began thinking of herself as a new person, a person without such strict bonds of her station in life. Penny Layton, the American, didn't have to worry about her parents' last wish as Lady Penelope Lytton, the English heiress, did. She was becoming a woman of independence who could now take care of herself.

"I'm sorry you weren't able to sleep, Penny," Mindy said. "Seems that since I've gotten used to the motion, I sleep like a baby."

"I'm glad I didn't wake you with my sleeplessness." Thank heavens her voice sounded calm. Still sensing Parker's gaze, she ignored the tightening in her stomach and smiled warmly, patting Mindy's hand. "I'm thankful you're feeling better." For a while there, Penny was really worried.

"So am I." Mindy grinned. "I can't tell you how horrible seasickness is. At one point, I truly wished I could die. Hopefully I'll endure the rest of the voyage without it."

Penny nodded.

Suddenly the galley door swung open when Jacques burst through with his usual energetic zeal. He placed Penny's breakfast in front of her. Then he sat and took a deep breath before saying, "*Bonjour, mademoiselles*, Parker. Such a *magnifique* morning."

"Thank you, Jacques." Penny offered a semblance of a smile, striving for cheerful. "The porridge smells heavenly. And it is a beautiful day. I'm enjoying the warm, sunny weather."

"I can't believe how hot it is. Certainly a change from London," Mindy added.

"A nice change." Penny wiped a trickle of perspiration off her forehead, unfazed with the heat. She loved it. "Sometimes I thought I'd never get warm, even in the middle of summer."

She glanced up to note Parker's gaze hadn't moved, only now his expression appeared more inquisitive. When she lifted her chin as if in question, he smiled, eyes flashing something she couldn't read.

"The air has more humidity," he offered. "The rainy season is upon us now."

Just the tone of his voice sent an unsettling spark of awareness through her. She hated that over the course of these past weeks, thoughts of the man had slowly taken over thoughts of Gerald Knightsbridge. That the thoughts of both men were of the same topic tormented her, and left her paralyzed with guilt. She'd been frozen with fear at the idea of having to mate with the earl, but the idea of mating with the man gazing at her now with humor-filled eyes had her shaking with another kind of fear—a fear of enjoying it, or worse, yearning for it. She closed her eyes, willfully pushing the images away and sent up a silent prayer.

Please, Lord. I only want to be that happy-go-lucky person I was a year ago. Back then, she'd had no worries about fighting men's lust, had no idea such a thing even existed. Now she fought her own.

Inhaling deeply, she opened her eyes and glanced at Parker. "The rainy season," she asked, raising a brow.

"We're veering farther south, due to the warm currents. We'll catch the Gulf Stream current taking us north once we cross to it. 'Tis much easier for the captain to ride the current at an angle than fight it," he explained, gracing her with another knowing smile.

If only her stomach would cease with the flip-flops his smile created. The man was simply too masculine for words. Penny's focus returned to her bowl. The sweet flavor of the molasses mixed in went down easily.

Done with her porridge, she then took a sip of coffee, a bitter brew she'd grown accustomed to, before beginning on her soft-boiled egg. A comment floated past her ears and she looked up. "Excuse me? I wasn't paying attention."

Parker chuckled. "I said I'm sorry you didn't sleep well."

Penny clenched a fist with the hand sitting on her lap. When fingernails digging into her palm became painful, she exhaled and relaxed her fingers.

Chin up, she met his gaze. "It was nothing but a case of homesickness," she boldly proclaimed, daring him to deny it with her glare.

"Of course. I understand. Being away from home and in different surroundings makes one behave differently."

Subduing the urge to throw more mental daggers, she smiled. "Sometimes it helps to be rudely awakened to the fact. Rest assured, my behavior will be a model of decorum from here on out."

Jacques seemed to take note of both the exchange and the charged atmosphere suddenly pervading the table. His smiling countenance turned to Parker and though his manner was jovial, his voice held a hint of warning. "It seems we all behave differently when away from the home. Very few of us have the vow of a promise to keep us in line."

Parker chuckled. Rising from the table, he nodded. "No worries, Jacques. I've no intention of breaking promises. I was just pointing out the obvious to the lady." He turned and bowed, catching Penny's focus and throwing her another mocking smile.

"Ladies," he said, before sauntering off.

ॐ

Parker located his brother on the deck below the wheelhouse, enjoying a pipe and searching the horizon as he did most mornings after being relieved. The scent of the salty, fishy sea air mixed with the smell of Lucas's burnt tobacco, a clean cherry flavor. He blew out another stream of white smoke that broke apart and instantly dissipated in the tropical breeze.

Since sailing into warmer waters, both men had donned the garb of the other sailors: a loose-fitting muslin shirt and baggy britches that could easily be rolled to the knees, allowing the breezes to keep them cool. Parker strode to the railing, absorbed with the tranquility, spying several dolphins frolicking and swimming with the ship as it glided through the calm seas.

"You seem content today," Lucas said.

"Aye. I guess I am," Parker replied honestly. He stared out at the blue-green depths as sights and sounds of sailing surrounded him. The ping of metal against metal clanged. One of the sails fluttered, then caught the stiff wind, filling it. The billowy white clouds floated in an azure sky and added to the tropical feel of the moist air blowing his hair about. He sighed. He did feel content just then. "I don't know why, as I'm anxious to get home."

In the days they'd been sailing, he hadn't dismissed the miners' ordeal from his mind. He'd tried to focus on their tragedy to figure out what he could do to help, rather than on other more disturbing people, namely one. The gnawing need because of a blue-eyed siren still ate at his gut, but observing Miss Layton's unease during breakfast acted as a balm, soothing his burning desires somewhat. A small smile formed at the edges of his lips. That she suffered too cheered him.

"We're making good time." Lucas's voice broke into his thoughts. "Unless we hit a storm, I don't anticipate any delays."

"Good, good," he murmured distractedly, still thinking of the expression on her face when he left the dining room. She might not be so quick to torment him now that she knew of the consequences.

"So, do you know what your next case will be?"

The question caught Parker off guard. Turning toward Lucas, his smile died. "No. My last instructions held no clue," he said, sighing.

"Why the sigh?"

Parker shrugged. "No reason."

"Then why the sudden change in mood?"

He massaged the back of his neck with one hand and glanced back at the water. His voice carried on the breeze a moment later. "I've been thinking of quitting."

Lucas's bark of laughter drew Parker's gaze. "You doubt my intention?"

"Yes. I can't see you quitting. You've been a marshal too long not to miss it if you quit."

Parker eyed Lucas thoughtfully. His comment rang true. He'd worked for the US government in one capacity or another since his teens. "It does seem like part of me, but lately it's a part I've come to hate," he whispered honestly a moment later, glancing away. He just couldn't stop thinking of the miners and their families. Even though he'd accomplished much, he'd also been very lucky. Somehow, he knew it was time to take up a different cause.

He'd been a fifteen-year-old heading into adulthood when the mine accident killed his father and left his family destitute. Not long after, Parker had learned the army paid well for needed information and had offered his services to work undercover for the Union Army before the War between the States. He'd been damned good at spying. Back then, there was nothing he wouldn't do if he could make money to send home, no matter the risk. Over the course of the war, he'd amassed a small fortune from his mercenary work, as his extraordinary skills hadn't come cheap. After all, he'd had a family to provide for and he could no longer allow men of means and position to take advantage of him or his talents.

A slight smile touched his face, thinking of all that he'd be giving up. "Remember when we first started out? Damn, how I loved outwitting not only those I spied on, but those who paid me to spy," he said wistfully.

Lucas gave a ready grin. "Aye. Father trained us well in the few years we had him." Lucas had done much the same type of work as Parker during the later years of the war, but he'd done his on the water.

The elder Davis began teaching all his boys when they were toddlers most of the skills that came in handy for spying. Both he and Lucas could track and hunt anything without their prey even being aware of being stalked. The brothers could live off the land, taking what they needed for survival, leaving no trace of their earlier presence.

"It was a challenge back then to make money and stay alive. A good game I enjoyed playing." More memories surfaced, as if he'd experienced them all yesterday rather than years ago.

Being born poor gave Parker an added edge in dealing with the foot soldiers he was sent to spy on. He understood them, blending in effortlessly and becoming one of them, because most were no better off than he'd been at one time, fighting for a cause that others who had more to lose held dear. But he could also change his personality and become the landed gentry, effectively imitating those men he hated because of his mother's tutelage, also started at an early age. He became a master of disguise, a chameleon readily changing to suit his environment, all the while learning the South's secrets for his government—a government that paid well for those secrets.

"It's been a lucrative means of survival." His thoughts shifted to all he'd acquired in the past seventeen years, including a sprawling farm along the Chesapeake Bay, outside Baltimore, an easy ride from Washington, DC. He'd hired a manager, placing his family there, ensuring their safety and well-being while he worked as an agent.

"True," Lucas agreed, nodding. "We've done well for a couple of boys from the coal mines of western Pennsylvania. I'm certainly not complaining."

"Neither am I." Parker grunted. "My work has given me the means to provide for the family, my most pressing need when Father died."

He broke off and watched the dolphins play, still chasing the ship. They seemed so carefree, a luxury he'd never enjoyed.

When the war had ended, along with the need for his special

talents, he'd tried his hand at riverboat gambling. Using the same skills of reading people without letting them read him and riding the big paddleboats up and down the rivers of America, also doing undercover jobs now and then for his government, he'd amassed even more money.

Gambling hadn't interested him for more than a couple of years, however. Looking for ways to increase his small fortune after winning a ship in a poker game, Parker had talked his brother into going into business with him, using Lucas's love of the sea for another type of risky venture, trading for monetary gain. With Parker's money and Lucas's cunning for bartering and trading, their lucrative partnership had lasted almost a decade. For too many years Parker had been happy to let Lucas sail the seven seas, increasing their wealth while he worked in an official capacity as a US marshal for President Grant.

"You're right, though. I'm rarely in Maryland to enjoy my home." He leaned into the railing, wondering why it mattered after so long. "I have no real complaint, except my work doesn't seem to be enough anymore," Parker added, keeping his gaze on the water. For the first time since he'd begun taking risks, he was no longer satisfied and realized he was ready to quit something he'd done his entire adult life. Why he felt this way, he wasn't sure. But disillusionment had filled him for months now. He turned back to Lucas and said honestly, in an effort to answer his own questions, "Maybe I will miss some aspects, but the job has changed and no longer holds my interest. I believe it's time to get out." He didn't add that maybe it was also time to do something about the Sterlings of the world.

Startled, Lucas glanced at Parker's face and his demeanor sobered. "You're serious, aren't you?"

Parker nodded. "I've yet to work with another partner I'm comfortable with since losing Harrington. Those boys they keep sending me are so wet behind the ears, I find myself watching over them and I don't like babysitting. Sooner or later, someone's going to get killed. I'd really rather it not be me. Then, there's my last case. To think I've wasted months being in a country I hate, only to find the culprit was nothing other than a spurned man who loved another man makes me cringe. I simply want something more from life."

"I didn't realize you felt so strongly." Lucas expelled a soft whistle, shaking his head.

"Funny, but until this very moment, neither did I."

"So, you're just quitting?" he asked with skepticism in his voice.

Shrugging, Parker's gaze moved unseeing over the various shades of blue in the water. "I don't know. I am thinking along those lines, and the more I do, the more quitting seems to be my next logical step. Still, it does seem a bit drastic."

"Aye, drastic seems an understatement," Lucas agreed. After a moment spent watching him, he asked, "Have you thought about what you'll do if you quit?"

"A little. Right now I have this driving need to go home. Maybe after a few months there, I'll feel differently yet again."

"At least you have a beautiful home to return to."

"Do I hear wistful yearning? What happened to 'my home is the sea'?" he teased, adding a little levity to their conversation.

Lucas offered a sheepish smile and admitted, "There are those times I need to find another home. If you're planning on staying put in Maryland for several months, I could be persuaded to visit."

"Oh?" Parker's eyebrows shot up in interest.

"Aye. I've one more scheduled trip to England. Then, this ship needs some maintenance. I've been wondering what to do during the months in between."

"You know you're always welcome. It would be nice for all of us to be together for more than a few days." Parker's smile grew wider. Movement caught his eye and he noticed another group of dolphins cavorting with the original three and racing along with the boat. An omen.

"I was thinking much the same thing," Lucas said.

"Mother will be excited to see you for an extended visit." The playful dolphins swam in front of him for a reason. "So will the girls."

Lucas grunted and moved to fill his pipe. After lighting it and taking a puff, he said, "You'd better not let Mother in on the fact that you're thinking of quitting before you figure out what you want to do, or she'll have your life mapped out for you in no time."

"Why do you think I seldom go home or stay very long when I

do?" Parker grinned at the image his brother brought forth of the vibrant woman who'd raised them. Elizabeth Davis was the rock that cemented his foundation, never letting him falter in times of despair and heartache. Her belief in him and her encouragement to do what he had to do in order to live with his grief over losing his father and brothers was as crucial to his success as his hatred of men like Sterling, who were born wealthy and made more money on the backs of others. He knew there would be a day when he'd do something to avenge his father and brothers' deaths. It seemed that time was fast approaching. Otherwise he might end up just like his nemesis. Greedy and uncaring.

"Same reason I sail." Lucas's reply drew his focus. "Is she still trying to marry you off?"

"Yes. And it's getting damned annoying." Parker snorted, his thoughts returning to his mother who never stopped mothering, despite his role in providing her a home and sustenance as a teenager. Unfortunately, her mothering included a need to see him settled, which accounted for the dozens of women she'd foisted off on him these past years. "I wish she'd concentrate on you for a while."

Lucas chuckled and took another puff on his pipe, his amused gaze meeting Parker's. "Mother knows I love the sea and would never be happy for long without it. But you, as the oldest, she has aspirations for and wants to see the grandchildren only you would provide."

"Rebecca and Sarah will satisfy that need in no time I'm sure," Parker said dismissively.

"You know she won't be truly content until she sees all of us married, tied with a ball and chain, along with a dozen children."

Parker bit back a laugh. No exaggeration there. "Her matchmaking ways, along with her 'eligible brides,' drive me to distraction. Maybe if Catherine became serious about someone, it would take the heat off me for a change."

"I thought Catherine was interested in some gentleman from Baltimore?"

"She was," Parker grumbled.

"He didn't offer for her?"

"He did and by then he no longer held her interest."

"Well, don't expect help from her," Lucas said, chuckling. "She's as bad as us with her fickle ways." Lucas remained quiet for a moment, lost in thought. A comfortable silence surrounded the two brothers for several minutes, intruded upon only by the soft sound of the water splashing against the bow of the ship now and then. "You know you really should reconsider marriage. Maybe that's what's missing in your life."

"Damn, you sound just like Mother." Parker gave a self-deprecating laugh and shook his head. "It's not something I want anymore."

"All women aren't like Lady Margaret."

Parker's back stiffened. He really didn't want to think of Lady Margaret and her perfidy. He'd gotten over the lady's treachery, but he wasn't about to put his feelings on the line for another woman. Love was a fairy tale…a dream that never came true. Women like Elizabeth Davis didn't exist. He now understood what women were really like, his sister included. The ones he'd come into contact with weren't much better than Lady Margaret, each trying to marry the most suitable man, suitable meaning the one who brought the most to the table. "Doesn't matter. She taught me a valuable lesson."

"Because you fell in love with her and she didn't deserve it? It's been five years. If you were willing to marry her, why not think about marrying someone more deserving?"

"Are you sure Mother hasn't been coaxing you?" Parker laughed. "I'm perfectly happy without a wife. What about you? Maybe you should take your own advice."

"I like the ladies too much to settle down with just one." Lucas grinned.

He grunted in reply and remained silent. Finally he asked, "So you say we're making good time? When do you anticipate our arrival?"

"Six or seven days, maybe more if we encounter a storm. Certainly no longer than ten days."

"I'll be glad to be home."

"I take it you've lost interest in our passenger?"

"I'm plenty interested in her, especially her secrets."

"Well, you've done a good job hiding the interest and haven't given me any reason to worry since we talked."

TEMPTATION

He shrugged. "I gave my word. What else is there to do?"

"She is a handful," Lucas agreed, chuckling. "But she seems to handle the crew well enough while on deck. I can't say when I've seen the seamen so enchanted. Having two ladies on board makes the journey go faster."

Parker nodded, disliking the surge of jealousy he suddenly felt. The journey certainly wasn't going faster for him. If anything, it seemed prolonged. Keeping annoyance out of his voice, he said more jovially than he felt, "Like I said, I keep my distance and try not to let the lady affect me." Then, not willing to dwell on the unwelcome irritation over images of the seamen's interest in one Miss Penny Layton, he added, "Miss Bowers seems to have her hands full as well."

"Aye. My return trip to England won't be near as entertaining."

Parker's thoughts then shifted to the conversation during breakfast and he voiced his concerns. "Doesn't it seem strange that they traveled so far from London to journey to America?"

"What do you mean?" Lucas's brow furrowed.

"It's something they said. If they were in London, why not embark on a ship docked there? Or if one wasn't available, seems they'd take a ship from Dover, Brighton, or Portsmouth."

"I still don't follow."

"During breakfast they both let on that they'd spent the summer in London. 'Tis odd they'd travel so far north, unnecessarily adding extra days of uncomfortable travel over land to make a ship that would extend the miles at sea. The voyage to America from Tynemouth has to have added on weeks to their journey than one started farther south."

"You did."

"I have a stake in this ship and I know it's faster," Parker said.

"You answered your own question. My ship is faster than some of the older ships farther south, evening out the time. Geoff trusted me enough to commission their passage when I docked in London, wanting the ladies to travel on my ship, but unsure of when they'd be ready to leave. So before I sailed north, I informed him of my scheduled stops for the next few months. I assumed my passengers would take my return trip, not this one," he added, shrugging off

Parker's concerns. "You're putting too much into the man trying to ensure his friends' safety."

"No. My intuition tells me there's more."

"Parker, you're just too damn suspicious."

"Maybe, maybe not," he said. "But the lady has secrets I mean to uncover."

"Everyone has secrets." Lucas chuckled and tapped his pipe on the rail.

"Doesn't it bother you that she claims to be of the serving class, yet she's a close playmate with a duke's brother? I thought it odd that first night at dinner, but never followed up on it."

"So?" Lucas stopped filling his pipe. His searching stare landed on Parker's face. "It doesn't matter. You'll just get into trouble if you persist. You know that, don't you?"

"I'm puzzled is all," Parker stated firmly, not yielding to Lucas's warning tone. "She's not of the serving class. Her bearing and clothes attest to the fact."

"What does it matter?" Lucas sighed. "Her secrets don't affect us." He continued eyeing Parker, who shrugged. "Oh no! Don't shrug like you have no idea what I'm saying. You've got that unbending expression on your face, and it worries me."

"You're not even a little bit curious?" His eyebrows rose. "The lady's story has too many inconsistencies."

"I've learned not to get involved in what doesn't concern me. My concern is making it safely to the shores of America, selling my cargo, and buying more to sell in England. I haven't time to worry over passengers I took on to help a friend."

"Well, I am curious," Parker said with a steely resolve. "And I'm not about to let it go."

"Which proves my point. Passengers are just too much trouble and not worth what I charge," Lucas said in a disgruntled manner. "You're not going to stop, are you?"

"No. It's not in my nature to let it go, at least not till I get some better answers."

"Your single-mindedness is wasted energy." Lucas's teasing grin formed, showing what he thought of his single-mindedness.

"It's my energy to waste. The lady's an enigma and her inconsistencies intrigue me."

"Why do you have to be so damned stubborn?" Lucas shook his head in defeat. He took a puff off his pipe, then added in a resigned voice, "We all have secrets. What can it hurt to let her keep hers?"

Parker didn't answer right away. When he spoke his voice was just above a whisper. "I wish I could let it drop. But I can't."

"Fine." Lucas nodded in the direction of the stairs. "I'm going below for a few hours of much-needed sleep. I'll see you later."

Parker watched him storm off and sighed. His interest in Miss Layton irritated Lucas. He wiped his face and raked a hand through his hair, trying to understand his motives.

Why this urgent need to find out more about her? He walked a fine line, his attraction held in check because of enormous willpower. Pulling tautly on the lines would only test his willpower further. Damn it all, he sensed she hid something, and more than anything, he wanted to know what. If he couldn't have her, he could at least appease his curiosity.

Suddenly a thought struck. He hadn't been this interested in anything in a long time. The surge of excitement strumming through his veins over discovering Miss Layton's secrets told him he was definitely interested now. The fact that he should be running in the opposite direction rather than appeasing his curiosity didn't faze him any. He could keep his needs in check. Hell, he'd already done so for two weeks. If nothing else, following up on gut instinct would keep his mind occupied on something other than his yearning.

With one last look at the water, his smile broadened. His mind churned, working on the task of figuring out how to best go about learning the lovely lady's secrets.

Chapter 7

Markham Collingswood tossed the bound file he'd just read on his desk and pulled the bell cord to summon Putnam. "Find Geoff," he said, the instant he spied his butler at his study door. "I need to speak with him as soon as possible."

"Yes, Your Grace." Putnam turned hastily around.

The report said it all. Geoff was definitely involved in the lady's disappearance. He glanced out the window and sighed, pulling a hand through his hair.

After interviewing his brother at great length weeks earlier, he'd found him as uncommunicative as ever. He'd obtained nothing useful, and probably never would. Not from Geoff. So he'd begun his own investigation into the lady's disappearance, calling in his man of business who'd always done all of his information gathering discreetly, albeit thoroughly.

Twenty minutes later Geoff strode into his office and up to his desk. He offered a perfect bow, asking insolently, "You requested my presence, Your Grace?"

"Sit down. I'm in no mood for your impertinence this morning." Markham stood and walked around his desk. Leaning nonchalantly against it, he crossed his arms and legs, snaring his brother's gaze. "I'm most put out with you at this moment, so you'd best drop the facade. I know you helped her get out of London."

All insolence faded as stunned disbelief replaced impudence. "How?" he asked, plopping into the chair in front of Markham without breaking eye contact.

"I've my ways." Markham mentally rolled his eyes and smiled. "Did you really think you could hide your involvement from me for long?" Heaving a sigh born of frustration, he added, "I'm on your side, Geoff. It will only take me a little longer to find out exactly where she disappeared to, so why don't you save me the effort and talk?"

"I can't just yet." He tilted his head at a determined angle and his eyes revealed a stubborn glint. "She needs time to make it to her destination."

"You were seen going north. How long do you think it's going to take Kentworth to ferret that out, if he hasn't already?"

"He won't." Geoff's confident mien had returned. "We were careful. She and her maid were dressed as boys."

"Don't be too sure." Gazes locked. The two entered a stare-off. Judging from Geoff's expression, he wasn't about to divulge any more than he had to. It was time to take another tack in dealing with his recalcitrant brother. "I know I told you honor dictates that I help him find her, but my first priority is to the lady. Since she's taken great pains to disappear, I'm thinking she has good reason. Let me help, if I can."

Noting indecision seep into Geoff's eyes, he pushed further. "I promise to keep your confidence. This is serious. My resources are much better than his, and my methods more thorough. Still, it will only be a matter of time and money before the earl learns of your involvement. I know his type too well. Greed will keep him from spending too much in the beginning, but once he becomes desperate, he'll increase his efforts. I've had him investigated. He's hurting financially and needs Lady Penelope's holdings and wealth." Something else his man of affairs had uncovered. "He won't let his heiress go without a fight. Lytton Mines are too valuable to give up, and given the manner in which he's been conducting business, it's evident he considers them his."

Leaning forward and gripping his arm, Markham said earnestly, "Please let me help."

Geoff sat back, his focus landing at some spot on Markham's desk. "You promise you won't put her back in that monster's clutches if I tell you?"

"I promise to do what's best for the lady, not Kentworth. But if he finds her first, you'll lose your opportunity to help her. Of that, I'm sure. Now tell me, and let me see what I can do to help."

Geoff was silent for a bit longer, his expression torn. "I can't let the earl near her," he whispered. "She hates him and is deathly afraid of him. She wouldn't tell me what he did to cause her reaction, but her fear is real and I've no intention of letting that man marry her. I'll kill him first."

Noting the depth of emotion in his brother's words, Markham had no doubt his brother meant them. "Talk like that isn't going to help Lady Penelope," he said, keeping his tone steady and not releasing Geoff's gaze. When it was obvious Geoff wasn't inclined to add more, Markham prodded, "Where did she go and what are your plans?"

Geoff averted his eyes and stared at his hands, remaining speechless.

Markham waited.

Finally his brother sighed. "She sailed to America."

"America!" the duke said a little too loudly and sounding totally stunned. "And you let her go?"

"It seemed a good idea at the time for her to follow Mindy. It was either that or Scotland and he'd find her there."

"My God, she must've been desperate to make such a journey, leaving all she loved behind."

"She was desperate. Now that her parents are dead, there's nothing here for her anymore. She told me that if she had to marry the earl, she might as well join them." He glanced at Markham, his eyes flashing a fervency all but shouting he believed his next words. "If I hadn't come to her aid, and they were indeed married, she would've taken her own life."

"She'd have never done that." Markham shook his head. "Ending one's life is a mortal sin."

"She told me she'd rather live an eternity in hell than be bound to evil in life."

"Was it truly so bad for her?" A sliver of guilt washed over him. Could he have done more to protect his friend's daughter? A girl who'd been like a younger sister as feisty and loveable as Geoff.

"Why do you think I helped her?" Geoff asked. "I've always loved her, but I understood her duty to marry the earl and was content to let her go." His gaze returned to Markham's desk in contemplation once more. Eventually he glanced at Markham, pain and honesty revealed in his eyes. "Though I hadn't seen her for five years, I still love her," he whispered. Pounding a fist onto the chair's armrest, he added, "I couldn't just walk away after she asked for my help."

Markham's eyebrows shot up. "How did you learn she was in London?"

"One of the earl's servants gave me her sealed message. The bastard had kept her a virtual prisoner, with Mindy her only company. We planned a chance meeting in the park. Later when I realized how desperate she was, I went to his house while he was out."

"Why didn't you come to me? I could've helped."

"Lady Penelope told me you'd argued about the betrothal, said you called her spoiled and ungrateful."

Marcus winced, remembering his careless words during their last meeting. "All right, I understand why she went to you, but wasn't going to his house a bit risky?"

"No." Geoff grunted derisively. "His servants hate him and you know how servants have always loved Lady Penelope. The earl's are no exception. They helped with her escape. I accompanied them, both dressed as boys. When we rode together, we acted as if we were traveling separately. I even split off from them, taking a later mail coach several times to avoid being together the entire journey. Mindy's brother met us at an inn a short ride from Newcastle upon Tyne to escort them the rest of the way, and I rode back to London without stopping so as not to raise suspicion."

"Why go north and not south?"

"I knew Lucas Davis's ship would be in port traveling to America and I knew I could trust him."

"You involved my business partner in this?" His voice increased tenfold in volume. "How could you?"

"I had no choice," Geoff said in his defense. "I trusted no one else. I didn't tell him exactly whom he'd be escorting across the ocean, just said that we were good friends and to treat them well. Mindy's mother paid her voyage and I paid for Penelope's. I also gave her all the funds I could, several hundred pounds, which should tide her over until we meet again after my birthday, when I finally inherit father's bequest. I'm joining her and we're to be married."

The words, spoken with such certainty, left Markham speechless and he could only stare silently at his brother. After several minutes, he straightened and walked over to the window, looking out without seeing the landscape, too absorbed in his thoughts. "So you were just going to disappear without telling anyone?" he asked, turning back to Geoff, not sure why his brother's lack of faith in him hurt.

"I'd have sent word once the deed was done and Penny was safely married to me," he whispered. "Because of your position I decided to keep you out of it."

"You didn't trust me enough?" He met his brother's gaze and couldn't stop the anguish the idea evoked from showing in his features. He'd failed in his role as surrogate father.

After holding his stare without flinching, Geoff cleared his throat. "I'm sorry. I know it grieves you to think I could be so cruel and you still think me a child, but she's my life now. I couldn't risk it. Not even for you."

The duke smiled wistfully. The unwavering resolve evident in Geoff's handsome features added years to his youthful face, giving him a mature wisdom Markham had never noticed before. Maybe he hadn't failed after all. The man before him knew exactly what he wanted and he'd do whatever it took to achieve it. "'Tis funny, but until this very moment, I didn't realize how much you have grown up. You are indeed a man with conviction to have risked my wrath for her." Sighing, he added, "I wish you happiness, Geoff, and I'll help you any way I can." Markham's gaze returned to the window. "It won't be easy. Knowing the earl like I do, he won't stop until he has her back under his control. The mines are too valuable. You're aware of that, aren't you?"

"Yes. It's why she was willing to travel to the ends of the earth."

Markham's smile grew at his confident tone. "Did she keep to her disguise on board ship?"

"No, I didn't see the need. In such close quarters, the crew would learn the ruse quickly enough, which might raise more questions."

"Then be prepared for the earl to find her," he said, shaking his head.

"No." Geoff's fist hit the chair's arm again. "The United States is a big place and he won't know where to look. We've planned well."

"Yes, I can see that. To be on the safe side, I think you should adjust your plans." When Geoff started to disagree, Markham held up a hand. "Hear me out. With an added inducement of money, Kentworth will eventually find someone who remembers her, as the lady is one who stands out in one's memory. By the time Lucas's ship returns, he'll most likely be desperate enough to spend whatever it takes to learn her whereabouts and I have no doubt he'll follow her. To the ends of the earth, if need be."

"What do you propose? Penny's supposed to write once she gets settled in California."

"California?" His head snapped up and he couldn't contain his horror. "Good God, Geoff, how could you let her travel across a wild country alone and unprotected?"

"I had little choice. It was her idea. She was set on going and you know her. She'd have figured out a way to do it with or without my help. This way, at least I know where she is, and in six months I'm to meet her and we'll be married."

Markham sighed, rubbing his temples. He should have expected something like this from the willful girl who'd always involved Geoff in her schemes. As a child, she'd been a handful, wrapping both Geoff and her father around her little finger with her charm and beguiling ways. Of course Robert Lytton's indulgence only encouraged her outlandish behavior.

Geoff undoubtedly needed his help in covering contingencies the naive lady wouldn't think of. His brother's plan seemed the best alternative for now, so Markham would go along with it, hiding his involvement at the same time.

In fact, the more he thought about it, the more he liked it, especially after learning of the mine accident that took ten lives. Penny's father would never have let the men work in such conditions. Like Markham, Robert had been an advocate for change, putting the miners' safety ahead of profits. The accident proved the earl was only interested in money.

"Lady Penelope shouldn't be too hard to follow. I'll have Jones make a few inquiries to see about departing ships." His man of affairs could be counted on for discretion. The couple could marry and settle in a country separated from England by an ocean. Hopefully, by the time Kentworth learned of it, he'd have no legal recourse, as his guardianship would have ended. Then he could help Geoff and Lady Penelope manage her inheritance. Markham had his own mines to run, so adding hers would place little burden on him. "Once I find out all the specifics, I'll travel with you on your journey, and we'll go a little sooner than planned. It won't take much to rework my schedule to accommodate a sea voyage." He rubbed his hands together, grinning, his mind spinning. "In fact, I relish the idea of seeing where my partner lives. He tells me it's nothing like the savage place I imagine. Now I'll have an opportunity to see for myself."

❦

"Mr. Terrance Winters to see you, my lord," Ferguson announced, interrupting the Earl of Kentworth's thoughts as he contemplated the dilemma of his missing ward.

Gerald nodded curtly. "Good, see him in."

A moment later Winters entered the room. "The younger Collingswood was seen climbing into a mail coach a day's ride from London several weeks ago," he said, halting a foot from the earl's desk. "Not your usual form of transport for the brother of a duke, wouldn't you say?"

"Any sign of Lady Penelope or her maid?" the earl asked, his eyes alight with excitement. He pointed to the chair in front of his desk, indicating for the runner to have a seat.

"No. None yet." Winters shook his head as he sat. "The duke's brother was headed north. I've only found this out hours ago. In response, I sent my men to the duke's holdings outside Newcastle upon Tyne to do more digging. I'm leaving on the morrow. I delayed my trip to talk to you."

"Of course. I should've looked there first." The earl leaned his head against the chair, absorbing the news. "Most likely he's keeping her there. Or maybe she's staying at her parents' estate, hiding in plain sight. Both seem logical steps." He snorted. "How stupid of me. I could have even passed them on my return trip. Good work, Winters.

TEMPTATION

Your plan is a good one, with one small change." His smile turned menacing. "I'll be accompanying you. It's time I headed north myself."

Chapter 8

The gentle sounds of the water splashing against the ship floated up and calmed Penny, even as the sun's rays warmed her. The ordeal of Parker's scrutiny at breakfast had taken its toll.

When a shadow blocked the warmth, it didn't take a genius to figure out who loomed.

She turned and squinted, noting his roguish attire. The wind whipped his hair and she could well imagine him a pirate if he'd existed in an earlier century.

When Mr. Davis sat down next to her, she inhaled a steady breath, tamping down annoyance. Her vexation over the ill-bred man who'd departed the table so smugly that morning only grew.

"I see you're wearing a locket. Is it from your intended," he asked, eying her with an amused grin plastered across his face.

Penny's hand covered her locket, fingering the heart-shaped piece of jewelry encasing small miniatures of her parents, her only memento of them. Unable to hold an intent gaze that saw too much, hers strayed to the water, and she shook her head no.

He chuckled. "I didn't think so."

Her back stiffened. "It was a gift from my father," she said curtly. "My most prized possession."

"You should drop the pretense." His sharp tone drew her focus and she was stunned to see anger in his eyes. "There is no intended, is there?"

She searched his expression, looking for meaning.

"I don't know who you are, Miss Penny Layton," he replied to the implied question she flashed with her eyes. "And though you kiss like an angel, you'd not be so quick to do so if you did indeed love another as you claim."

He would have to remind her. Hating herself, she closed her eyes as more shame filled her, if that were possible. She *had* enjoyed his kiss. The breath she took was deep. She let it out slowly to quell her nerves, and said with more serenity than she felt, "Then you would be wrong because I do plan on being married and I do love him."

His smile mocked her. She jutted her chin out and maintained eye contact without blinking. "It's the truth," she finally said.

His gaze narrowed, and still grinning, he nodded, which only added to her discomfort.

"Why this sudden interest?" Exasperated, she threw up her arms. "Why not just leave me be and I'll leave you be, like you suggested last night?"

"I have too many unanswered questions."

"That's your problem, not mine." She tucked a strand of hair that was blowing in the stiff breeze behind her ear. "We're strangers on a ship bound for a new world."

"Are we?" He chuckled and his amused glint was back. "Just strangers who kiss in the night?" he whispered as shivers crept along her spine. "That's all?"

He held her stare. The entire time her insides did somersaults.

Then he shook his head, breaking the spell. "No, I doubt it—just as I believe there's more to your travel on board this ship. I'll find my answers, Miss Layton. Of that you can be sure."

"No. Please." Now she shivered for a different reason. "There is nothing to find." She stood. "I think it's time I went inside." She then turned and ran, vowing to stay far away from him, too afraid of what his questioning might uncover and of her reactions to the man.

◌◈

Penny stepped onto the deck three days later, needing fresh air after hiding from Parker all morning in her stifling cabin. She walked over the railing and heaved a sigh of relief. Thank God there was no sign of him. Still, no matter how careful she tried to be in avoiding him, it usually wasn't enough. Anytime she came on deck, she could only enjoy her solitude for a scant few minutes before he'd usually appear out of nowhere.

"Ah, there you are, Miss Layton."

She groaned. Obviously this morning was no different. She smiled and nodded in greeting. "Mr. Davis. What a surprise."

Parker stalked toward her, tsk-tsking. "If I didn't know better, I'd say you're avoiding me."

"Of course I'm not avoiding you," she replied in a sardonic voice that belied her claim.

Chuckling, he said, "You never answered my question. Why would you travel all the way to Northumberland to journey to America, if you started from London?"

"Will you cease with your endless questions?" She offered her back and crossed her arms, holding in frustration and resisting the urge to stamp her foot. The man was forever vexing her with his maddening presence, asking his infuriating questions, taunting her with his amused gaze that seemed to miss nothing, and annoying her with his outwardly unaffected demeanor. During dinner last evening, his nosiness had been especially pointed. Her unwillingness to talk caused many uncomfortable moments at the table, but Parker didn't seem to notice or care because he never stopped.

And here he stood again, asking more and grinning in the same manner she quite determined she hated.

"I'll stop when my curiosity is satisfied and not until then."

"I have nothing to say to you," she practically yelled, hurrying toward the portal leading to her cabin.

The sound of his amused laughter echoed as she ran to the only place with any amount of privacy. At the door, she halted. Uncurling her fist, she took a steadying breath before going inside.

When Mindy looked up and smiled, Penny rolled her eyes, moaning inwardly.

Even this bit of privacy had drawbacks because Parker Davis was all Mindy could chat about. Mr. Davis had befriended her ex-maid in the last few days, but his actions hadn't fooled Penny. Oh no! He used Mindy as a tool to ferret out information. She had no doubts Parker Davis knew how to worm secrets out of people, and Mindy was surely easy prey for any information she possessed.

"Please, Mindy. Don't forget I'm keeping my past private," Penny said, closing the door. "You can't breathe a word of my true identity." Despite imparting the same warning too many times, Penny desperately feared her friend would give her away somehow. She sensed it was only a matter of time before Parker discovered something useful.

"Don't worry," Mindy said smugly. "I can keep your secret."

"This is not a game." Penny stepped in front of the small bureau and poured fresh water into the basin. "It's my life. I don't think you realize how important this is."

"Of course I do." Indignation spread across her face. "I would never say anything about who you really are."

"I know you'd never say anything intentionally."

"Or unintentionally. I'm getting used to Penny Layton, though truth be told, she isn't much different from the Lady Penelope Lytton I once knew. In these past weeks I've seen my childhood friend return from a world of grief and fear. Do you think I want to take that away from you?"

Feeling a little churlish, Penny offered a half smile. "I'm sorry for doubting you. It's just that I'm afraid of Parker Davis."

Mindy shrugged. "We only discuss silly things, mostly my family. His farm isn't far from my sister's, and we have much in common. Sometimes he tells me stories about his sisters when they were growing up. He thinks I should meet them once we've landed." Mindy then added solemnly, "He doesn't ask any questions about you. And if he did, I wouldn't betray you."

"I don't trust him. He seems too tenacious. Lord only knows what would happen if he discovered I've run away from my guardian. Captain Davis is the duke's business partner. Word would surely get back to the duke, and based on his comments when we last spoke, His Grace thought Gerald the perfect match for me. He'd insist I return to the earl."

"I can't believe the duke was so taken in by that horrid man."

"Gerald hides his cruelty behind smiles and charm. There's only one way to keep out of his control, and that is to make it to America without anyone knowing about my past. Once I make it to those shores I'll be safe. After all, from what I've read, English earls don't carry the same weight in America as they do in England." Penny wiped a refreshing wet towel over her arms and face, easing some of the unbearable stuffiness of the cramped, heated room. She placed the damp cloth on the hook. Then heaving a huge sigh, she padded to the edge of the bed and sat. "Maybe I'm going about this all wrong."

"All wrong?"

"Yes." Too much pent-up energy flowed through her veins for her to sit still. She jumped up and began pacing. "I'm running from the man's presence, which appears to amuse him no end."

Mindy nodded. "He does seem to delight in pulling a reaction from you."

"It's payback."

"What?"

"For my behavior in those first few weeks of sailing." Penny halted. Glancing at Mindy, she shrugged and confessed, "When I'd try and do the same. I admit, I enjoyed goading him."

"No?" Mindy sat up straight and leaned forward, her eyes growing wider in scandalized excitement. "Do tell!"

"I chased him a bit." She grinned. "And he took great pains to avoid me."

"I don't know, Penny." She shook her head and practically clucked her disapproval. "I'd not goad a man like him, if I were you. He's nothing like Geoff, who you've always been able to sway with a few words or a look. I don't think Mr. Davis is so easily swayed."

"Humph, don't I know it." Stomping her foot, she hit a fist to her palm in frustration before continuing to pace and to think. She had to do something to stop the man. "I know he's not immune to me." Maybe she could use the fact against him. Use his own game to thwart his attempts.

"I know that look in your eye." Mindy's gaze narrowed. "And that scheming expression."

Penny gave an unladylike snort. "There's no such look. No such expression. I'm merely coming up with a plan."

"Your plans always backfire. If I were you, I'd put whatever you're thinking totally out of your mind."

"Oh, Mindy, don't be such a goose." Penny laughed. "I'm not going to goad him. I've learned my lesson." She rubbed her arms, remembering his warning about riding tigers.

TEMPTATION

"Somehow that doesn't ease my mind." Mindy's worried glance as well as the hint of concern in her voice added weight to her statement.

"You're being a worrywart. My plan is simple. I'll not avoid him anymore. And you can help."

"Me? What can I do?"

"Nothing. I plan on being present whenever you're with Mr. Davis. That way, I'll be solving two problems with one solution."

"You aren't going to annoy him, are you?" Mindy warned, her glare accusing.

"No, of course not." Penny threw her shoulders back and winked. "I plan on being a model of decorum. He'll have nothing to complain about." Grinning, she said conspiratorially, "But if it annoys him, then all the better."

"Hah!" Mindy placed her hands on her hips. "I know you. You're never a model of decorum."

Stunned, Penny gaped. "How can you say that?"

"Because it's the truth and I know you."

"I can be." She held her head high. Noting Mindy's skeptical expression, she inched her chin higher. "You just wait and see."

"It's a horrible idea," Mindy said, her tone pleading. "You'll only make him angry."

"Well, what would you propose? I've tried everything else."

"I don't know. Just keep away from him."

"How?" She crossed her arms and tapped her foot. "The man never lets me avoid him." Her temper flared just thinking about it. "My only alternative is to stay inside this cabin for the rest of the voyage. That, I simply can't do. It's too confining. Too stifling." Penny added more heatedly, "I refuse to hide any longer. If I use you as a buffer and you're always around, there's nothing to be afraid of."

"I only hope you know what you're doing." Mindy exhaled a resigned sigh.

∞

"How much longer before we reach the shores of America?" Penny asked excitedly and set down her spoon. The seaman's specialty was always delicious. Still, she couldn't eat another bite of stew filled with various abundantly available fishes. Jacques told her it also contained potatoes, leeks, onions, and spices from places he'd visited.

Parker hadn't asked any annoying questions thus far, so she began to relax her guard. She stretched out her legs, feeling quite satisfied.

"We'll be pulling into the Chesapeake in four days, unless we encounter a storm," Lucas replied, lounging in his chair at the head of the table and puffing on his pipe.

"This has been a wonderful trip. I love sailing." Penny looked directly at Parker, her grin turning mischievous. "Mindy said you were teaching her how to play chess. I take it you know the game well?"

Startled out of his thoughts and clearly not expecting her question to address him specifically, Parker hesitated a moment. "You assume correctly, Miss Layton." He bestowed on her one of his engaging smiles. "How about you? Do you play?"

"A little." She lifted her shoulders in an innocent shrug. "Would you mind if I watch?"

"No, I don't mind. I'll even challenge you to a game." Parker sat back, eyeing Penny with interest. "Chess is a good way to alleviate the boredom of sailing," he finally added, still observing her.

"I'd love nothing better than a game of chess. But I should warn you, I haven't played in a while." She smiled smugly, all but laughing. Her attention returned to her empty bowl. Her plan was already working. He clearly wasn't expecting her to horn in on their chess game. Ha! She'd show him. Her smile widened.

Lucas laughed. "Are you sure you want to play against Parker? I don't even like playing him."

"That is because you are a terrible chess player, *mon capitaine*," Jacques said.

"I seem to remember beating you a couple of times during this trip," Lucas teased good-naturedly.

Jacques snorted. "I have to let you win sometimes. Otherwise I have no partner."

"Well, a game of chess will help pass the time," Penny said, laughing along with the others at the table as Lucas stood to refill his bourbon. While he poured, his eyes searched for others at the table who needed a refill. Penny waited until he finished before she looked purposely at Parker. "Maybe you can even give me some pointers."

"I'd be happy to." Parker nodded.

"Since Penny's playing, do you mind if I watch a bit before I make a bigger fool of myself with my lack of knowledge." Mindy pushed her empty plate forward and grinned. "But I should warn you, Penny is better than she's letting on."

"Is she, now?" Parker slanted a glance at Penny, the heat of his expression sending warning signals to her brain. Considering the warm, tingling sensations his look generated, Penny wondered how great her idea truly was. She breathed a sigh of relief when Parker turned to Mindy and nodded encouragingly. "You're still learning. It's really a game of strategy." After speaking, his focus landed on Penny once again and that knowing, amused smile was back. He captured her gaze for far too long before releasing it.

In a dismissive gesture, Penny glanced at the captain and smiled sweetly. "So, tell me. Do you think this beautiful weather will hold for the rest of the trip?" She would win this mental game with him or her name wasn't Penelope Lytton.

☃

"The mademoiselle is no novice. Eh, Parker?" Jacques said not more than fifteen minutes later. "She has definitely played the game before."

Parker nodded as he and Penny played chess in the officers' game room.

Lucas was on watch and Mindy sat across from the Frenchman.

After a few moves on both their parts, more of Jacques's laughter rang out.

Grinning, Parker shrugged. "I had a feeling she'd played before, especially after Miss Bowers's comment." With frank admiration, his stare moved slowly over Penny, catching her gaze once it finished the caressing journey. He added, still grinning, "I've always savored playing with a worthy adversary, and I find this is a pleasant surprise. Very pleasant indeed."

A slight blush rose up her under his perusal, causing a tug of awareness. He looked back at the board. Maybe he shouldn't have been so quick to agree to this game. His attention, when not on the board contemplating his next move, had been directed solely at her and he was now having a hard time ignoring the fiery sensations such blushes generated.

When more than an hour had passed without an obvious winner, Jacques glanced at Mindy and whispered, "I think I will leave the chaperoning to you, *mademoiselle*. Mornings come too quickly for me, and the men are too hungry."

Mindy nodded. Parker waved distractedly, but Penny was too absorbed in their game to notice his departure. Eventually, Mindy put her head back against the settee and closed her eyes. Soon her soft snores accompanied the sounds of water lapping against the sides of the ship.

"I wouldn't do that if I were you," Parker said when Penny began to move her bishop to a precarious position. In answer to his warning, she tipped her head in a challenging tilt and let go of the piece.

Parker deftly took her bishop and realized his error a few moves later when his queen came into jeopardy. Grinning and shaking his head, he said, approval clearly in his tone, "So, who taught you to use such daring strategy, Miss Layton?"

Laughing, she moved to take his queen. "My father. He used to always say it was the biggest mistake he ever made."

"Oh? Why is that?"

"Because I beat him regularly and, up until he taught me the game, no one in the area could except for Collingswood." Her hand shot to her mouth as she realized what she'd said. An alarmed blue gaze sought his.

Their stares locked for endless seconds.

"How is it your father plays chess with a duke?" His voice was barely above a whisper.

She closed her eyes and shook her head. "Please, I can't answer that." She opened eyes that now glistened with pleading.

Her beseeching expression disturbed him, had him questioning his motives. "Why all the secrets?" He studied her features and noted something else he hadn't expected. Pain. The thought of his questions placing such heartache in those blue depths left him feeling empty.

"Why is my past so interesting?"

TEMPTATION

"Your past is not what interests me. What interests me is that you're so quick to hide it," he replied truthfully.

"I've done nothing wrong."

"Do your parents know you're sailing to America?"

"My parents?" Her eyes narrowed in confusion.

"Aye. At first I thought you might be running from them, but the obvious pleasure in your voice when talking about your father negates the notion."

"My parents are dead and I'm on my own."

Hearing the sorrow in her words, Parker dropped his goal of questioning her further, not comfortable with destroying their earlier camaraderie any more than he already had. He rose. "Well, I concede defeat. Hopefully you'll let me regain some of my dignity by playing another game. Tomorrow night, perhaps?"

She offered one of her beguiling smiles and readily agreed.

While Penny woke Mindy, Parker left the room, wondering why the enchanting woman affected him so. Would he ever get over his lust for her? It was bad enough when she was mocking him, but when she'd sent him that smile a moment ago, it took every bit of willpower to walk away as if it meant nothing. In reality, the thought of her bestowing one on him so easily increased this need she stirred tenfold.

❦

With chessboard in hand, Parker stood on deck. A brisk, steady wind eased some of the tropical heat beating down on his neck when the sun came out of hiding from the billowy white clouds forever present in the blue skies above. His gaze swept over the ship. Catching sight of Penny, he bit back a smile when he spied Miss Bowers perched next to her. The damned minx had figured out a way to not only put a cog in his plans of using her friend to dig deeper into her past, but also to foil his attempts to rile her.

Penny no longer avoided him, yet always had her cabin mate close by, which amused him no end. He glimpsed a bit of a challenge in her actions, and he could no more ignore that challenge than he could quit breathing. Of course, after their shared chess game, his quest for knowledge of her past dimmed somewhat. For the last two days, he'd been working to enchant the lady and he could tell she'd warmed a bit to his charm, though she took great pains to hide her reaction.

He now looked forward to the next few days rather than dreading them, so much so that he wished the voyage wouldn't be over quite so quickly.

Pushing that thought aside, he ambled toward the two women sitting in a shady spot, obviously enjoying the afternoon breeze. Neither seemed bothered by the continual rocking of the schooner under full sails.

"Ladies." He nodded, dropping onto the empty bench next to them. He then started setting up the board on a nearby table.

"Mr. Davis," Mindy gushed, smiling. "How nice to see you."

"I'm sure it is. But I'd thought we were ready to dispense with formalities. You're to call me Parker. If you don't, there's no way I can return the favor and call you anything other than Miss Bowers."

"Of course. I forgot." A blush darkened her already pink cheeks as she cleared her throat. "Parker. After all, we are friends, are we not?"

"Exactly, Mindy." Grinning, he turned his attention to the blonde beauty next to her. "And what about you, Miss Layton? Are we to keep up the formalities?"

Due to the tropical humidity, both women dressed in less formal attire than their first night on board the ship. Penny wore a light blue muslin gown that, without petticoats, pantaloons, or the whalebone stays of a corset, outlined her lush, compact figure, sending the usual signals to his brain that incited his senses. Whenever near her, those senses were on full alert.

"I have no problem with formalities." She smiled sweetly, yet he caught the bit of mischief displayed in her eyes before she shuttered the look. "I prefer to allow only close friends the privilege of using my given name." Her new expression definitely said he didn't fit into the category.

"I must be doing something wrong." His grin only widened and he clutched his chest over his heart. "I thought we were friends."

"You thought wrong." Her chin rose an inch, presenting her usual stubborn mien. "We'll never be friends."

"My mistake." His smile quickly died and he remained silent, lost in thought. Finally, he seized her gaze again and asked solemnly, "What would it take to ensure your favor?"

He held the stare, unwilling to mask the intensity he felt just then. After being in her company, trying to charm and cajole her for days, he realized his plans had been a double-edged sword. He'd been the one charmed. More and more he loved seeing her impish smile. In fact, he said things just to put one on her face, because her smile could warm his heart for the entire day. And this concerned him.

Penny broke eye contact and glanced at the hands she nervously wrung. After an uncomfortable moment, she sighed. "Why do you need my favor? Isn't Mindy's enough?"

Parker shrugged. "One cannot have enough friends."

"You really think we can be friends?"

"Don't you?"

She shook her head and cast her focus upon the water. His followed. The gentle splashing was the only sound until a fish jumped, its plop dispelling the quiet.

Eventually she spoke, her soft voice barely audible. "No, I don't."

"Why?" He hated that his whispered word held a note of desperation, as if the answer was too painful to bear.

"Because friends don't pry." She inhaled deeply and let it out slowly. She glanced up, allowing him to see the honesty shining from her eyes. "They realize some things are better off left alone."

Parker sucked in a breath. The sound of her clipped English accent never ceased to tug a reaction from his gut. The raw anguish in her tone had him questioning his motives again. Maybe her secrets were better off left alone. He leaned against the rail and scrutinized Penny's face, as if by staring he could discover the reason her secrets mattered. Why did he have the urge to uncover them? Why did she intrigue him? "Maybe you're right," he finally said, still eyeing her. He really did see her as a friend. And as one, Parker felt her best interest would be served by getting her safely to her destination so she could marry her intended, however fishy those plans seemed.

He nodded. "Go ahead and make your move. I'll not ask any more questions today."

Ꮟ

"Good evening," Penny said, breezing into the dining room. The captain, Mr. Hillman, Mindy, and Mr. Davis were seated along with two other officers, their dinners already on the table.

Jacques came up behind her carrying two bowls. "*Bonsoir. Ça va, mademoiselle?*" He placed one on the table in front of her chair and one at his spot. Then he sat.

"*Très bien. Merci,* Jacques." Penny smiled warmly. "It smells delicious." Her bowl appeared to be filled with the usual bean and seafood soup they'd had too many times in the past two weeks, complete with scallops and potatoes.

She shook her napkin and laid it on her lap, purposefully ignoring Parker. Thank God she'd soon be able to escape his confusing presence. "I'll miss the balmy weather once our journey ends."

Penny chanced another glance at him and forgot to breathe. In the past few days, he seemed to smile at her more and more, and when he did, like right now, the dangerous element in his expression disappeared. Heavens! Parker was far too attractive. She looked away, fighting the urge to return his grin, and ate a spoonful of soup instead.

"When are we reaching land?" Mindy asked.

"We should be spotting land sometime tonight, and enter the Chesapeake in the early morning hours. We'll reach Baltimore tomorrow after the noon hour," Lucas replied. He took a sip of bourbon. "We're all excited at the prospect of finally ending our journey." Turning to Penny, he asked, "So, what are your plans after we dock?"

"I'll need to secure passage to San Francisco. I'll be taking the train."

"You're traveling by train across the country all alone?"

"My plans are set and I'll be fine. What can happen on a train?"

Lucas shrugged. "I only hope you'll be careful. Transcontinental travel isn't easy and there are many dangers, especially for a woman alone."

"Of course I'll be careful." Penny caught the silent communication that passed between the captain and his brother. Her annoyance grew. "I made it this far, didn't I? The rest should be easy."

Parker cleared his throat. "We're only worried about your safety."

TEMPTATION

"You have no need to worry." His sincerity did what all his other ploys over the past few days failed to do, push through the rest of her resistance. The admission, along with the genuine concern in his voice, made Penny feel as if her safety were the most important thing in the world to him.

"I could accompany you and provide escort for a day or two, just to make sure you're all right."

"That's a kind offer." She should be scandalized at the thought, but she wasn't. Not when the earl had wiped most of her maidenly sensibilities away with his behavior. It might even be nice to have such an escort, but she couldn't allow it. It became harder and harder to keep her distance, to keep thoughts of their kiss out of her mind. And when he gazed at her as he was doing now, she could almost feel his lips again—was ashamed to admit she'd love nothing more than to feel them again.

Heat flared on her face. She shook her head, using the movement to avert her eyes. "But like I said, I'll be fine," Penny stated firmly, once she could speak without giving her inner thoughts away. She couldn't risk spending even one more hour in the attractive man's company. She already dreaded leaving him, and now more than ever, she had to remember her plans with Geoff and stick to them. Nothing had changed in these past weeks. She was still running from a monster. Her beloved would be meeting her soon enough, and until that happened, her life would never be safe. Sensing the determination of the men at the table to foist Parker's solution on her, Penny added quickly, "Besides, Mindy and her sister will be escorting me on the train and stay until my betrothed meets me in San Francisco. Isn't that right, Mindy?"

Mindy looked up, clearly startled. "Um, yes. That was the plan," she said, blushing furiously at the obvious lie.

Both men eyed each other again, but neither spoke.

Penny let out a sigh of relief when Hillman got up to leave, changing the focus of their thoughts. She had one night left and then her adventure would begin in earnest.

ଔ

After dinner and another game of chess, Parker watched Penny and Mindy maneuver toward their cabin as the ship rocked back and forth. He then climbed the narrow stairs to the top deck to find his brother.

"I'm worried about Miss Layton," he said, seeing him at the wheel and hurrying to his side.

"What?" Lucas chuckled. "No longer interested in finding out her secrets?" He waved a hand. "Parker, you need to quit obsessing over her."

"I'm not obsessing, just concerned. Mindy's sister is with child and in no condition to travel. Which means it's a lie and Penny's going alone with no one to help or protect her," Parker said, his irritation rising. "You can't tell me you're not thinking the same thing because I saw it in your eyes at dinner. 'Tis obvious she's on her own." And running from something, he added mentally. The thought of the fragile young beauty being out in the world without protection bothered him more and more. There was no way he could simply let her walk away without ensuring her safety.

Lucas sighed and lit his pipe, sucked in a long puff, then blew it out. The sweet scent of burnt tobacco filled the air. "Yes, but it seems she doesn't want our help."

"She's your responsibility. You said so yourself. Are you denying that?" Parker demanded and leveled his now narrowed gaze at his brother.

"No, and I am worried about her. Maybe you could keep your eye on her—at least until she's safely on board her train. Once she's traveling, she does have some amount of safety in the other passengers. My biggest worry is what happens to her when she gets to California. Unfortunately, the moment she's off my ship, it's out of my control."

Parker grunted. Lucas had a point. The two stayed silent, absorbed in their thoughts. Finally he said, "I'll watch out for her because I'm going along, and she won't even know I'm there."

Lucas's loud laughter rang out.

"What's so funny?"

"You! Have you lost your senses?"

"Maybe. But damn it all, I can't have her going out into the world alone." Plus, he'd have a purpose, a perfect solution to this new need to help others. What better way to start than making sure she was safe? He'd simply delay his trip home a few more weeks, after which he'd planned on staying put. "Since you're going to see Mother, you could inform her of my delay."

"I thought we'd go together. My ship's only in port for unpacking, reloading, and provisioning, so I won't have but a couple of days before sailing to London," Lucas said with a rueful smile. When Parker didn't respond, he asked, "Why would you go to such great lengths to help her? Seems she has her life planned out and those plans don't include you."

"I can't explain it. I'm sure she's running from someone, but it's not her parents as I once thought. They're both dead and she has no one else."

"If I didn't know better, I'd think you were in love with her."

"No." Parker laughed outright. "Enchanted, yes. Attracted, yes. But love? No. You know love doesn't exist for us."

Nodding, Lucas took another puff on his pipe. "It's not a bad idea. Just don't let the lady see you."

Parker rubbed his hands together, feeling energized. "Don't worry, she won't."

Chapter 9

"Good-bye," Penny yelled as she waved to the group of sailors hanging over the sides of the ship. "I'll write." She never realized how hard leaving would be. Parker, his brother, the captain, and even Jacques had become her surrogate family, and saying her good-byes to them had been heart wrenching.

She turned back to the noisy dock filled with seamen, travelers, and their families. Everyone had someone to meet but her. She pushed the scary thought aside. This was a new adventure. America was a perfect place to hide and full of promise. Gerald Knightsbridge would never find her in this big, open country. Still, ignoring the stench of fish, foul water, and sweat while darting through the throngs of rough-looking dockworkers unloading not only Lucas's ship but also two others now docked, she was glad she had an escort of sorts. She now understood Parker's concerns.

To alleviate those concerns, Penny kept to her deception. She trailed behind Mindy, her sister, and husband after her friend explained Penny's plight, letting them think she was traveling to meet Geoff in California, rather than the other way around.

Less than an hour later, with the trunks on board, Penny tried not to gawk as the horse and buckboard drove toward the center of town and the train station. Once away from the docks, Penny's fears ebbed. Baltimore looked no different from London, and she and Mindy had ridden those streets often enough to add to her comfort level now. She had to remember Geoff would be joining her soon.

"Your belongings will be safe here, ma'am," the burly stationmaster said, taking the tip Mindy's brother-in-law handed him. "Just bring proof of ticket purchase, and I'll make sure they're loaded properly when your train arrives."

She took the claim check he held out and smiled.

TEMPTATION

Dressed in black pants and an open vest over a white muslin shirt with rolled sleeves, he looked no different from any stationmaster she'd encountered in England.

Except for their rough speech, Americans seemed very much like her British countrymen. They dressed the same, the men wearing somber suits and top hats, and the women wearing dark-colored skirts topped with white blouses and matching hats and gloves.

Penny adjusted her hat to wipe her forehead with her handkerchief and smiled, enduring the stifling heat without a complaint. She loved the hot, humid weather she'd experienced on the ship.

The crowds had thinned to only a few stragglers who hadn't gone inside yet.

"Please stay in touch after you're married," Mindy said, pulling her into a bear hug once Penny's trunk was secured.

Blinking back tears, she watched her friend climb into the buggy. It rolled down the cobbled road, mixing among other similar conveyances. When she could no longer see them, she turned back to the station's entrance. The imposing brick building appeared familiar in its opulence. Exhilaration as well as trepidation filled her. Ignoring the small amount of fear at feeling very alone, she headed inside to buy a ticket. The rest of her grand adventure was only a train ride away. San Francisco was a city of opportunity. She had the travel brochure to prove it.

The heavy doors closed behind her and she glanced around. Americans had to have some culture and artistry, given the marbled floors and grand columns. She'd never stepped inside London's train station, but she figured if she had, she'd note more similarities.

She followed a family of five to the ticket booth. The mother, father, and three children dressed and acted much like the higher classes in England, which eased her sense of isolation. As did the travelers hurrying past her, most likely going off to find adventure just like her.

When it was her turn, Penny flashed a confident smile at the man behind the caged window, "I'm traveling to San Francisco." He was just like the ticket makers in England, his bespectacled face partially hidden with a visor and a pencil tucked behind one ear.

So far, so good. She'd be fine.

"Just one?" he asked.

"Yes," Penny nodded, paying no heed to the two men on her left. "Just one."

He acted none too pleased with her answer but he took Penny's money and wrote out a ticket. Earlier Lucas had exchanged her British pounds for American currency, so she was all set with American dollars.

"Platform two." He pushed the ticket as well as her change under the bars. "Train going west leaves at ten thirty tonight."

"Thank you." She stuffed her change into her reticule and ambled through the station, taking note of all the activity of other well-dressed travelers going about their business.

She was about to pay a vendor for a pastry to eat when someone shoved her aside and ripped her small bag from her hands. Stunned, she watched in horror as two men sprinted toward the entrance with her money.

It took a moment to gain her wits and she yelled, "Stop, thief!" She ran in the direction they'd shot off, but her half boots and traveling skirt hampered her speed. Pushing past the passersby who were eyeing her with speculation, she lost sight of them.

Tears sprang to her eyes. Oh dear Lord! The thieves had stolen her means to live while she waited for Geoff. Looking down, she was relieved to see the ticket still in her hand, but the fact didn't stop the emptiness from growing in the pit of her stomach. Bereft and all alone, she walked over to a bench and sat. Though she fought them, her tears wouldn't stop flowing. Except for the value of her ticket and a few pieces of jewelry in her trunk, she had no means of supporting herself and no idea of what to do now. And even worse, her prized locket had been in her reticule.

◌ℨ

"Are you all right?" Parker asked minutes later, sitting down next to Penny.

Staying out of sight, he'd followed her to the station and had observed her tearful good-byes to Mindy. While keeping to his task, he'd noticed the men's interest. Then, hanging back further, he'd seen them make their move. Only he'd been much faster than Penny. He'd tackled the one who'd grabbed her purse. The thief eventually got away, but he'd retrieve her money, along with the other objects in the small bag. After placing them in his pockets for safekeeping, he'd returned to help Penny.

"Mr. Davis? What are you doing here?" Penny sniffed, wiped away her tears and flashed a brave smile. "They took my bag."

He gripped her elbow, turning her to him, slowly sliding an intent gaze over her body, looking for injury. Under his scrutiny, her tears increased.

"I lost my locket, my only memory of my parents, along with all my money," she said in between sobs. "I can't travel without money."

"Shush," he whispered, wrapping her in his arms and holding her as she continued crying.

"What am I to do now?" Her soft, accented words filtered past his ears not long after her tears subsided.

Parker's arms tightened. "We'll work it out." He kissed the top of her head, not about to tell her he'd retrieved her money and locket. The little fool just didn't realize how dangerous it was to be alone and unprotected in the world. He couldn't let her go now. While holding her, his mind churned, thinking of some way to keep her in his company until he could come up with a better plan.

"You still have your ticket, right?" When she nodded, he smiled. "All right. Let me see it."

She placed the ticket into his outstretched hand. "What good does it do me, if I haven't the means of supporting myself?"

"This is good for travel anytime," he said, reading the ticket. "Which means your trip will only be delayed." He met her tear-filled gaze. "When did you say you were meeting your fiancé?"

"Six months."

"Plenty of time to make it on the train at a later date. I've booked a hotel room for the night," he told her, suddenly coming up with the lie. "Let's get you a room and we can discuss what to do once we've had dinner and can think clearer."

"I can't." Shaking her head, Penny said in a more confident voice,

"I just realized I can sell my jewelry, but I don't have the funds to squander on a room." She looked off in the distance, lost in thought. "I hate selling the pieces, though. They were my mother's and all I have left of her now that my locket is gone."

"It's not a wise idea to keep to your original plan, Miss Layton." Parker's voice became more urgent. "It's really best to secure a room and postpone your trip."

"Oh?" she said, eyes widening. "Why would I do that when I won't be needing one? Hotels charge money. I have until ten thirty to sell some jewelry. Then I can make my train. I'm sure I can get some type of employment once I get to California." Her voice lacked conviction, but her eyes flashed determination.

Parker bit back a retort and held in his frustration. Was she jesting about still traveling to California alone? And selling jewelry for more money to live on once she arrived there? Hadn't one lesson of being robbed been enough? Sweet Jesus, she was too trusting. Too naive. There was no way he could let her leave his side, even if it meant taking her screaming and kicking off the street.

"I can't in good conscience let you get on the train tonight." He shrugged. "I'll pay for an extra room and even help you sell your jewelry. Today's Saturday. Not the best day to do business. Might do better to wait until Monday. Better yet, if you don't want to sell them, why not come home with me and work on my farm. Surely that's a more viable solution than me leaving you to make your trip and find nonexistent work in California."

"I don't know." Penny eyed him thoughtfully, chewing on her bottom lip. "If only my bag hadn't been stolen." She sighed. "I was so looking forward to my train trip."

"You'll still take your trip west." He hesitated. "You're only changing your plans a bit."

She smiled wanly, then admitted sheepishly, "This incident has left me a little shaken."

"It's a perfect solution." He grinned and he added more enthusiastically, "Gives you a chance to think about what you want to do. Sell your jewelry and go now, or stay awhile, earn some money, and keep your jewelry."

Penny nodded. "You do make a good case. I'll pay you back for the room." She stared at him for the longest time, as if weighing his suggestion before her focus shifted to a distant spot. Watching her facial features go through several changes, Parker prayed he wouldn't have to coerce her any more than he already had. He hated deception. Yet if he told her the full truth, she'd leave him only to become an unwilling victim to some other horrible fate, and he couldn't allow that to happen.

"Maybe it would be best to delay my trip. At least for a day or two."

"Come along then." He stood and held out his hand. "Let's go retrieve your trunk and make our way to the hotel."

Chapter 10

"Hope you and the missus enjoy your stay at Baltimore's finest, Mr. Davis." The gentleman behind the desk who'd registered Parker handed him a key.

"Thank you." Parker smiled, enjoying the idea of this man mistaking Penny for his wife. For some reason, hearing him address her as such provided an odd feeling. Pushing his thoughts aside, he handed the bellman his key and pointed to where Penny waited with their belongings. "Can you have those sent to our room as soon as possible?"

"Yes sir, Mr. Davis," the young man said, before hurrying to do his bidding with Parker right behind him.

"Our room?" Penny whispered once he stood in front of her. "I thought you were getting two?"

"There's a cattlemen's convention in town. Seems they only had the one left," he murmured, pulling her toward the stairs and out of the bellman's earshot. "I don't see a problem."

"That's ridiculous." She stopped suddenly and crossed her arms. "I can't share a room with you."

"We have no other alternative." He wasn't any happier when he'd be suffering her alluring presence. At least he'd know where she was and could keep an eye on her until he figured out what to do next.

Penny gaped at him. You'd think he was asking her to lie naked in the streets, rather than help her out of a difficult situation.

"It's unseemly and simply not done," she stated in the clipped English accent he'd come to love, holding her nose in the air and looking much like the lady to the manner born. "I'd bring scandal on myself if anyone ever found out."

Parker chuckled. "Miss Layton, who's to find out? I'm virtually unknown in Baltimore and no one certainly knows you."

TEMPTATION

When she met his gaze, he sucked in a huge breath. The torment mirrored in those vivid blue eyes tugged at him and did nothing to ease the attraction he felt.

"Can you honestly tell me being in your company any more than necessary won't be a huge mistake?"

She had a point.

He swallowed hard, wondering at this lunacy. Spending the night with her wasn't the brightest idea he'd ever had. But what choice did he have? He wanted her with him and he'd keep his lust in check. Hadn't he been doing it for weeks now? "I give you my word, you can trust me to act as the perfect gentleman."

"You promise?"

The lady had spunk, Parker thought, biting back a smile. With no options left, she still bargained as if she held all the aces in the deck. "Yes, Miss Layton, I promise."

One of her impish grins emerged and sent a signal directly to his groin in the form of liquid heat. Watching her lips now begging to be kissed, Parker shook his lustful thoughts, reminding himself of her situation and of his promise. She was an innocent, engaged to some other fellow, or so she claimed. Damn! Why had he set himself up for such temptation?

Parker placed his hand on Penny's elbow and said gently, "Come, my dear. We're on the second floor."

They were in the room for a brief period when the bellman knocked. Parker waited patiently as he placed the luggage in the spacious, richly furnished room, including a large canopied bed on one side and a formal sitting area on the other.

Once the bellman finished, he turned to Parker. "Enjoy your stay, Mr. and Mrs. Davis."

Watching him leave, he heard Penny's horrified, "He thinks we're married?"

"He doesn't know us and he'll never see us again, so what difference can it make?" Parker answered, his voice revealing a slight annoyance over her appalled expression. "Wouldn't you rather he believe you were my wife since we're staying in one room?"

"I expect you to behave as a proper gentleman, Mr. Davis." All of a sudden she paced, reminding him of a caged tiger. "Otherwise I'll be forced to carry out my original plan and leave on the train tonight," Penny threatened, rubbing her arms. She stepped to the window and looked out onto the bustling street below. "I don't know how I ever agreed to this arrangement."

"Miss Layton, my intentions are honorable. If you'll recall, we spent several weeks on board ship without incident, thanks to my efforts." Chuckling, he removed his jacket and hung it up. He started for the wash closet, saying over his shoulder, "I'm going to freshen up. Rather than stay cooped up, maybe we can take a stroll around town before we find someplace to eat dinner."

慑

"That would be nice," Penny said too quickly to Parker's back as he closed the door. She continued to pace and said a little louder, trying to sound normal, "This is an adventure and I'd love to see all I can. Baltimore doesn't appear to be much different from London—noisy, crowded, and dirty."

If only she didn't like him so much, she thought, wishing she could be braver, more adventurous, and not so relieved to not have to take the train just yet. She wanted to be independent. Yet she'd never been totally on her own before and had never thought about how daunting not knowing a soul in the world could be.

Now that she was safe with Mr. Davis, she reflected on exactly what had happened at the station. Her shoulders slumped in resignation. Women alone were vulnerable.

"True." Parker's voice from the small room infiltrated her thoughts. "Baltimore isn't as big nor as old, but most big cities are similar, whether here or England." There was a pause before he asked, "I take it this is your first trip to America?"

"Yes. Until eight months ago I'd never been more than a few miles from Newcastle upon Tyne, the village close to where I grew up," Penny answered honestly.

"So eight months ago you traveled to London? And that was your first visit?"

Seeing no reason to lie, she said, "Yes. I really didn't like London. Too big and crowded."

TEMPTATION

Coming out of the room, Parker wiped his face with a towel wrapped around his neck. He'd taken off his shirt while in the wash closet. He halted at his bag, pulled out a fresh shirt, and put it on while he spoke. "You never did answer my question about why you traveled so far north to sail to America. Or for that matter, you never told me why you'd travel so far to marry. Why not get married in London?"

Penny had to purposefully avert her gaze back to the street as heat seeped up her face. Heavens, did he have to affect her so? In his sleeveless undershirt, his well-muscled upper body was too hard to ignore and she liked looking at it too much. Unwilling to dwell on how attractive he appeared, she turned her attention to a wagon being unloaded across the street, working to quell the emotion in her voice. "I wish you'd quit with your nosy questions. I'm not going to answer them."

"Still being evasive, Miss Layton?" Parker chuckled and finished buttoning his shirt. "You know I'll find out eventually."

"Not from me, you won't," she said, thankful to use his nosiness as a diversion to her attraction. Irritation over his curiosity she could handle much more than his half-naked torso. "I thought we'd become friends."

"We are friends," he said cheerfully, ignoring the annoyed look she sent. Parker reached for his jacket. Once done shrugging into it, he bestowed on her another wide grin, showing beautiful straight teeth. "Are you ready or would you prefer to freshen up?"

"I'm fine. Let's go." Unable to stop the flush of pleasure that his smile educed from spreading, she hurried past him. The walls were closing in on her because his male presence filled the room, leaving no space to avoid him.

Out on the streets, she could breathe easier and had plenty to keep her mind occupied. Everywhere her glance hit, busy passersby rushed about, street vendors hawked their wares in loud voices, and horse-drawn wagons rumbled by. The startling blue sky was marred only with white billowy clouds that added to its beauty. The sun's heat added balminess to the air, yet felt good on her skin.

Penny relaxed her shoulders and let out a heavy sigh, taking delight in just being free.

She'd escaped the earl. He couldn't touch her here. It was exhilarating to be walking around Baltimore with a handsome man who did his best to entertain her and keep her mind off her earlier mishap. She decided to enjoy the rest of the afternoon and not worry about her attraction to her escort.

Their hotel was located in the center of Baltimore. The two walked past a bakery and a general store.

At a jewelry store, Parker stopped.

"Those would bring out your eyes." His nod indicated a pair of sapphire earrings in the window. "Come. Let's go in and look around." He reached for her gloved hand and led her into the shop.

The bell tinkled as the door closed behind them.

"May I be of service?" The jeweler looked up from the glass case he was polishing.

"I'd like to see the sapphire earrings in the window." Parker pointed to the display.

"Ah. A nice selection—perfect stones. I also have a matching necklace and bracelet. Would you care to see those?" At his nod, he removed the earrings from the display and handed them to Parker. "Over here," he said, going behind another case and removing two stunning pieces of jewelry.

"What do you think?" Parker glanced at Penny, lifting a brow and smiling.

She gaped. "I can't remember when I've seen more beautiful sapphires."

"So you like them?"

"Of course. What's not to like?" Penny fingered the pieces with reverence.

"Then try them on," Parker urged. When she shook her head reluctantly, his grin stretched. "I'm thinking of getting them for my sister. She's fair like you, so if you try them on, I can get an idea of what they'll look like."

"All right." Penny took the earrings from the jeweler and put them on. She glanced in the looking glass and added the necklace, presenting her back to Parker.

He fastened the clasp, before capturing her gaze in the glass.

"They do bring out my eyes." She turned to him and smiled. "Are your sister's eyes like mine?"

"Similar." Shaking his head, he said, "But somehow after seeing them on you, I don't think they'd do for Catherine."

"That's too bad. They are beautiful," she said wistfully. "There are other pieces here, if you're looking for a gift." Penny took the jewelry off and laid the pieces on the velvet pad the jeweler had placed on the counter.

She then roamed through the shop, looking at other displayed items while Parker talked quietly to the proprietor.

With his business clearly concluded, she ambled in his direction.

"Well, shall we continue?" He offered an arm, as well as a brilliant smile.

Penny nodded and after placing her hand in the crook of his bent arm, they walked out of the store.

"So, tell me about Catherine," she said, after traveling half a block. "Mindy said you had sisters. Is it her birthday? Is that why you're buying her a present?"

Parker halted and gave her an amused look while patting her gloved hand. "How about this? I tell you about my family, only if you tell me about yours."

"I have no family left, so I don't have much to tell," she countered, fighting to keep a straight face.

"Then you can tell me how is it that you're such good friends with a duke's brother."

"Which I might answer if you tell me something about yourself."

"You're evading again." He laughed. "I think you should tell me first. That way I can be sure of getting an answer."

"Oh no," she said, unable to keep the teasing quality out of her voice. "I know nothing about you and you already know too much about me."

"Not true. You know Lucas and I are brothers."

"That's all, though." Her half laugh rose up. "How many sisters do you have?"

"Three. Rebecca, Sarah, and Catherine."

"Where do they live?"

"Catherine lives with my mother, who lives on my farm. Rebecca and Sarah are both married and live in neighboring towns with their husbands."

"I take it Catherine is the youngest?" she asked, only too glad he answered her questions without making her reciprocate.

"Yes, she's the baby." No one could miss the warm affection in his voice.

"Any other brothers besides the captain?"

Parker stiffened. For a brief instant pain flashed in his eyes before he schooled the look and shook his head. "No. Just Lucas and me."

"I didn't mean to pry," Penny murmured in an apologetic tone, noting the change in his demeanor.

"How could you know I had two younger brothers who died tragically?"

Penny stopped and gripped his arm. "I'm sorry. I understand what's it's like to lose someone you love." She waited a heartbeat and added, "It might help to talk about it."

"Oh?" He eyed her a long moment before shrugging and looking off at a distant point. She'd begun to think he wouldn't say anything when his sad voice filled the air around them. "My father and two brothers were killed in a senseless accident." He clenched his fist and his expression became as hard as granite. "I can never remember their deaths without thinking about why it happened. Though Henry Sterling didn't outright cause the accident, his negligence did nothing to prevent it, either." He ran a hand through his hair and met her gaze again, his now mirroring pain. "Greed killed my father and brothers—a love of profits over a love of humanity. Since leaving England, I can't seem to push the memories away."

"I'm so sorry," Penny said softly, squeezing his arm, trying to add comfort, now sensing a kinship with him because they shared a deep sorrow.

Parker grunted, but added nothing more to the conversation. They meandered toward the hotel, both lost in their thoughts.

Minutes later, his voice rang out. "I'm hungry. What about you?" When she nodded, he asked, "Would you like to stop in one of these restaurants, or would you prefer the hotel dining room?"

TEMPTATION

"The dining room is probably more convenient." Penny shrugged, glad they weren't going back to their room so quickly, especially after his earlier confession, which left her more torn than ever. She glanced up to see his mood had lightened. As disconcerting as it was, his warm gaze made her heart race.

He held the door while she entered the hotel dining room. All remnants of Parker's pain had dissipated and he was once again the charming, entertaining man she'd come to rely on. In moments, they were seated. A waiter greeted them pleasantly.

Any remaining uneasiness with Parker fled as he regaled her with story after story of his sister Catherine and her unruly behavior.

"We've lost all hope of finding her a match," he said, finishing up with Catherine's last debacle with her suitor from Baltimore.

"Well, a good match isn't always what it appears to be," Penny stated, thinking of her own situation.

Something in her tone must have given her away, because Parker's expression changed slightly. Eying him warily, she thought, Uh-oh, I'm doing it again. If I'm not careful, he'll have all my secrets out and I'll be back under the earl's control in no time.

"Why would you say that?" he asked, picking up her gloved hand. He kissed it and eyed her intently. "Are you running from your intended, perpetuating a lie? Is that why he let you sail across the ocean alone and unprotected? You think to hide in California?"

"No," she cried, alarmed at how close to the truth he'd come. She chewed on her bottom lip nervously as a streak of fear raced through her system. Covering her trepidation under a nervous laugh, she withdrew her hand. "Why are you so concerned? I'm fine. Surely once I leave, your duty to protect me will be over."

"I see. And you need no protection?"

"No. I can take care of myself."

"And that's why two men were able to abscond with your bag? Because you were taking care of yourself so well?"

"That was just a minor setback and could've happened to anyone." She wouldn't believe otherwise.

"It's never happened to me or anyone I was protecting. If you were mine, I would never let you roam the countryside by yourself."

Despite feeling safe under his protection, she stiffened. Just like a man to make such an autocratic statement. One who thought he owned women. Of course in her world, men did. Men like Geoff and her father were rare. "I don't belong to you or any man, so it's a moot point," she said, before going back to her food and remaining silent.

For the rest of their meal, their jovial mood of the afternoon had fled to be replaced with one of guarded reserve.

CB

Parker heaved a heavy sigh as they walked back to the room, wishing he didn't care about Penny's secrets. Though he'd tried, he couldn't stop the vision she'd presented in the jewelry store from invading his thoughts. The blue sapphires had highlighted the creaminess of her pale complexion while bringing out the blue in her eyes, and too many times over the course of the evening he'd wondered what she'd look like wearing only the jewelry without clothing. He had to quit thinking such things.

Outside their room, Parker cast a glance at her and sighed, noting a closed expression. Hell, maybe it was for the best. With her demeanor shut tight, his own lust died somewhat, making it easier to be around her without wanting to wipe that impish grin off her face with kisses, as had been his most pressing daydream much too often during the last few hours.

He held the door open, allowing her to go ahead of him.

It would be a long, long night.

"It's still early. Would you care for a game of chess?" Parker asked.

"I'd love one." She smiled, but remained silent as he set up the board.

The two played for over twenty minutes with neither speaking.

"I was only trying to help, Penny," he finally said, no longer willing to put up with the depressing mood in the room.

Seeing her stunned expression when she glanced up at him, he shrugged. "Don't you think it's a little silly for us to be so formal when we're sharing a room?"

Penny's spine straightened. She inhaled deeply and met his gaze. "Mr. Davis—"

"It's Parker." When she opened her mouth to argue, he reached over and placed a finger to her lips. "Shush and make your move."

He chuckled at the annoyed barbs her gaze tossed at him. "We're friends. As such, I expect you to call me Parker from here on out and I'm going to call you Penny," he said, not giving her a chance to say what he knew was on her lips. "I promise not to pry into your personal life, but I can't let you go off by yourself. Will you come home with me and forget going to California for the time being? You can help my mother and Catherine with their duties on the farm."

"We're friends and you're not going to pry?"

"Yes, if you'll you agree to come home with me." Relief swept over Parker at her nod. "Thank God you've come to your senses."

Penny's lips flattened into a straight line. "Just remember. You don't own me. I'm only doing this because I feel it's the right thing to do, especially since I don't want to sell my mother's jewelry."

"I'll keep that in mind." Parker chuckled, moving his knight into position. "Check."

"Oh, you think you're so smart. My mind wasn't on the game, that's why you trounced me so easily," she said.

"Make your move, so we can end this game and play another. I rather like playing a better adversary. Your distraction wasn't much of a challenge." He flashed a smug smile, only too happy to have convinced her to his way of thinking.

Later, after another long game that finally ended in a stalemate, the room filled with tension. Penny stood and flitted about, nervously going from space to space, too preoccupied with whatever she focused on.

"Will you stop?" Parker finally said, annoyed that she seemed ill at ease. "I'm not going to ravish you, so you can relax."

She froze and a heated blush stole up her face. "I didn't think that."

"Then why the blush?"

If eyes could kill, he'd be dead, given the look she sent him. Grinning, he patted the divan next to him. "Come here." When her expression turned skeptical, he laughed. "You need to trust me. You can't trust me if you're afraid of me." He patted the seat again. "So come here."

Penny rolled her eyes, before flashing another irritated glare. "I don't think that's going to help. I need air." She continued her pacing.

Chuckling, Parker rose and walked toward her, moving in slow motion as she took reflexive steps back, but was hampered from retreating farther when she hit the wall. With purpose, he gripped her arm, tugging her with him to the settee.

He sat and gave her no choice but to follow.

"See?" He bit his cheek to keep from laughing at her stiff posture. If he laughed at her discomfort now, she might never forgive him. "There's nothing to fear. Relax." His hands slid up her arms in a soothing manner. "Remember, we're friends." He nodded, indicating the bed. "You'll be safe over there, and I'll be right here." Parker kissed her forehead and pulled her closer. "I gave my word. Do you trust me?"

He smiled when he felt her nod. Eventually, her stiffness ebbed somewhat and he leaned away, his grin growing. "See? Nothing to fear." Another blush stole up her face. Suddenly he couldn't breathe. Lord, would she ever stop looking at him like that? When she did, it was hard to remember his promise.

Dropping his hands, Parker straightened and cleared his throat.

Penny smoothed her dress, glancing guiltily at her lap.

"Damn," he whispered, standing. The lady's innocent gestures were too much to bear. He raked a hand through his hair, keeping his focus on the floor. "Maybe it would be best if I went for a walk to give you a chance to get ready for bed. I meant my words. You have nothing to fear from me, Penny." He strode across the room. "I'll be back much later in order to give you plenty of time to fall asleep." He stopped at the door and nodded. "Good night."

Once outside the room, Parker leaned against the cool wood. Good God, he'd come so close to kissing her, especially after catching her blush, leaving him no doubts about her thoughts. Invitation to taste her lips was written clearly in her eyes and more than anything, Parker wanted to accept her invitation.

He headed toward a saloon, needing a drink. Hell, he needed the whole damn bottle.

Chapter 11

"No," Penny cried. "Please." She'd awakened from a sound sleep to find he'd invaded her bedchamber. She tried to cover her nakedness, but her wrists were bound to the bedposts. "Why are you doing this?"

And like that first time, no matter what she said or how she begged, it did no good.

"You can't fight, my dear, so you should just enjoy it."

"No. I won't. Please. Leave me be."

"You'll get used to my touch. I'll make sure of it." A menacing laugh laced with cruelty filled her ears, letting her know he took pleasure in her fear.

She looked around. Oh, dear Lord. Somehow he'd found her and she was back in London at the earl's townhouse, where he'd forced her to endure his depravities.

"Once we're married you'll be under my total control, never to escape me. Then I can enjoy all your charms, and not have to worry about what I do." He loomed over her, stroking her suggestively. "That bastard Collingswood won't be able to protect you then. You'll be mine! Mine to enjoy as I want, for as often as I want. Do you hear me?" he asked, whispering in her ear before licking it, then biting it, hard, causing her to clamp her eyes shut and move her head back and forth to avoid his lips and teeth.

She tried harder to ignore his touch and pretend it didn't bother her. When she felt his manhood rubbing against her, getting closer to the juncture where her legs met, she couldn't bring them together because her legs were spread, tied to the lower bedposts. Her nightgown was pushed above her breasts, baring her skin to him. She tugged on the restraints, crying out louder in fear. "No. Stop. Please stop," she yelled, finally breaking down in tears.

Though he didn't actually invade her body, his movements as he pleasured himself revolted her. She averted her gaze as much as was physically possible, not wanting to see what he was doing. Once satisfied, he got up to leave and cruelly grasped her chin, forcing her to meet his demented gaze.

"You're mine. And no one will dispute the fact. All of your father's lands are mine, as well as his wealth. I'll hunt you down to the ends of the earth to find you and when I do, you'll never escape again. Do you hear me?"

His threat as well as the crazed look on his face sent a surge of terror through her.

"Please," she whimpered as her tears increased.

ଓ

Penny's shouts pulled Parker out of a sound sleep. For a moment he wasn't sure where he was, but he quickly got his bearings. He was on the settee in the hotel room and Penny was in the throes of a bad dream as more of her cries rent the air.

He reached for the shirt he'd taken off in order to fall asleep in the stuffy room, but it lay forgotten as her increased yelling had him rushing to the canopied bed barely visible in the moonlit room.

"Penny, wake up." He gave her a gentle shake. When she only offered mewing pleas, he shook a little harder and said a little louder, "Come on, sweetheart. Wake up. You're having a nightmare. It's all right, you're safe."

By the time he did wake her, she was crying uncontrollably. He sat on the edge of bed, pulled her into his arms and let her cry.

"Shush," he murmured, stroking her as he would a small child. "You're safe."

"Hold me, Parker," Penny said, shivering. "It seemed so real," she eventually whispered.

"There's nothing to fear."

"I know. You're my friend and I trust you." She stopped shivering and her breathing evened out. "I feel safe with you." She snuggled closer.

"Nothing can hurt you now. I'll make sure of it." His embrace tightened. He kissed the top of her head.

"Thank you." She let out a long sigh. "I can't imagine why I'd have such a bad dream."

"Do you want to tell me about it? Sometimes voicing your fears helps. It always did with my sisters when they had bad dreams."

"No." She shook her head. "It's too horrible and not something I can share."

Since she seemed calmer, he didn't pry further. He held her a bit longer, watching as she closed her eyes. Eventually, her board-like rigidity dissolved and she sighed, her breaths becoming long and deep. When he thought she slept, he moved to disentangle himself from her.

Penny grabbed his arms, stopping him with a strong, panicked grip. "Please don't go."

He sat back down, positioning himself fully on the bed, lying prone and taking her with him. Parker closed his eyes, enjoying the feel of having her right where he wanted her.

"Remember that night you kissed me?"

"Yes," he replied warily, stiffening.

"Kiss me again."

He almost choked as her fervently whispered plea sent a signal directly to his groin. Loving nothing better than to shower her with kisses, he could only stare into the darkness with her in his arms, grasping at the little bit of control he had left.

Once he found his voice, he offered a strained, "Kissing's not a good idea right now."

"Why? Don't you want to kiss me?"

Parker ignored the hurt in her voice, fighting to rein in his warring emotions. Was she serious? Damn, how could he not want to kiss her again? But she was too tempting, and his need too great.

He replied honestly, whispering, "Yes. But that's not the point. If I start, I may not be able to stop."

"One kiss." She kissed his bare chest, the contact shooting white-hot lust straight through his body. "What can it hurt?"

His manhood responded instantly.

"I trust you, and a good night kiss will give me a different memory to go to sleep with other than my nightmare."

"Penny," he said a little more firmly, sitting up. "We are not going to kiss. It's a bad idea."

"Please? To make me forget," she pleaded, bending over him and timidly placing her mouth over his.

The minute their lips touched, more lust heated Parker's blood and his tenacious grip on his desires slipped. He knew he should pull away, especially since he still had some semblance of control, but her soft mouth sucked him in farther. Instantly, like a match to dry tinder, need and want burst to life inside his soul, flaming out of control. He could no more stop kissing her than he could stop breathing. Her low moan floated above his head, infiltrating his brain. He fought the impulse to deepen the kiss and returned to some modicum of reality.

"As much as I love kissing you, we have to stop," Parker whispered, breaking their contact, reaching deep inside for restraint. He rested his head back on the pillow, bringing her with him in the crook of his arm. When he realized he was still massaging her breast in an unconscious motion, he closed his eyes, willing his hand away from her body, but it wouldn't budge. He knew he was in serious trouble the minute Penny shook her head and leaned into him, her expressive eyes begging in the moonlit room, clearly telling him she was having none of his rejection.

"I love kissing you. Please, Parker, don't stop," she whispered, her voice as pleading as her eyes.

He watched in stunned fascination as she lowered her head, brushing her lips over his, using her mouth like a seasoned courtesan, yanking him back into an abyss of desire so hot his blood boiled. He wanted her. The more he kissed her, the more he wanted her. It was like being sucked into a vortex; the harder he fought, the greater its strength. He shook his head, abruptly pulling away. "My God! You kiss like an angel, but we have to stop. Penny," he ground out, breathing heavily. "This isn't a good idea. You don't know what you're doing."

"I'm enjoying your kisses. Aren't you enjoying mine?"

"Yes, but if you continue, I won't be able to honor my promise to you."

"Then I release you from your promise. I trust you and I love kissing you."

She kissed him again and again Parker broke away.

"This will only lead to trouble. I promised Lucas I'd leave you be and I can't break my word."

"We're no longer on board Lucas's ship, so that promise no longer holds you. Besides, it's my decision, not your brother's, and I'm willing."

"I can't believe this. I must be mad." He rubbed his hand over his face and stared at the ceiling, praying for divine intervention.

"Don't you want me?" she asked, her innocent question more seductive than anything he'd ever heard.

"Of course I want you, but what about your intended?"

"This has nothing to do with him," she stated firmly.

"Nothing to do with him?" Parker glared at her, totally incensed at the notion. "Penny, he's your betrothed. You owe him loyalty and fidelity."

"I'm not married yet," Penny hissed, just as incensed. "After we're married, I'll be faithful. But until that time, he doesn't own me. No one does." When he looked at her as if she had three eyes, she asked, "Why is it men can have countless affairs and no one questions them before marriage?"

"It's not the same thing and you know it. We men are animals."

"That's not true," she said, a quick grin spreading across her face. "Not all men."

"You doubt me?" he asked incredulously.

Penny nodded. "If that were true, then why are you stopping? I want this, Parker. Please. Kiss me," she whispered, just before her lips found his again. This time, her tentative hands began roaming over his naked upper body, her strokes growing bolder each second. She then undid his trousers and pushed them down, before her hands continued their exploration.

Her actions did nothing to quell his raging desire. He couldn't determine if this was heaven or hell because at the moment he experienced a little of both, and he knew he was sinking fast. When her timid fingers brushed over his bulging erection, he almost disgraced himself. Finally, he couldn't fight both her and his need any longer. Didn't see any reason to. Once he overcame his internal battle, he kicked out of his restraining pants. He took over as the pursuer, intent on inflaming her as he was inflamed.

He fought the pleasure, knowing he should go slower. She was an innocent, but the feel of her wandering hands left him with no will to cease his hurried pace and an overwhelming need to possess her—to stop the flames from consuming him. Her lips and hands were everywhere, yanking the same reaction from him. Damn, he hated himself because he was out of control. The only thing he wanted was to be inside of her. That became his driving force.

His hand caressed lower, grazing her womanhood. She flinched. The movement acted as a bucket of cold water, drenching his desire, yanking him out of an erotic fog and halting his advance.

"Why are you stopping?" Penny asked, when it became obvious he'd stilled his movements.

"I can't do it. You're an innocent and it's not right," Parker was able to get out after closing his eyes and gaining a bit of his control. At that moment, his body screamed for release. God, he had died and gone to hell for trying to seduce an angel. What had he been thinking?

"No. You can't quit."

"Yes, I can." He groaned at her insistent voice and offered a self-deprecating laugh. "Don't ask me why because I'll never be able to understand it myself."

"Oh no, it's not your decision." She pulled her nightgown over her head and threw it on the floor. Daringly, she reached for his manhood, holding it in her hand and stroking, watching him the entire time.

"Penny," he ground out in a warning tone, covering her hand. "You don't know what you're doing," he whispered, tormented beyond reason.

"Yes, I do. I'm ridding myself of a nightmare," Penny the temptress boldly answered, pulling out of his grasp and growing more courageous. As if knowing she held the secret to providing unlimited pleasure in her fingertips and that she controlled it somehow, her strokes became more insistent.

Flames shot through his veins. His resistance slipped and slid into the night, along with his reasoning. All his thoughts centered on possessing the angel from heaven, unconcerned over spending an eternity in hell for doing so.

Parker couldn't bear her touch one additional minute without exploding in her hands and shaming himself. Once again he became the aggressor, pushing her back on the bed and looming above her. But his finesse ended there. His control spent, he had to possess her. Now. That he'd not readied her properly for her first time no longer mattered. In a fluid movement, he pushed inside her, stopping the second he felt her cringe beneath him...felt her maidenhead.

He lifted up on his forearms.

"Are you all right?" he asked through clenched teeth, fighting the urge to plunge deeper into her moist depths.

She smiled. "Now I know what unleashed power feels like," she whispered, reaching around his neck and pulling him closer for a hot, soul-searing kiss.

Her words and mouth seduced him beyond his endurance. When the blonde goddess he possessed shifted beneath him, meeting him stroke for stroke, Parker thrust, veering completely out of control. And though he tried, he couldn't last long enough to give her pleasure. In seconds, he emptied himself inside her with a mind-numbing release before collapsing on top of her, too sated to stir.

The earth had surely moved and Parker needed a moment to collect himself. He'd never lost control before. Not like that. And worse! The one tempting woman who caused such actions claimed to be betrothed to another man.

She stretched beneath him. "So, that's what it's all about?" Penny whispered, interrupting his thoughts. "While it is nice, it does seem to be missing something."

Hearing the hint of disappointment in her voice, Parker couldn't help laughing. What irony. Damn if the innocent angel didn't amuse him, extending his nightmare because he was bound and determined to wipe the discontent from her voice. Parker pushed up on his arms, his smiling gaze caught and held hers. "There's more. You never gave me a chance to show you. Now that my lust has been sated somewhat, I can finish what *you* started."

Her eyebrows rose in question, clearly not understanding. Another chuckle rumbled from his chest and he flashed a seductive grin.

When Penny bestowed on him her siren's smile, he responded, instantly filling her once more.

"What have you done to me? Though my need has been met, I still want. Much more than I should," he whispered as his mouth sought hers. Unhurriedly, he kissed her, gentling his lips, coaxing her, and drawing out her desire a sip at a time. Again his need spiraled. Parker fought doubly hard to keep a tight rein over his body's reactions. He blocked the craving to plunge wildly into her warmth and concentrated solely on bringing her to completion.

She moaned. Her hands and lips caressed. Though an innocent angel, she was a natural at lovemaking. His muscles flexed under her fingertips. He gritted his teeth, fighting the fire her touch ignited. Still, he meant to give her a release this time, so he kept his thrusts slow and drawn out. Relief swamped him when she cried out with force and he could let go as his seed burst forth in one long moment of unadulterated bliss.

When Parker could move again, he pushed up on his elbows and looked down, noticing tears streaking down her face in the moonlit room.

Her tears unmanned him. This was entirely his fault. He should never have touched her. He rolled over, taking her with him and not breaking contact, so that she was now on top.

"Shush, shush. It's all right," he said, not hiding the emotion he felt.

His soft words caused her tears to increase. Parker held her, letting her cry, feeling a knot in the pit of his stomach over what had just happened moments ago. Damn, what was he going to do now?

"I'm sorry, it got out of control. We shouldn't have done that," he whispered once her tears subsided.

"No. It was the most beautiful experience of my life. You'll never know how tonight has changed me." Penny lifted up and he glimpsed the honesty in her eyes. "You've given me new memories to take the place of those that leave me cold. Thank you. I'll always treasure the memory of our lovemaking."

Her avowal made him even more uncomfortable. Rolling her over to the side, he pulled out of her and went to the wash closet for a wet cloth. When he returned, in an act of servitude because she humbled him, he wiped away the signs of her virginity. He then climbed back into bed and pulled her to him.

"Get some sleep, angel," he whispered, kissing the top of her head.

Holding Penny close while she peacefully slept, Parker lay awake, thinking of the beguiling woman he held and wondering about her past. What was she hiding? He no longer believed she was meeting her betrothed. No woman who loved another man would yield to him what she had. So that meant she was probably running from one. Well, she wasn't running anymore because she was marrying him. He didn't love her. He wouldn't allow himself to love any woman again after Lady Margaret, but he craved what they'd shared together. There was no way he could let her go after their mating. Lying there now, no more than two hours after having her, he still wanted her.

Chapter 12

"There are several ships sailing to America within days, but two are making other stops along the way and none are making port in Baltimore as Lucas's ship does," Markham said, after reading the missive from Jones with news about various ships and their schedules. He nodded as Geoff sat down in front of him. "I'm inclined to wait for Lucas. His ship is scheduled to be back in port in three more weeks."

"I thought you wanted to sail right away."

"I have my reasons, trust me."

"I do trust you." Geoff stood and paced, impatience radiating from him. "But now that I have your blessing, I'm eager to find her."

Markham smiled. "If we sail with Lucas, we can keep our trip confidential. Our partnership is a silent one and he's not in the habit of taking on passengers. Hopefully Kentworth will overlook his ship. No doubt he's following our trail to find the lady, so no need to make his job any easier. Besides, waiting on Lucas won't set us back much and this will work to confuse the earl, especially if we act normally." When Geoff looked at him with eyebrows raised, he added, "Go about your usual business. Quit hiding out in the house as if waiting for news. Take interest in a few of the ladies around town to throw him off more."

"All right." Geoff nodded, concentration moving to a paperweight situated in the middle of Markham's dark mahogany desk. "I want to be married as soon as we meet up with her."

"I expected as much." Markham leaned into his chair and regarded his brother. "Are you planning on staying in America?" he asked.

"That was the original plan." Geoff smiled. "With your support, we can return home after making a tour of it. She'll reach her majority a month after I turn twenty-one. By then we'll be married, and the earl's power over her will be diminished."

TEMPTATION

Markham sighed. "Somehow, I don't think it will be that easy. We have to be prepared for his reprisals and make sure he can't have the marriage annulled somehow. Maybe it would be better to plan an extended stay until well after her birthday and get her with child so an annulment will be completely out of the question."

∞

"Mrs. Bowers," Gerald Knightsbridge said to Lytherton Manor's head housekeeper. Lady Penelope's loyal staff surely knew much more than they imparted. He'd already spent countless hours riding hundreds of miles to arrive at his ward's childhood home, all to no avail. His patience had long waned.

"Do not waste my time." He added a bit of menace to his voice in an attempt to intimidate the woman in front of him. "Nothing will let me believe you have no knowledge of your daughter Melinda's whereabouts." Penelope had to have had help and her maid was also missing. If he found the maid, he'd find his heiress.

Desperation ruled his actions. His ward had been gone more than a month and time was of the essence. While he still had faith he'd find the bitch, her disappearance filled him with rage.

"Now, either you tell me or I'll have no choice but to set you out and let it be known that you stole from the lady. I can assure you, Newgate is not a pleasant place to spend your last years."

"You wouldn't," Jane Bowers cried, her confident expression crumpling. "You have no cause. I've worked here all my life and have always seen the manor well cared for."

"That is beside the point," he said with a sneer, his smile now matching the sinister tone in his voice. "I have no use for thieves. I should've fired the lot of you the moment Lady Penelope became my ward. Now talk or I'll bring you up on charges."

Jane cringed in obvious fear as he'd hoped. Her eyes blurred with tears. "Please, my lord, I've already told you! I don't know where the lady went."

"That may true, but you do know your daughter's whereabouts and you will tell me." His anger erupted. "Now," he bellowed, pounding the table. He would find her, by God. He'd sail to the ends of the earth for this heiress—his greed and lust demanded it of him.

Once he'd gotten his use out of her, both physically and monetarily, she'd be expendable, just like her parents. Little did the couple know they'd signed their death warrants at the same time they'd signed their betrothal agreement. He'd counted heavily on the money she'd bring to the marriage, not to mention the Northumberland mines, property they'd bequeathed to her. Gerald would never let them go.

Something in his manner must have convinced her he meant his words, because Jane Bowers closed her eyes, letting the tears fall unheeded, before whispering, "Mindy is in America. A farm not far from Baltimore, Maryland. She went to help her sister in her time of need and for a better life than being a servant here in England."

"Was that so hard?" His answer was more tears, which became more pronounced when he added, "You're of no more use to me and I expect you off this property within the hour."

"Please, I told you what you wanted."

"Yes, and I'm sure you helped her escape. For that, I'll make certain you won't find work in any respectable household ever again."

"You're nothing but evil, my lord," she said, brushing her tears away, her spine stiffening. "I now see why she was so quick to run."

Gerald backhanded her, his vicious slap sending her back a step.

Jane Bowers took a moment to recover, and then she gave a throaty laugh. "You'll never find her. Even Mindy doesn't know where she went." Watching the earl, her scornful laughter increased. "Ah. I see you now 'ave doubts. Good. Try as you might, you'll never find her, my lord. She hates you."

The woman departed the room, her laughter filling the air, fueling Gerald's rage and mocking him. He had no one to blame but his own lust and stupidity. He'd miscalculated his treatment of her and his actions had the opposite effect of what he'd intended. How had he missed the bitch's spunk hiding under her cowering, simpering disguise?

He'd been too hasty in giving her a taste of his needs. But he'd had a hard time resisting her lure. Bloody hell! What an understatement. The girl's innocence had driven him to distraction. Just thinking about having her under him caused his groin to fill. Slamming his fist on the mantel, he swore. Damn the bitch. She was a curse, bewitching him with her purity.

What ate at him more? The duke's threats had kept him from taking what he wanted while she'd been under his control. He'd not fully tasted her, yet but his desire had only grown to an all-consuming mass of want that ate away at him.

Still, he was thankful he'd not done anything that could be questioned. He'd taken great pains to ensure she came across as a spoiled, willful child with no appreciation of all he'd done, so no one would believe her. If Collingswood found her, it would be an earl's word against hers, and the duke would have no choice but to return her. His ward had no proof of his abuse—only memories.

Soon, he'd have her and his wait would be over. The thought of using Collingswood to bring it about pleased him even more.

Turning, intent on making a swift return to London, Gerald walked briskly from the room.

Chapter 13

The next morning Penny woke before Parker. In the light of day, her nightmare had totally receded. A continent away, Gerald Knightsbridge couldn't touch her. Thoughts of Geoff filled her mind and guilt consumed her as memories of last night followed. She'd betrayed him in the heat of the moment. Worse, she'd do it again. She'd do anything to erase the bleak images of being a powerless and helpless victim. Last night she'd been anything but the victim, she had to admit. Nestled in Parker's arms, she felt very safe, as she'd sensed she would, but she'd paid a hefty price for such safety. Well, she wouldn't think of that now.

Penny untangled her leg from his and sat up to study his face. In sleep, the angular lines softened somewhat, making him appear boyish. He was ruggedly handsome, so much so that she wished there was something about him besides his autocratic nature that she could find fault with. It wouldn't do to let him think he could control her. She'd had enough of controlling men.

With this in mind, she climbed out of the bed being careful not to wake him, and padded to her trunk. She opened it and took out the necessary items she needed to dress. Once done with washing and dressing, and too impatient to sit and wait for Parker to wake, she began tidying the items of clothing scattered about the floor in disarray. She placed his trousers neatly on a chair. They slid to the floor. When she reached inside the armoire and grabbed the jacket off the hanger to place the pants underneath, something fell out of the pocket. Bending to pick it up, she spied her locket on the floor and froze in horror.

He'd found her locket and hadn't told her? Confusion clouded her mind. Glancing at the bed and watching him for a moment, she fought to understand. Maybe he didn't realize how important the locket was to her, but what was he doing with it to begin with? How had he gotten it from the thieves? Or worse, maybe he'd hired the men to steal it from her to scare her into staying with him. Anger rushed up, distorting her thoughts.

Clutching the jacket, she went through all the pockets only to find everything she'd placed in her bag, including her wad of American money. Unable to control her rage, she marched over to the man sleeping so peacefully.

"How dare you!" she yelled, pushing him as hard as she could. "You planned it all, didn't you?"

Groggily, Parker opened his eyes just in time to dodge her fist. Snatching her around the waist, he pulled her off balance, with her kicking and striking out the entire time. He rolled, positioning her underneath.

"What the hell are you doing?" he asked, clearly stunned. He pinned her down, seizing her wrists with a firm grip.

She squirmed and furiously worked to yank her arms free, her eyes snapping fire.

"What's the matter? Didn't get enough last night? I can remedy that," he said, chuckling and nuzzling her neck while holding her hands above her head.

"Get off me," she cried, feeling his erection nestled in the V of her lower body. She froze, alarmed at how quickly her anger dissipated, to be replaced with excitement and worse—desire.

"In a minute." He unhurriedly spread kisses along her neck.

Goodness, he knew how to use that mouth. She melted into him, unable to withstand the pleasure it evoked on its magical journey to her ear. After he spent glorious moments kissing, sucking, biting, and tugging on it, his tongue plunged inside. Thankfully, he'd released her arms so she could touch his exquisite masculine torso.

"Do you know how lovely you are?" he whispered. "Can you feel my want?"

A low moan was her only answer.

Parker nuzzled his way to her breast that he'd somehow exposed. She arched, allowing him more access as sensations of pure bliss shot from her core ending in her soft moans, only to regenerate and begin anew.

Oh heavens, she wished he wasn't so skilled a lover. She fought the heat building, the warmth spreading, and the yearning to have him inside her. It seemed a losing battle, especially when he added such practiced hands. One now lifted her dress to her waist, and did away with her underclothes as his fingers found her center, stroking and eliciting more sensations out of her, one after the other in wave after wave of pleasure. So much so that she thought she would die if he didn't continue.

"God, you're ready for me, and I haven't even begun to make love with you," he murmured, just before his lips found hers.

She shut her eyes tight, willing the need away. She didn't want to be ready for him. She broke the kiss, said softly into his lips, "No," and hated herself because she didn't mean it. Her actions of last night were justified, but right now? How could she mate with him again when she loved Geoff? Self-loathing filled her.

Parker touched his hand to the side of her face and stroked her cheek.

"Penny?" His lips hovered inches above hers. "Look at me, sweetheart."

She met his gaze, unable to disguise the passion roiling inside her, and noted the same mirrored in his expressive blue-gray depths.

"I don't believe you. Tell me you don't want this and I'll stop."

He gave her a choice, yet she had no choice, the temptation too strong. "I can't," she answered truthfully.

His mouth lowered. As if they had a mind of their own, her arms wrapped around his muscular back to pull him closer.

When he entered her, she met him stroke for stroke, touch for touch, until she found her release. Pure ecstasy spread throughout her every pore. The force of the release tormented her further with Parker not far behind, spending his seed as he shuddered violently above her.

When the sensations ebbed, emotion overwhelmed Penny, evoking tears of shame. How had she so brazenly wanted to lie with him when she knew Geoff loved her and she loved Geoff? And God in heaven, how was she ever going to be free of Parker if he could control her so easily with passion?

Parker lifted up onto his elbows and noticed her tears. "Shush," he murmured, pulling out of her, rolling onto his side and bringing her with him. "Please don't cry," he whispered fervently, kissing her closed eyes. "You have to know I mean to marry you. I'll take care of you."

When the significance of his words set in, she sat up abruptly and jerked out of his grasp. Wiping her tears away, she said, "Heaven forbid. I can't marry you." She sprung from the bed and righted her clothing.

"And why not?" he demanded, his voice taking on a hard edge.

His autocratic tone could easily belong to a peer of the realm—a controlling peer, much like the duke or worse—the earl. Her spine stiffened. "Because I told you. I'm already engaged to be married. Nothing has changed."

Parker glanced at her, his expression a mask of disbelief. "You can't really think that after last night. After what just happened?"

Penny bit her lip nervously, not quite sure how to handle him. It was hard to ignore the blatant sexuality of the man, especially when he all but lounged in naked splendor, not seeming to care whether she stared or not. She took a deep breath to still her racing heart. Lord knew she couldn't deny that she liked looking at him.

She looked away and reached deep for resolve. No! He was twisting this around. Nothing had changed. Yes, she found him attractive. But that was only because she missed Geoff.

Her golden prince entered her mind just then, changing her focus to what she'd done. The unthinkable, but he'd never know it. She'd go to her grave keeping her attraction to Parker a secret. Penny pushed the draperies aside to stare out the window, also pushing aside her shameful behavior. Other thoughts replaced those she banished, like those of her locket and how Parker happened to have her property.

Anger rose up once again and using it as a crutch, she turned on him. "Did you plan it? Did you have those men rob me to keep me with you?"

"What are you talking about?"

"My bag. My stolen property. How is it that you happen to have the contents of my bag in your jacket?" she demanded, picking up her locket and shoving out her hand, the piece centered in her palm.

The guilty look crossing his face confirmed her worst fear. He was somehow involved.

"You did plan it. Heavens, you're no better than Knightsbridge."

"No, I didn't plan it. You're damn lucky I was there to circumvent a tragedy." He hesitated a heartbeat. "Who's Knightsbridge?"

"That's none of your business," she shouted. "I don't recall asking for your help."

"Then who the hell was in my arms crying her eyes out?" he yelled back. "You're driving me to distraction with this damned independence."

"I had the means to leave." She pointed at him accusingly. "You held me here against my wishes."

"Sweet Lord. Give me restraint." He closed his eyes and leaned his head against the headboard. "I did nothing of the kind," he said with a sigh a moment later.

"If that's so, then how did you happen to have my things in your pockets? How am I to trust you had nothing to do with those men taking them?"

"I don't believe this. You're questioning my motives?" he asked, his face reddening in anger. He rose from the bed, stormed toward her, and loomed above her. "I was following you to make sure you were safe and just happen to see the entire scene unfold. I'm a trained investigator and know when someone's being stalked, and you, dear lady," he said, pointing a finger at her chest, "were being stalked. I just waited until they made their move and then went after them. No way was I going to give back your things to let you go on your merry way only to have a reoccurrence. You're just too damn trusting and naive. You need to be taken care of, and I'm the one who's going to do it. You got that?"

"No." She stomped her foot. "You do not own me, Mr. Davis. I told you the first night we met. I'm dependent on no man and I meant it. Nothing has happened to make me change my mind. I've made my choice for my husband, and there's nothing you can do about it."

"So last night and this morning meant nothing?"

Sensing hurt in his voice, she looked closely at his features, trying to understand what he was saying. Maybe she'd read him wrong and he did have feelings for her—that he wasn't only enamored of their mating. It seemed as if that was all Gerald was after. If Parker could love her, then it would mean she could trust him as she did Geoff. "Are you saying I mean something to you? That you could love me?" she tentatively asked.

"You mean something, but love's a silly notion," Parker scoffed, waving a hand and reaching for his trousers. Stepping into them, he added, "I'm not the loving type, sweetheart, but I will do my duty by you and see that you are protected and taken care of."

His statement, spoken in such an aloof manner, sent a wave of disillusionment through her. No, of course he couldn't love her. At that moment, he seemed no better than the earl, using marriage as a means of achieving what he wanted. "That eases my mind," she retorted, hiding her disappointment in a flippant demeanor. "And who's to protect me from you?"

Parker placed his hands on his hips and practically leered at her. "I didn't hear any complaints earlier. In fact, you started it, lady. I'm just finishing it, as usual." He grabbed his shirt and shook out the wrinkles.

"Humph." He sounded so like the duke, Geoff's older brother. Seemed all men wanted to do was control women. "Just because we mated doesn't give you the right to control me." She brushed past him, stilling an urge to slug him. "I'm keeping to my plans to marry Geoff and that's final."

"You're marrying the duke's brother?" Parker asked incredulously, stopping in the middle of donning his shirt. "He's your betrothed?"

"Yes," she admitted, none too happy he'd goaded her into revealing her secret. But having done so, she'd use it to keep him at a distance.

"Then why isn't he here? Why would he let you sail halfway around the world alone?"

"Geoff doesn't let me do anything. I do it on my own. That's what I'm trying to tell you," she yelled. How obtuse could a man be?

"You mean the duke's brother is so enamored that he let you go off on your own?"

She clenched a fist, squelching another urge to wipe his amusement away as Parker laughed uncontrollably, holding his stomach.

"Good God, lady. You need a keeper. Does Lucas know that his business partner's brother is your intended?"

"Argh!" She threw up her hands. "This has nothing to do with the duke or your brother. Geoff and I are going to be married just as soon as he reaches his majority and comes into his inheritance."

"Ah, I see. So the duke's family disapproves of you because of status?"

Penny remained silent, neither agreeing nor disagreeing. The less he knew of her situation, the better off she'd be.

Parker's grin didn't die, in fact spread. "And you'll marry your Geoff, even though you don't love him?"

"I love him. I've always loved him," she stated, jutting her chin out, daring him to contradict her. Even though she somehow suspected Geoffrey's love might be a bit more ardent than hers. But she wouldn't think about that now. She did love him and she'd make him a good wife.

"And marriage to me is unthinkable because I care enough about you not to let you go gallivanting around the countryside unescorted?"

Keeping her defiant stance, she nodded.

"All right. Fine," he relented, tucking in his shirt. He strode toward the wash closet. "You don't want to marry me. I can accept that, but you're coming home with me."

She breathed in a sigh of relief. Thankfully, she could hide on his farm until Geoff came for her. Somehow she'd make it up to her beloved for no longer being a virgin. The thought gave her cause to ponder. What would he think when he learned the truth? The enormity of her actions the night before suddenly hit with the jarring force of a slap to the face. Dear Lord in heaven. Her head fell back against the wall as tears welled in her eyes. What had she done?

⊗

After shaving, Parker perused his face, looking for flaws in the mirrored glass, contemplating his conversation with Penny. What was wrong with him? He'd bet he had everything her Geoff had. Plus, the lady wasn't immune to his kisses. How could she so easily dismiss his gallant offer of marriage, especially when the duke's brother might not want her now that he'd ruined her? The nobility he'd met were a mite touchy about things like that.

TEMPTATION

Parker closed his eyes, stilling the desire to march back out there, tell her she had no options, and show the recalcitrant lady just how well they did suit.

No! That wouldn't work.

Her stubborn stance when imparting her news of Geoff being her betrothed, along with her undying love, told him she believed her words. Only he didn't. If she loved the man as she claimed, there was no way she'd give so much to him while in his arms.

Oh, hell. Why not admit the truth?

Her refusal twisted his gut in knots. He hadn't liked the feelings of unease her heated outburst evoked, nor did he understand the sense of loss he felt right now.

Why should he care?

He snorted mentally.

He shouldn't.

The bit of baggage was trouble. Pure trouble.

If he were smart, he'd just let it go and not let it bother him. Hell, he should just let her go on her way to California. Except he knew damn well he'd never allow her to go off on her own. And as for marriage? Once the idea formed last night, he hadn't been able to shake it. He still wanted her. Despite being willful and hoydenish, she'd do very well as his wife.

Oh yes, Parker thought, rubbing his hands together. Very well indeed.

Penny definitely needed a keeper, and since his angel was going home with him, he had months to sway her to his way of thinking.

He smiled as another thought struck. She might be carrying his babe at this moment. If not, he'd get her with child. Then she'd have no option but to marry him. Wiping his face and grinning back at his reflection, he turned to face the challenge of seducing the beguiling minx into marriage.

Parker entered the room and, noting Penny staring at the street below appearing distraught, his good mood dimmed.

"Why so glum, angel?" he asked more jovially than he felt, walking toward her.

"What have I done?" she whispered, peering at him with such

unhappiness shimmering in those periwinkle eyes. "He won't want to marry me now." She turned her gaze back to the street below. Ribbons of water flowed along the ivory perfection of her face, marring her beauty with grief.

An uncomfortable sensation flitted through him. He stepped behind her, embracing her stiff shoulders. "Please don't cry. I hate it when you cry."

"What a fool I was to let a moment's pleasure change my course."

"Shush. It can't be that bad." Instead of easing her hurt as intended, her tears increased. All the while, he couldn't stop his own hurt from forming once he grasped the full impact of her words. "It'll work out," he whispered, kissing her cheek. "If he loves you, it shouldn't matter."

"You think so?"

Penny's question, so innocently asked, produced a guilty twinge. Her distress had him rethinking his strategy. Maybe she really did love Geoff.

What a nightmare!

Images of her lying with her fiancé flashed through his mind. Dismissing them, he refocused on one thought. He had months to change her mind.

Parker ignored the discomfort of consoling her about another man and said with more conviction than he felt, "If it were me, I'd forgive you." Then, hoping to cajole a smile, he added, "You said it yourself. Why can men have countless affairs before marriage and not women? Well, he doesn't need to know who or when, does he?"

The questions seemed to cheer her.

When he felt her smile on his chest, Parker glanced down and forgot to breathe for an endless moment. He would surely rot in hell now. Not only had he told this angel to be duplicitous to her intended, but he also planned on keeping her for himself. Yet, hating his actions didn't change the situation. He wanted her.

"Come, it's getting late," Parker said, pulling Penny along toward the door. "Let's go have a hearty breakfast and then I'll make arrangements for transportation home."

Somehow, someway, he'd make sure she wanted him just as much.

Chapter 14

"How long a drive is it?" Penny prayed her voice held none of the apprehension Parker's ominous nearness generated in the close confines of the well-sprung open carriage loaded with trunks.

The driver sped south, leaving the cobbled stones behind as the road eventually smoothed into a well-maintained dirt path.

"A little less than two hours."

She nodded and ignored the intimacy of Parker's thigh pressed against hers with his arm perched along the seat behind her, paying more heed than necessary to her surroundings. They now passed the outskirts of the city. Houses and buildings became scarce, swallowed up by green open spaces dotted with trees and late summer wildflowers.

Thankfully, the morning breeze negated the heat seeping into her skin, which had more to do with the warmth emanating off his body than the heat of the sun's rays peeking out from leafy branches now and then. That he seemed to be so unaffected while she could barely breathe, chafed.

"Tell me about your home," she said, grasping on to the topic as a distraction to his looming presence.

"What would you like to know?" Leaning away from her, Parker seized her gaze and his eyes lit up with humor. He'd obviously picked up on her discomfort. And worse, found it amusing.

Two hours couldn't pass fast enough. "Whatever you wish to tell me," Penny murmured, going for nonchalant as her focus returned to the passing scenery flying by in a whirl of greens, browns, and yellows.

Parker thought a moment. "It's now a fairly large parcel of land. I've increased the size over the years—not that I needed it, it just happened as surrounding land came up for sale. I've also added on to the original house." His grin expanded. "My mother thinks it's too big now. Says she was perfectly happy with the old one and thought I wasted my money improving what didn't need improving."

"Was she right?" Penny smiled, not missing the warmth in his voice when he spoke of his mother. Somehow it made him more human.

"Maybe. It was certainly bigger than what she'd been used to, but not what she deserved."

"That's an odd statement."

He laughed. "My mother isn't one to be taken in with wealth. Always said the measure of a man wasn't the gold in his possession but what he did with his life that spoke about who he was."

"That sounds like something my father would've said," Penny said wistfully. "So your mother lives with you, even though she thinks you spend your money frivolously?" When he nodded, she sighed. "You're so lucky to have one parent still living. I'd give anything to see my parents again, especially my father. We were really close."

"Mine died much too young." Parker turned his attention to the road ahead and remained silent. Finally he said, "They all did."

"I'm sorry. I shouldn't have brought it up."

"It was a long time ago. I should be over it by now."

"One never recovers from the tragedy of losing parents before their time," she said softly.

"Could be." His gaze sought hers, and he shrugged. "My father was what my mother termed 'a great man,' no matter that he had very little gold. His wealth was in his spirit, which lives on in all of us. So maybe 'tis enough?"

Penny nodded, fully comprehending Parker's sadness. Her voice reflected hers when she said, "I don't think I'll ever stop missing them. They were all I had as family besides Geoff and Mindy."

"So their deaths were fairly recent?"

The understanding she glimpsed in his eyes caused her to drop her guard for a moment, allowing her to answer honestly without thinking about what she was saying.

"Less than a year. I'd still be in mourning but my guardian doesn't like black and wouldn't hear of me dressing in anything so somber after six months. I really didn't get to mourn them much before being whisked off to London. Besides, what good does mourning do? It doesn't change anything."

"Tell me about your father. When you spoke of him just now, your eyes sparkled."

"My father was also a great man." Penny's voice filled with admiration. "It was so easy to love him, because he was easy to love. My mother and I were his life. I miss him dreadfully."

"He sounds like a man worth knowing."

"Yes, he was," Penny said, remembering their shared love of horses. Besides teaching her chess, he'd taught her to ride, treating her no differently than other fathers treated their sons. Her father used to go head-to-head with Penny's mother over her behavior and his indulgence. He'd been her biggest ally in allowing her freedom other young ladies never had, including the ability to ride the countryside, sitting astride a horse rather than using a sidesaddle as expected of ladies of her station. "He always sided with me when my mother tried to make me do ladylike things like sewing or playing the piano, telling her that I had plenty of time to learn such boring stuff."

Penny broke off and chuckled at the memory. Then added, "To this day, I still can't play a note or make a clean stitch, but I can hit a target at fifty paces and jump any bush on our property," she declared proudly, eliciting Parker's amused chuckle.

"You remind me of Catherine. She's too busy pursuing unladylike endeavors. So much so that Mother has lost all hope of her ever marrying. I guess Lucas and I are to blame, as we always let her tag along with us when we went hunting. Funny, but we could never let on that we took her with us because, even as a child, she had the uncanny ability to find our game much better than we could. She's also a better shot than either Lucas or me. I was hoping this gentleman from Baltimore would suit. That way, I wouldn't feel so guilty over my part in creating such an unsuitable bride."

"You don't think she'd make a suitable bride, given her lack of ladylike endeavors?" Penny asked, wondering why women had to fit into such rigid constraints of society. Even here in America, it seemed women had very little choice in the world. This only reinforced her intention of marrying Geoff. He'd be the perfect husband because he indulged her, like her father had. Plus, she did love him. How could she not? He cut a dashing figure. He was tall, and his blond good looks matched hers perfectly. Together they'd make beautiful children.

Thinking of him made her realize how much she missed Geoff— missed all the fun they used to share. Oh, how she wished they didn't have to wait to put their plans into action. She smiled as all their earlier exploits flitted into her consciousness. No matter what mischief she'd conjured up, he'd always gone along. He'd always been her champion. Yes! Geoff would be the perfect husband. They'd both get what they wanted from the union and she'd make him happy. After all, he'd saved her from a fate worse than death. Without a doubt, she'd have more control over her life with Geoff as a husband than the man sitting next to her.

Parker's laugh pulled her out of her musings. When she looked up with the question in her eyes, he said, "I just got a mental glimpse of my sister acting like some of those suitable brides I met at the balls I attended in London." He shook his head and his grin added to his rugged good looks. "She's definitely not the biddable type. But she's easy on the eye, so her lack of suitors hasn't been a problem. She's just being fickle. Says she's looking for a man as great as Father was. Of course, I don't see her remembering much about him. She was only seven when he died."

"You must've done a good job of keeping his spirit alive." Penny smiled. "Maybe she's looking for someone like you and Lucas."

Parker let out another hearty laugh. "I certainly hope not. In fact, sometimes I wonder if he's not rolling over in his grave at the things I've done, and Lucas likes the ladies too much. No. My father was a great man as my mother believes and neither of us fits that description."

Though he smiled, Penny caught the hint of sadness in his expression before he shuttered the look and focused on the passing scenery.

"Why don't you think your father would approve of the things you've done?" she asked, unable to stop the words or keep the compassion out of her voice.

Seeming uncomfortable with the sympathy her question held, Parker shrugged. "Though a common man, he was one of peace and was content with his life, though he actually owned very little. I don't think I ever saw him raise his voice in anger at anyone in the short time I knew him. I've been content with nothing so far and my heart has been driven by hate and anger for too long, neither of which he'd admire." As if he'd revealed too much, he deftly changed the subject. "I do think you and Catherine will get on well together." When she flashed an impish grin, he added, "Or maybe I'm making the mistake of my life putting the two of you together."

Penny couldn't help but laugh. "Surely you can't be afraid of two women?"

He grunted. "Now I am worried."

For the rest of the ride Penny was happy to note they stayed on less personal topics, mainly talking about the differences between their two countries.

Just as the carriage turned onto a narrow tree-lined drive, Parker said, "You know, you're starting to lose your English accent. Except when you get annoyed. Then it comes out, along with the lady of the manor look."

"I have no such look," she said indignantly, crossing her arms in front of her and looking out of the carriage, wondering if she should be insulted or amused.

Parker threw back his head and laughed. "I rest my case." He squeezed her shoulder and kissed her cheek.

She wasn't expecting his actions. Eyeing him warily, she bit her bottom lip after her tongue made a sweep of it. She cleared her throat.

She was just about to disagree when Parker gently placed his finger on her mouth. He whispered, "You tempt me, angel. You sorely tempt me."

Then he stroked her bottom lip with his thumb. The heat generated from his soul-searing stare spread warmth everywhere. Heavens, when he looked at her like that all she could think of was their joining. She knew he was about to kiss her, and that she should break away. Kissing him wasn't in her best interest, but somehow she couldn't find the will to resist when his lips followed his thumb.

His soft mouth, covering hers with a feather-light and gentle touch, begged her to yield all to him. She didn't refuse, in fact allowed the kiss to continue for too long, too engrossed in the sensations filling her.

Eventually she reluctantly pulled away. "Please," she whispered. "You've got to stop kissing me. It's unseemly. I'm betrothed to someone else."

Parker released her and dropped his hands to his side. "Oh?"

He caught her gaze. The expression in those blue-gray eyes had her wondering at the lunacy of staying with his family. She had to quit acting on such decadent feelings and remember she was engaged to another.

"Otherwise I'll be forced to make other arrangements," she was finally able to say with a bit more conviction than she felt.

"No need to do anything so drastic. I'll behave." He sighed and nodded. "We're here."

The carriage slowed.

Penny recovered from their kiss and her focus landed on a sprawling Georgian manor house, almost as big as her parents' country estate. She peered at him with new understanding. Parker Davis was a man of influence and means.

The driver reined in the horse and set the brake.

A woman bounded from the house and sprinted down the porch stairs.

"There's Catherine now." Parker jumped out. Meeting his sister halfway, he picked her up and engulfed her in a bear hug. Spinning full circle, her feet left the ground. "You're a sight for sore eyes," he said, laughing and setting her down. "Where's Mother?" He glanced around.

"She's resting. We didn't expect you after Lucas's account of how you decided to traipse across the country on a mission of mercy, delivering some woman to her betrothed." Catherine's laugh was infectious. "I take it this is the lady?"

Parker released Catherine before turning back to Penny, who stood in the stopped carriage. With hands on her waist, he lifted her to the ground, then grabbed her gloved hand. Grinning and pulling Penny with him, he said, "Catherine, this is Miss Penny Layton. She's going to be our guest while waiting for her intended, rather than traipsing over the country, saving me the bother of chasing after her." He nodded.

TEMPTATION

"Penny, my sister, Miss Catherine Davis."

"Oh, Parker, how lovely." Another gurgle of laughter bubbled up and his sister's voice held genuine pleasure. Holding out her hand in welcome, she added with more warmth, "How do you do?"

Placing her hand in Catherine's, Penny could only stare when she actually met her friendly gaze. The beautiful woman towered a good six inches above Penny, just a few inches short of her brother's height. Though the lady was fair in complexion, her hair was a rich auburn color. With those emerald green eyes, Penny wondered how Parker could ever think she shared similar looks with his sister while in the jewelry store. Penny paled in comparison to the vivacious Catherine Davis. The thought was quickly extinguished when the lively woman pulled Penny behind her, talking a mile a minute.

Parker chuckled. "You might let her freshen up a bit before you ply her with questions," he teased, laughing outright when Penny glanced back at him in bewilderment. "I'm sorry, Penny. Catherine's inquisitive nature runs in the family, but she means well. Go along, she'll take care of you," he urged, still smiling.

∞

Inside the house the family butler walked quickly toward them. "Mr. Davis!" he said. "What a pleasant surprise. Miss Elizabeth will be only too happy to know you're home safe and sound."

"Thank you, Jason. It's good to be home." Parker clapped him on the back.

Parker had no more than taken off his jacket and handed it to Jason, when he caught sight of his mother moving at a fast pace down the stairs.

Elizabeth Davis, now into her fifth decade, still had a youthful look about her, giving him a glimpse of what his sister Catherine would look like in twenty-five years. Except for the small lines surrounding her eyes and a few telltale gray hairs, she favored her youngest daughter more than any of her other children who, like Parker, took after their dead father.

"Parker!" she gushed. "Thank God you're home. Lucas said you might not be back for weeks."

"It's good to be here." He hugged her. "You're looking well, Mother."

"That's because all my babies are close by. Catherine is all excited about the houseguest you brought home. You'll have to fill me in." Her smile increased tenfold as she linked arms. "How long are you staying?"

Arm in arm, they headed for the inner room.

"I'm not sure about my schedule."

"Oh?" Elizabeth said. "I thought for sure Jonathan would have you out and about in no time."

"I may take a little time off after my last case," he said evasively, not wanting to discuss tendering his resignation when he met his superior. "What has Lucas said about our houseguest?"

Elizabeth stopped and eyed her son.

"Mother, you're being obvious." Parker ignored the feeling in the pit of his stomach he always got when she gave him that look. "I can see your brain working from here."

She raised her eyebrows. "Really?"

"Yes. So let me put your speculations to rest. The lady followed me home, at my request, because it was much easier on both of us for her to do so. She's meeting her fiancé and I mean to keep her safe until she does."

"Humph," she grunted in a most unladylike fashion. "I must be slipping. I remember a time you had no idea what was on my mind."

Grinning, he kissed her cheek. "You forget, I've had years to perfect reading people's faces and you've been out of practice for years." Parker led her to a plush chair in the richly decorated room with varying shades of crimson and gold. The russet velvet draperies were drawn to let in the midday breeze that drifted through the floor-to-ceiling windows overlooking a veranda with the view of the bay. Parker sat in a settee across from her, stretching out his long legs, and sighed.

"I asked Jason to have Pearl bring in some leftovers from the noon meal," Elizabeth said, pulling his attention. "I'm sure you're famished. I instructed him to tell Catherine to bring your guest down as soon as she's ready."

TEMPTATION

"Thank you, Mother. I'm sure Penny will appreciate it."

"Penny?"

Chuckling at his mother's sly grin, especially after noticing more speculation in her eyes, he admitted, "It seemed silly to use formal names when we've been in such close proximity for three weeks."

At the knock on the door, her attention turned to a woman carrying a tea tray.

"Place the tray on the cart and move it over by Parker, would you, Pearl?" Turning back to Parker as the woman pushed a tea cart toward them, Elizabeth said, "Lucas called her Miss Layton."

"Your youngest son was too busy sailing the vessel to become familiar with anyone. Besides, you know he avoids such obvious marriage traps like the plague," Parker said, shaking his head.

Elizabeth chuckled softly. "I have to meet this woman. She must be lovely to have you calling her a marriage trap."

Parker cleared his throat, wishing his mother weren't so astute. "She is, but she's also engaged to another."

"Where is this fiancé? I thought the English were much more protective of their females. How is it she sailed unescorted across the ocean?"

"Ask Lucas. She's a close friend of the family of one of his biggest clients. I think Lucas was that escort, if you want to know my thinking," Parker said, none too happy his mother's questions were some Lucas should have asked before letting the woman board his ship.

Just then Parker remembered her mention of a guardian during their drive. He was almost certain she hadn't even realized she'd spoken of one. Definitely something to ponder.

He took a cup and poured coffee, filling his plate with food while saying with irritation, "I'm not privy to the lady's dealings, nor was I there when Lucas guaranteed her journey. All I know is I didn't feel comfortable letting her out of my sight. Which was a good thing too. I interrupted a robbery." When his mother's eyes grew larger, he gave a disgusted snort. "Two thieves relieved her of her bag and I thwarted their activities. Not wanting a repeat scenario, I convinced her to come home with me, telling her she could work here rather than in California while she waited for her fiancé."

"Surely you don't expect her to work? Not a friend of Lucas's business associates." Elizabeth's appalled expression said it all. No one could be so cruel.

"I hadn't planned on it, but the lady's a bit stubborn and may have other ideas. It was hard enough getting her here without the promise of a job. I was hoping you could find something to make her feel useful?"

"She means to work? Really?" Her gaze flew to the door. "How interesting. I thought all well-to-do Englishwomen were spoiled."

"This one's a bit different. Reminds me too much of Catherine. Maybe that's why I like her."

"Even more interesting," she added, watching her son's face closely.

"I see that look in your eye, Mother," Parker chastised before taking a sip of coffee. "Do not even think of playing matchmaker here. You'll only be meddling where you're not wanted."

"Humph, as if that would stop me. But I know when to quit. I've already thrown the best of the area at you and not one holds your interest, so I'm giving up."

Parker grunted. But he almost choked on his coffee when she said, "No, I was wondering what it is about this lady that brings out both my sons' protective sides."

She paused for a moment, then asked, "So she reminds you of Catherine?" He examined her expression, which was still far too assessing for Parker's peace of mind.

"Mother," he ground out.

"Oh, go on with you." She dismissed his warning with the wave of her hand. "I'll drop it for now."

"Good. Where's Lucas?" he asked, intentionally changing the subject.

"He left early to work on provisioning his ship. He'll be here for dinner and then he's leaving at dawn to sail back to England. I gather after this trip, he'll be spending some time with us?"

"So he says." Parker smiled at the pleasure in her voice.

"You can't know how much it will mean to have all my children close at hand."

"Yes, well, please try and remember we're adults and don't need mothering anymore."

"I'll try." Her soft laugh burst forth. "But it's hard to stop mothering simply because your babies grow up. You wait until you have children of your own. Then you'll know what I'm talking about."

"You don't give up, do you?" He rolled his eyes and counted to ten.

Elizabeth shook her head. "It simply isn't in my nature."

"No, I don't guess it is." Parker broke off a piece of bread to add to his cheese.

"Beth Thompson had her baby. A six-pound boy. The papa is quite proud."

Parked drank his coffee and ate, listening with half an ear while his mother updated him on the happenings in the area during his latest absence.

"Maryanne Walters is betrothed. She'll marry her intended next spring. I was surprised, especially since she claimed to have such strong feelings for you."

He grunted. "Her strong feelings for the state of matrimony were no doubt aided by my obvious success."

Elizabeth shrugged, then added, "Emily Anderson is expecting. Gertie had almost given up hope of having grandchildren, much like me."

This comment earned Parker's short burst of laughter. "Mother."

Undaunted, she continued without missing a breath.

A few minutes later Penny's clipped English accent drew Parker's attention, just as she and Catherine stepped into the room, interrupting Elizabeth's monologue. A sensation, not unlike the first time he spotted her, rolled over him. The lady was simply the most beautiful woman he'd ever seen. Earlier, during the drive, he'd had a hard time ignoring her, especially when her delicate fragrance had wafted over his nostrils any time she'd point something out. It had been pure torture. How could one woman be so enchanting? After seeing the countryside through her eyes, he realized how much he enjoyed showing her his world. That thought was even more disconcerting. Ignoring his uneasiness over where his thoughts drifted, he let his gaze follow her progression into the room.

She stopped short, sparing him a glance as pink stole up her face.

"Ah, here we are. Come over here and have some tea." Oblivious to the suddenly charged atmosphere, Catherine chatted on, pulling Penny to a chair next to Parker and patted the seat. "Though it's not teatime yet, you must be hungry and exhausted after your drive. Mother, this is Penny. Isn't she charming?"

Penny stood beside the chair, appearing bewildered. Parker grinned. Catherine had that effect on people.

When Parker happened to look up at his mother, noticing her total interest, his grin died. He rolled his eyes, swearing under his breath.

Elizabeth stood and smiled, holding out her hand. "My dear Miss Layton, I'm Elizabeth Davis. My son wasn't embellishing tales of your beauty."

"I'm pleased to meet you." Penny took her hand and curtsied. "Parker didn't tell me how lovely you were."

"You're too kind." Elizabeth sent Parker an "I was right" look as Penny sat in the chair Catherine indicated.

"I'd love a cup of tea and I have to admit I'm famished," Penny said to Catherine, who was now pouring.

"Cream? Or we have honey to sweeten it?" Catherine asked.

"Honey will do fine," Penny murmured as Catherine added a teaspoon, then handed it to her.

Penny filled a plate with meats and cheeses.

No one spoke while they ate and drank.

Once Parker sipped the last drop, he stood, brushing nonexistent crumbs away. "You said you enjoyed riding. I'm going this afternoon, Penny. If you'd care to join me?"

His plans included visiting his sisters, in hopes of persuading them to join the family for dinner. Elizabeth Davis relished any opportunity to have all her children under one roof, if only for a short while, and tonight would be no different.

"I'd love nothing better, but I'm a little overwhelmed right now." Penny smiled, yet wouldn't look at him. "Perhaps another time."

Parker waited until she looked up. He caught her gaze and held it without hiding his thoughts. He didn't believe her. When her chin jutted out, daring him to refute her words, his smile tugged free. "As you wish. Perhaps another time," he said in a mocking voice, before giving his mother a peck on the cheek and striding out of the room.

ᙦ

"Interesting."

The one word drew her attention and Penny looked up in time to see Elizabeth's gaze follow Parker's departure.

Catherine glanced at her mother with raised eyebrows. "What's interesting?"

"Nothing," Elizabeth replied, smiling too brightly, her focus returning to Penny and her daughter. "So, you two seem to have become fast friends."

"We are." Catherine heaved a regretful sigh. "It's too bad you're overwhelmed. I was going for a ride before I spotted the carriage."

"I love to ride," Penny said before taking a sip of tea.

"Didn't you just say you were overwhelmed and wanted to rest?"

"Yes, I guess I did." Penny stared wistfully at her plate, swallowing her regret at her choice of excuses. A ride sounded perfect.

"Maybe it was the company that was overwhelming." When Penny's questioning gaze met Elizabeth's, the older woman shrugged. "Parker can be a bit intimidating at times."

Penny let out a long breath. "He does like to take charge, which is nice." Only she wasn't inclined to let him take charge of her.

"Don't mind him." Catherine's unladylike snort was telling. "He likes to lord it over anyone he thinks is under his protection."

"He is the head of the family, Catherine," Elizabeth chided.

"I guess that's why he reminds me of my fiancé's brother," Penny stated honestly. The duke was also the head of his family.

"Are you sure you're not too tired to ride," Elizabeth asked. "I'm sure Catherine would love the company."

"Oh yes, Penny. You can rest later."

Torn, Penny set her cup in the saucer. "I suppose I could delay my rest."

"Good." After nodding to Catherine, Elizabeth rose, sighing

loudly. "Remember, she's a guest and try not to kill her on her first day out." She placed her hand on Penny's shoulder, squeezed gently, and said, amusement showing in her tone, "You'll do. I'm delighted to have you as a houseguest." She then left the room, her step lively.

"Well, she seems happy all of a sudden." Catherine stared at the door her mother exited with a confused look. Shrugging, she turned to Penny. "Come on. Let's change and I'll show you one of my favorite places to ride. Do you jump?"

Penny laughed with pure abandon. Imagine! After weeks at sea, she had the opportunity to ride a horse.

Chapter 15

"Parker, I can't believe you managed to get all of us together again," Elizabeth said later that evening at dinner, drawing Penny's attention.

The boisterous affair included all of her children, even Sarah, Rebecca, and their spouses, who'd shown up unexpectedly.

Elizabeth exhaled an audible sigh as her contented gaze roamed around the table, resting briefly on all those present. "However did you do it? You must've been busy today."

"I needed a diversion." Parker glanced at his mother, his satisfied expression in place. "An enjoyable horseback ride was a nice change from being cooped up on a ship for weeks, but nothing compared to seeing the joy on your face when you found everyone at the dinner table."

"Imagine my surprise when I saw his ugly mug in front of me after opening the door this afternoon," Rebecca replied, sticking her tongue out at Parker when he grunted. "Short notice aside, it was a perfect idea. I wouldn't miss dinner for the world."

"Hear, hear," added Sarah. "It's not often we can sit at the table and have Mother consumed with something other than the two of us providing grandchildren."

Elizabeth chuckled. "Neither of you are cooperating, I might add. Catherine's a lost cause, and since Lucas and Parker are avoiding marriage, you two may be my only hope. You do know that I'm not getting any younger?" Elizabeth stopped long enough to pass a bowl to Sarah on her right. "So, Miss Layton. Parker tells us you're to be married?"

Penny nodded and swallowed a bite of delicious smoked ham. "Yes. Our original plan was to meet in San Francisco, but Parker convinced me that I should wait here and travel across the country with my fiancé's escort." She sat taking in all the interactions of the large, rowdy family, amazed that Parker's two married sisters shared such similar good-looking features with the men—fair complexions, reddish-blond hair, and blue-gray eyes. All of the Davises were tall, towering over her five-foot-two-inch frame.

"Thank God," Lucas grunted. "Markham and Geoff would have my head if I let anything happen to you."

"You have no idea how right you are." When Lucas looked up with raised eyebrows, Parker added, "Her intended is none other than the duke's brother."

"You and Geoff?" Dropping a forkful of food, Lucas turned toward Penny with a stunned expression.

"It was meant to be a secret," Penny hissed, sending daggers of annoyance at Parker. She glanced at Lucas. Smiling sweetly, she said with more calm than she felt, "Since you now know, I'm hoping you'll honor my privacy and keep the news from Geoff's brother."

"So that's the way the wind blows." Lucas gave a soft whistle, eyeing her thoughtfully. "Markham doesn't know?"

Penny squirmed under Lucas's scrutiny. Fear streaked through her at how easily her plans could be thwarted if the duke were to find out too quickly. She grabbed the bowl of potatoes Rebecca handed her and added a helping to her plate, thinking of how she could gain his support. "No," she said, deciding on the truth. "The duke doesn't know. Our impending marriage is between Geoff and me and doesn't concern him. I really would appreciate your silence on the matter."

"I hope you'll honor her request, Lucas," Parker chimed in, as if just realizing the consequences of his revelation. "It's really none of our affair."

"I'm not in the habit of keeping things from my business associates." Lucas heaved a heavy sigh. "I'll not offer any information. But if asked, I won't lie."

"See?" Parker grinned, adding a conspiratorial nod. "Your secret is still safe. You can remain here, and Lucas can relay the information of your whereabouts to your intended."

"I can pay you," Penny offered, relieved to be staying with such a welcoming, loving family until Geoff came for her. Unwilling to think about what would happen should the duke discover their plans, she focused on how safe she felt here and pushed all negative thoughts away.

Lucas brandished a hand in dismissal. "We wouldn't dream of taking money, would we, Parker?"

"No. You're a welcome guest in our home as long as you want," Parker agreed.

"I don't expect charity. I can work."

Turning to his mother, Parker laughed. "Told you she'd be a little stubborn." Then his jovial gaze moved to Penny's. "You're certainly not working for bed and board and we wouldn't hear of you paying for our hospitality. Consider yourself family."

"Thank you," she murmured. Paying close attention to the beautifully set table, she resumed eating, uncomfortable with the feeling of warmth his sincere offer generated. She fingered the exquisitely cut crystal goblet. The sterling silver place settings and fine china, a rose pattern she recognized as one of the most exclusive, could grace any table of a peer of the realm. This room featured dark blues and golds on the walls and in the upholstery, which matched the tasteful and expensive dark wood furnishings. She also recognized authentic Chippendale when she saw it. Though Parker told her he was a common man, there was nothing common in the man or in this room.

"We had a wonderful ride this afternoon," Catherine said. "I'd venture to say she's as good a horsewoman as I am."

Penny sensed Parker's gaze, but she wouldn't look at him while Catherine elaborated about their excursion, one she hadn't wanted him to know about. Not when he'd given the kind offer of his home for as long as she needed, and she'd turned down his earlier request.

"I thought you were too tired to ride," Parker said.

"I felt better after I rested." Penny shrugged and concentrated on her plate, praying the heat hitting her cheeks wasn't a blush of embarrassment.

"So that means you're not avoiding me and will in fact ride with me sometime?" he asked, lifting an amused brow.

His perception annoyed Penny. Wanting nothing more than to

disavow his claim, she met his laughing blue-gray gaze with her head held high. "Surely you're suffering from delusions. I'm not avoiding you," she said, her clipped English accent becoming more pronounced.

"Good, then you'll join me tomorrow afternoon when I return from my meeting." He eyed her thoughtfully, the gleam of amusement flashing brighter. "Around four? Is that acceptable?"

Her eyes sparked anger, but Parker ignored her signal. She clenched the fist draped across her lap and bit her tongue to keep from telling him what she really thought of him and his idea of a ride. When her nails cut into her palms, she relaxed her hand and nodded, offering a frozen smile. "Of course."

"Since you're not avoiding me, I expect a game of chess in the library after dinner."

Penny stiffened, the excuse of retiring early due to tiredness on her lips, yet something in his taunting stare stopped her cold. Despite the strong urge to say no, the urge to wipe that smug, knowing leer off his face and prove him wrong was stronger. "Fine. Prepare to lose."

Parker's grin was quick. "We'll see who loses."

Irritated, she refused to look away first.

Finally he shook his head, chuckling. "Should be interesting."

Penny glanced around the table to note the others' attention riveted on their discussion. "I'm so sorry. I sometimes forget myself," she said, filled with shame because she'd acted so rudely.

"No need," Elizabeth said, patting her hand. "Parker has a habit of getting his way and I assure you, it can be most annoying at times."

Nodding, Penny picked up her fork and ate without saying another word as conversation continued around her.

"Penny?" Elizabeth was glancing at her and Penny realized she had addressed her.

"I'm sorry," she said, offering an apologetic smile. "I was daydreaming and didn't catch that."

"I said, since you'll be in the library." Elizabeth then directed her gaze toward Parker. "We'll have our after-dinner drinks in there before everyone leaves."

"Sounds perfect." Parker nodded before turning to Penny and offering another dangerous grin. "Though we won't have time tomorrow, maybe we can take a ride to see your friend Miss Bowers on another day." He added, glancing at the others, "Her sister's farm isn't but an hour's ride."

In a heartbeat, Penny's unease vanished and she bestowed on him her most enchanting smile. "Thank you, Parker! I would love to see Mindy."

"How solicitous of you, Parker," Elizabeth said, still watching him intently.

He cleared his throat. "Just being hospitable, Mother."

"You've always been too busy to go visiting before this."

"I'm still busy." He shook his head and directed his next words more toward Penny. "And will be for the next week with business. Besides meeting with President Grant and Jonathan Morgan, my superior, I need to meet with my farm manager."

"I can wait. You can't know how much it means to me to be able to see her. She's my family." Penny glanced around, realizing what she'd just said and added, "Not that you all aren't like family, too. It's just that I've known Mindy all my life."

"Of course, we understand how you feel." Elizabeth reached for her hand and gave it a reassuring squeeze. Her generous smile reached her eyes. "One cannot have enough family like your Mindy. Having someone to love makes the hard times we all face in the world easier to bear."

"I never thought of it like that before, but you're absolutely right," Penny replied, thinking it an accurate sentiment. "Mindy was there for me when I lost my parents. In fact, she and Geoff have always been there for me."

She chewed on a bite of creamed spinach as another thought struck. From the moment she'd boarded the ship, she'd felt safe and secure for the first time since her parents' deaths. It was a good feeling. Safety and security had been something she hadn't even realized she'd taken for granted in her young life, assuming it her due, owed to her because of her station. She'd never had to think about things like that before. Over the course of the last year, her eyes had been opened to the hardships in life, especially for women who were at the mercy of men. Sitting at the table now, she felt doubly lucky to have this family's support.

"It's nice to know she's close by," Lucas said, interrupting Penny's thoughts. "You two certainly kept things lively on our voyage. My men have never been so entertained, myself included."

Penny kept her smile in place and didn't add any more to the conversation. Soon, talk revolved around the farm and all that had taken place since Parker's last homecoming.

CR

When dinner ended, Parker trailed behind the large group retiring to the library. The tall windows on either side of double doors were open, allowing the late summer breeze to freshen the room. His mother loved color, a detail exhibited in full view out the double doors opening to the large wraparound porch leading to a garden in full bloom, adding bursts of reds, pinks, blues, and yellows to the green bushes and trees in the background.

Within minutes, he set up the chessboard and nodded to Penny. "You ready?"

The smile she provided said, "Prepare to lose."

He smothered a laugh and sat, determined to do the opposite.

The fierce battle they engaged in still continued an hour later when his two sisters, along with their spouses, stood and bid their good-byes.

Once they left, Lucas rose. "It's been a long day, plus I have to be up early to make my ship." He gave Catherine a quick hug and a kiss before turning to his mother. He kissed Elizabeth's forehead, pulling her into a bear hug. "I love you. If I don't see you on the morrow, I'll be back as quickly as possible."

"Sleep well," she replied, hugging him back. "I'll make sure I'm up to see you off."

"I'm leaving before dawn, Mother. No need for you to rise so early."

"Then have a safe journey," Elizabeth said wistfully, sitting back down as Lucas turned to Penny.

"I'll see you when I return. I'll also let Geoff know you're safe and where to find you, using discretion, of course," Lucas offered, interrupting their play. Parker stood. The two men shook hands and gave each other a brief hug.

TEMPTATION

When Penny stood, she was engulfed in Lucas's embrace. "I'm glad you decided to stay, rather than travel by yourself," he said. "You'll be safe here."

"Thank you." She smiled shyly. "I appreciate all you've done for me, and I'm sure Geoff will be happy to know I'm safe and sound."

Parker's irritation rose. The name of her intended, spouted so earnestly from her lips, chafed like a hair shirt. Though she'd done nothing to indicate otherwise, he couldn't believe she actually meant to follow through on her plans. She was a stubborn one, he'd give her that. He just needed some time alone with her to help her see the error of her ways.

He glanced up and caught his mother's knowing grin. Parker straightened and placed an answering smile on his face, effectively disguising his rising annoyance.

"Come, let's get this game over with," he said a little too abruptly, so only Penny could hear.

Nervously biting her bottom lip, Penny's focus flew to his face and she spent a few moments searching his expression. "We can finish at another time, if you'd like," she finally murmured.

Noting her subdued demeanor, he sighed and added a little more politely, "I'd prefer now, if you don't mind."

Penny nodded. Both returned to their seats.

The two played for another fifteen minutes before Elizabeth stretched. "Well, I'd love nothing better than to watch you two play all night, but I have correspondence to catch up on." She rose from her perch a few feet away and added, "I need your help, Catherine."

"My help?" Catherine frowned. "What can I do? Mother, you're not making any sense."

"Trust me, my dear. I need your help." Elizabeth's tone allowed no argument.

"If you say so." Catherine shrugged and stood. "Good night." She nodded to Parker. "I'll see you in the morning."

He waved her off and watched her follow her mother, closing the door behind her and leaving the two alone for the first time since their arrival.

Penny took her time, her attention more focused on the board than on the two departing women. Once she moved her rook, she looked about, her gaze all but shouting the realization. She'd lost her chaperones.

He ignored another surge of irritation and stood. "Would you care for more sherry? I'm having a second drink." He headed for the bar located at the end of the room. "I need reinforcements. You have me stumped."

She eyed him for a lengthy moment, indecision sliding over her expression. Parker had to bite his cheek to keep from laughing outright when she nodded, taking him up on his implied challenge. "I'd love another."

"Perhaps you'd care for something stronger?" He flashed a disarming grin in an attempt to twist the lady's mischievous streak to his advantage.

"You're not teasing?" Just as he'd intended, his suggestion intrigued her. "You'd really allow me to drink what you're drinking?" At his nod, she giggled. "I can't believe I'm agreeing to this, but I'd love one," she said, throwing caution to the wind, exactly as he'd hoped.

The woman was nothing if not daring.

"You'll appreciate a smooth Kentucky bourbon. There's nothing quite like it." Parker poured two drinks before sauntering back to her with his smile in place. He handed her one of the glasses. Resuming his seat across the table, he held his glass over the board and nodded. "Cheers."

Another burst of laughter bubbled out of Penny. Boldly, she clinked her glass with his, apparently enjoying the moment. She then swigged a hefty drink and almost choked, coughing and sputtering.

"There's a bit of a kick if you're not used to strong spirits. It's better if you sip it," Parker advised, chuckling.

"So why are you allowing me to drink this?" she asked, without containing her grin once her coughing fit ended. "You have to know it isn't done."

He laughed. That clipped, aristocratic English accent of hers never ceased to entertain him.

Parker sat back and kept an amused gaze on her. "No, I don't suppose it is in England. Let's just say I think the British are a little stuffy. Here on my farm, things are different. Both my mother and my sister imbibe once in a while and I've learned it doesn't really matter. Besides," he teased with a wink, "I need all the help I can get with this game."

"Ah, I see. Ulterior motives. You're a sneaky devil, Mr. Davis." She bestowed on him a sly smile and took another sip.

Enchanted, Parker watched her. He ignored the knot tightening in his gut because her jesting held too much truth. Her edginess disappeared as the effects of the drink took hold. Just as he'd hoped. He wanted her pliant and accepting, not nervous and panicky as he sensed she was when his mother and sister had left.

She glanced at him, her soft smile in place, assessing him with half-lidded eyes. Heat from her gaze shot straight to his groin.

Ignoring her blatant message, he managed, "Drink up. As long as we play chess in the evenings together, you can do whatever you want in this room and no one else will know. I'd even let you'd smoke a pipe like Lucas if it would make you happy."

"Really?" Her eyes wide as saucers, Penny's grin spread, her joy completely taking over her face.

"It will be our secret," he whispered seductively.

Penny nodded, breaking eye contact, her mien suddenly not so confident. Still, he'd noted the spark of awareness in those liquid pools of blue as the air crackled with renewed energy neither could miss. She took another long drink that went down easier. And ignoring the urge to flee that he'd also caught in her expressive eyes, the rigidity left her shoulders, clearly a result of her bourbon-enhanced courage. A heady laugh pushed out her last bit of wariness. "I know I shouldn't trust you, but for some reason, I can't quite remember why."

"Maybe you shouldn't drink any more then," Parker said, unable to resist grinning. "After all, if I win this game, I don't want you crying foul."

"I would never." She straightened in indignation. "But you won't win. I've boxed you in but good. It will take a clever mind to get out of my trap, an even more than clever mind to win the game."

Glancing at the board, Parker shook his head. "You have done a pretty good job of it, but I've figured a way out."

"If you can find a way out, you'll earn my utmost respect," she replied confidently, lounging back and sporting a smug smile.

"I'd rather earn a kiss," he said playfully, watching her face closely.

"Shush." She placed a forefinger to her lips, giggling. "You mustn't say such things."

"Why? It's true." He enjoyed the sound of her light laughter. "I would rather have a kiss than your respect."

More laughter bubbled up. Suddenly, her teasing expression vanished and her eyes narrowed suspiciously. "Why are you looking at me like that?" she asked a little too breathlessly.

"Like what?" he asked, increasing the intensity of his gaze.

"Like you want to gobble me up."

He chuckled. "Maybe that's because I'd like to." His attention went back to the chessboard. After making his move, he inquired softly, "So are you going to make it worth my while to win this game?"

She took another sip of bourbon and studied the board, following his move. Her smile reached her bright blue eyes when she peered up and said, "Why, sir, I have to tell you. You are resourceful, but alas not resourceful enough." Her focus then returned to the board, and she spent a long moment thinking. "And because you haven't got a prayer, I will take you up on your request and make it worth your while." Her secure tone all but shouted that she fully believed he had no way of winning. "It should be over in a matter of a few moves, so go ahead and try, because if you win, it will be worth a kiss to see such skill."

For the next thirty minutes neither spoke while the game went on in earnest. When it was time for Penny to make another move, her face said it all. Any confidence at winning the game had completely shattered.

"I think I need another one of these." She lifted her empty glass in the air. "I don't see how you wiggled your way out of my trap."

Parker stood to do her bidding. The dismay in her strained voice was hard to miss. "It's only a kiss," he stated nonchalantly while pouring.

"Oh no. It's much more than that and you know it."

"Oh?" His eyebrows rose and he glanced back at her. "How so?"

TEMPTATION

"Well, you say it's for a mere kiss, but you're playing as if there is more at stake—as if this means something. My mind's a little befuddled right now, so I can't quite figure it out. You're the only person I've ever played who has beaten me, once I had him in the position you were in not twenty minutes ago."

Parker's eyes flashed amusement and his grin spread, showing all of his teeth. Picking up the drinks, he started back toward the table. "You have a point, which should tell you how potent your kisses are."

He presented an unreadable expression as Penny watched him. All of a sudden, the room seemed to shrink and a flush of color spread up her face.

"I think it's time I concede defeat," she said much too quickly, looking entirely panicked at the thought of kissing him again.

Parker handed her the glass of amber liquid and stood next to her. Eyeing her intently, he took a long drink. When she stood, avoiding eye contact, he said in a soothing voice, "Penny, look at me."

Reluctantly, her tormented gaze slowly made its way to his. He placed his drink on the table, then reached for hers and did the same. Gripping her shoulders, he gently pulled her closer.

"It's just a kiss," he whispered, before his head lowered.

Like that night on board ship, he kept his pace unhurried and leisurely, using skillful lips to slowly draw her response, despite the fact that want and need exploded inside him the second their mouths connected. The maddening urge to give in to the impulse, to let go, to allow his lips to consume her drove him to the brink of an all-consuming desire. With an iron will, he tamped down yearning and continued as her innocent kisses and mewling cries propelled him completely out of his mind. Though he could control his mouth, he couldn't control his hands. One wrapped around her neck, bringing her closer. The other found her perfect breast, gently squeezing and touching and rubbing, and luxuriating in the feel of her response.

⚙

No, Penny thought, lost in a sea of sensation. It wasn't just a kiss. It would never be just a simple kiss with this man, she realized too late. Once his lips touched hers, Penny knew she fought her own craving

163

much more than she fought his. She hated herself because at the moment, she never wanted his kiss to end—in fact, yearned to feel him inside her again.

All of her senses were magnified. She tasted the bourbon still lingering on his lips, could smell the male scent of him, and the sensations playing behind her closed eyes were enough to make her knees weak. Heat surged through her system when his hand stroked her breast and she couldn't stop herself from giving him more access or responding to his incredible touch. His hands, now roaming freely over her body, felt too glorious. With full knowledge she should end things and run away because Geoff deserved her fidelity, she gave in to the driving, coursing pleasure. Wrapping her arms around him, stepping closer to his warmth, she touched him as she was dying to do.

"God in heaven, I can't stop," he whispered, slowly pulling her down on the thick carpet with him as the kiss careened completely out of hand, his mouth and tongue growing more urgent, demanding more from her. Once on the floor, his hands worked to release her breasts fully, before one moved to lift her skirt and petticoats, pulling them around her waist. He then found her warmth, where the heat from her body had to have singed his hand as he began readying her for receiving him, stroking in and out. He was so good at drawing the waves of sensation as they swamped her, coming faster and faster before she shuddered to completion beneath his hand.

"I'm at the point of no return," he murmured, kissing his way along her neck, nibbling and biting as he went, before whispering urgently into her ear, "I need to know you want this as much as I do." When she didn't answer, couldn't answer, he pressed, saying savagely, "Do you?"

She nodded her reply, giving him a low moan while moving her hands over his manhood as all rational thought fled. At that moment, she met him head-to-head, her need matching his.

He quickly undid his trousers, pushed them down, and kicked them off. Then he buried himself inside her. The entire time he moved in and out, Penny held on, knowing she'd pulled the tail of the tiger too hard. His prediction after their first kiss on board ship had come true. She was receiving the ride of her life.

TEMPTATION

Penny's violent groan burst free as pleasure she'd never realized existed engulfed her, washing over her in wave after wave like the sea lapped at the beach until it slowly ebbed.

When the feeling had totally faded, reality rushed in. Mortified that she'd lain with him once more, self-derision filled her. Tears welled up. She had no one to blame but herself. She'd allowed him to continue, even though she'd sworn earlier in the day this would never happen again.

Eventually Parker lifted up on his elbows, searching her face. "Shush, love. Please don't cry."

His endearment brought on more tears. Parker rolled over, disengaging from her, and pulled her into his warmth. He lay there for several minutes, gently stroking up and down her arm while she quietly sobbed.

"It's not that bad," he whispered once her tears subsided.

"Yes, it is. How can I lie with you when I'm engaged to another? I'm a horrible person."

"No, you're not. But I do think you should rethink your plans."

Stiffening, she closed her eyes, saying on a sigh, "I can't."

"Sure you can. You can marry me instead," Parker explained all too smugly. "It's the perfect solution to your dilemma, given your response to me but a moment ago."

"What about love?"

"I've already told you that's something I can't give, but I'll take care of you. I promise."

His tone was simply too overbearing. Heavens, how had she gotten into this predicament? When she tried to pull away, he held her steadfastly in place. Panicked at how controlled his movements were, she tried to reason with him. "It's not what I want. I mean to marry Geoff and that's final." Her clipped English accent grew more pronounced with each word. "I'll not change my mind."

"But you don't love him."

"Yes, I do."

"You can't love him," he ground out. "Not when you respond to me like you do." He released her to right his trousers, buttoning them up.

"I don't want to respond to you," she stated vehemently, letting him help straighten her dress.

Once done, he stood, grabbed her hand, and pulled her up with him. An intent blue-gray stare sought hers, and his eyes mirrored disbelief. "Why would you marry him if you don't love him?"

"But I do love him," she cried, pounding a fist in an effort to convince him. "I do!"

"No, you don't," Parker said, waving her avowal of love away. "I know it in my very soul."

"Well, your soul is wrong then." She threw up her hands, completely annoyed with his single-minded tenacity. It seemed he wouldn't give up with his insistence that she marry him, and marrying him would not do. Penny paced the room.

"What's wrong with marriage to me? Surely we have something between us, even if it's not love?"

"You don't understand," Penny whispered, wishing she hadn't heard a bit of hurt in his voice.

"No, I don't," Parker snapped angrily. He moved to pick up his unfinished drink and took a deep swallow, watching her the entire time.

"Why would you marry me when you say you don't love me?" she asked, searching his eyes for something, but feeling let down when his expression became closed and unreadable.

"That's easy. There's our heated attraction. Surely you feel it."

"But what of love?"

"Men don't marry for love," he insisted, shaking his head in denial. "Marry me. I promise to take care of you. We can tell Lucas before he leaves, saving Geoff the trip here."

"I can't," she said softly, turning her head away from him to hide her disappointment.

"Hell, we can't keep our hands off each other. Which is a lot more than most marriages have."

"Well, you'll have to start keeping your hands off me, because I'm marrying Geoff and that's final," she stated firmly, crossing her arms in front of her with her chin jutting out.

"You could be carrying my babe right now. Would you foist

another man's child on him?" he shot back heatedly.

She hadn't thought of that. Her expression revealed the horror she felt, and she started pacing the room again, rubbing her forehead. "Hopefully that hasn't occurred. Until we know for sure, no more kisses." She stopped and gave him a steely look. "No more kisses or I'll leave."

Parker's annoyance showed on his face. Warily, she took an involuntary step backward as he stalked up to her. He placed his hands on her shoulders, effectively stilling her retreat and closing their distance until his mouth hovered an inch above hers.

"I still say you're making a mistake. This means something. You know it does," he said softly just before their lips met.

His tongue plummeted, sliding inside her mouth to begin a seduction she had little will to fight.

Still, she knew if she succumbed to the knee-weakening pleasure, she'd regret it to her dying day.

"It's not enough," she whispered, pulling away and wishing more than anything that he was different, that he could fall in love with her and not just want to make love with her. She shook her head, and walked toward the door. Once there, she turned around and said in a determined voice, "Kiss me again and I swear I'll leave."

ℭℬ

Parker stood, rooted to his spot, watching her leave the room. Once she was gone, he picked up his drink, finishing it in one swig. Then in a fit of rage, he threw the glass at the fireplace, where it shattered into tiny pieces before he stalked out of the room, his face taut with anger.

Chapter 16

A knock woke Penny. As she sat up, a maid breezed into the room with a bowl of fresh water and towels.

"Come, Miss Layton, you don't want to be late for breakfast." She tugged the draperies open, bound them with a sash, and attached the sash to the wall as sunshine burst through the windows.

Shame and regret washed over Penny as memories of the night before resurfaced. Would Geoff want her now that she'd lain with Parker? Somehow, she'd make it up to her beloved. She just had to.

The maid opened the armoire door and Penny glanced at her timepiece. It was odd to see the woman in her room at a quarter to seven. Must be an American custom, she thought, slowly climbing out of bed.

Usually an early riser, she wanted to take the coward's way out today and remain under the covers for as long as possible. Still, it was always better to face unpleasantness sooner rather than later. Penny began washing while the maid readied her clothes to wear.

"Ah, good, you made it to breakfast," Parker said when she entered the dining room a little later.

Determined to act as if last night hadn't happened, Penny nodded, then frowned. "I didn't realize your household is on such a tight schedule."

Elizabeth patted the seat beside her. "Come sit next to me. Parker's a stickler for the family eating together whenever he's in residence."

Without glancing his way, Penny sat and another maid poured her a cup of tea. Penny added a dollop of milk and brought the cup to her mouth.

A noise at the door drew everyone's gaze.

Catherine rushed in, adjusting her skirt and tucking loose auburn curls behind her ear. She slowed and, smoothing her gown, walked sedately into the room when she realized all eyes focused on her.

"You're late," Parker said, glancing at his pocket watch. "As usual."

"I overslept." She took her time pulling out a chair. Once seated, she offered a beautiful smile. "I didn't dare miss breakfast on your first day home."

Parker only grunted, but looked none too pleased.

Out of the corner of her eye, Penny watched the two. "If Catherine's always late, why does breakfast have to be so early?" she finally said.

He turned her way, capturing her gaze with a cold icy stare. "Because I deem it so."

Without flinching, Penny held his stare. The autocratic tilt of his head reminded her of Markham, Geoff's older brother.

"Parker!" Elizabeth chided. "You sound like a despot."

"Can't have that." He inhaled a deep breath and forced a smile before adding, "I leave early and sometimes miss dinner. I like connecting with my family, which is why breakfast is at seven sharp."

Penny looked down at her cup and prayed the others at the table didn't see her burning cheeks. He was obviously still mad at her for refusing his offer of marriage after what went on in the library.

After that she remained silent. Thankfully, no one seemed to notice as Elizabeth kept the conversation going with more news of what had gone on during Parker's absence.

From her perch in the front parlor window seat an hour later, Penny watched Parker mount his horse. As he rode off, her shoulders slumped in relief.

What was she going to do? God forbid, what if she carried his child? How foolish of her to not consider the consequences of her actions.

As it was, women had few options in this world and she had fewer still, especially with no living relatives, and her rightful inheritance in the hands of a madman.

"Would you like to do something fun today?" Catherine asked

from behind her, interrupting her musings.

Penny nodded, but her thoughts weren't so easily dismissed. She needed a husband. Someone with power behind him, like Geoff, to take on Gerald Knightsbridge.

"Excuse me," she said once it registered that Catherine had spoken again.

"I said, now that he's off, we can enjoy ourselves to the fullest."

"You mean you he doesn't allow you to enjoy yourself?" Penny shook off her melancholy and turned her full attention on the animated woman.

Catherine scrunched her nose. "He's a tad overprotective. Of course, his wishes have never stopped me and I always make use of the time he's away." She tugged Penny off the seat. Still holding her hand, she started up the stairs. "He's worse than Mother. Now that he's back for a lengthy stay, I'm sure he'll be a nightmare to handle."

If his actions at breakfast hadn't already confirmed her worst suspicions, Catherine's statement certainly did. Parker Davis wasn't like Geoff. He was a controlling man who expected everyone to follow his commands, just like the duke. Marrying him would be another huge mistake. After enduring hell under the earl's thumb, Penny wasn't about to kowtow to anyone.

"He thinks he's responsible for me," Catherine said. "Both he and Lucas do. If I were truthful, I'd have to say he means well, which is why I pretend to do his bidding. He pretends I obey him and we both go on pretending to keep the illusion alive."

Intrigued, Penny asked, "Are you saying he doesn't have control over you?"

"Well, no," she mumbled, then said more cheerfully, "What would you say to going hunting? My brothers have been too busy lately. They hate for me to go alone, and it's really not as much fun, so I seldom do anymore. But now that you're here, we can have a grand time."

"I've never hunted before," Penny said honestly. "It sounds like an adventure." Her time in the Davis household had suddenly taken on a new dimension and provided her with the perfect distraction. She shoved her negative thoughts away. Nothing good would come of fearing the worst until it came time to face Geoff. Then she'd worry.

In the meantime, she would avoid Parker like he was horse manure.

"Great," Catherine said when she nodded. "We'll make a day of it and have Pearl make us a lunch. First, we have to find just the thing for you to wear." She headed for her bedroom.

Penny trailed behind, feeling as if an anvil of worry had been lifted from her shoulders.

"I have some trousers and old shirts from when I was younger that should fit." Catherine moved to a bureau and rummaged through drawers. "Ah, here they are." She pulled out a faded dark pair of boys' homespun trousers as well as a worn muslin shirt the color of mud. "You can wear your riding boots. What do you think?"

"Trousers? What fun." Penny took the items, warming to the shocking idea of wearing boys' clothing while hunting. In front of the cheval glass, she held them up to gauge what she'd look like in them.

"You can't dress here," Catherine warned when Penny started to unbutton her blouse. At her questioning look, she rolled her eyes. "Mother would never let us out of the house if she saw us in something that scandalous, so we need to act as if we're going for a ride. Once we get to my hiding place, we'll change. It's near impossible to catch prey in a day dress and my riding habit is too uncomfortable." Wearing a conspiratorial expression, she put her finger to her lips. "What Mother doesn't know won't hurt her."

Penny grinned. How novel! "So Lucas and Parker don't care that you gallivant around the country in boys' clothing?" The thought amazed her.

"They've tried to dissuade me, but have learned to tolerate it. Both know they can't stop me if I really want to do something. I never do anything too outrageous. And since I can hunt and shoot better than either of them, they keep their mouths shut about what I wear when we're hunting."

Penny nodded, suddenly feeling right at home as memories of her younger years with the freedom to run around the wilds of northern England flitted through her mind. More laughter bubbled up. "This surely has to be the most scandalous thing I've ever attempted." Or almost the most scandalous. She decided not to dwell on her misadventures with Parker, as those were mistakes never to be repeated.

"It's not really as scandalous as it sounds," Catherine said. "After all, I only hunt on Davis property, which is certainly not dangerous. And since you've never been before, we'll go for something easy, like wild turkey or quail."

She presented her back. "Here, help me into my riding habit, and I'll help you. Then we'll ride out to my hiding place."

The next thing Penny knew, she was following Catherine down the back stairs to the kitchen. Pearl handed them a basket with their lunch. The two ran out the door, heading in the direction of the stable.

"We'll leave the horses tethered once we make it to our starting point," Catherine said, mounting.

Penny did the same.

Catherine took the lead, galloping toward the woods as if the devil were after her, and Penny stayed hot on her trail.

Eventually they slowed to a walk. The midsummer sun was still low enough that the lush green landscape shaded them from the burning rays. Leaves rustled in the gentle breeze as they continued on a trail that led through the dark, dense forest. At a huge rock, Catherine stopped, dismounted, and tied her horse to a branch where the gelding could graze.

"Well, what are you waiting for?" she said, glancing at Penny, who watched from atop her mare. Penny didn't need any further encouragement before jumping off and leading the mare to the same tree.

She followed Catherine around the big boulder that led to what looked like a cave. The small amount of space in between the rock and the opening made it a tight squeeze.

"This is my special place," Catherine said, hiking farther into the deep cavern high enough to stand upright. "Hold on a minute while I light a lantern." She struck a matchstick, engulfing the spacious interior with light.

Though hot outside, the cooler temperature inside the cave felt good on Penny's skin as she took a deep breath, inhaling a musky, earthy scent that pervaded the cavern.

Catherine headed purposefully toward several bundles packed

away in a corner. Undoing them, she had everything out and began undressing. "We can leave our things here, and come back when we're done."

In moments, she'd changed into male attire and looking every inch a female because the clothes did little to hide her curvaceous figure and long legs. In fact, if nothing else, they accentuated them.

Penny quickly donned the pieces Catherine provided, loving the freedom to move about without heavy material hampering her. She certainly felt like a hunter.

"Put your clothes with mine so they stay dry. The earth is damp," Catherine said, indicating the neat pile next to the big canvas bag she unpacked, pulling out two rifles, a six-gun, and a bow with several arrows.

She nodded, folded her split skirt and blouse, and then added her clothes to the pile.

"Have you ever fired a rifle before?" Catherine asked, loading one of the rifles.

"Yes. I'm also good with a bow, but I've never hunted before," Penny stated honestly.

"We won't go after a deer today. It's better to have Lucas or Parker around for large game because they can deal with cleaning and dressing it better than I can." Her scrunched-up nose indicated her thoughts on the subject.

Catherine buckled a holster around her waist and tucked a gun into it before tying the holster to her thigh. To Penny, she looked like one of those gunslingers she'd read about who embodied the Wild West. She handed Penny first a bow and then a loaded rifle, while she finished loading the other one.

"They have fox hunts in England, but I've never actually been on one," Penny said, eyeing the items with interest.

"Fox hunts? I've heard of them." She started for the mouth of the cave. "Seems like a waste of time to me. What do you do with the fox when you kill it?"

"I've no idea," Penny said, following. "I only know there are those who love the thrill of the chase with the hounds running wild and everyone following on horseback."

"Humph. It also seems as if the dogs do all the work. Where is the skill in that?"

"I'm sure you're right." Penny smiled at Catherine's disapproving frown. "So, what do we do now?" she asked once the two were outside.

"Now we stalk our prey." Catherine pointed out what tracks to look for. Then she taught her how to sneak up on a bird or another animal, staying downwind to avoid detection, also showing her how to camouflage herself.

They eventually took a break for lunch before going back to tracking and waiting, which seemed a big part of hunting, as the day was more than half over and that was all they had done so far.

While patiently covered with dried leaves and twigs, Penny froze and prayed that a family of skunks sniffing not two feet in front of her wouldn't notice her hiding spot. She exhaled a relieved breath when they sauntered on one at a time, the mother in the lead and the three kits following. After that, several raccoons and a couple of groundhogs visited long enough to sniff around her. When a deer ventured nearby, Penny stared in awe. She loved watching creatures wander so close and never detect their presence. Suddenly the idea of killing them didn't seem like sport and she said as much to Catherine.

They were just getting ready to leave their hiding spot when something caught Catherine's attention. Silently signaling for Penny to stay quiet, Catherine emerged and stalked noiselessly away, disappearing into the brush.

Sounds of the forest penetrated Penny's thoughts. Bees buzzed, birds chirped, and tree frogs croaked. Suddenly all noise died. There was another rustling sound in front of her, before all was still. Penny didn't move. Where in the world was Catherine? All alone, fear streaked through her.

A twig snapped.

Catherine's laughter rose up, followed by her voice. "Give it up, Parker. I've got you in my sights."

Penny shifted and looked out through a break in the leaves. Sure enough, Parker stood a few feet away, dressed much the same as she and Catherine.

"Damn. I was so careful," was his amused reply. "How did you know to get around me? I swear you have a sixth sense."

Penny had no idea how he came to stand in front of her. Nor did she know where Catherine hid, even though her voice had come from somewhere behind Parker.

More laughter followed as Catherine stepped into view holding a rifle at the ready. She appeared much like what Penny imagined an Amazon warrior would look like, her rich masses of auburn hair falling around her shoulders and her emerald eyes flashing triumph. Only she wore boy's trousers in place of a loincloth and carried a rifle rather than a spear. "You never used to let me get behind you. You're getting rusty."

He snorted. "No, I'm not. I found you, didn't I?"

"Hah! That's just because you know where I hunt. You know darned well if I'd been stalking you, you'd be dead right now."

"Maybe," he conceded. "But next time I'll catch you unaware. Part of stalking is knowing the habits of those you seek." Parker walked over to where Penny still hid and sat down next to her. "You can come out now," he said, snaring Penny's gaze, confirming her suspicion that he'd known exactly where she'd hidden all along.

"Don't scare her," Catherine admonished, coming up and plopping down beside him. "She's done well for her first time. Although she's a little squeamish when it comes time to pull the trigger."

"My, I have raised a bloodthirsty sister," Parker said, chuckling as Penny moved from her spot, brushing the leaves and debris off her dungarees.

"I never kill anything without a reason. I find more sport in finding prey and only kill it if we can eat it. So, how did you know I was hunting?"

"I put two and two together when Mother told me you'd gone out for a long ride and took along a lunch. You shouldn't corrupt our guest, Catherine."

"You're just out of sorts because you had to work instead of hunt."

Penny could only stare at the two as they bantered back and forth about killing, finding prey, and corrupting her. The fact that both she and his sister were dressed as boys didn't seem to faze him a bit. He also seemed very relaxed today, a contradiction of the controlling man at breakfast and too attractive for words. Parker definitely fit the part of the rugged American adventurer in her mind's eye. His trousers, tucked into scuffed boots, fit him like a second skin, and his muslin shirt with open collar accentuated the V of his throat. His shirtsleeves were rolled, showing his strong forearms and beautifully shaped hands.

Her heart skipped a beat as she remembered where those hands had been.

"And did you have a reason to kill anything today?" Parker asked, thankfully interrupting her wandering thoughts, yanking Penny's attention back to his face.

Catherine shrugged. "Pearl said a turkey or some quail might be a nice change for dinner, so I thought I'd have a bit of fun showing Penny what we cloddish Americans do for entertainment."

He glanced at her, grinning. "Has my sister totally ruined your idea of what sweet, genteel American women are like?"

Penny returned his grin. Catherine seemed so different from any woman she'd ever met.

"Humph." Catherine crossed her arms. "We both know that doesn't describe me."

"I can always hope you'll change," he teased. "What did you get for Pearl?"

"A nice big gobbler and several quail," she stated proudly. "They're back in the cave." She eyed her brother thoughtfully and asked pointedly, "Why are you here? I thought you'd be in Washington all afternoon."

"So did I. President Grant didn't like what I had to say. Neither did Jonathan. Both sent me on my way. I'm to return next month after I've had time to reconsider."

"Why would he not like what you had to say? You're not quitting on him, are you?"

"As a matter of fact, I did tender my resignation," Parker said in a quiet voice. His gaze moved to Catherine's before he warned, "But it's just between you and me. God knows I don't need Mother planning my life before I figure out what I'm going to do next."

"You really quit?" Catherine squealed, jumping up and hugging him. "So that means you'll be around more?"

Parker's soft chuckle could barely be heard above Catherine's animated reply. "Like you really want me around telling you what to do," he stated in a disgruntled manner, when her excitement died down and she released him.

"Of course I want you around." No one could miss the exasperation in her reply. "How could I not? You're much easier than Mother to handle."

Parker grunted. Companionable silence pervaded until his voice rang out again. "Hey, would you be interested in shooting something bigger than turkey?"

"I don't think Penny wants me to kill a deer. She thinks the bucks look too majestic."

Parker's amused gaze wandered to Penny's, where it stayed. Finally he looked away. "I was thinking more along the lines of wild pig. I noted signs of one not too far away."

More of Catherine's enthusiasm burst free. "You'd let me help you bag a boar?" A pleased smile split her face.

"Like I have any choice?" Snorting, he stood, pulling first Catherine to her feet and then Penny. "Come on, you can help me figure out where he's hiding."

It was such a natural move. Penny had no time to react to his touch before it was over and he'd let go of her. Watching him out of the corner of her eye, Penny could only marvel at how calm he was— as if last night hadn't happened. She dusted her bottom off and followed. If he could so easily pretend the events never occurred, then so could she.

For the next hour the three stalked wild boar. Or rather Catherine and Parker stalked. She observed, totally amazed at how the two worked noiselessly together, searching for signs of an animal Penny was beginning to think didn't exist.

All of a sudden Parker tensed and signaled silently to Catherine. She caught his signal and nodded. He turned to Penny and whispered, "Wait over there, behind that big rock. You'll be safe enough if you stay there."

Penny did his bidding and watched the two disappear. For a quarter of an hour she stayed put, listening to only silence. Then a loud shot rang out. She waited patiently another half hour without hearing another sound. She was starting to become concerned when movement from the direction the two had disappeared earlier drew her attention.

"If you ever do anything so dangerous again I'll flay you myself." Parker's angry voice reverberated through the forest.

"There was nothing dangerous about what I did. Admit it. You're just mad you weren't in position to get the first shot," Catherine said just as heatedly.

Within seconds, Catherine and Parker walked out of the brush while carrying between them a huge trussed-up pig with horns tied to a sturdy branch, arguing the entire way.

"For your information, getting in front of a charging boar is not my idea of a safe endeavor."

"I snared him, didn't I?" Catherine countered. "It was child's play."

"What if you hadn't? What would've happened then?" he argued, still incensed.

"Then you would've had a shot," Catherine said, grinning. "And I have no doubts you would've hit him dead-on. But you knew as well as I did, I wasn't about to miss, so I don't understand why you're all in such a dither."

"I swear you'll be the death of me, Catherine. You take too many risks," he chided, his anger dissipating somewhat.

"Oh?" Catherine gave a heady laugh. "And you never take risks?"

"It's different for me and you damn well know it."

"Humph. Come on, Parker. Don't be a killjoy. Instead of chastising me, you should be congratulating me on my skill. It was a brilliantly executed kill and you know it. I hit him right between the eyes."

By this time they'd hiked to where Penny waited.

"The animal does look dangerous." Her eyebrows furrowed as she carefully eyed the massive beast. "You actually killed it?" she said, glancing at Catherine in awe.

"Of course." Catherine stood taller, clearly pleased. "Did you have doubts that I could?"

Parker rolled his eyes and said under his breath, "Why do I bother?"

He and Catherine placed their burden on the ground. He took his rifle from around his shoulder and leaned it against a tree. Then he unclipped a canteen from his belt, drank, and handed it to Catherine, who took a couple of swallows before handing it to Penny.

Watching Parker out of the corner of her eye, Penny lifted the canteen to her lips. A trickle of sweat wormed its way down the side of his face before he brushed it aside with his shirtsleeve, wiping his brow at the same time.

Her gaze centered on the hand attached to that arm and something clenched inside her stomach. She sucked in a huge breath and let it out slowly. Closing her eyes and willing the thought of those hands touching her out of her mind, she gulped a big drink.

Parker took the canteen from her, placed it back on his belt, and said, "I think it's time to get back." Turning to Penny, he asked, "Can you handle our two rifles so Catherine can help carry the boar?"

Keeping her gaze averted, Penny nodded, reluctant to risk giving her thoughts away by speaking or making eye contact. She took their rifles and followed the two once they picked up their burden and started back toward the cave where the horses patiently grazed.

At the cave, both Catherine and Penny changed clothing after Catherine helped Parker lift the boar along with the other dead animals onto Catherine's gelding for the trip back to the house.

"Catherine can ride the mare and you can ride with me," Parker said nonchalantly, as if the thought of being so close to her didn't affect him. When her facial features grew pensive, revealing a little of her dismay, he explained in a low voice, "It only makes sense. You're much smaller than Catherine, making it easier on the stallion. We're not riding far, but I'd really rather not overtax either horse."

He then placed those beautiful hands on her waist, hoisted her onto the horse, and easily mounted in one quick burst of energy. Penny's breath caught in her throat and she sat frozen, too afraid movement might worsen the situation. His arms came around her, pinning her against his chest with one hand that stayed glued to her middle. Then he lifted the reins with the other and urged the horse forward. It was all Penny could do to ignore those hands now so close, when all she really wanted was feel them roaming over her body again.

CB

"Relax, angel," Parker whispered near her ear after they'd ridden less than a tenth of a mile. "You're safe enough."

From the first moment Penny had emerged from her hiding spot, she seemed wary of him. Her wariness ate at him like an acid of uncertainty. He couldn't decipher her mixed signals and wasn't going to try. He only knew he had to tread carefully; not an easy task, especially when she looked far too fetching in trousers that did nothing to hide her feminine figure. So much so, he'd used total restraint in not yanking her into his arms and smothering her with kisses.

He closed his eyes, remembering their last encounter. He could still taste her lips and wanted to taste them again. How was it possible that this was the same woman who'd met him stroke for stroke last night? Gone was the siren who'd melted in his arms, and in its place was this frozen creature who acted as if he had some contagious disease.

Penny's parting words after their lovemaking entered his train of thought. Parker damn sure had no intention of having to track her down if she made good on her threat, so he decided to humor her. At least until he figured out a way to make her yearn for his touch the same way he yearned for hers. Once he did, he had no doubts she'd marry him.

Unfortunately, his plan took a taxing toll.

His hand flexed involuntarily. It was next to impossible to be this close to her and not wrap his fingers around her breast as he wanted.

When she mumbled something and moved in the saddle in front of him, his groin came alive, causing her to stiffen.

"Stay still," he hissed in a strangled voice. "I told you, you're safe. I have no intention of going where I'm not wanted."

"You're horrible," she whispered back.

TEMPTATION

"You didn't think so last night, angel." He tightened his grip on her waist.

She froze. "You're no gentleman to bring that up."

He chuckled and couldn't resist the urge to nuzzle her neck and give her a few kisses. "As I recall, I gave you the choice." She was simply too tempting. His smile deepened when he noticed the quick racing of her pulse along with goose bumps before she tried to cover her reactions.

She scooted farther away from him, but in the end all her scooting accomplished was a derriere nestled closer to his arousal.

"Stop," he said. "You're making it worse. If you continue rubbing me like that, I'm not going to be able to take your threats of leaving seriously."

Immediately Penny froze, not moving a muscle. She stayed in her uncomfortable position for several minutes before Parker's hand firmly pulled her toward him. "Relax. I promise to behave. Like I said, angel. You have nothing to fear from me."

His grin turned more confident when she complied with his request. She wasn't immune to him, that much was true, but she was denying their attraction and building a wall of resistance.

He stayed silent the rest of the trip, plotting ways he could tear down the wall and melt that resistance.

Chapter 17

"You've a green thumb," Penny commented to Elizabeth, who was vigorously weeding in the garden outside Parker's library. She walked in between flowers of all types, roses in every color, lavender, pink azaleas, yellow day lilies, and maroon begonias. "I've always loved gardens," she said, admiring the beauty of this one. Several days had passed since the ride with Parker back to the house. Mornings were the only time she could avoid him.

"It's my obsession." Elizabeth sank back on her heels, shading her eyes with a hand and smiled. "I love roses. These were my husband's favorite when he was alive," she said, indicating a bush with the most beautiful red roses Penny had ever seen. "I propagated this from a clipping that I brought from Pennsylvania." She sighed. "Makes me feel closer to him." She went back to weeding. "I'm usually out here in the morning, to avoid the heat."

"Would you mind some company?" Penny asked.

"Surely you don't want to spend your time weeding with an old lady?" Elizabeth's question held a hint of amusement that said she was teasing. "Where's Catherine?"

"She's off painting. I love to garden and spent many hours helping our gardeners at home in England." Penny looked around and added wistfully, "I'd like to feel useful."

"You've already made yourself useful helping me with the tenants, not to mention helping around the house. I could get spoiled with all your usefulness."

The smile she offered warmed Penny's heart. "I enjoy staying busy."

Elizabeth chuckled. "If you're determined to help, I'd love the company. You might want to go and change, though. I have another old bonnet to keep the sun off your face as well as an extra pair of work gloves in the shed."

"I'll be right back." Penny couldn't contain her grin as she hurried to change.

The two had spent several hours working side by side when Penny looked up.

Catherine stepped into view. "Would you like to go for a ride?"

Penny nodded. "I'd love to, if that's all right with your mother."

"Oh, go on with you. You don't need my permission to enjoy yourself," Elizabeth scolded good-naturedly.

"Thanks for letting me help you." Penny rose, taking off her gloves and bonnet.

"I'm the one who's thankful. I enjoyed the company." Elizabeth smiled warmly. As Penny left, she added a little louder, "I'm out here most mornings, if you get the urge to get your hands dirty again."

Penny only laughed and said, "I'll be here tomorrow morning."

After that, Penny spent most mornings helping Elizabeth in the garden.

❦

Over the next three weeks, her life on the Davis farm settled into routine. Parker played the perfect gentleman, not once giving her cause to mention her threat of leaving. He still required her to play chess with him in the evenings, even letting her drink more of his bourbon, but she was careful to avoid being alone with him. The minute the others retired, Penny would take her leave and Parker never said a word. No, but he always wore an indulgent smile when he'd say his good night—a mocking grin shouting louder than words that he knew she was running from him and he found the fact amusing.

Today she sat with Catherine and Elizabeth in the library as they did each afternoon.

"Take a look."

Glancing at Catherine, who'd been engrossed in sketching something with a piece of charcoal, Penny nodded and her eyes focused lower. "What are you working on now?"

"One of the tenants' boys." She presented the picture. "What do you think?"

"That's Tommy. You're quite good. This has definitely captured

183

his spirit," Penny said, impressed with the likeness of the sweet child she'd met while helping Elizabeth.

The picture brought forth a ready memory of the first time Parker's mother asked Penny to go with her to check on the sick child. Penny smiled. Parker's tenants not only farmed on his land, but they paid rent with part of their yield each year. This similarity to estates in England made her feel even more comfortable with her temporary home. And more comfortable with Parker, despite the great lengths she took to avoid him. All to no avail.

During the day, when he wasn't working with his farm manager, he would seek out Catherine and her out to go riding. He caught on early on that riding was her passion and Penny couldn't resist taking him up on the offer. Nor could she help but enjoy the daily rides, in fact begin to live for them. Racing both Catherine and Parker through the Maryland countryside in an effort to come out on top was something she relished. One thing marred her happiness. He was still too darned attractive, and keeping a level head around him became harder by the day.

"I wish Catherine was as adept at household duties as she is with hunting and drawing," Elizabeth said with a sigh, attracting Penny's attention. The elder woman shook out the shirt she'd mended and gently folded it, placing it in a basket and picking up another to work on. "You can't know how nice it is to have someone to share them with, now that Sarah and Rebecca are gone. Until you came, Penny, I was starting to feel as if I was the only female in the house."

"Mother! How can you say that? I'm female," Catherine declared in a shocked voice. "I simply have other interests."

Penny's smile stretched. Despite her unwanted attraction to Parker, Penny felt as if she really was part of their family, and her time spent with them was something she treasured. Besides her early morning gardening and going hunting with Catherine a couple more times, Elizabeth had taken her under her wing, showing her things within the household that needed tending and taking Penny along with her more and more when she went to visit Parker's tenants.

"Yes, I know," Elizabeth said. "But you can't tell me you'd rather not be outdoors riding or hunting with Lucas or Parker than sitting with Sarah and Rebecca talking about fashions or decorating. How are you ever going to find a husband, when you outshoot and outride every man within a fifty-mile radius?"

"Why do I need to marry?" Catherine asked huffily, returning her attention to her charcoal.

Elizabeth's eyes flew to Penny's and her expression seemed to say, "See what I have to deal with?" Instead, she murmured, "Why indeed?"

"You never married again after father died."

"We're talking about two completely different subjects, and you know it. I guess I should be content with your offer to help me with our ball next month."

"You're having a ball?" It seemed ages ago that Penny had attended one.

Catherine nodded. "It's our Harvest Ball," she explained to Penny. "An annual celebration held at the end of the growing season, usually the last Saturday in October. Everyone within riding distance attends—tenants and landholders alike." Catherine chuckled. "See, Mother. I'm not totally without merit. I do love creating the perfect ambience." She then went back to her drawing, while Penny picked up her book again and Elizabeth mended.

They all glanced up when Parker sauntered into the room a short time later. He bent to give Elizabeth a quick peck on the cheek. "You're looking content today, Mother." He straightened and looked at his sister. "Are you two ready for our ride?"

Catherine shook her head and replied in a disappointed voice, "You and Penny will have to go without me today. I promised Tommy I'd finish his picture by this afternoon."

Parker looked to Penny with raised eyebrows. "Well, angel. How about it? Are you up for a ride?"

Penny frowned, wishing he'd quit with the nickname he'd started using soon after that first night they'd played chess and had made love. "I think I'll stay and read."

"But you love to ride," Catherine said. "There's no reason you have to lose out just because I made a promise."

"Go on and have a nice ride, dear," Elizabeth chimed in. "The fresh air will do you good."

Feeling stuck, Penny nodded, even though Catherine wouldn't be around to provide a buffer. "Just give me a chance to change." She set her book aside and stood, hiding her dismay behind a stiff smile.

"Good." Parker met her gaze. "I'll meet you in the stables in ten minutes. Since Catherine can't join us, we'll ride someplace special."

As Penny rushed out of the room and up the stairs, she wondered where somewhere special was.

She soon found out when she and Parker rode to a scenic spot overlooking the bay, a part of his property she'd never been to before.

The sun, high in the sky, warmed the air and created a perfect late-summer day, neither too hot nor too cold.

Parker dismounted and tied his horse to a nearby tree before heading for a big boulder. She watched as he sat, pensively looking out over the water.

"You love it here, don't you?" Penny had tied her horse to the same tree and now stood behind him. Her eyes swept over the panoramic view of the bay and shoreline. From this spot, she could see for miles. The view of the water filled her with peace.

He shrugged. "I do love it here. Catherine has her cave, Lucas has the sea, and I have this spot. This is why I bought the property all those years ago," he said, meeting her inquisitive gaze. Then his attention returned to the bay. Two ships sailed on the horizon and he silently studied their progress. "The scenery is spectacular, don't you think?"

She nodded. His mood seemed more brooding today—different. His gaze held nothing of his usual amusement. Instead she caught a glimpse of yearning, or hunger would be a better term, before he quickly shuttered the expression. Licking her lips nervously, she hesitated, not quite sure how to proceed. "It is beautiful. Makes me wonder if heaven is like this," she said, finally moving to sit beside him.

"I would imagine if anyone knew what heaven was like, it would be an angel such as you," he teased lightly.

"I'm hardly an angel." Penny couldn't stop the grin from touching the corners of her mouth. "In fact, my father used to say I had a bit of the devil in me because of some of my exploits when I was younger."

"Maybe that's why I find you so intriguing. You're a devil disguised as an angel, come to earth to torment me. It's my living hell, part of my penance for being the way I am."

"Why do you say that?" she asked, wishing she could understand his strange mood.

"No reason," he replied abruptly, his manner indicating he'd shared too much. "You're right about this spot being heavenly, though. It's so peaceful here. Maybe that's why I love it."

Penny accepted his answer and remained silent, lost in her thoughts. The serene spot elicited images of her past. "I've often wondered if my parents watch over me from heaven," she said sheepishly, voicing her thoughts and keeping her eyes on the horizon. "Sitting here now, I believe it, and the idea of them up there somewhere looking down warms my heart." After a moment of reflection, her focus returned to his face. "As if such a thing were possible. That's so silly, isn't it?"

"No. It's a very pleasant thought. I wonder if my father is watching over me." Smiling, he held eye contact. Then his smile turned wistful and he sighed, shaking his head and releasing her gaze. "If so, I don't think he'd like what I've become."

"That's not true. You've much to be proud of."

"Not in my father's eyes."

He'd mentioned something about his father on the trip from Baltimore. At the time, she'd let it go, unwilling to pry. Now she was curious because she sensed he was revealing something about himself he didn't usually share with others. Her curiosity got the better of her. "Would you like to talk about it?"

"About what?" His reluctant gaze met hers again.

"About the accident that killed your father and brothers," she said softly. "I know it still pains you."

Parker refocused on the water as another passing ship sailed below. Penny wasn't sure he would say more until his deep voice penetrated the quiet.

"It happened a long time ago. A mine caved in. We were coal miners—my brothers and I—following in our father's footsteps. It was how we survived back then."

Well aware of such accidents that killed people and too stunned to do much more than stare, Penny remained speechless. Her father had owned several coal mines, now hers, in Northumberland. Having had a strong social conscience before his death, he'd worked tirelessly with the miners to improve working conditions, especially for children. She remembered several long discussions between her mother and him over his concerns for safety. So much so, he'd proclaimed if he couldn't be profitable without killing people, he would shut them down. Penny knew he worried over that scenario. Shutting them down would then deny hundreds the means of support, which was why Lytton Mines were still in operation today with her guardian overseeing them. Only Lord Knightsbridge didn't possess her father's social conscience.

"It must've been hard," she said, shaking her disturbing thoughts of her guardian's control of her property. Somehow she'd regain control of them.

"It was my father's way of life for generations, even though he'd also made sure we'd taken the time to learn what my mother had to teach us. My grandfather on my mother's side taught at the university, and my father used to say education was a way out. At the time, I didn't know what he meant, but now I do." He heaved a heavy sigh and rubbed the back of his neck. "'Tis funny. That accident shaped my life. Once they died, I was no longer content to break my back for the profit of others. It took my father's death for me to figure out what he was trying to tell me all those years ago."

"I'm sure he'd be proud of you, if he could see how you've taken care of your family."

"I doubt it," he said ruefully, then added after meeting her questioning eyes, "Oh, I took care of them, but he'd abhor the way I let the hate for the one responsible guide my life. My father would never be proud of that." Parker shook his head. "It simply wasn't his way. But as God is my witness I still hate Henry Sterling for his part in my family's loss. I'd love to shut down his mines." He stopped talking and stared out at the water, as if lost in thought.

Penny was just about to say something when he continued in a more heated voice. "His greed knows no bounds. I guess you could say in a way I owe the man for the life I now have because it's what drove me out of a living hell." Parker's sad smile appeared. "Without hate, I'd probably still be content to live and mine in western Pennsylvania for a few dollars a day, living in a shack owned by the company, shopping at the company store, just as my father and grandfather had done before me. Instead, I vowed to escape—to give my family a different sort of life."

After ending his tirade, he shrugged. "I can't fathom why I told you so much. Nor do I know why I'm so maudlin today." His pensive gaze refocused on hers. "You're a good listener. Has anyone ever told you that?"

Offering a slight smile, Penny shook her head. "No. No one's ever spoken to me as you are now except my father."

"Well, you are. Would you ever expect I came from such humble beginnings, seeing all this?" His hand swept out to indicate what surrounded him. He sighed again and his stare returned to the water. "Sometimes I feel I'm twisted because, despite rising so far, I'm not one of them, but I'm not what I used to be either. What's worse, I can't help the prejudice I feel toward the higher classes for their mistreatment of those socially inferior, those masses whose servitude the upper class feels is owed to them simply because of their lower status."

"Not all are that way," Penny said. He seemed so lost and more than anything, she wanted to ease the pain in his voice. "I think you are perfect the way you are." In a way, she grasped his meaning. His words described how she was beginning to feel about her life. She was no longer that privileged girl of a year ago. Nor had she come from poverty, so she had no idea what his earlier life must have been like. Still, she did feel a connection with him because she also felt torn, like she didn't belong anywhere either.

Their gazes locked and before her eyes, his expression heated, taking on a new dimension. He wanted to kiss her and more than anything, she wanted his kiss. But he didn't follow through.

Instead he shook it off and stared out at the water. "Are you still planning on marrying him?"

Penney cringed. "Parker, please don't ask me that," she pleaded, not sure of what her answer was anymore. She'd been relieved to find she wasn't carrying his babe, but didn't understand her regret when that moment of truth came. It was simply something she didn't want to think about, even now a week later. She focused on her hands.

"Why?" When she didn't answer, he added, "You know there's something between us."

Trepidation ran through her at how true his words rang. "I can't explain it. I can't tell you why. I can only tell you it's something I must do to survive."

She sensed his searching gaze before he gently placed his hand on her neck, cradling her head in his palm and forcing her to look at him as he guided her lips closer.

Penny closed her eyes, wishing she didn't love the feel of that hand on her, his thumb skimming her cheek in a soft caress. If only she could ignore the burst of pleasure exploding inside her when his lips grazed hers, barely connecting.

"You're a stubborn one, Miss Penny Layton, but alas not as stubborn as me," he whispered, just before their mouths touched for the softest of kisses. One that was over much too quickly.

Penny had an even harder time pushing away disappointment when all of a sudden, with his lips gone, she was abruptly pulled from her seat as Parker stood and grabbed her hand. "We'd best get back."

Dazed, she could only follow him, wondering why he seemed so unaffected, especially given her most pressing thought was to pull him back and continue kissing him, with the idea of encouraging him to use those wonderful hands again.

Chapter 18

"I understand you had a couple of interesting passengers on your last voyage to America."

Lucas Davis almost choked on his drink, not expecting Markham Collingswood's words. He'd made port that afternoon and had sent word to the duke, asking for a meeting. Surprised that his request had been granted so quickly, he had accepted the duke's invitation to dinner with pleasure.

Working to keep surprise off his face, Lucas glanced at the duke, who added, "I owe you my gratitude for bending your rule. I'm sure Geoff is dying to know how one particular lady is faring."

As a guest of honor, Lucas had spent a good part of dinner thinking of a way to let Geoff in on Penny's change of plans without alerting the others at the table, including Markham's mother, Hermione, and his younger sister, Vivian. And now it seemed he needn't have bothered. They were all obviously aware of this. Lucas turned to Geoff with eyebrows lifted, searching for confirmation.

Geoff grinned and shrugged. "Markham has a nasty habit of finding out all my secrets. He knows all about Lady Penelope's escape to America."

"Lady Penelope?"

"Oh, that's right." Geoff had the grace to blush. "You still don't know. She didn't want anyone to learn of her true identity, so she went by Penny Layton."

"Penny Layton is a lady? As in nobility?" he asked, unable to stop the stunned expression from taking over his face.

"Yes." Markham nodded. "Lady Penelope Lytton, as in heiress." Markham cleared his throat. "It seems she and Geoff concocted a plan to run away to America. Geoff plans to meet her there."

"An heiress? Good God, I don't believe this." Lucas chuckled. "Parker was right about the lady hiding some big secrets. I'll never hear the end of it."

"I'm sorry for the inexcusable duplicity. Geoff placed you in an untenable position, but from what he told me, the lady was desperate. Her parents were the Earl and Countess of Lytherton. Robert Lytton was one of my best friends until he and his wife died in a tragic carriage accident nearly a year ago," the duke explained.

"I'm sorry to hear of your loss," Lucas said sincerely. "So Penny lost her parents, just as she'd told my brother she had?"

"Yes."

Lucas nodded and was just about to take a forkful of food, but he halted the fork at his mouth, unable to hide his curiosity. Flashing a grin, he shook his head. "Why travel to America and why change her name?"

"The answer's a little complicated," Markham said, his expression turning solemn. Swirling his wine, he glanced at it. After taking a sip, he set his glass on the table, still fingering the stem in an obvious attempt to gain his words. "Lady Penelope disguised her birthright and ran away to keep out of her guardian's control. She planned on meeting Geoff in California." He cleared his throat. "She's too damn headstrong for her own good."

"An apt description," Lucas said just as solemnly. "We wouldn't let her go off by herself. You should know Parker found out what she was really about and talked her into waiting for Geoff at his home." When the duke and his brother's eyes met in silent communication, Lucas quickly added, "My mother and sister live with him, so there's no impropriety. I know how you English are with your rules."

"That wasn't my worry," Markham replied.

Lucas sat up straight. "There's more to this than you're letting on, isn't there?"

Markham nodded, and then explained in detail everything pertaining to the lady, her guardian, her betrothal, and ending with the news that he and Geoff planned to sail to America on his ship when it left port.

"You're both more than welcome. But your return journey may be delayed as my ship's going into dry dock for maintenance the minute we land," Lucas replied, once he had time to digest the information.

The news didn't faze Markham. "I've cleared up pressing business in anticipation of a trip."

"It would have to be for an extended stay. I don't plan on sailing again for several months," Lucas warned. "Of course, you can always travel to New York or Norfolk where my other ships dock to return earlier, but I don't have their schedules off the top of my head."

"An extended stay might be nice. Geoff was already planning on spending several months there, plus Jones, my man of business, can handle anything that comes up in the meantime." Smiling, the duke rubbed his hands together. "I quite like the idea and see no problem with waiting for your ship to come out of dry dock." Markham glanced up and asked sheepishly, "That is, if you don't mind houseguests? I hope I'm not being too forward."

"Of course not. I'm staying with Parker, and I've no doubts he'll welcome you with open arms," Lucas lied. He picked up his wineglass and took a lengthy sip. Now all he had to do was convince Parker that the duke's visit was worthwhile for their business interests.

"Good, good. Our plans are set then." Markham smiled. "I'm looking forward to it, as I'm sure Geoff is looking forward to seeing Lady Penelope again. Everything should work out splendidly. I doubt the earl can interfere. By the time we're back, his influence over the heiress will have ended." Markham held up his glass of wine and said to all at the table, "Here's to Geoff and Lady Penelope. May they find happiness together once they are married."

Chapter 19

"Are you planning on making a move, or are you going to concede defeat?"

Parker's voice startled Penny out of her thoughts. Her focus lifted from his strong hands to his chest, then moved higher. She inhaled deeply to stop guilt in the form of warmth seeping into her face at being caught covertly studying his fingers while pretending absorption in the chessboard.

He stood and headed to the bar at the far end of the library. "'Tis obvious this is going to be a long night, and I need reinforcements. Would you like one?" he asked, holding up a glass.

Spying the usual amusement in his blue-gray gaze, she clenched a fist, fighting the urge to punch the expression away. "No, I'll pass tonight," she declined politely, though she didn't want to. She'd love one. Only now she understood how much she needed all her wits about her to deal with him. Penny was simply too susceptible to his charm, especially during evenings like this when in the company of his family.

Her thoughts then shifted to her situation.

Soon after their ride to his special place weeks earlier, Parker's demeanor had changed. Oh, he never gave her cause to worry about his conduct, which was always above reproach and very appropriate, but he no longer hid his yearning.

Ignoring the need ever present in his eyes was next to impossible, made even more so when her own desires simmered in her soul as well. The thought of those beautiful hands roaming over her was a constant one, making her forget at times she was supposed to be waiting for Geoff. And thoughts along those lines only made her feel guilty and undeserving of Geoff's love.

TEMPTATION

"How about you, Mother?" Parker said, drawing Penny's attention back to the room. His nod indicated his sister who sat reading across from her. "Catherine? Can I get you something?"

"Of course." Catherine smiled warmly. At the same time Elizabeth shook her head and said, "Not tonight, dear."

Parker poured another drink. Penny watched as he handed it to Catherine, the smile on his face speaking of amused indulgence. Though in command at all times, he seemed different with his family. He took care of them, but it wasn't lost on her that Catherine had a certain amount of freedom, a freedom to be different from most young women of Penny's station. He could be totally protective while also accepting, an amazing aspect in her mind and so like her father.

Ambling back to the table, Parker curled his lips at the corners. "Well?" He sat and lifted a brow. She looked at him with the question in her eyes and that same disarming grin spread, causing the thousands of butterflies in Penny's tummy to flutter. "You know I have you, so give it up."

Pushing the sensation away, she rolled her eyes. "You're so sure?"

"Yes, and so are you." He chuckled. "Maybe you'll win the next game," he offered, taking a sip of his bourbon and holding her gaze.

The challenge in those eyes seemed to mock her. Seemed to be saying he was winning and there was more than a chess game at stake. Her chin jutted out and she said haughtily, her accent becoming more pronounced, "We'll see about that."

Parker only laughed. "Spoken like a true lady of the manor."

Penny made her move and tried very hard to ignore the pleasure surging through her at his obvious approval.

ᑲ

"Just the person I was looking for."

Shielding her eyes, Penny glanced up and noted Parker sauntering their way as she weeded in the garden next to his mother. "It's a beautiful fall day. You don't mind if I take advantage of it and steal your helper for a ride, do you, Mother?" he asked, halting behind them.

Elizabeth sighed, and sat back on her feet from her kneeling position. "Of course not. I never meant for her to spend all her time helping me, but she seems determined to make herself useful." She wiped her forehead with her arm.

Parker chuckled and bent to pull Penny to her feet. "Come on, angel. You've earned a ride."

"I guess I could be persuaded." She brushed a bit of dirt off her dress.

"I thought we could ride over to see your friend Mindy."

"Really?" Penny's delighted squeal filled the early October air. "I had almost given up seeing her."

"I've been too busy for such a long ride, but I remember promising you." He nodded to his mother. "We'll be gone for several hours."

"Enjoy your ride," Elizabeth said, still on her heels. She stared after them with a huge grin lighting her face as Parker led her through the garden.

Their trip on horseback took more than an hour before ending at a tidy farmhouse centered among fields being harvested.

Parker and Penny dismounted at the same time.

Penny started toward the house just as Mindy burst out the door, not stopping until she had her in a hug.

"You're still here? I was so worried," Mindy said, laughing. "I can't believe you've come for a visit."

"I know we didn't give you any notice. I hope it's all right?" Penny asked tentatively.

"Of course it is. You know both Mary and I owe your family much," Mindy scolded, keeping an arm around her while she led her up the whitewashed porch stairs.

Mary Johnson, Mindy's sister, stepped out onto the porch. "Lady Lytton. What a wonderful surprise. Please come in."

Penny winced. She was a countess in her own right, and after marrying, her husband would acquire the title of earl. Her family's title had passed to her, due to an earlier provision from an eccentric pair of great-great-grandparents. She hadn't informed Mary of her ruse, thinking it wouldn't matter.

Out of the corner of her eye, she flashed a quick glance at Parker, who now tended the horses, to judge his reaction. She heaved a relieved sigh, relaxing her shoulders a bit when his face showed no emotion. "We're in America now, so please call me Penny," she said softly, in an attempt to brush aside Mary's use of her title.

"I'd be honored, my lady," Mary gushed. "Penny it is."

Turning toward Parker, Penny couldn't meet his gaze as he strode up to stand beside her. She ignored her rising trepidation and said with more calm than she felt, "Parker Davis, allow me to introduce Mary Johnson, Mindy's sister."

Parker took Mary's hand, kissing it while saying in a most charming voice, "It's a pleasure to meet you, Mrs. Johnson. Mindy has told me all about you."

Blushing, Mary patted her hair. "The pleasure is mine, Mr. Davis," she stammered. "She's also told us all about you and your brother, Captain Davis. I know I have the two of you to thank for her safe passage. Please! Come inside. Can I offer you both some tea?"

Penny and Parker drank tea, catching up on the last six weeks before talk centered on the ball the Davises were hosting. Elizabeth had instructed both Parker and Penny to invite Mindy as well as her sister and her husband. When nothing in Parker's words or facial expression indicated he'd overheard Mary's slip, the rest of Penny's apprehension eased.

They were just about to leave when Mindy grabbed her hand. "Penny, you have to see my new room. Mary let me decorate it any way I wanted. We ordered pillows and material from Baltimore."

Looking at Parker with a question in her eyes, his answer was an indulgent smile along with, "Go ahead. I'll wait here."

The two scampered off.

Once they were out of earshot, Mindy whispered, "So, how is it you're still here? I thought you determined to make your way to California."

"I was, but my plans changed." Penny explained her mishap at the train station and Parker's intervention.

"Thank heavens you're safe. Now that I know you're in the area, we can visit more often."

The two friends spent another few minutes oohing and aahing over her room, before heading back down the stairs and into the parlor, where Mary and Parker stood talking amicably. Amid hugs, Penny reiterated Elizabeth's invitation to the Harvest Ball.

On the trip back, Parker stayed silent, letting Penny carry on the conversation, grunting occasionally to let her know he was listening to her rambles.

When they approached the bend in the road leading to Parker's bluff, he asked unexpectedly, "Are you in a hurry to get back?"

"No," she answered truthfully, wondering what was on his mind. Something in his voice had the hairs on the back of her neck standing on end, eliciting a feeling of impending doom.

Parker dismounted near the same rock the two had sat on and talked weeks earlier. He turned and placed his hands on her waist, easily lifting her off the horse, his expression unyielding.

Penny hurriedly moved out of his grasp once she was on the ground, but stopped short when his voice cut through the air with rapier sharpness.

"Were you ever going to tell me?"

"Tell you what?" Stalling for time, she spun away from him and walked past the big boulder, keeping her gaze on the serene scene below.

"Who you really are." He'd moved with her and was now directly behind her.

"I'm not sure I understand what you're asking," she said evasively.

He chuckled, but the sound was anything but humorous. "I had a pleasant and illuminating chat with Mrs. Johnson while you were occupied with Mindy. Would you care to know what we discussed?" He reached for her arm, forcing her to turn around and face him.

Penny heard the bitter edge to his voice and she couldn't meet his eyes. "I wouldn't know," she murmured, looking at the ground.

"I'm sure you can hazard a guess. Go ahead and try."

Penny chanced a glance at his eyes and was stunned to see a cold glare emanating from his gaze. Everything in his stiff demeanor said he was livid and his anger scared her. She'd never seen him like this, and while watching him, fear, much as she felt when she'd been back with the earl, streaked through her.

"No? Cat got your tongue?" he sneered savagely. "All right, if you can't remember, I'll tell you. You are none other than Lady Penelope Lytton, daughter of the late Earl and Countess of Lytherton. Ring a bell?"

"Please! You don't understand," she whispered, growing more concerned.

"Oh, I think I do. God, you're a countess, an heiress to Lytton Mines, no less. How you must have secretly laughed at me when I first brought you here to this very spot and bared my soul about my past. Me, a lowly coal miner, thinking to marry a lady and the owner of the mine. What a fool I was," he hissed.

"That's not true. Please don't look at me like that. You're scaring me," she begged, cringing from the unyielding glimmer of hate written over his features, before his expression became an implacable frozen mask. "Why are you acting so horribly?"

"You're a goddamned aristocrat—one of those simpering, spoiled misses I can't abide. Not only that, you own mines that suck the life out of its workers."

She shook her head. "No. That's not true."

"Now I understand why you won't marry me. I'm good enough to use for pleasure, but not for a husband. You need the brother of a duke for that," Parker said, ignoring her denial, not keeping the fury out of his voice.

Tears blurred her eyes. "How can you say such a thing?"

"I say it because it is true."

"No."

"Then prove it," he ground out. "Marry me."

The accusations he hurled at her stung. This hidden irrational side terrified her. He hadn't spoken of marriage since the afternoon they'd ridden to this very spot. If he had asked the question before now, she might have accepted. That she was coming to think more favorably toward the idea made her realize how out of control her feelings had gotten. During the past few weeks, she'd begun to think he might actually love her as she had come to love him, even though he never spoke of it. Right now, with fear guiding her, she wasn't sure about anything. And because indecision filled her, she offered her most honest answer.

"I can't," she replied softly.

"I see," he whispered in a tone that belied his words. "Damn, how was I so stupid as to think someone like you could actually be happy with someone like me?"

"What have I done to make you hate me all of a sudden?" she asked, holding her head high, her clipped English accent slipping into her speech.

Noticing her stance, he shook his head and said with derision, "Ah, the lady to the manor born. You do that so well. I don't hate you. I just have no use for you."

She flinched as more tears threatened. But she would not cry. Fury filled her, and using it as a crutch, she flung it back at him, "Why are you so angry? What have I done besides keep my past a secret?"

"You exist. You're all the same, money-loving bloodsuckers of the lower classes, thinking it's all right to suck them dry for your own gain and amusement. Is that what I've been? An amusement? An adventure?"

"No!" she yelled, her voice horror-struck. At this point she couldn't halt the tears now streaming down her face. His words struck at her very core, sending a cold feeling throughout her system. How could he think those things after all they'd shared? She stared at him with tear-glazed eyes. "Surely you know the person you describe is not me."

"Isn't it? It's all right to share a bed with me, but not my name? No, you'd rather have a man you don't love, your Geoff, brother to a duke, than a mere cloddish American commoner with neither title nor breeding who once toiled as a miner."

Again she shook her head.

"You want proof?" he all but shouted, gripping her shoulder and pulling her toward him. "I'll show you."

The next thing she knew his mouth ground into hers in a hot, demanding kiss, the emotion of it catching her off guard. Penny didn't push him away, which was her first mistake. Responding was her second. She should have known he affected her too much. The minute Parker's lips softened, begging her to yield to him instead of commanding, she wanted more. The heat of her anger and fear altered to a different sort of heat. One of passion. Though his words and anger terrified her, his kisses scorched her. She burned from the inside out. She knew she should stop this when rage drove his actions, but for weeks she'd wanted his lips and hands on her.

Right now, warmth filled her and all she could do was feel the sensation of pleasure seeping into her that his kisses generated. She'd deal with her remorse and his anger later.

೮೪

He'd meant the kiss to be punishing, but his lips had slowly softened of their own volition. The minute they connected with hers, Parker couldn't stop the hunger from overtaking him. He'd been holding it in check for too long. When he felt her arms go around him and her determined hands pulling him closer as her mouth and tongue met his, all sanity deserted him.

God in heaven, she was part angel, part demon sent to torment him and Lord help him, he still wanted her. No matter that he hated what she was, he still yearned for the heat between them.

Desperately Parker continued kissing her, sinking to the earth without breaking contact. In moments, he had her blouse unbuttoned and his hands found her breasts, releasing them. He then undid her riding skirt and pushed it down, exposing her center, where he spent the next few minutes using his mouth and tongue, as well as his hands, to bring her to the edge of her release.

On the brink of losing his mind and before he lost total control, his lips moved higher, grazing her bare midriff, breast, and shoulder, all the way to her ear. He whispered, "Tell me you don't want this, even though you say you're going to marry another man."

When it clearly dawned on Penny that he'd stopped kissing her, with his lips an inch above hers and his tormented gaze meeting hers, she shook her head, sincerity shimmering from her eyes. "I can't. You know I can't."

Her honesty took away some of his anger, but he still heard himself ask, not bothering to keep the hurt out of his voice, "You still mean to marry him?"

Penny contemplated his words before asking, "Do you mean to say you love me? Is that why you're so insistent?"

"God in heaven, I should hope not. I've experienced your actions firsthand when you admit to loving someone," he scoffed. Her eyebrows shot up in question and he added in a voice dripping with derision, "Like when you threw yourself at me, though you professed to love Geoff? More like you love his status and his place in society. I'd never give one such as you my heart. Not when you toss my offer of marriage in my face to marry someone you don't love. So let's leave love out of this, shall we?"

"Then let me go," she begged, tears glazing her eyes, making them look ten times their size.

He glimpsed something else before she shuttered the look—a spark of hatred for him mixed with self-hatred. He understood exactly how she felt. At that moment, he hated himself for the driving need coursing through him almost as much as he hated her for tempting him.

"I can't," Parker answered in a voice full of anguish, doubling his efforts to bring her pleasure. His lips sought hers at the same time his hands roamed lower, one finding her breast and the other seeking the moist heat he'd tasted only seconds ago.

"Please," she moaned, tearing her mouth away moments later, panting, her flushed body writhing under his fingers telling him she was on the precipice of pleasure. "I want you," she pleaded, her hands moving to release his manhood and stroking it boldly.

Her actions inflamed him, sending his need out of control. Heaven help him! He was surely in hell. He had no will to resist her. Parker despised his lack of restraint. Despised the inability to hold her at arm's length. He'd only meant to prove his point, to drive her insane with want and then walk away, sending her to her Geoff.

He hadn't intended to make love with her, yet he couldn't seem to stop himself and the fact filled him with more self-loathing. This Lady Penelope Lytton or Miss Penny Layton, whoever she was, was in his blood and he needed to drive her out somehow. His most pressing thought was to have her, but he also had to use the mating to extricate her from his system once and for all.

He pushed her back onto the ground, and in one fluid motion he slid inside her, plunging furiously as if his life depended on it. That she was as wild made him that much more feral, his actions more untamed, and their mating continued with both of them spiraling into the abyss together. Penny reached the precipice first, her yells proclaiming intense pleasure. Her unending contractions pulled Parker's release from him. He exploded violently, unable to contain his loud groan as his seed spurted into her.

Neither moved for the longest time.

Once Parker could think again, he reached for the strength to lift up, but his arms seemed like jelly and he could only lie there for another few minutes, too spent to muster any energy. Slowly, he gained his wits and his strength returned, allowing him to push up on his elbows. His gaze touched Penny's beautiful face. She had her eyes closed, looking more like an angel than he'd ever seen before and so help him, he still wanted her.

Self-disgust filled him when he spoke. "So tell me now after you've lain with me how you're still going to marry him?"

Gazing into his eyes, her expression saying she saw the disgust he couldn't hide, she sucked in her breath. "I can't marry you," she whispered, her fresh tears falling.

Without speaking he nodded, rolled off her, and stood, righting his trousers. He moved to sit on the rock, keeping his gaze on the water below. Finally his tormented voice rang out, disturbing the silence. "I understand."

He glanced at her as she quickly redid her buttons.

"No. You don't," she said, shaking her head, her words just as tormented. "You've made sure I could never be happy with Geoff, and marriage to you would be no better than marriage to Gerald Knightsbridge." After speaking, she turned and walked back to her horse.

Parker's dumbfounded gaze followed her. "What do you mean by that? And who the hell is Gerald Knightsbridge?" he yelled, watching her take the reins. She'd mentioned the name before.

Ignoring his questions, she mounted her horse. She then turned and leveled a hate-filled gaze at him. "Listen and listen well. If you ever touch me again, so help me as God is my witness, I'll shoot you dead."

In a heartbeat, Penny flicked the reins and was gone, galloping toward the bend in the road.

Chapter 20

The ordeal of dinner couldn't end fast enough for Penny. She had no clue how she'd survive the evening with the man seated at the head of the table, acting so unaffected, especially if he expected her to play a game of chess in the library afterward.

Secretly, she watched him. And after imitating his impassivity, pretending as if nothing out of the ordinary had happened, she had to admit—he affected her.

"I'm afraid I don't have time tonight for our usual chess game. I need to work on some problems with the farm." Shortly after eating, Parker rose, releasing her from further suffering. He offered a polite bow and said aloofly, "If you will excuse me?"

Penny nodded, and pushed the pang of regret out of her mind. After all, he was honoring her wishes. Still, observing him turn to kiss his mother on the cheek, it stung to have him treat her so coldly, as if he'd spoken to a spot on the wall rather than someone he'd shared earlier intimacies.

Shrugging off Parker's behavior, Penny decided to keep to the tasks that had become routine during her short time in the household.

The next morning, her mood lifted as she walked sedately down the stairs on her way to the garden.

"Good morning, Penny," Elizabeth said warmly when she stepped out into the sunshine.

"Good morning." She hurried to where Elizabeth was busy pruning, happy to note some things stayed consistent.

When Penny plopped down next to her, she added, "You're looking chipper this morning."

"I am. It's a beautiful morning." Penny's smile broadened. At that moment she did feel chipper. Things had to work out, she thought, keeping her gaze on Elizabeth and listening with half an ear while she prattled on.

"A little on the nippy side, but it'll warm up when the sun hits. I love fall. I don't even mind that winter follows because the weather is so crisp and clear."

Penny spent the next few hours with nothing more serious on her mind than pruning and weeding.

For days after that, Penny rarely got a glimpse of Parker. Except for the few minutes at dinner, he completely avoided her, no longer available for their daily rides. He was gone from the house before she arose and left the dinner table the moment he finished eating, saying he had work to do, always apologizing to Penny for not partaking in their usual chess game. Penny suspected his polite gestures were given more out of courtesy for his mother than for her.

Parker kissed Elizabeth, having just imparted another such apology more than a week after their heated session on the bluff. Watching him hurry from the room, Penny's thoughts returned to an incident earlier that morning when she happened to meet him by chance in the stables.

"You must be busy," she'd said, greeting him and smiling warmly, unable to keep the joy out of voice. "We rarely see you anymore."

He'd shrugged and had peered at a point past her shoulder. "I am busy. There's a lot to be done." He'd walked away, saying, "If you will excuse me."

"Penny, I'm recruiting you to help with our ball." Elisabeth smiled kindly and placed a warm hand over hers, yanking her attention back to the dinner table.

Nodding, she discreetly turned her eyes away from the doorway. His cold indifference, no better than his treatment of a complete stranger, hurt. She couldn't stop the surge of disappointment as sadness engulfed her.

Elizabeth, who never missed much, had noted his behavior. The compassion she bestowed on her whenever she caught Penny staring after him, only added to her torment. Tonight her sympathy was simply too much to endure. To sit at the table night after night, pretending nothing had happened when everything inside felt broken, became a nightmare.

"Catherine loves the planning, but she's not so good when it comes to the actual decorating. We've only two weeks left. I'm only too glad you're here to help."

Penny opened her mouth to decline, hoping to escape to avoid any more pain, but Elizabeth gripped her hand harder.

"You will not hide in your room as if you've done something wrong. Do you hear me, child?"

Stunned, Penny looked up at her.

"I'm very aware of the rift between you and Parker." She snorted as irritation mingled with impatience in her expression. Elizabeth glanced at the empty doorway Parker disappeared from not five minutes ago. She sighed. "I'll never understand that boy. You both seem too stubborn to see what I see, but you will not allow him to dampen your spirit," she added, turning her attention back to Penny.

"Parker's only abiding by my wishes." After all, she did threaten to shoot him dead.

"Even better." Elizabeth clapped her hands and presented a pleased laugh that ended in a grin. "Parker has to control every aspect of his life or he's not happy. He tends to be a tad overbearing, especially with those he cares about. Obviously whatever you are doing is having some impact, and all the more reason not to let him run roughshod over you."

"You don't understand. He despises me. Despises what I am and represent," Penny said in an attempt to enlighten her. It wasn't Parker's fault, but hers for not being honest, and there was no way she could have been honest with him.

"Oh?" Elizabeth eyed Penny thoughtfully, then shook her head. "Most likely he's having difficulty accepting your breeding. You've obviously come from money."

Penny stared, her mouth dropping open. "What do you mean?"

"Come now, child." Elizabeth waved a hand. "Surely you didn't think you could hide what you are? It's as clear as the nose on your face. I figure you're probably one of those stuffy aristocrats Parker hates so much, and that's what's eating him. Trust me, if he wasn't interested, he wouldn't ignore you. He'd stick around, accepting your presence with his veiled amusement, mainly because he knows it would get my goat. Just let Parker stew. He'll get over it eventually."

Nodding, Penny had her doubts. Elizabeth hadn't seen the hate and anger emanating from her son right after they'd made love that day on the bluff. Nor had Elizabeth heard his denial about giving his heart to her. She believed every word. Penny meant hers too. She couldn't marry him. After escaping her horrible destiny, she'd never willingly marry such a controlling man who didn't love her.

Suddenly her mood lifted. Though she missed the times spent with Parker, their shared rides during the day and their chess games in the evenings, she accepted the truth. He'd never love her. So what if her world hung upside down and her plans for marrying Geoff totally ruined. The situation wasn't hopeless. She was a continent away from the Earl of Kentworth and another month closer to reaching her majority. She'd finagle something. Thoughts of still making her way to California flitted through her mind just then.

Elizabeth rose from the table, placed a hand on her shoulder, and squeezed gently. "Come and help Catherine and me with the ball."

Her smile broke free as the idea took a firmer hold. Penny didn't see how she could in all good conscience marry Geoff, not when she loved another and had behaved so badly, but maybe he'd accompany her to her destination. Then maybe between the two of them they could figure a way to wrest her money and holdings from her guardian's control.

As she followed Elizabeth out of the room, her confidence returned. She couldn't wait to see Geoff and put her plans into motion.

ଓ

Penny didn't let Parker's attitude affect her any longer after her talk with Elizabeth. In fact, she began to find his actions amusing. What's more, her amusement seemed to have some effect on him, as his efforts to avoid her became more infrequent. Though he didn't accompany her on the daily rides she took with Catherine, he did begin lingering at the table after dinner.

"Would you care for a game of chess this evening?"

Penny almost bit her tongue when she realized Parker had directed his question to her. She quelled the excitement running amuck in her system, chastising herself mentally. Nothing had changed, yet with his request, everything had changed.

"I thought you had work to do," she said nonchalantly, not daring to meet his gaze for fear he'd see how much his request meant. More than anything she'd love to play a game of chess with him.

"It can wait," he replied, shrugging and pushing his empty plate away. "Tonight I'd rather share a glass of bourbon with my family than work."

Elizabeth gave an unladylike snort. "It's about time you decided to join us."

"I've been busy," Parker said evasively.

"Oh? For all we've seen of you these past weeks, you might as well have been gone away on one of your cases again," Elizabeth grumbled.

Parker grunted and said while rising, "Like I said, I've been busy. If you're set on badgering me, I'm sure I can find something else to keep me busy tonight."

"Is that what I'm doing? I thought I was just letting you know how much I've missed your company."

Parker shook his head, and amusement flashed in his eyes. He bent to help Elizabeth out of her chair after planting a kiss on her forehead. "I know damn well what you're doing."

He then held out his arm and turned to Catherine, holding out his other one. "Shall we?"

Catherine laughed gaily and placed her hand in the crook of his bent arm. "There's no elbow for Penny."

Parker's grin was quick and reached his eyes. "I'll come back for her."

"That's all right." Penny rose. "I can follow just fine."

She stayed behind them as Catherine said, "Mother's right, Parker. We've missed you. I hope you're not going to be too busy to enjoy your family a little, otherwise you should just go back to working for the president."

Parker gave his sister a hard look and then glanced at his mother. When Elizabeth's attention seemed absorbed by something else, he visibly relaxed.

After seating the ladies and setting up the chessboard, Parker walked over to the sideboard. "Would anyone care for a drink tonight? Mother? Catherine?"

Both women gave their assent and Parker slanted a glance at her, his eyebrows raised in question. "Penny? Surely you can have a glass of bourbon?" When she eyed him silently in an attempt to discern his mood, he added in a teasing voice while pouring, "Come on and join us. I think I'll need the advantage tonight."

Unable to stop her grin, Penny nodded. "I'd love one."

With drinks in hand, he gave one to his mother and the other to his sister, before going back and picking up the last two glasses.

Penny surreptitiously observed Parker as he advanced toward her, his expression guarded. Though his friendly demeanor seemed so different tonight, he still kept his distance. Which suited her fine. Distance would make it easier to stick to her plans for when she had to leave.

Chapter 21

A clatter in the yard drew Parker's attention on the way out of the library. He turned toward the open windows with draperies drawn to let in the warm autumn breeze. "I wonder what all the fuss is about," he said more to himself, since his mother, Catherine, and Penny were too busy working on their decorations for the Harvest Ball in two days to pay him any heed.

The others must have heard it too because Elizabeth and Penny stood and followed Parker across the room to peer over his shoulder as a carriage rolled into view.

"Oh my heavens," Penny cried. Hands on her face, she turned and hurried out of the library.

Parker started after her. On the bottom porch step, he halted and hung back as she ran toward the carriage and jumped into a tall blond man's outstretched arms. The man hugged her tightly, lifting her off the ground in obvious delight.

"Geoff, what are you doing here?" she asked after he let her go a moment later, not hiding her excitement.

"Pen," he said, laughing. "It's so good to see you. I've been dreadfully worried about you."

"I'm fine, as you can see." Smiling warmly she stepped away, and after grabbing his hand, she pulled him toward Elizabeth, now gliding down the porch steps followed by Catherine, who never glided.

Out of the corner of his eye, Parker spied Lucas and another man climb out of the carriage.

Penny obviously noticed them too. Halting and leaning closer to Geoff, she whispered loud enough for Parker to overhear, "Why is your brother with you?"

"It's all right, Pen. He's on our side." When her eyes grew wide in question, he snorted. "You know Markham. Can't keep a secret from him. He knows all about our upcoming nuptials and we have his full support."

After hearing his statement and viewing their reunion, the gut-wrenching knot in Parker's stomach tightened. His desire for the blonde beauty had never died; in fact, it ate at him. If he were honest, he'd have to admit to wanting her more than he'd ever wanted her, with his need building over the last two weeks.

Though Penny had said she wasn't marrying Geoff, Parker couldn't believe it. Not now, when faced with the truth. The picture of the good-looking young man gripping Penny's shoulders as if she belonged next to him didn't lie. Neither did the joy on her face that all but shouted she loved the man.

Thank God she hadn't lied about that. He blew out his regret on a resigned sigh. From his vantage point, the scene appeared intimate and Parker felt like an interloper for watching. As hard as the thought of her leaving him was to endure, he faced a worse nightmare—knowing that when she left, she'd be with a duke's brother. Damn, it was Lady Margaret all over again. No! He pushed the hurt away. Penny had never led him on with the same lies. And because of that, any lingering anger toward her vanished. Shaking off his regret, Parker joined his sister and mother.

"Introduce us to your intended," he said, smiling at Penny.

She nodded and introduced Geoff to the three of them.

Just then, Lucas and the man Parker determined to be the duke caught up with the small group.

"Your Grace," Penny said, offering a perfect curtsy.

"Stop." Markham laughed. "You're as bad as Geoff." He glanced around and met Parker's interested gaze. His smile remained intact. "You must be Lucas's brother. I'm Markham Collingswood." He stuck out his hand in such a friendly manner that Parker didn't respond right away.

"It's a pleasure, Your Grace. I'm Parker Davis," he finally said, changing his demeanor to match the other man's.

"Please. We're in your country and I'd prefer just plain Markham if you don't mind."

Parker nodded, unable to hold back his grin. Turning to his

mother and sister, he said, "Markham Collingswood, allow me to introduce my mother, Mrs. Elizabeth Davis, and my sister, Miss Catherine Davis."

"*Enchanté,* madam." Bowing at the waist, Markham took Elizabeth's outstretched hand and kissed it.

When his dark eyes fastened on Catherine, Parker noted the usual spark of male interest. No one else noticed his sister's blush as the duke brought her fingers to his lips before releasing her gaze and bestowing on her another perfect bow. "Mademoiselle." He straightened, and flashing her a secret smile, added flirtatiously, "I can see America is full of beautiful women."

Catherine quickly pulled her hand away as if burned, clearly flustered.

Parker bit back a laugh. The duke's attention wasn't unexpected. Not when she had a long list of brokenhearted men up and down the Eastern seaboard. Still, few had actually produced his sister's blush so effortlessly. Yet, if the man thought her an easy conquest, he was in for a rude awakening. Parker trusted Catherine's ability to keep any over-interested males in their place. In the event her tactics weren't enough, both he and Lucas were strong deterrents.

The moment was lost when Lucas cleared his throat and said, "The duke and his brother have graciously accepted my invitation to stay here while my ship's in dry dock."

Parker met Lucas's gaze in a silent communication and nodded. "Of course." Though not excited one whit at the prospect of entertaining and housing aristocrats, he deferred to his brother's judgment. Lucas wouldn't have invited him without good reason. Turning to the duke, he held on to his smile. "It will be our pleasure to accommodate you. You're both welcome for as long as need be."

"Why don't we all go inside and I'll have Pearl make us some tea," Elizabeth said, herding the group up the porch stairs.

Parker fought to ignore the streak of heated jealousy rising when Geoff placed a proprietary hand on the small of Penny's back and said good-naturedly, "I see I had no need to worry. It warms my heart to know she was in such good hands."

The duke snorted. "She shouldn't have left England." He shook his head and directed a stern look at his brother. "You both know that, don't you?"

A bit of red rushed up Geoff's face. "Penny has an adventuresome spirit and felt America the perfect place to hide." He stuttered apologetically, "I…um…I wanted to elope to Gretna Green, but she would have none of it, saying we'd be found out and the marriage somehow annulled." He shrugged. "She made a strong argument."

"Seems you were right," Lucas said, slanting Parker a glance. "The lady was hiding some big secrets."

Parker rolled his eyes. What understatements from both men! "If you're referring to the fact that she's a titled English noblewoman and an heiress to boot, I already know." He then turned to Geoff and Markham. "You don't have to convince us of her adventurous nature. We're all well aware by now how willful Penny can be."

"Oh, for heaven's sake," Penny chimed in, flashing an irritated grimace. "I was perfectly safe and could take care of myself. You all seem to think I'm a complete cake. Everything worked out."

"Yes, it did," Lucas agreed, smiling. "I now see why you placed her in my care. You knew I'd ensure her safety."

"We no longer have to postpone our plans." Geoff clapped his brother on the back. "See, Markham, sometimes things just work out the way they were meant to be."

Watching Penny's irritation evaporate, Parker hung on to his weak smile. He didn't want to think of what the impact of not delaying their plans meant. He'd never been so grateful for the diversion of his mother's voice.

"You've arrived just in time for our Harvest Ball the day after tomorrow." By this point they were at the parlor doors. Elizabeth opened them and gestured for the others to go ahead. "Make yourselves comfortable while I go and see about refreshments."

Markham glanced around, clearly impressed. "I thought I'd be coming to a savage place. Instead I find big cities, and manor houses to rival those in England. And now you tell me there's to be a ball."

"Though most Englishmen don't believe it, we're not heathens here in America," Lucas joked.

"Don't tell them that." Parker waited at the double doors while

214

they filed in one by one. "If they think we're heathens, it'll keep them away."

Curtains billowed as warm autumn air filled the room from the open windows and French portico doors. Markham chose a chair near the window. Lucas and Parker sat in chairs opposite him. Catherine hung behind Penny and Geoff, who sat side by side on one of the settees.

Elizabeth breezed into the room, her intent gaze on Catherine. "What are you doing hiding in the background, dear? Come and join me."

Then grabbing her hand, she tugged, leaving Catherine no choice but to follow. Parker didn't miss either the duke's amused smile or his sister's blush as she moved to sit across from Penny and Geoff.

"I gather you're home to stay awhile, Lucas?" Elizabeth's question was more a statement laced with joy.

Lucas nodded. "I don't plan on leaving until well after Christmas," he said with a huge grin, not bothering to hide his amusement.

Elizabeth's smile brightened. "Imagine! All my children will be home for Christmas this year. I must be doing something right. Tell us about your voyage."

Lucas did just that, spending the next twenty minutes regaling everyone with his story. When done, he looked at Geoff. "So, when is the lucky day?"

"As soon as it can be arranged." He looked at Penny with what Parker, who'd been surreptitiously studying the two, determined was pure adoration. "The sooner the better."

At least they loved each other, he thought.

"I agree," Markham said. "The earl's not a fool. He'll eventually guess our whereabouts, especially after our disappearance from London is noted."

"He won't find me," Penny stated.

Parker was certain her voice held more conviction than she felt, given the streak of fear he caught glimmering in her eyes at the mention of the earl.

Markham shook his head. "Don't be too sure."

"Is this earl named Gerald Knightsbridge?" Parker asked.

Penny's gaze to fly to his. With eyes wide in stunned awe, she asked "How'd you guess?"

He snorted. How could he not put two and two together? "Correct me if I'm wrong, but the way I see it, he's someone with whom you were arranged to marry—a guardian, perhaps?"

His reply earned another shocked intake of air from Penny.

Lucas slapped the arm of his chair. "Damn if you don't surprise me." His head went back as a hearty laugh escaped. "I should've known you wouldn't let it rest. That you'd find out her secrets before anyone."

"Penny's parents betrothed her to Gerald Knightsbridge, the fifth Earl of Kentworth, just before they died in a tragic carriage accident." Markham sat up straight, his handsome features hardening into an implacable wall of granite. "He's not a very nice fellow and happens to be her guardian for another four months, which is why time is of the essence and these two need to marry as soon as possible."

Remembering her nightmares, Parker said, "He can't touch her here." He would kill the bastard first.

When the smile Penny offered didn't quite reach her eyes, Parker steered the conversation to other topics in an attempt to alleviate the dread still lurking. He much preferred her spunk to the fearful creature she was reduced to by thoughts of the earl's finding her.

Eventually Elizabeth rose. "Luncheon will be an informal affair with food displayed on the buffet. That way you all can eat at your leisure. Dinner, however, will be formal and I expect you all to dress," she added, before walking sedately out of the room, disbanding the impromptu gathering.

CR

Penny floated down the stairs later that afternoon and smiled brightly at Geoff, who strode purposely toward her.

"Pen, Mr. Davis told me we could make use of his horses and go riding. Would you like to?" he asked, not hiding his excitement over the idea.

"I'd love to." Her smile faded on a sigh. Her brief reprieve was over. How she wished for more time to prepare for what she would say to him once they were alone.

They rode for a mile in silence before Geoff slowed and indicated with the tilt of his head a copse of trees. "Let's ride to that spot and talk."

Penny nodded and followed.

When they'd both dismounted and had the horses tied, Geoff pulled Penny into his arms and kissed her gently. "I've been dying to do that since I saw you this morning," he whispered, just before his lips met hers again.

Penny closed her eyes, allowing the kiss to continue because it felt so good to be in his familiar embrace. More than anything, she wished things were different. That she didn't have to hurt her best friend.

Finally he lifted his head and met Penny's gaze. The warmth emanating from his eyes spread through her. She could clearly see the ardor and acceptance she'd always felt from him in his expression.

"I've always loved you." His declaration was spoken so earnestly she had to look away. "I truly thought I'd lost you when I found out you had to marry the earl."

Penny stepped back. Licking her lips nervously, she couldn't meet his eyes again, keeping hers downcast while he continued speaking.

"I can't wait 'til we're married and I can be near you all the time. These past months seemed unendurable without you." When she remained silent, Geoff's demeanor stiffened. His grip on her shoulders tightened. "Pen?" When she didn't say anything, he placed a hand under her chin, lifting it up and forcing her look at him. A confused expression slid over his face. "What's wrong?"

One glimpse of the love and concern in his eyes and her tears flowed freely down her face.

When he tried to tug her back into his arms, she pulled away and started pacing, not quite sure how to broach the subject. Oh dear Lord, how had she squandered his love for pleasure? How was she going to tear her own heart out, hurting him at the same time? He certainly didn't deserve her infidelity and she didn't deserve his love.

"Pen?"

Her gaze flew to his at the desperation she heard in the one word.

Holding her stare, he waited patiently for her to explain. Finally, she closed her eyes and whispered in a tormented voice, "I can't marry you."

"Yes, you can. You still love me, don't you?"

"I'll always love you. You know that. You're my best friend, but you don't understand," she said.

"What's to understand? Markham will back you. You have no reason to fear reprisals from the earl. He can't touch you, especially if I can get you with child before we return to England."

More silence followed because Penny couldn't bring herself to say anything. Closing her eyes again, she blurted out, "It's not the earl."

"Then what? I see nothing standing in the way of our union."

"Please, Geoff, I can't marry you because I've lain with another," Penny admitted, unable to hold the information inside any longer.

"What?" he asked, clearly not grasping her meaning. When the moment of realization hit, he only stared at her with eyes wide as saucers.

Watching his features change, Penny's tears increased. "I never meant to hurt you. You have to believe that."

"Do you love him?" Geoff finally asked. "Are you going to marry him?"

Penny heard the pain in his voice and hated herself for her infidelity all the more. "It wouldn't be wise for me to love him, since he doesn't love me. And as for marriage to him, well, I'd rather die than marry someone who doesn't love me."

"I see," Geoff said softly. He remained silent, lost in thought. "If that's the case," he added in a shaky voice, "then I see no reason why we can't be married as planned."

"No. We can't. It wouldn't be fair to you."

"You think I care?" he shouted, not bothering to hide his anguish. "I lost you once, I'll not let you go again."

His manner turned more passionate, making Penny realize how much she wanted to give in to his request. Instead, she countered, "What if I carry his child?"

"I don't care," he stated heatedly. "I simply don't care. You're all I care about."

"You'd raise another man's child? And you'd continue loving me even though I don't deserve your love?"

"Yes," he said so adamantly that Penny wished she could believe him.

More moisture blurred her eyes. "I can't let you do that." She wiped the tears away.

Geoff turned away from her and paced back and forth. After minutes of pacing and thinking, he stopped and faced her again. "Who is he?"

"No one you know."

"Then what will you do if you are with child? Your child will need a father."

"I'll think of something, but I won't allow you to sacrifice your life for me." Penny shook her head, unwilling to let him even think of giving up so much for her stupidity.

"Pen, how would it be sacrificing my life when you are my life? It's better than being totally without you."

"You deserve someone who loves you enough to be faithful." When his head moved from side to side with a ready denial on his lips, she put a hand over his mouth. "You know I speak the truth. Eventually the fact that I was unfaithful will change your love."

"You're being stubborn. But I'm just as stubborn as you and I'll not give you up."

Arguing at this point was futile. And she couldn't stay here seeing the unhappiness she'd wrought any longer. She turned and rushed to her horse. Untying it, she quickly mounted. "Marrying me won't change what I did. I don't think I could endure your scorn," she added as she glanced back, her soft voice carrying on the breeze. She then kicked the horse's flank to get him moving.

"Wait! Pen! Please don't go. We can work this out. Please," he yelled as she rode away. She pretended not to hear him, urging her horse faster as his voice penetrated her being. "I don't care. I'd take you any way I can get you, even if I'm second in your affections."

ᘓ

Dinner that night was a subdued affair, mainly because most at the table seemed preoccupied. Parker didn't say much. Penny felt his gaze the entire meal, except when every now and then he'd look at Geoff, drawing her attention. Then he'd meet her stare, and he didn't bother to hide his confused expression. To make matters worse, Elizabeth's amused gaze landed frequently on both of them before moving to Catherine, who was also acting strangely. Only Lucas and the duke seemed oblivious to all the drama, too caught up in a discussion over business for most of the meal.

Once the ordeal of eating had ended, Penny stood. "If you'll excuse me." She flashed a semblance of a smile and swiftly left the table.

The next morning Penny dressed for gardening and rushed outside, looking for solitude. When she spied Parker's mother on her knees faithfully pulling weeds, a surge of relief went through her. Weeding with Elizabeth was even better than solitude. Reaching for her gloves, hat, and a mat to kneel on, she hurried up to the woman. She placed the mat on the ground and plopped down next to her.

"Good morning," Penny said. "I didn't expect you to be here, given last night was so late."

Elizabeth rocked back on her heels, eyeing Penny thoughtfully. "No rest for the weary," she said pleasantly.

Nodding, Penny returned her smile, then began to pull weeds, using the time to let her mind wander.

The two weeded quietly for a long while before Elizabeth's voice broke into Penny's thoughts. "Geoff seems like a nice young man."

"He is."

"When are you to be married?" she asked quietly.

Penny sighed, brushing a stray hair off her face with the back of her gloved hand. Her eyes took in a perfect red rose, where her focus remained. Finally she shook her head. "I'm not sure we are going to be married."

"Oh?"

The simple one-word question, spoken so softly, held sympathy and was Penny's undoing. Tears seeped from her eyes. "I'm not sure of anything anymore," she whispered, her voice full of anguish.

"Shush, don't cry." Elizabeth stretched an arm around her shoulder, squeezing gently. "Tell me what's wrong." When Penny didn't offer any words, she prodded, "In the short time you've been here, I've come to think of you as a daughter. You've added much to our household. I'd like to help, if I can."

"I'm more confused than anything." The two had grown close these past months. Penny had recognized in Elizabeth the same consistency and strength of her own dead mother. She could almost believe her parents in heaven had guided her to this house, a haven of warmth and love, something sorely lacking in Penny's last year. Oh, how she missed both her parents' guidance now.

"Do you love him?" Elizabeth asked, scrutinizing Penny's face.

"Of course. How could I not? He loves me and he'd never hurt me," she said, meeting Elizabeth's sympathetic eyes once she could talk again. "When we decided to marry, I wanted marriage to him more than anything." Her gaze went back to the rose. "But now I'm so confused. I don't know what to do."

"Oh, child, yes you do," Elizabeth said earnestly, taking Penny into her comforting arms. She smiled warmly and added convincingly, "You have to follow your heart."

"How do I determine what my heart wants?" Elizabeth's warmth felt so good—a port in a ravaging storm—the storm raging inside of her.

"Now there's a good question. That's never easy. In fact, figuring out what we want in this life and then grasping on to it can sometimes be the hardest thing we mortals ever do."

Finally Penny could smile. When she leaned back, Elizabeth brushed her tears away. "It's been my experience to understand events happen for a reason. Problems always have a way of working out as long as you follow your heart and are honest with yourself."

Penny sighed and nodded. What did she want? She did love Geoff. Maybe he could forgive her and she could still be happy with him.

Chapter 22

"Good day, everyone," Penny said cheerfully to the group in the dining room later that day. Ignoring Parker, who she could see out of the corner of her eye watching every move she made, she breezed toward the table.

Elizabeth's words still played in her mind. Maybe things could work out with Geoff. Her spirits rose, giving her newfound hope. Maybe she could get him to stick to their original plans of going to San Francisco. She rather liked the idea of having that adventure before making the trip back to England. She still had several months until her twenty-fifth birthday, but she certainly didn't want to stay here any longer. There were just too many memories. Too many reminders of what would never be.

Geoff stood at her approach. "Good day, Pen. I missed you at breakfast." He bestowed a quick peck on her cheek after holding out her chair. "I hope you're not avoiding me," he added a little lower so that only she could hear.

"Of course not, Geoff." Smiling warmly, she sat down. "I slept late and then I helped Mrs. Davis in the garden."

"Yes, the dear has been helping me get the beds ready for winter," Elizabeth chimed in. She sighed heavily and her voice turned wistful. "I'll miss all the beautiful flowers when the first frost hits. That we haven't had one yet is definitely a blessing."

"I hope this beautiful whether holds enough for the ball tomorrow night," Catherine said.

"Surely the weather won't affect the ball, will it?" asked Markham. Then he added jovially, "If we waited for perfect weather in England, there'd be no fancy balls."

"Of course we have the ballroom, but I was hoping to use the patio and gardens like we've done in the past." Catherine's expression turned dreamy. "I love dancing under the stars."

"Ah, a romantic," Markham said, amusement showing in his voice. His smile softened his harsh features, making him appear boyish and approachable, not at all like the formidable picture he presented earlier. "How nice."

"Not our Catherine," Lucas chortled. "There isn't a romantic bone in her body."

"That's not true. Dancing under the stars is romantic and I do love it," Catherine said, jutting out her chin.

"Now, now, Lucas. Quit teasing her. You both could learn lessons about romance," Elizabeth said, not bothering to hide her exasperation. "And wipe that smirk off your face, Parker. You're no better than your siblings. All of you are disappointing in the romance department."

"At least I've tried," Parker said. Though he kept his expression serious, his eyes danced with good humor.

"Asking the wrong person doesn't count. Lady Margaret was wrong for you and you know it," Elizabeth chided, her annoyance growing. "What I want to know is what you've done since."

Parker's gaze touched Penny's briefly, and his smile was quick. "Like I said, Mother. I've tried."

Casting her glance lower, Penny felt heat rush up her face. When she noticed his hand resting on a goblet, fingering the stem, the warmth deepened. She looked back up to see if he'd caught it.

Parker's grin spread. "It just didn't work out," he said, shaking his head. "And since we're so disappointing in our romantic pursuits, I think you should concentrate on those grandchildren only Sarah and Rebecca can give," he teased.

"Humph," Elizabeth said, dismissing her errant children with the wave of her hand and picking up a fork.

"I'm sorry," Penny murmured, turning to Geoff and quelling the flood of sensations seeping through her system that only now were subsiding. "I didn't catch that. I was daydreaming."

"How about a ride later?" Geoff leaned closer. "We need to talk. We left things unfinished yesterday."

"I'd like that." Penny offered a soft smile, happy to have

something else to think of besides the man sitting across from her who seemed too impossible to ignore. Time with Geoff was just what she needed to put her plans into motion. "A talk would be nice," she answered honestly, her eyes searching Geoff's. Noticing her handsome best friend's earnest expression, she exhaled a deep sigh. Her smile deepened. All was not lost. He certainly seemed to accept her perfidy. Maybe he really could forgive her.

C03

Penny and Geoff rode off on horseback, acting much as they used to when younger.

"I bet you can't beat me to that fence post," Geoff challenged, goading her into a race.

Penny took off, letting the wind blow through her hair. She felt freer and happier than she had in a long time.

As they neared the post, Geoff shouted, "Stop. I concede defeat." Laughing, he galloped closer once she'd slowed. "You always could outride me, Pen."

Once he caught up, they ambled, neither speaking.

"Why can't it be like it used to be?" he asked moments later, interrupting their companionable silence. "We had so much fun back then."

Her eyes focused on the surrounding scenery. "That's true. We did." Fall hadn't made much of a presence yet and the trees still appeared more green than yellow or red. Keeping her gaze on the horizon, she added, "I guess we've grown up. Things have happened in the past year that have changed who we were."

"Did you lie when you said you still love me?" he asked, halting his mount, his intent gaze traveling across her face.

His whispered plea gripped her soul. She reined her horse to a stop and answered honestly. "No. How can I not love you after all we've shared? But you have to admit, your love has always been stronger."

"I don't believe that." Shaking his head, he urged his horse forward. Penny did the same. "I don't know what happened with the earl. Nor do I know how you came to lie with another man. I really don't want to know or think about either. It eats at me. I blame myself.

I can't change the outcome and I should've done more to prevent both. But I refuse to believe you've changed so much. What I see before me when I look at you is the same engaging minx I used to follow all over the wilds of Northumberland before I went to Eton."

"No, I'm not," she said. "I'll never be that girl again."

"Maybe. But know this. I'd still follow you anywhere." Judging by his fervent expression, he meant it. "You need me, Pen. I'll take care of you."

All of a sudden, her doubts prevailed. "I don't know, Geoff." Her trepidation grew. "I'm confused."

"How can you be confused?"

"Because I don't know what to do right now."

"It's very simple. You marry me. After you reach your majority, we'll go back to England and you can take your rightful place as your parents' heiress. The earl won't be able to do a thing about it, especially if you've conceived. If not, it's easily remedied."

"I thought I could marry you, but now I don't think it's what I want." She pulled on the reins and dismounted. Looking around, it dawned on Penny that she'd led Geoff to the same spot where she and Parker had made love weeks earlier. She shook away the memory when Geoff stormed up to her.

He put his hands on her shoulders. "It's a perfect solution. But we don't have a lot of time. The earl could find you and then where will you be?"

His words brought to mind that first time Parker told her she should marry him. They were so similar. Was marriage to Geoff what she really wanted or just a solution to her problem? Glancing at him now as he paced and rubbed his neck in obvious dismay, she came to a sudden realization. She had changed. His love didn't seem to be enough anymore. Instead of voicing her thoughts, she said, "I'm not in England and I'm not afraid of him any longer. He can't force me to marry him. Not here. I'll figure out a way."

"I don't understand why you won't marry me," he said, halting in front of her, his expression becoming sullen. His gaze went out toward the water before returning to hers. "No one will love you more than me."

Penny sighed and placed a hand on his face, lovingly tracing his firm jaw. Always her golden champion. Oh, how she wished she loved him as she did Parker. And because she didn't, she had to let him go. "I know. You deserve someone who loves you just as much."

"So you're saying you love this other man? The man you've lain with?" he asked, taking her gloved hand and kissing her wrist. "Tell me that and I'll leave it alone."

"I don't know what I'm saying. I'm confused and because I'm confused, I'm not marrying anyone," Penny replied, pulling her hand out of his. She turned and walked to the rock, her gaze resting on the water. Holding it there, she said, "In fact, I'm leaving here. I'm going to California as we originally planned. I'd hoped you'd accompany me."

"So you will marry me?" Hope swelled in his tone.

"No. You misunderstand. We'd travel together, but I won't marry you. I'm going whether you accompany me or not."

"You want me to accompany you without being married?" Geoff asked, clearly incensed at the thought. "I can't do that."

"Come now, Geoff. Surely you can't be afraid for my virtue. I have none," she teased, amusement sliding over her expression.

Her teasing only made him angrier, which came out in his voice. "You're being unreasonable, expecting me to bend propriety. It simply isn't done."

"Now you sound like Markham. I didn't think you'd changed, but I just realized you have. You never used to be so bound by convention."

"Why? Because I want marriage to the woman I've loved most of my life? You're just as bound. You'll never change the fact that you're an English heiress. You should stop all this talk about such nonsense."

"It's not nonsense. The Davises have taught me much. I like it here in America. I think you will too. You're the younger son. You can make your fortune here."

"Penny, you're not thinking. What will you do for money to live on?"

She hadn't thought about that. "I still have the money you gave me." And she still had her mother's jewelry to sell.

"That won't last long."

"After my birthday, I'll fight the earl for my money." Once she attained the age stipulated in her parents' will, she could find a barrister who'd take her case. Of course, it wasn't lost on her that her case would be strengthened if she had a husband.

Geoff swore under his breath, kicking the ground in obvious frustration. "You're an Englishwoman. An English heiress. You can't hide from who you are."

"I know that part of me will never change, but I don't think I can go back to being Lady Penelope Lytton. I like Penny Layton too much. I think she's been with me always, hiding underneath." She grabbed his hands and squeezed, trying to make him understand. "Come with me. It will be an adventure. Think of the fun we can have."

"No. I'll not do it, and neither will you. Do you hear me? I'll give you time to come to your senses and realize that I'm your best solution. I love you, and I expect you to marry me. After your birthday, we'll be going back to England, where you can take your rightful place in society."

Penny kept her eyes on his stubborn expression, which said he'd never back down. "It seems we're at an impasse." Sighing, she shook her head. "I'm not marrying you, nor am I returning to England to live."

"You will marry me and once you're my wife, you'll have no choice but to obey me. You have several months to get used to the idea," he said before turning and stalking to his horse.

Penny watched in stunned silence as he mounted. She never thought to see Geoff acting so much like Markham.

Her spine stiffened when he glanced at her without bothering to conceal his irritation. "It's time to go back."

Keeping her chin up, Penny walked resolutely to her horse and mounted. "I'm not changing my mind, Geoff."

"Nor am I, my lady," he replied, clicking the reins to get his horse moving.

❦

Standing in front of the mirrored glass in Catherine's room, helping her dress as well as receiving help, Penny tried to muster up some of the same excitement Catherine couldn't hide. She simply wasn't in the mood to pretend happiness when she had nothing to be happy about.

The day had been impossible. It had been hard enough to keep from thinking of Parker, but every time she looked up and caught Geoff's resolute gaze, her task of remaining sane became more arduous. Geoff had then dogged her heels and wouldn't let her be. Somehow she had to make him understand. She meant what she said. It annoyed her that he didn't listen to her. He acted like every other man she knew, thinking she should obey him and that he could fix what was broken rather than accept what was.

At least no one else had paid her any attention, as all had been wrapped up in the ball, which would take place in less than an hour.

A knock at the door interrupted her thoughts.

Laughing, Catherine rushed to open it. "Parker?" she said, drawing Penny's attention. "What are you doing here?"

"Bending the rules." His nod indicated the room. "Is everyone decent?"

At Catherine's grin and yes, he strode over the threshold, and spotting Penny staring, his grin spread. "Ah, there you are and looking much like the angel I know you to be."

He was dressed in formal evening attire. His debonair looks could grace any ballroom in England. She spun around and glanced at her reflection in the cheval glass in an attempt to dismiss him from her mind, not wanting to find him attractive any longer.

He moved to stand behind her while taking something out of his pocket. In the next moment, he placed a sapphire necklace around her neck, the same one she'd admired during their outing in Baltimore. The warmth of his fingers seared her neck as he secured the clasp.

Penny's confused gaze caught his in the mirrored glass and her hand went to the beautiful piece, fingering it lovingly. "Parker?" she asked. "What's this?"

"They don't suit Catherine. Never did. In fact, from the moment I saw them I knew they'd suit no one but you."

Smiling wistfully, she said softly, "I can't accept these. Surely you know that."

"Yes, you can. Call them a wedding gift from a friend." He held out the earrings. "You need these to complete the picture."

Spying his earnest gaze in the glass again, Penny was torn. His expression was one of acceptance and friendship. Sincerity shone from his eyes. Still, she shook her head and said more firmly, "No. Such a gift is too valuable. You should keep them for someone you care about."

As she lifted her arms to remove them, Parker placed one hand on her shoulder, stilling her attempt and turning her around. When Penny wouldn't meet his eyes, he took her chin and raised it up, forcing her to look at him. "Take them as an apology for all the pain I've caused you. Please? I won't take no for an answer. I care about you and I bought them for you because they match your eyes perfectly."

Then opening her hand, he placed the earrings in her palm and closed her fingers around them. He kissed her forehead, before pivoting and walking out of the room.

Penny stared at his departing back in bewilderment.

Catherine, who'd silently watched the whole scene unfold, whistled softly. "Wow. I don't think I've ever seen Parker like that."

Penny's brow furrowed. "Like what?"

"Smitten. My Lord, he gave you sapphires. Do you know what this means?"

"No," Penny shook her head, having not one clue. "What does this mean?"

"He cares about you."

"I don't think so," she quickly said, dismissing Catherine's claim. "But you have to admit these sapphires make this dress. I can't possibly keep them, but I'll definitely wear them tonight." All of a sudden her mood lifted and she turned back to the glass. After putting on the earrings, she glanced at Catherine. "What do you think?"

Catherine gave a hearty laugh. "I agree they make that dress, and I think if he feels he's done something to warrant giving you these, you should definitely keep them."

The idea sounded like something Catherine would do just to snub her nose at convention. How she got away with it and could be so bold, Penny wasn't sure. She just didn't think she could be as bold. "I'll think about it," Penny said, grinning.

Penny followed Catherine, who did a better job of gliding while all dressed up, down the stairs. Guests had started arriving. Geoff caught sight of her and headed their way.

"I hope you'll give me the honor of leading you in the first waltz," he said once she reached the bottom stair.

"Of course." Seeing no way out, she bestowed on him a smile and took the elbow he offered. He led her into the ballroom, staying resolutely by her side while people flowed into the room. His proprietary manner annoyed her. The entire time he stood next to her, his stance dared anyone to challenge his right to be there. By the time the orchestra finally started up a waltz, relief swept through her as Geoff took her into his arms, adroitly leading her around the room.

"I don't remember seeing those sapphires. Are they new?"

She swallowed her irritation. There was something in his tone, and she leaned back to search his handsome features. "They were meant as a gift. I'm not keeping them, only wearing them tonight because they match this dress so well."

"I see." But his expression belied the two words. He remained silent, clearly sulking. "Are they from him?" he finally asked in a clipped, angry voice, his features distorted with resentment.

"Him?"

"Don't play coy, Pen. It doesn't become you."

"And jealousy doesn't become you," she shot back, her ire getting the better of her.

"I'm not jealous. I'm annoyed. There's a distinction."

A realization struck. The more she was in his company, the more like Parker and Markham he became. Penny shook her head, saying sadly, "I used to think you were different. I thought I knew you."

"Then I guess we're even. You're nothing like the innocent girl I thought you to be."

His comment, spoken with such scorn, hurt. Penny's patience snapped. "Well, know this. I'm not marrying you. I'm sorry I'm not abiding by your wishes and falling into your arms, ready to do your bidding. I'm sorry for what I've done but I've never lied to you, and

I'm not going to start now."

Geoff glared at her for the longest time. His gaze then went to somewhere beyond her shoulder while the orchestra continued playing. When the music died, he released her and bowed politely. "My lady," he murmured, before stalking away.

Watching his stiff back, Penny's heart hurt because of the pain she'd glimpsed in his eyes. Hating herself for causing the pain, she blinked back tears and tried not to let Geoff's behavior dampen her spirits. She tried to smile as Lucas claimed her for the next dance.

When the music slowed, Penny spied Mindy, who'd just arrived. Turning to Lucas, she pasted a smile on her face. "I see Mindy at the door. I need to go and welcome her. If you'll excuse me?"

He nodded and Penny hurried across the dance floor. "Mindy! I'm so glad to see you."

"I can't believe I'm here. Look at me. I look like I'm you," she said with a laugh. "This would never happen in England."

"America does seem to be a magical place. One where we can be whatever we want to be." Penny hugged Mindy tightly.

ᙏ

Parker stood off to the side, unable to keep his eyes off Penny. No matter where she was in the large ballroom, his attention wandered back to her. She was the most beautiful woman he'd ever seen, dressed in the stunning gown she'd worn when he'd given her the necklace, which accentuated her eyes and still hung in a place of honor around her neck. He fought to ignore the stirrings and to forget the feel of possessing her, yet the desire to have her in his arms one more time overwhelmed him.

In an attempt to appear indifferent, Parker danced with several ladies, working his way in her direction.

"I think this is my dance, Penny." He whisked her glass of champagne out of her hand and placed it on a nearby table. Then he pulled her into his arms and led her around the dance floor.

"Why aren't you with Geoff?" he finally asked.

"Why would I be with him?" Her chin inched up.

"If you were mine, I'd keep you with me at events like this, never letting you out of my sight. Too many eligible men are ogling you for my liking."

"Then it's a good thing I'm not yours," she snapped, her annoyance rising out of her like steam rising from a boiling kettle.

"Oh?" Though he tried, he couldn't keep the amusement out of the one word.

"Yes, because I don't do well being caged," she said in her patrician tone.

He rejected an urge to capture her and do just that. "Fine. Ignore my callous statement. But I'm still curious. Why aren't you dancing with your intended?"

"He's no longer my fiancé."

Stunned, Parker leaned back and ensnared her gaze. "Why?"

She rolled her eyes, mumbling something under her breath about males, before she added in a more distinct voice, "I told you I couldn't marry him. On our last encounter? Don't you remember?"

"But it's obvious you two love each other. I thought you wanted him?" Now he was even more puzzled.

"Let's talk about something else, please," she demanded, tossing her head back, appearing as regal as any queen. "This ball seems quite the success. Your mother must be proud."

"Yes, she is." Parker nodded distractedly, still wondering at her admission. He meant to dance with her for one dance and then let her go. Only now he had questions. Wanting answers, he led her out the double doors. He maneuvered her through a gaslit pavilion filled with dancers from an overcrowded ballroom, heading toward the edge of the stairs to the gardens.

He was aware of the exact moment Penny realized his motives because she suddenly stiffened under his hands. "Why are we dancing out here?"

"Why not?" he countered noncommittally, tightening his hold.

When the music died, they pulled apart. He observed her as she stood frozen, assessing him and nervously licking her lips. Parker raised an eyebrow and she jutted out her chin, just as he'd hoped. In an effort to further goad her into staying with him, he taunted, "Afraid to be alone with me? Is that why you're nervous?" He headed down the steps.

"I'm not nervous," she denied a little too abruptly, following him and earning a quick grin.

"What're you up to?" She eyed him suspiciously as he walked through the gardens to a secluded spot.

"Too late. We're already out of earshot from the house," Parker teased as he grabbed her hand, dropped to a seat on a hidden bench, and pulled her next to him. Penny looked around. Parker had to bite his cheek to keep from laughing outright. Her dubious expression was worth a thousand words. After watching her watch him for too long, he couldn't stop the chuckle from erupting, nor could he stop his smile from reaching his eyes. "All right, tell me about him."

"There is nothing to tell," Penny replied, back to her lady-of-the-manor tone he'd come to love.

"If not, then why aren't you with him?"

"Why should I be with him?"

"You're evading. Why?" he asked, his amusement turning to curiosity.

"Parker, this is my business and I'll thank you to keep your questions to yourself."

Her English accent became more pronounced than ever.

Squinting, Parker fought to understand. "You're not going to marry him?"

"No. I seem to remember telling you that. Many times," she said with complete exasperation as her focus landed on bushes a few feet away. "No one listens to me or takes what I have to say seriously."

"I do," he said softly.

Her gaze flew to his, giving him an idea of her thoughts. For a brief moment he spotted the same desires that he felt in those fiery blue depths before she tried to hide them by hastily closing her eyes.

"I love seeing these on your neck," he said, his voice a notch above a whisper, his hand moving to the sapphires and fingering the stones as well as her soft skin. "They were made for you. You know that, don't you?"

"Parker, please."

"Please what?" The back of his hand slid higher, grazing the side of her face in a loving gesture. "I tried to stay away, but I can't. You tempt me too much, angel." The whispered words came out just as his mouth lowered. His hand wrapped around her neck, drawing her closer, and he luxuriated in the feel of her soft lips yielding to his. Deepening the kiss, he slid his tongue into her parted lips, barely able to contain the need she so easily elicited.

"How could you, Pen?" Geoff's angry voice rang out in the crisp night air.

He broke the kiss and released Penny only to glimpse the man standing in front of them with an accusatory glare. Parker swore under his breath.

"What a fool I've been," Geoff said, his hurt unmistakable.

"Geoff." Penny's expression was one of horror. "What are you doing? Spying on me?"

"No. I came to apologize after thinking I may have overreacted. It appears my imagination wasn't wrong." He turned and stormed toward the house.

Penny looked at Parker, her sad eyes begging. "I'm sorry. I need to make him understand."

Nodding, he watched her disappear into the night to find Geoff, wondering why the thought of her tearing after the man left him feeling bereft.

He pushed himself off the bench and stilled the desire to rush after her to show her what was between them. Heading in the direction Penny had taken, he wished he could get her out of his system. Halfway to the edge of the garden, he spotted the two and stepped closer to wait in the shadows.

ભ

Penny caught up with Geoff and grabbed his arm to stop him. "Geoff, please."

"Please what?" he hissed, spinning around, wild-eyed and tormented. "Watch you kiss another man? Is he the one? The one who won't give you his name, but implants his seed?"

"You don't understand."

"I understand what I saw." He rubbed his neck, his attention focused on the ground as if working to gain control. He met her gaze, his harsh expression turning to sadness. "Face it, Pen. You've made your choice. It's obvious you love him."

"No. You don't understand. He's not my choice. I'm leaving. I'm going to San Francisco."

"I can't let you do that," he said, shaking his head.

"What do you mean, you can't let me do that?"

His jaw dropped and he stared at her, dumbfounded. "Have you forgotten the earl?"

When a more determined demeanor slid over his features, she wrung her hands and her apprehension increased. How had this whole mess gotten so out of hand?

"Have you forgotten the reason you sought me out in London? Well, I haven't. You need protection and if you won't marry me, then you can damn well marry him."

"No." She stamped her foot in frustration. "I'll not marry someone who wants to control me. That's all men want to do and I don't want that for my life." She broke off for a moment before pleading further, "Please, Geoff. Be my friend. Try to see this my way."

They eyed each other for a long while, before Geoff shook his head. "I can't, Pen."

"You're no better than he is and just as controlling."

"It appears so. My biggest mistake was not taking you to Gretna Green when I had the chance. I love you too much to let you go off by yourself." His voice lowered to a tortured whisper. "If you've lain with him, you've made your choice, and I mean to see you honor that choice." He then turned around and left her.

Watching his back as he stalked away, Penny's unease grew, changing to stubbornness. After coming this far, she had no intention of letting any man dictate her actions.

Chapter 23

His attention on Penny once Geoff strode angrily away, Parker remained motionless. Finally, he started toward her, coughing to alert her of his presence.

Penny glanced at him, and if an expression could harm, Parker figured he'd be a dead man, given hers.

"So, you're not marrying me or Geoff because you think we're controlling?" he asked softly, halting in front of her. "It's a mistake, you know. You should marry him, especially since it's obvious he does love you and I can tell you love him."

"I don't need your advice," she said, still frowning. "You're the reason I'm in this muddle."

"Tell me about this earl," Parker demanded gently but firmly, ignoring another frozen glance.

Penny rolled her eyes and started pacing. She stopped abruptly and turned back to him. "Why are you badgering me? From the moment I met you, all you've done is pester me with questions."

"You're a lady with secrets." He flashed an amused grin.

"I don't find anything funny in my situation." She threw out another crushing look and started pacing again.

"I'm sorry," he whispered sincerely. In response, Penny stilled her pacing. When she turned back to him, he prodded, "Talk to me so that I can understand your predicament." With a thumb and forefinger, he lifted her stubborn chin and gazed into her eyes, his showing total sincerity. "I want to help, Penny. As a friend. I promise."

Her facial features softened and he asked, "Is this earl as big a threat as Geoff and Markham think he is?"

"He's not a nice man," Penny said, letting out a deep sigh and nodding, breaking eye contact. She shuddered. "He seemed to take pleasure in inflicting fear in me. And yes, I would agree with Markham and Geoff's assessment…he's probably not going to let me go easily, considering what my parents left me. But he'll never find me," she stated vehemently. "Especially if I disappear in this country. San Francisco is a continent away."

"You're still not thinking of traveling across the country alone?" he asked incredulously.

Penny's back stiffened. "That has always been my plan, if you'll remember."

"Ah, yes, the lady adventurer." He sighed. "How could I forget?" Parker's sarcastic comment drew another scowl and he had a hard time holding on to his sober expression. He schooled his features not to smile and asked seriously, "So he's after your money as well as your other assets?"

"I guess so." She shrugged. "It does fit. Of course, he has a time limit. He won't have any say over anything I do once I turn twenty-five in February."

"I don't think that will stop him," he warned. When her eyes narrowed, he added, "He sounds a bit desperate. I know about such men, and they don't stop looking, Penny. Marrying Geoff is a sound idea. At least you'd be safe, given his affiliation with the duke."

"Geoff is no better than you and you're no better than Gerald. With choices like those, I'd rather take my chances alone in California."

Her chin went up and that clipped accent was back. Parker couldn't help flashing another grin. "Give him a chance. He loves you. Surely you can see that. When a man loves, it's instinctive to protect those he loves. Trying to control is just part of that protection."

"Is that what you do with those you love?" she asked, her eyes searching his.

"I've never thought about it before, but I guess it is."

"Well, I have no intention of being controlled. I've a mind of my own and I mean to use it."

Parker shook his head, grinning like a fool again. "Damn if you don't remind me of Catherine. And because you're so much like her, I'm betting you can control Geoff just as easily as she controls me. Think about it. If you love him, marriage to him is a perfect solution to your dilemma." He grabbed her hand. "Come on, angel," he said, walking toward the house. "It's time for another dance."

CRWORL

Geoff stalked into the ballroom, his mood totally bleak. Seeing Penny wrapped in Parker Davis's arms with their lips locked together left no doubt in his mind. The man was her lover. He hit his fist. The bastard wouldn't get away with taking her innocence without paying the price for seducing her. He'd call him out.

Damn, but the thought of putting her into his hands hurt. He closed his eyes, pushing out pain, wishing he'd never come upon the scene. Penny had never looked at him as she had Davis just before she kissed him. If she had, he'd never give her up. From his vantage point, there was no mistaking her expression—one that said she'd follow him anywhere. It hurt too much to think about, so he thought about how to force the bastard into making an honest woman out of his beloved.

He scouted the crowded, music-filled room, looking for Markham, and spotted him dancing with Catherine. When the music died, he worked his way toward them. Acting nonchalant, as if his heart weren't breaking, he said the moment he was within earshot, "Markham, I need a word with you."

Markham gave Geoff a curious look. "Can't it wait? I've finally convinced Miss Davis to walk in the gardens with me."

"It's fine, Your Grace," Catherine said, seeming relieved at the interruption. "I've duties to attend to for my mother. If you will excuse me." She curtsied before scurrying toward another group of people across the room.

Glaring, Markham put his hands on his hips. "What's so urgent it can't wait until later? I was hoping to sit next to her at dinner."

"Sorry to intrude, but I wouldn't do it if I didn't think it necessary." He looked after Catherine, and added, "Besides, judging from how quickly she ran away from you, I'd say your chances for dinner are nil."

"Have you no faith in my charm?" his brother said, his quick grin transforming his stern features.

"You? Charming?" Geoff drew back his head in a loud guffaw. "'Tis a pity she's not aware of how sought after you are in England. Then you wouldn't need the charm you're so lacking."

"I hate it that you're so loose with your tongue and have no respect for your elders," Markham said, his annoyance replacing amusement.

"Give over, Markham. That look doesn't work on me." He shook his head and said more seriously, "I truly do need to talk to you, but it can wait until morning." He nodded toward Catherine and grinned, suddenly feeling better. "Go and see if you can charm her into sitting with you at dinner. If so, I'll be impressed." Chuckling, he walked away.

"You doubt I can?"

Geoff stopped and turned. "Would you care to wager?"

A determined expression passed over Markham's face. "Twenty pounds," he said. "She'll eat next to me and we'll share another dance. A waltz."

"You're on, old man." He pivoted and strode aimlessly through the dancers, his mood ten times lighter than when he'd entered the ballroom.

"Geoff? Is that you?"

Upon hearing his name, he glanced around. Mindy Bowers, looking so beautiful, floated up to him. His smile broadened. "Look at you! I hardly recognized you."

"Like it?" she asked, doing a full circle and earning his chuckle as well as a nod. "You're looking very pretty yourself, Geoff." Her gaze took a trip up and down his person before landing back at his eyes. "Very handsome and dashing, I'd say," Mindy added as pleasure lit her face. "It's good to see you."

"Come, let's dance." Geoff held out an inviting hand to his childhood friend. "A man always loves flattery, especially when it comes from such a beauty."

Mindy took his outstretched hand and looked around. "Where's Penny?"

"She's dancing with him." Geoff schooled the look of annoyance, replacing it with another smile that didn't reach his eyes.

"Him?" Mindy asked.

"A man she should be avoiding."

"What?" Confusion flitted over her expression. "Surely the earl's not here? That man's a monster."

"No, not him." Geoff took Mindy into his arms, remaining silent while they danced. "What do you know of her time with the earl?" Geoff finally asked. "Do you know why she's so afraid of him?"

His question drew Mindy's gaze. "Please don't ask," she said hesitantly, shaking her head. "Penny swore me to secrecy."

"I'm worried about her. She told me she wasn't marrying me because she says I've changed and become too controlling."

Mindy chuckled. "What did you do?"

"Nothing but try and protect her from her betrothed, but I don't even know why. I'm beginning to think she may have had another more willful motive for running away." Geoff broke off, thinking about the maddening woman. He'd known since Eton, the chance at marriage with her was nil. Neither her family nor his had been amenable to the idea, which was why he surmised her parents planned an arranged marriage. Finally, he shook his head and said in a wistful voice, "Maybe it would be best if Markham took her back to England so she can abide by her parents' last wishes."

"How can you say such a thing? Putting her in that monster's clutches would be the worst possible thing you could do," Mindy said with horror.

"If she won't marry me, I may have no choice. You should know she means to travel to California by herself."

"Surely she won't do something so ridiculous. Not after being robbed at the train station."

"She was robbed?"

Mindy spent a moment telling him the gruesome details of her misadventure, ending with, "It worked out. Mr. Davis was watching after her."

He hated feeling beholden to the man, especially for his stupidity of letting Penny travel by herself, but he had to admit to more than a small amount of gratitude.

"I can't believe she's still planning to go off on her own now that you're here. You have to stop her."

"Yes, I do. She's too willful." Geoff snorted. "Too determined. And you're right. She won't go off alone again, even if it means sending her back to her guardian."

"No!" Mindy's alarmed voice rose. "You can't."

"Then give me more information as to why I shouldn't." Eyeing her, Geoff waited.

She sighed. "There's a reason why she doesn't like controlling men. He was cruel to her. Did horrible things to instill fear." Mindy lowered her voice and leaned in. "You have to promise you won't let her know I told you. She would die of embarrassment." When Geoff nodded, she continued. "The first incident happened when she disobeyed one of his directives of not wearing what he'd stipulated. She didn't like the lewd cut of the garment and argued with him, saying she was still in mourning. The next day she went out to the stables and found Jezebel dead."

Geoff remained stoic while Mindy recanted the chilling tale of how the man had shot Penny's favorite mare her father had given her the year before, and then left the horse for Penny to discover.

"The vile man then began withholding privileges or destroying things she loved. Eventually, his brutality increased. I happened to be in the dressing room when he came into her room one day and said something Penny didn't agree with. When she questioned it, he backhanded her, sending her flying a few feet, as there was force in the blow. Never before had anyone lifted a hand to my lady. I could tell she was as shocked as I was. But that wasn't the worst. He then strolled over to her, helped her up, and said if she ever told anyone about the incident, her maid would meet with an accident. He used her love for me to control her. The look on his face, when he imparted his threat, kept Penny silent, because it was obvious he meant what he said. After that, he'd strike her whenever he felt like it."

Mindy broke off. Geoff didn't think she had anything else to add until she began speaking again.

"One night I heard her cries and went in to see what was wrong." Her soft voice held sadness. Then her tone changed to anger. "The beast had her tied to the bed, doing all sorts of depravities to her. I couldn't help her, could only watch in hiding while he tormented her. I didn't even want her to know what I'd seen, so I waited until he'd been gone for several minutes before I went in to comfort her. God only knows how many times he'd gone to her like that."

Geoff stared at Mindy, barely able to continue dancing while he absorbed this information.

"Please, Geoff," Mindy begged. "He's a monster. No telling what he'll do to her if he has the chance to marry her. Penny swore when we left London that no man would ever control her again."

His fury erupted. He damn sure had to make sure Penny was safe from the earl's clutches, and if her safety meant marriage to another man, then so be it. Despite the pain the thought brought on, he was certain she loved Davis. He'd force the bastard to do his duty and he'd force Pen to do hers.

"Don't worry. She'll never know what I know. It'll be our secret," he said, meeting Mindy's gaze. He flashed a brilliant smile. As they continue dancing, he mentally resolved how he'd achieve his goal.

Chapter 24

Geoff sought out his brother the next morning, finding him in the library. "Markham, I really do need to speak with you," he said, entering the room.

Markham glanced up and a sardonic expression crossed his face. "Ah, yes, the charming brother." When Geoff offered a confused look, he chuckled and withdrew a wallet from his lined jacket. He opened it and pulled out a twenty-pound note. "You won the bet. I take it you want your money."

Relieving him of the money, Geoff grinned. "I figured I would, but that's not why I'm here."

"Oh?" Markham's eyebrow lifted.

He cleared his throat. "It's about Penny."

"Has this to do with the two of you marrying?" Markham's attention went back to the books on the shelves he'd been perusing.

"In a way." Suddenly not sure how to broach the subject of Penny's situation, Geoff began pacing, practically wearing a hole in the beautiful woven rug as he reached for the right words. Finally he stopped. Rubbing the back of his neck, he hesitated.

Markham glanced at him. "Well? Let's hear it, now that you have my attention."

"Penny's not cooperating," he blurted out.

The duke laughed. "Since when has she ever cooperated? Geoff, just marry the minx and get her with child. Once that's done, she'll have something else to focus on besides causing problems. In my mind, you should've dragged her to Gretna Green when you had the chance."

"This isn't something to joke about," Geoff said hotly, not bothering to hide his irritation, though in hindsight, he wished he'd done exactly that. "Penny's talking about staying in America and going to San Francisco."

"All the more reason to hurry with your plans. She's the most willful woman I've ever known. The sooner you have her under your control, the sooner your problem will be solved."

"That's just it, Markham. She won't marry me."

"What? Of course she'll marry you."

Without saying more, Geoff's pain-filled gaze moved to the scene in the rug and he silently studied it.

"Why?" Markham asked. "What's happened?"

"She's in love with another man. He's seduced her." Thinking of it all brought Geoff's anger to the surface. He could do very little to hide this fact, so his voice held fury when he added, "He'll not get away without paying the price for his seduction because if he doesn't marry her, I'll call him out. I'll kill the bastard."

"Calm down. Talking like a hothead's not going to solve the problem. What do you mean she's in love with another man? Who is he? Who seduced her?"

"Lucas's brother, Parker Davis." He shoved a hand through his hair. "It's a big mess, Markham. I don't know what to do."

Markham's eyes grew round with shock. "You're saying our host seduced her."

"Yes, and Pen has some harebrained idea about leaving here and going on to California. By herself. She says she won't marry me because I deserve someone who loves me more than her, and she won't marry him because she'd rather die than marry someone who doesn't love her. My God. It's such a bloody coil."

"Wait!" Markham held up a hand. "You lost me. Start from the beginning."

Geoff took a big breath and let it out slowly. Then he recounted to Markham all that he'd learned in the past few days about Penny and Parker Davis, also telling him about the earl's coercive actions and striking her, leaving out the last horrible details Mindy had mentioned.

"So, you see why the bastard has to be forced into marriage with her?" Geoff asked once he finished.

Lost in thought, Markham's gaze remained glued to Geoff. "Maybe she'd be better off marrying you," he finally said, his expression turning more serious.

"No." Geoff shook head. "She loves him. I saw that with my own eyes." He wiped his face, becoming agitated once again.

"Are you sure? I can use my influence to bring the man to the altar, but you have to be sure you're willing to let her go," Markham said quietly, his scrutinizing eyes searching for some sign.

"Though she denies it, marriage to him will make her happy. I love her enough to want her to be happy. Maybe that's stupid, but it's how I feel."

"My God. You've grown up in front of my very eyes," the duke said, smiling wistfully. "It takes maturity to make a decision like that. I'm proud of you."

"It bloody well hurts to be this mature," Geoff said with a self-deprecating laugh. Mere breathing became too painful to bear. "I'd rather have her love."

Markham placed his hand on his shoulder and squeezed reassuringly. "I know, son. Letting go of childhood dreams is hard."

"I'm not mature enough as the desire to hurt that bastard is a strong one."

Chuckling, Markham wrapped an arm around his shoulder and started for the double doors, urging him along. "I'll take care of this. Though it doesn't seem like it, she is doing you a favor by not marrying you. You'd never be happy with just part of her."

"Please, save your platitudes. I'm not in the mood."

❧

Parker glanced around the table. Despite the Harvest Ball being a huge success, lunch was a somber affair and no one attempted to lighten the mood with conversation.

When done, Parker rose, followed by Lucas.

Markham's voice interrupted as they reached the door. "Might I have a word with both of you?"

"I have a few moments to spare," Parker said, shrugging as Lucas said, "Is everything all right?"

"I have a problem that needs to be addressed. It won't take long." Markham stood and threw down his napkin.

Once in the library, Parker went to the bar, sensing the note of seriousness in the duke's request. He filled a glass and held up the bottle. "Would either of you care for a drink? I have a feeling I may need one."

"Not a bad idea." Markham smiled.

Except the smile didn't quite reach his eyes, Parker noticed.

He glanced at Lucas and earned a grin and a nod. Parker poured two more drinks before handing them out. Then he settled into a chair, keeping his gaze on Markham and sipping as the man took a seat across from him. "What's on your mind?"

While Lucas sat in another chair, the duke cleared his throat, taking a moment before he spoke. "I'm not sure how to put this. It concerns Lady Penelope."

"What about Penny?" Parker sat up taller in the chair.

"It seems there's been a bit of impropriety going on," the duke said, his focus resting on Parker. "The lady's father was one of my best friends and I cannot allow her mistreatment to go unnoticed."

"Mistreatment?" Parker grinned. "Of Penny?"

"You know damn well what I'm alluding to. Do you deny you seduced her?"

"I don't believe this." Parker snorted, shaking his head. He glanced at his brother, who appeared stunned.

"Is that true, Parker?" Lucas asked once he could speak.

"This is too much," Parker said, chagrined at being taken to task for something he'd tried so hard to avoid. To have to explain his behavior to either of these men, especially over Penny, didn't sit well.

"You seduced her? After you gave your word?" There was no mistaking the anger in Lucas's tone.

"No," Parker denied quickly, then amended, "Yes. Hell, I don't know how it happened." His gaze moved to the duke's and he flinched at the fury those piercing ebony eyes held. "I don't believe I owe either of you an explanation. This is between Penny and me."

"You believe wrong and you'd better readjust your thinking," the duke ground out. "I've already explained the duty I feel for the lady and I'm not dropping your mistreatment of her." He pounded a fist into his palm. "I demand satisfaction."

"Oh?" Parker's entire body stiffened at the air of command in the duke's tone. His voice became just as angry and just as loud. "You demand?" He glared at Markham, not backing down. He'd be damned before he'd allow a man such as the duke to order him around.

"Parker, you have to see how this affects him and how he views it," Lucas chimed in when it was obvious neither man was willing to relent. "You know you'd feel the same about Catherine. We've already had this conversation, so I'm expecting you to do what's right."

"I don't like being dictated to," Parker warned, holding on to his patience by a silk thread. Nodding to Markham, he taunted, "You can't force me to do a damn thing, so don't even try."

The duke's silence produced a satisfied smirk, but taking in Lucas's frown, Parker added, "And before you get all riled up, you should know I offered marriage right after it happened, in fact insisted on it. She only cried and said she had to marry Geoff, so I dropped it."

The duke's demeanor softened somewhat as the man cast his eyes down before he spoke again, his voice a little more controlled. "She's now talking about going off to California by herself. I can't allow that to happen."

"Yes, I'm aware of her plans to follow through on her adventure." Parker clenched his fist, totally annoyed with Penny and her goddamned plans. He exhaled a long breath. "I can't force the lady to marry me. I've already told her I think she should marry Geoff." When he caught Markham's startled expression, he added, "'Tis obvious they love each other."

Markham's gaze stayed on Parker's for a moment before curiosity formed in his eyes. "Really?"

Parker shrugged. "Like I said, I've already asked the lady to marry me. Several times. 'Tis clear I'm not what she's looking for in a husband."

"I fear she no longer can be so unaccommodating." Markham sighed. When both Parker and Lucas looked at him with eyebrows raised, Markham spent a few minutes telling them what Geoff had told him about the earl, finishing his diatribe with, "I think it's time to confront the lady and let her know her options are limited."

"I'll not force anything on her," Parker said. Noting both men's challenging stances, he put up a hand. "I can see she's in a difficult position, but she either wants to marry me or she doesn't."

"As Geoff said, the lady has made her choice. She'll have no alternative but to honor that choice," the duke replied just as firmly.

"We'll see," Parker murmured doubtfully. He rose from the chair and strode over to the bell pull. When the servant came into view, he said, "Please find Miss Layton and have her come into the library, would you, Jason?"

"Yes sir, Mr. Davis. Right away."

Parker moved to the fireplace and turned to both men. Leaning his elbow on the mantel, he said skeptically, "Just remember, I'll not force anything on her. The lady has an aversion to controlling men, and I'm about as controlling as you can get, so don't expect miracles."

Markham didn't add to Parker's statement, but his expression clearly said, "Yes, we will see."

A few minutes later Penny appeared at the library's entrance. After gracefully closing the double doors, she took her time advancing into the room, stopping in front of Lucas and Markham.

A smile touched Parker's lips when expectancy filled her lovely face.

"You wanted to see me?" she asked in that aristocratic tone he loved.

Parker's smile progressed to a full-out grin. "It seems the duke has something he needs to discuss with you," he said, trying to keep his tone solemn. He turned to Markham and added sardonically, "Your Grace?"

A displeased scowl flitted over Markham's features. He cleared his throat. "I'm not too sure how to put this delicately, but I'll try." He took a big breath and let it out, obviously stalling. "It has come to my attention that the two of you"—he indicated Parker and Penny with a nod—"have been behaving in an unseemly manner. And because of this, I'm expecting you both to do the right thing."

Penny glowered first at Markham, then at Parker, and finally back at Markham. She spent a moment schooling her expression before she spoke. "Excuse me? I'm not sure I understand what you're saying," she said, placing a smile on her face. Her voice was soft and questioning, showing none of the earlier anger on her face present right after the duke's words.

"I'm not Geoff, Penny, so don't try that on me," Markham said in a curt tone. "You know precisely what you did and I expect nothing less than marriage. Is that clear?"

Irritation flashed in her eyes. "No." She crossed her arms in front of a puffed-out chest.

"What do you mean, no?" yelled Markham, who'd come off the sofa.

Parker hid his grin. The tiny woman going head-to-head with the imposing man towering over her in an obvious attempt to intimidate was a sight to see.

"I choose not to marry."

"You should've thought of that before you acted because you no longer have the choice."

"Why?" Penny's chin inched higher. She did self-righteous indignation very well. "Does it automatically mean marriage for a man?"

"May I remind you, you are in no position to argue the point," the duke said, his voice becoming cold and unyielding.

"We are not in England, and you have no control over me. No one does."

Her gaze turned to Parker, hurt glinting in her eyes. His amusement died.

"I thought you understood how I felt. I thought you were my friend," she whispered, then turned and ran from the room.

"Damn," Parker said under his breath before rushing after her.

"Let her go." Markham waved a dismissive hand. "She can run all she wants, but it won't change a bloody thing. The two of you will be married post-haste."

Parker halted in midstride. Whirling on the duke, his anger erupted. "In case you hadn't heard, the lady said no." He lowered his voice, but no one in the room could miss the cold fury in the next words. "And because there seems to be some confusion, let me make myself perfectly clear. I'll not force her."

‌cs

When he left the library, Lucas and Markham eyed each other with curious glances.

Lucas grinned. "Two hundred pounds says he can get her to the altar without forcing her."

"You're on." The duke held out a hand, chuckling. "If he gets that stubborn bit of baggage to the altar without force, it'll be worth every pound."

Chapter 25

Parker looked everywhere for Penny. He was just about to give up when he came out of the house in time to catch her riding off at a good clip. Based on the direction in which she rode, he had a good idea of where she'd gone. Smiling, he rushed to the stable to saddle his stallion.

In a matter of minutes, he galloped after her.

He cleared the bend in the road that led to his bluff and saw her sitting on the rock looking out over the water, tears streaming down her face.

He swallowed hard as a knot in his stomach tightened. After dismounting, he stepped quietly up to the rock and stood behind her without speaking.

As if sensing his presence, she said, "I wish people would listen to me and quit trying to decide my future."

Parker moved to sit next to her.

"I know." He stared out at the water.

Several ships dotted the ocean on this cloudy afternoon. The biting breeze seemed to go right through him, but he paid it no heed. After watching the scenery below for some time, his gaze sought her face.

"But I am curious. I'm wondering why you don't marry Geoff, when it's obvious you love him."

His whispered words carried on the wind, and he wasn't sure she heard him because she sat silent for too long before she shrugged. "That's precisely why I can't marry him."

When Parker's expression turned questioning, Penny smiled wanly and shook her head very slowly. "He deserves someone who loves him enough not to lie with another."

Too much sorrow was in her voice. Parker didn't like it that he, or rather their shared passion, had brought about such unhappiness. He couldn't peer into her eyes anymore, knowing he'd put that sadness there. His gaze wandered over the water once again and his voice was still low when he spoke. "I know he loves you. He'll get over it."

"It would come between us eventually," she said, sighing. "He's always loved me. But I don't think he's ever known me. I think he loves the innocent girl I was at one time. I'm no longer that girl."

For quite a while they both stayed silent, taking in the view.

"So your mind is set then?" He glanced back at her face, searching.

"Yes." Penny nodded. "I know what I want."

Her chin rose defiantly and Parker bit back a smile at the stubbornness lurking in her expression.

"I don't mean to change your mind, just present another offer."

That got her attention. She peered at him expectantly, curiosity concerning his offer reflecting in her eyes as the wind whipped strands that had come loose from her tight bun.

"Markham tells me this earl is a very dangerous man. I know you don't want to be controlled by any man, especially one like me. But you need protection." His grin appeared when she stiffened. Her expression closed as her eyes reconnected with the water. He placed his thumb and forefinger under her chin, forcing her gaze back to his. "Penny, you know it's the truth. Life for a woman without the protection of a man is hard." When she tried to yank away, he tightened his hold. "Answer me this. If he finds you in California, will you be safe on your own? Will he be a threat?"

His meaning set in as fear streaked through her beautiful features, marring them. Penny sucked in a deep breath and let it out. "I am afraid of him. He's evil and he most likely won't stop."

"If you won't marry Geoff, marry me. I'll take you to California. I'll even stay with you for several months, ensuring your safety, giving you the protection of my name. When I return here, you'll have the choice of staying or coming back with me. I'll not force you to do anything you don't want to do. I promise."

"And what if I'm with child?" she asked, wringing her hands nervously. "What then?"

Parker sobered. Releasing her eyes, he lowered his gaze to her lips, "Are you?"

TEMPTATION

"I don't know."

Her voice hung in the air, wrapping around Parker's soul, making him wish for things he shouldn't. That she could even imagine leaving under such circumstances left him shaken. That it gave him a promise of tomorrow with her left him even more shaken.

"You weren't thinking of leaving here, if you were?" he asked as she cast her gaze at the ground and shrugged, her motions indicating it was exactly what she was thinking. "You can't think to keep my child from me? Not after all we've been through?"

He expelled a lengthy breath and stared at the water. When he finally spoke, his words were just above a whisper. "A child would change our agreement and I'd expect you to return with me." His focus landed on her face, remaining until she eventually looked up. "I'll abide by your wishes, and try not to control you, but that's non-negotiable."

Penny lapsed into silence. Her attention moved back to the horizon and she seemed lost in thought.

"Well?" He smiled when she jumped. "Have we an agreement?"

Her grimace was quick as she glanced at him. "I'm still thinking." Her cheeks turned a pretty shade of pink as she asked, "What about—you know?"

Parker's eyebrows shot up. "You know?" A sly grin slid over his expression.

"You know what I'm talking about."

He chuckled as more red stole up her face. "Have I ever forced you?"

She closed her eyes and shook her head.

"The *you know* will be up to you," he said. "Just so there are no misunderstandings, I want to clarify this in the beginning. If a child results from your decision, you and I are bound for life. Are we clear?" He waited until she nodded slightly before adding, "And if that happens and I can't have your love, I'll require your loyalty and fidelity."

"You'd settle for loyalty and fidelity because you don't believe in love?" she said, watching his expression.

He nodded. "I'd not ask for something I couldn't give."

"I see," she replied, nodding slowly. "Then I guess I'd be a fool to turn it down. What choice do I have with a monster on my heels."

Although Penny said this with a smile, Parker caught the sadness in her eyes and it sent a small pang of regret through his system. Pushing the feeling away, he smiled and wrapped his arms around her, bringing her closer.

"We should seal our bargain with a kiss, don't you think?" he whispered just before his lips found hers.

Their kisses usually turned hot and heated quickly, but Parker kept this kiss gentle and loving. When he pulled away and looked upon her lovely face, his breath caught in his throat. God in heaven, she was the most beautiful woman he'd ever known, and he understood at that moment, he'd promise anything to keep her by his side. He'd probably burn in hell for coercing her, as well as praying for a child, but he'd never been able to resist the temptation of having her and he was tired of fighting it. Holding on to some semblance of control, he released her and straightened.

"We should marry as soon as possible," he said, clearing his throat. "I'll take care of the arrangements. Is that agreeable?"

Penny nodded.

Parker stood, offering his hand. She took it, and he led her to the horses, helping her mount.

ᛡ

Neither spoke during the ride back to his house.

Penny's thoughts were on her impending marriage. So much had happened in the last three months. Marrying Parker might be a huge mistake, but she had to face the truth. The idea left her giddy with relief. Secretly keeping her focus on Parker's hands holding the reins as he competently rode the stallion along the trail, she swallowed hard. How she wished to have those hands on her and that desire disturbed her. If somehow she avoided being with child now, it would be only a matter of time before it happened in actuality. Then she'd be bound to him for life.

Searching his implacable expression, she wondered. Would she be able to handle living with him as his wife and loving him as she did without his love if he couldn't return the sentiment?

Eventually they made it back to the house. They entered the main hall and all but Catherine were present in the library, as if waiting for news of their encounter.

"Seems nothing is private around here," Penny said, noticing their curious expressions. Except for Geoff's. He sat in surly silence without making eye contact. Guilt rolled over her and she looked at Parker, who offered an encouraging smile.

Elizabeth laughed. "Of course nothing is private. This is the Davis family, after all." She rushed over to Penny, wrapped an arm around her, and led her farther into the room. "So tell us! What have you decided?"

"Mother, gloating doesn't become you." Parker headed toward the bar, then glanced at the three men sitting. "Would any of you like something? Lucas? Markham? Geoff? I'm having one."

"Pour one for each of us," Lucas said. "And please don't keep us in suspense. Are we celebrating or commiserating?"

"It's all a matter of perception. I for one am celebrating, but I'm not so sure about Geoff." Parker lined up glasses and picked up the decanter of bourbon. "Penny and I will be married as soon as I can arrange it."

Geoff's gaze went to the floor. "I can't say that I'm happy but I accept your news." Geoff's attention moved to Penny, and his expression softened. "Congratulations are in order. I do wish you happiness, Penny." He then turned to Parker. "You seem successful in dealing with her and I think you'll keep her safe. You damned well better or you'll have me to deal with."

Parker grunted an assent. "I'll take care of her. I promise," he said sincerely, drawing Penny's gaze. He glanced first at her and then his mother. "How about you two? Would you like something so we can toast to a happy union?"

CB

As promised, Parker had made arrangements for the wedding. Though the church pastor was none too happy about the participants wanting a hurried affair, a large donation had him bending his rules on announcing the banns. He arranged for their wedding to take place the following Saturday, telling Penny and Parker that, at the very least, the couple seemed very much in love.

Hours seemed like seconds, and before Penny knew it, Catherine and Elizabeth helped her dress on the big day.

"Don't you look lovely." Elizabeth's eyes misted with tears. "I'm happy you chose to join our family."

Penny nodded. "I'm proud to be part of it." She loved both women. Catherine was like a sister, as close as Mindy ever was, and she'd come to view Elizabeth as a surrogate mother, as warm and caring as her own mother had been.

"You do look lovely. Look at how the sapphires bring out your eyes, Penny," Catherine said, her voice filled with awe. She'd just finished clasping the necklace around Penny's neck and stepped back. "Parker knew what he was about when he bought them for you. He also has excellent taste in gowns. The color of this dress with its hint of blue is perfect with those jewels."

"This gown is exquisite." Penny smiled wistfully, looking down and fingering the soft ice-blue silk folds. The material hung in an elegant gather from the waist, below the form-fitting bodice. "It seems like a dream."

Her gaze went back to the cheval glass and she caught her expression. Her earrings danced as she turned her head this way and that, looking for imperfections. Though she appeared serene, disturbing thoughts filled her mind.

"It's no dream, child. Just reality," Elizabeth said, gripping her shoulders. "And you are the one who is exquisite. You make a beautiful bride, with or without sapphires or expensive gowns."

Penny tried to see what Parker would see when she walked down the aisle. Was she pretty enough to hold his attention? Would marrying him give her the one thing she prayed for daily—his love? Or would he become bored with her over time and look for another as so many men of her class did? Though Parker expected loyalty and fidelity from Penny, and promised Penny the same, she didn't expect it. Not when the last year had taught her that few men were like her father.

How quickly her worries had changed over these past months, she mused. The memory of her guardian became a distant irritation. Concern over how she'd survive mating with Parker night after night, having his body but not his mind and soul, weighed heavily upon her heart. With or without the child she felt sure grew inside her womb because of that day on Parker's bluff, she sensed the two of them would be forever connected. She didn't know if she was strong enough to endure a loveless marriage, but she couldn't leave. Not when she'd determined the truth of never truly meaning to carry out her plans, the temptation of having him—even without what she yearned for—too intense. She simply loved being with him. Craved the passion they'd shared. At this point, she couldn't imagine not marrying him, and she'd grown weary of pretending otherwise.

"Let's get this veil on and then you'll be ready." Elizabeth slipped the headpiece over her head and stepped back, her face showing visible joy. She sniffed and wiped her eyes. "Oh, my! You're breathtaking. Leave it to Parker to pick the one perfect bride for him."

"He's only marrying me out of honor." Penny couldn't believe otherwise. Though she hadn't told Parker about the child yet, she knew the news would make him feel even more honor bound. "He's only protecting me."

Elizabeth gave an indelicate snort. "If you think that, you don't know him very well. Parker has always had a way of twisting situations to work for him. I'm sure this is no different." She fussed a little more with Penny's veil. "No. I've seen the way he looks at you. You're the woman he wants and it's clear he means to have you."

Penny's tears worked free. Meeting Elizabeth's gaze in the mirror, she wiped them away as the older woman gently asked, "Why the tears, dear? Surely you can see what I see."

"I don't think so."

"Shush. Don't let sad thoughts ruin this day. I know he admires you, as do I."

"But he doesn't love me."

"You're so sure?" Elizabeth still held her gaze in the mirror.

Penny smiled through her tears. "I'm not sure about anything anymore." She had to look down, uncomfortable with Elizabeth's searching stare. "I know he likes being with me, but is that enough?"

"Humph." Elizabeth dismissed her words with a wave of her hand. "Men can be fools, and Parker's no different."

"Parker's not a fool," Penny declared hotly, unsure of why she was defending him. To his mother, no less.

"Of course he is, if he can't see what's in front of his nose. What is love? When does it start and when does it end?" Elizabeth's voice trailed off. She fiddled with the veil and added distractedly, "I'm betting he's done everything in his power to keep you at arm's length and to what end? He's giving you his name, and believe it or not that's an honor I never thought to see him bestow on anyone after his fiasco with Lady Margaret. He may not realize it, but the deed speaks volumes. Trust me on this," she said confidently.

"I've heard the name before. Who is Lady Margaret?" Penny asked.

"She was a noblewoman Parker fell in love with," Catherine interjected. "When he asked her to marry him, she declined because she was engaged to an earl, something she neglected to tell Parker when they were together. From what I've gathered in snippets I've caught between Lucas and him, it seems she still wanted Parker as a plaything. Someone to dally with after marriage."

"You shouldn't be eavesdropping, especially about something so delicate."

"Oh, Mother! I'm not an imbecile."

Catherine's statement drew Elizabeth's long, resigned sigh. "The incident affected my son, though the lady certainly didn't deserve the attention." She then stood back and smiled warmly. "There! I think you're ready. You're simply beautiful."

Penny had no more time to think about their conversation, because within minutes she began her wedding march as Markham Collingswood, the sixth Duke of Wyndham, led her down the aisle, sealing her fate forever.

Walking toward the altar and her destiny, hand resting in the crook of Markham's bent elbow, Penny felt Parker's gaze. Meeting it, excitement rushed through her. Heat emanated from those blue-gray eyes, giving her a sense of security. If nothing else, she knew he wanted her and maybe, over time, she would gain his love.

TEMPTATION

A huge reception followed the wedding in Parker's ballroom.

There was no missing Parker's possessive demeanor as he introduced Penny to his ex-partner Simon Harrington and his wife, Giselle. Parker rarely left her side, even standing off to the edge of the room and watching while others claimed her in a dance, not bothering to hide his impatience for her return. Only Lucas and the duke seemed immune to Parker's dark looks of annoyance. It was obvious they took pleasure in his displeasure when someone new tapped him on the shoulder, asking for a turn with Penny.

Though Penny knew Parker's patience had drawn to an end, she couldn't ignore Geoff when she saw him across the room. He'd avoided her for the past week. The idea of losing his friendship had devastated her. Somehow she had to make things better between them. At the very least, she had to talk to him.

She placed her hand on Parker's arm and bestowed on him a warm smile. "I need to speak to Geoff." Noting his spine stiffening and sensing his irritation, she pleaded, "It won't take long."

He nodded, but his features snapped shut.

Penny felt his gaze while she started in Geoff's direction. Offering a friendly smile, Penny purposefully put herself in her friend's path so that he had to stop and talk to her.

Geoff nodded. "Penny." His smile didn't quite reach his eyes as he added, "Congratulations. You do make a beautiful bride."

"Will you dance with me?" Penny asked hesitantly. When he appeared about to decline, she pressed a finger over his mouth. "Please?"

His smile seemed more strained, but he nodded stiffly and moved to take her in his arms.

Out on the floor, Geoff peered down at her. His expressive eyes seemed to say, "Well?"

She blew out a soft breath and ventured forward. "I am sorry for the turn of events. I never meant to hurt you. You have to know that." She met his gaze, letting him see the honesty in hers. "I do wish I could have been different. Can you ever forgive me?"

Geoff shook his head. "There's nothing to forgive," he said in a sad voice. "It wasn't meant to be and I see that now. Markham was right about something else." He hesitated and eyed her steadfastly. When she arched a brow, he offered a semblance of a smile. "As much as I love you, I would never be happy with only part of you." He nodded toward where Parker stood keeping his diligent vigilance. "You've never looked at me like you do him. Makes me realize I'd have given my right arm for one of those looks." His smile turned wistful. "Maybe someday I'll find someone who'll view me in such a way."

Penny's eyes watered. Blinking back tears, all she could do was nod. For the rest of the dance neither spoke.

When the music ended, they drew apart and he kissed her forehead. "I want you to be happy, Pen. I also want you to know that if you ever need me, I'll be there for you."

She nodded and said quietly, "Thank you."

He took another step back and cleared his throat. "I think I'd better lead you over to him as he looks ready to kill me." Geoff held his arm out. "I gather he doesn't realize I'm no threat."

When they reached Parker's side, Penny swallowed a pang of sorrow and watched Geoff offer a polite excuse, leaving the two together.

"I've endured enough," Parker murmured, drawing her attention. He pulled her into his embrace. "My turn, angel. I'm tired of sharing you," he said, before leading her into a waltz.

As Parker spun her around the room, Penny meekly followed without showing any of the turmoil churning inside her. During the dance, thoughts of disappointing Geoff dissipated as others formed. She couldn't help but feel Parker's muscular upper body while he moved. She tried not to think of the evening ahead. Still, her gaze settled on his hand intertwined with hers and heat engulfed her. Visions of his hands roaming over her body caused a feeling of hope to burst inside of her.

Chapter 26

Parker relaxed the rigid line of his shoulders, loving how well Penny fit into his arms, as if she were meant to be there. He towered over her, which made her appear even more delicate. A protective surge swept through him as he took another deep breath. The fragrance of her hair produced memories of their first night together. How he'd fought his desire for her and now she was his.

Thoughts of the evening to come filled his imagination. A smile touched his lips while he glided with her in his arms in time with the music surrounding him.

The music died and they stepped apart. Parker kept his hand possessively on the curve of her back and leaned closer. "It's time to leave, Penny."

Noticing her questioning look, he sighed. "I don't think I can tolerate much more of this. I've stood patiently by while you've been ogled and groped. I know I'm not supposed to be this way, but you have to know patience has never been one of my virtues and these past two hours have been torture." He grabbed her hand, pulling her with him as he walked toward the double doors. "No one will miss us. In fact, I'm sure most are surprised at my restraint."

The two entered his vast bedroom where an enormous four-poster bed, the centerpiece of the space, shouted overwhelmingly of what would come next. A matching armoire and desk graced opposite corners. The masculine dark blue hues and dark furniture suited him, but Parker wondered at Penny's thoughts as she walked farther into the room, glancing around wide-eyed.

He shut the door, drawing her attention. The room automatically shrank and suddenly shyness seemed to besiege his bride.

Parker faced her.

She took a few steps back, smoothing her hair before wringing her hands. A pink hint of color appeared on her cheekbones.

His intense gaze caught and held her fiery blue depths, not letting her look away as he strode purposefully toward her. When he got to within a foot, he slowed his progress, still holding the intimate contact with her eyes.

He stroked the side of her face with the back of his hand. Cupping her neck, his thumb still stroked. His voice strained on his words. "Do you have any idea how lovely you are?"

As if inundated by the heat she saw reflected in his eyes, she cleared her throat and more pink infused her face. Her heart raced under his fingertips.

Licking her lips nervously, she broke eye contact and studied the designs in the thick rug.

"Surely you're not afraid of what's between us, angel?" His thumb and forefinger lifted her chin, forcing her gaze back to his. "But if you don't want this, I'll honor my promise. It's your choice."

He waited, eyeing her unreadable expression. When she gave a slight nod and said, "I want this," he blew out his breath in complete relief.

"You are without a doubt the most beautiful woman I've ever known, and I thank God you agreed to marry me," he whispered just before his mouth found hers.

Still sensing her uneasiness, he kept the kiss light for the longest time, using soft lips and a gentle touch to quell her apprehension.

His tongue skimmed along her lips. Her mouth opened on a low moan, giving him more access. When his tongue invaded, demanding her response, Penny's louder moan escaped and she wrapped her arms around him. As if he'd set a match to dry tinder, her flames erupted, pulling him in deeper, scorching him with the heat of her fire.

Their flames spread. Mouths and hands became more urgent. More demanding. Parker effortlessly lifted Penny, quickly carrying her to the bed. Laying her down, he hastily undid her gown. He couldn't get it off fast enough, but Penny didn't seem to notice, too intent on relieving Parker of his own clothes. No more than seconds passed before both were naked except for the sapphires around Penny's neck.

Parker viewed her through half-shuttered eyes. His grin turned wicked. He fingered the necklace and felt her shivers.

TEMPTATION

"Did you know I've longed to see you wearing these, and only these, since I bought them?"

Penny's head moved from side to side. He stilled it and leaned closer, whispering, "They look just like I thought they would."

Watching her watch him, he lowered his head until he could no longer see her expressive eyes. Slowly his mouth grazed hers, back and forth before fully connecting. He kissed her unhurriedly, tasting in slow motion and drinking her passion thoroughly. Sensations of heat coursed through him, and lapping tentacles of fire reached everywhere.

Working in tandem with his mouth, his hands caressed, touched, stroked, and discovered every inch of her, leaving no spot on her glorious nakedness untended in order to bring her pleasure. Parker stilled his body's response, subduing the strong urge to slide into her warmth.

"You have the softest skin and your breasts were made for my hands." He cupped a round mound, fingering the fullness.

"For my lips," he whispered, before suckling one and then the other, taking the whole areola into his mouth and tugging gently with his teeth.

He happened to glance at her face just then. The sheer passion shimmering in her eyes said one thing: she wanted him inside her now. Impatiently, she reached for him, clearly tired of waiting for him to determine the moment he'd enter her.

Giving in to her silent command, he thrust home in one swift motion. Her heat enveloped him. Parker soon lost the rest of his control, control he'd been holding on to by a thin thread. He plunged in and out, unable to contain the pleasure building. She was too intoxicating, too tempting, and he'd denied himself for too long. She moved with him in wild unison until both became frantic for completion.

When it happened—when Parker felt her shatter, her contractions gripping his manhood—he exploded, sending his seed inside her. He'd never felt such pleasure, and his release seemed to last forever. Much time passed before he could think again. Once he could, he raised up on his arms. Looking down at her and seeing her satisfied, serene smile, he knew right then. No other woman would ever do but her. He closed his eyes and kissed her forehead, thanking God for giving him this angel in his arms. Though he wasn't about to risk his heart, he'd honor his promise. She'd never have cause to regret her decision to marry him.

CB

"Are you all right?" Parker's voice broke through the languid haze of Penny's thoughts. Opening her eyes and peering into his intent gaze, she nodded, not trusting her voice. If she spoke, he'd surely know about the love bursting from her heart, and she didn't trust him with that knowledge just yet.

He pulled out of her, fluffed the pillows, and situated her head in the crook of his arm and shoulder. Silence blared while he slowly stroked her arm in a soothing manner.

"So when would you like to make your trip to San Francisco?" He picked up her hand and kissed it.

"I don't know." Penny shrugged. Somehow the trip didn't seem as important. "I'd still love to go. From what I've read it sounds like an exciting place, but I'm in no hurry to get there. I'd rather stay here with your family for an American Thanksgiving holiday your mother has mentioned, and then I can't miss Christmas. It sounds even more wonderful."

Parker's smile softened the angular lines along his jaw, making him appear years younger. He kissed her forehead. "Fine, we'll plan on a delayed honeymoon right after the first of the year. I'll make the arrangements."

He held her close with his eyes shut. Moments later, his even breathing tickled her neck. She felt the rise and fall of his chest.

Penny watched him sleep for the longest time, luxuriating in being right where she'd longed to be. She couldn't resist pushing an errant lock of hair off his forehead, allowing her hand to trail along his strong jawline, enjoying the rough feel of his slight day's beard under her fingers. He was everything she wasn't. Tall and powerfully muscular to her small, curvaceous frame and where her skin was soft and yielding, his was firm and more solid. Her eyes moved to his beautiful hands now wrapped around her, holding her as if he'd never let her go. She smiled, remembering what those hands did only moments ago. Feeling very safe and secure in his arms, she closed her eyes.

CЗ

Life as Parker's wife settled into a routine for Penny, even as Geoff and the duke left on an extensive train trip across the country. Markham told the Davises they would be back by Thanksgiving, but they couldn't miss this opportunity to see America. Lucas traveled off and on to see to his ship.

"I could stay here all morning, wrapped in your arms," Parker said one morning weeks after their wedding.

"You'll not find me complaining." Penny kissed his naked torso. Though he seemed to be overly preoccupied with the farm and his secret business dealings with the president during the day, she had his attention at night and in the early mornings. She treasured the moments, like now, when he'd linger after making love before going down to breakfast. She could block out the rest of the world and pretend that he'd come to love her as much as she loved him. Trailing her finger where her lips had been, she added playfully, "The time would be well spent. I can't wait until we travel to San Francisco."

He chuckled, climbed from the bed, and grabbed a shirt. "Get dressed, sweetheart. You're too big a temptation for a busy man like me."

"I rather like being a temptation," she said boldly, leaning back, not bothering to cover her breasts.

After donning the shirt, Parker bent over and kissed her—a long and lengthy kiss that always generated heat. Lifting his lips, he yanked the sheet higher and said in a strained voice, "Have a heart. I've no time to dally."

Quashing her disappointment, Penny said, "Catherine wants me to go hunting with her today if it's not too cold."

"You'll take care?" he asked, eyeing her cautiously, his expression turning blank.

"Of course." She smiled reassuringly. "I know you're concerned because of the babe, but you needn't be." At this point, she knew without a doubt that day on the bluff had yielded a child now growing within her. Her monthly bleeding had ceased for almost two months.

"Is it wise to ride and hunt?" When she started to object, he put out his hand, touching a finger to her lips. "I know I promised not to be controlling, but 'tis slowly killing me. I only want to keep you and the babe safe." He sat, pulled her into his arms, and kissed the top of her head. "I like having you here and I don't want anything to happen to you."

His concern sent warmth spiraling through Penny. Though he'd not mentioned love, at times like this she felt it. The more she was with him, the more she prayed for him to declare it.

"I promise to take care." She smiled into his chest, loving the feeling of being wrapped in his arms. "Since you're so busy, it helps to have something to pass the time before the cold weather sets in."

Parker nodded and planted another kiss on her forehead. "I'll hold you to that promise, angel." He stood and headed toward the washroom.

∞

A US cavalry soldier led Parker through the halls of the White House to President Grant's office.

"Mr. President," he said, nodding to the man who sat behind a huge mahogany desk.

"Ah, Davis. Good to see you on time." The president indicated another man who'd stood. Parker hadn't noticed him until now. "I think you're familiar with Mr. Henry Sterling. I wanted you two to meet because of your impassioned pleas weeks ago. You have much in common."

"Mr. Sterling," Parker murmured, shaking his outstretched hand, totally surprised and completely unprepared to greet someone he'd spent more than half his life hating. He didn't see what they shared in common and couldn't contain his curiosity. "I'm wondering what you assume we have in common, especially when my ideas will definitely affect his company? And not in a good way." He worked to hold all contempt out of his voice.

Parker watched the good-looking, distinguished older man sit back down, unruffled by his words. He certainly never expected to meet him here, not in the context of what he'd proposed to the president a month after his resignation, especially since it involved mine safety practices men like Sterling would abhor and fight to the death to prevent their implementation.

The capitalists he'd come into contact with, men like Sterling, wanted less government intervention, not more, citing the usual platitudes, especially in coal mining. Safety cost money. Coal was in high demand. They had a tremendous job to do and didn't need more government restrictions tying their hands. He'd heard every excuse in the past two months from congressmen to senators. No one wanted to upset the balance of a rising commodity that held industrialization in its grip.

Change might cost votes…from all walks of life. From the lowly tenement dweller using precious coal for heat, to the industrialists needing the steam it produced to power factories and fuel railroads. Owners of mines had been given a free rein for too long due to America's voracious appetite for progress. Someone had to look out for the humble man digging it out of the ground and Parker determined he'd at least put a few ideas into the president's ear. Yet Parker wasn't as concerned with the men who worked those mines. After all, they had families to feed and most were astute enough to understand the risks. It was the children he hated to see enslaved in their situation. Childhood should be a time of learning, not toiling.

"Sit down, Davis," President Grant said, ignoring his comments and pointing to a chair opposite Sterling. "What would you like to drink?"

"Nothing, thank you, Mr. President." Parker sat, then glanced at Sterling leaning forward. "Aren't you a ways from western Pennsylvania?" he asked, his voice barely civil.

"I know my presence here isn't wanted, but the President and I have been in contact for some time, working on the very topic you've brought to his attention. When he mentioned your involvement, I asked to be included today. But I've an ulterior motive, a mission of mercy," Sterling said. "I'm hoping you'll at least hear me out after traveling so far. What I have to say may be of interest."

Parker held his gaze, making the man squirm before President Grant cleared his throat, drawing his attention. He sat up straight. "I believe I'll take you up on the offer of a drink. A bit of bourbon might make it easier to endure the meeting."

The president nodded to a servant at the back of the room, who quickly proceeded to the bar.

"That's as far as my magnanimous patience goes."

"Parker, that'll be enough," President Grant chastised.

Sterling put up a hand. "No, no need to intervene, Mr. President. I expected some animosity." Smiling, he turned to Parker and waited until he had his drink before holding his out in a toast. "Here's to accomplishing the impossible."

Eyeing Sterling, Parker clinked glasses and took a long swallow of the warming liquid.

"All right. You have my full attention. Now tell me why you're really here," Parker demanded, his gaze still on the man.

"I hear congratulations are in order. Is your wife nearby?" Sterling asked.

Parker's smile didn't quite reach his eyes. "I'm sure you didn't spend all those hours on the road simply to congratulate me or ask after my wife."

Unperturbed, Sterling took a sip of his drink. "Yes, well, this concerns the lady."

"How?" There was no missing the deadly tone of Parker's curt question.

When the president started to object again, Sterling shook his head, then set his drink on the table in front of him. "I'm sure you're aware that your wife is an heiress to one of the best-producing coal mines in England?"

Parker flashed him an ominous look at the mention of Penny's legacy. "What has this to do with my wife and her property?"

"Quite a bit, actually. I've been corresponding with her guardian in the last year, working on negotiations for acquiring Lytton Mines. The purchase was to be concluded the day after the earl's marriage to one Lady Penelope Lytton, the same woman you married. From what Lord Knightsbridge had imparted, they have a betrothal agreement and their wedding was delayed due to mourning her dead parents. Were you aware of that?" he asked.

Keeping his expression guarded, Parker nodded.

TEMPTATION

"The earl is convinced the lady is still going to marry him, and he assured me the sale would go through without a hitch as recently as two weeks ago," Sterling added. "Imagine my surprise when the very next day, your wedding made headlines in our little town. Seems you're still a bit of a hero to some fellows there and nothing you do goes unnoticed." He chuckled. "Also, the lady's unique status as an heiress makes her newsworthy. I'm digressing, however." He stopped talking long enough to take a swallow of his drink. "Very good bourbon, Mr. President."

"Continue, please," Parker prodded, when it seemed the man was procrastinating.

"I'm not sure how to present my concerns, so I'm just going to blurt them out," Sterling said. "Gerald Knightsbridge, the Earl of Kentworth, is here in this country. He gave his assurances in person."

The news definitely drew Parker's concern. He stiffened and the angular lines on his face tightened with tension.

Sterling nodded. "I gather you didn't know. I believe he's planning something sinister involving your wife."

Frowning, Parker dismissed his worry with a negligent shrug. "I don't see how. The lady is no longer his affair." Penny was safe on his farm. The earl couldn't touch her.

His assurance didn't faze Sterling, whose voice became more insistent. "When I questioned him days later and showed him the newspaper's account of your vows, he ranted for a solid five minutes before he managed to rein in his temper. Then he told me to disregard the news. Said nothing has changed. He'll have the marriage annulled and the sale will still go through without delay." Sterling leaned in before adding, "He was very emphatic. According to the earl, the matter would be resolved the moment he had the lady under his control again. He was a bit off-putting, so I questioned him further, which seemed to enrage him more. I have to tell you, from our conversation, the man is clearly unbalanced. Quite mad, I fear. I think he means to do you or the lady harm." Lifting his shoulders, he opened his hands as if to say, now do you see why I'm alarmed?

"I appreciate your concern, but I can handle him," Parker said, unconvinced the earl held any true threat to him or Penny. Still, he mentally calculated how long his ride home would take. No sense taking chances. "But I am curious. Why would you care? You never did before."

"That's not true."

The quick outburst spoken so fervently got Parker's attention, causing him to eye Sterling with contempt.

Sterling cringed. "But I knew it would do no good to let you in on that information."

Parker's bark of laughter held no amusement. He snorted. "Surely you don't expect me to believe you have a heart? Men like you haven't one."

He bit back a snarl when the president interjected in a mortified voice, "Parker!"

It was simply too much to share bourbon while listening to Henry Sterling espousing concern for him and his family. Parker was beginning to think his quest had been a fool's errand. The president seemed more interested in his image and Indian uprisings in the West, than solving what Parker considered a huge problem.

Sterling sat quietly, most likely contemplating his next words. Finally he said, "I know you'll never believe this, but I was as horrified as you were when the methane gas exploded and the mine caved in, killing your father and brothers. Your father was my most valued employee. I depended on him."

"You had a good way of showing it, considering it was your greed that allowed the cave-in. You might as well have buried them yourself."

"That's not true, son."

"Don't call me 'son,'" Parker ground out. "You did nothing to make the mines safer."

"I know you believe you have cause to hate me, but it's time you heard the truth," Sterling said, shaking his head.

"What truth? That the mines are somewhat safer because my family died? That you were forced into making them safer? I don't know how you sleep at night."

"Parker," President Grant said firmly. "That's enough."

"No, Mr. President, it's quite all right," Sterling said. "I understand his need to lash out." He turned to Parker. "Believe what you want, but you should know that I was working with your father to make the mines safer for all, just as I'm working with a committee on mine safety now. Your father had several inventive ideas and we were in the process of implementation when the accident occurred. After his death, I implemented every last one of them and there hasn't been an accident in Sterling Mines since. And as for being forced into it, there are no laws on the books requiring me to do what I did. Yet."

"I'll bet that hurt your bottom line. Imagine, humanity before profits. Don't expect me to declare you a saint because you suddenly acquired a conscience," Parker said dismissively. "The end result is the same. Men are dead—my father and brothers included—because of your lack of concern."

"You're right, of course, no matter that I tried to make amends to you. You'd have none of it, but I've more than paid for my imagined crimes. And because of how successful your father's ideas have been, I'm working with other owners to convince them of the value of safety. I also gave your father what he wanted most. And I believe he would forgive me."

"Henry, Parker is out of line," President Grant said, his voice drawing both men's attention, and interrupting the charged atmosphere. He nodded at the older man and stated firmly, "You don't have to justify yourself."

"I disagree." Henry sighed. "It's time I told the complete truth." Henry eyed the president, letting the statement hang in the air. He kept his gaze steady, seeking acquiescence, until he got a nod.

Parker noted the exchange. "What truth?"

Henry straightened. He cleared his throat and pulled on his bow tie as if it were too tight.

"I secretly helped you acquire the job with the government. Jonathan Morgan, your superior, and I are good friends. He needed someone with special skills and I told him about you and your brother."

"You're lying." Totally stunned, he shook his head. "No," he yelled. "I'll not give you credit for something I did." Feeling betrayed, he turned to the president and demanded, "Did you know about this?"

"I knew of the connection as it's in your file, but from what I've read, you more than proved your worth on your first mission, so you are right on that account. However, I doubt, given your background, we would have used you in such a way without a strong recommendation."

"Your mother is well aware of it also," Sterling said. "We talked after the accident. I had to make sure she agreed with my plans."

"Elizabeth? You brought my mother into this?"

"We didn't dare tell you because you wouldn't take the offer if you knew where it came from, and that offer gave you a way out," Sterling said softly. "It was your father's last wish. I had to honor it. You far exceeded Jonathan's expectations," Sterling went on. "But did you really think you'd sway men looking for experienced, seasoned soldiers without some kind of help? You were a green, hotheaded boy, bursting into manhood with rage in your heart. I only gave you a little bit of help and redirected that rage. Put it to good use. Of course you would never accept help from me, so I kept it hidden as did your mother."

"This is too much." Parker stared in disbelief at his drink, absorbing the information as his thoughts raced. No one spoke or moved a muscle. The clock above the fireplace mantel bonged twelve times, the only sound disturbing the quiet.

"All right," Parker finally conceded. "Why would you? I was every bit as valuable in your mine as my father. He taught me everything he knew about mining. I can't see you doing that out of the goodness of your heart."

"I had an arrangement with your father. I could have him for life but not his sons. He wanted more for all of you."

"You expect me to believe that, when you killed his two youngest?"

"They weren't supposed to be part of what we were doing. He needed their size to shore up one of the tunnels. No one else could get to them. He took the chance because he thought what we were doing was worth the risk. Unfortunately, fate intervened and they died," Henry said, heaving a heavy sigh. "No one, least of all your father, expected gas in that part of the mine. I wouldn't have let anyone near it without his say-so."

TEMPTATION

Though Parker didn't want to accept what Sterling was saying, the man's words rang true. Benjamin Davis knew the mines better than anyone. It was also true that Parker's father never wanted his sons to live and die as miners. His father had made that fact known with every breath he took. His grandfather's slow and painful death from black lung disease had profoundly affected Ben Davis and he'd always been on Parker about rising above mining, telling him education was a path to a better life. He could now see his father making such a bargain with Sterling. Sadness engulfed him as he listened to the rest of Sterling's story, and heard the sincerity in his voice.

"I had no way of circumventing that accident and I'll be damned if I can let the earl's threat go unheeded. That's why I'm here. I couldn't save your father or your brothers, but I can warn you. That man means mischief and you'd be a fool to ignore his threat." Sterling placed his empty glass on the table. He eyed Parker and added with much conviction, "I know you're anything but a fool." He turned to the president and nodded. "Now that I've said my piece, we can get back to business. I've learned I have only so much control over fate. Whether or not he follows up on my warning isn't up to me."

"We'll have to discuss business another time." Parker gulped the last sip of bourbon and stood. "If you will excuse me, Mr. President. Mr. Sterling." When both men nodded, he added, "I think I'll take your advice and check on my wife's safety." Parker headed for the door, his equilibrium bent. Sterling's news affected him more than he wanted to admit and he had to escape. With his hand on the knob, he turned back and smiled. "Merely a precaution; I certainly don't see how the earl could pose a real threat."

"I don't know, Parker. The man's a little too scary for my liking," Sterling said.

Parker grunted. "Scary or not, he's an aristocrat after all. Appearance is everything to someone like him."

Chapter 27

Catherine cautioned Penny with a finger to her lips to ensure silence. Then, spying something in the brush, she signaled for Penny to halt, whispering, "Wait here, I'll return after I track and kill him."

Penny nodded and watched her stalk into the woods, content to let Catherine do what she did best—by herself. She relaxed with her back against a tree, enjoying the feel of the sun on her face.

A twig snapped. "Now you're the one getting rusty, Catherine." She laughed, turning toward the sound. "I heard that."

Her amusement died the moment she spotted the man a few yards away, holding a gun pointed at her heart. She stared, too dumbfounded to speak.

"Lady Penelope." Gerald Knightsbridge smiled, a nasty one that sent shivers of panic up Penny's spine. "Expecting someone else?" He chuckled, a purely evil chortle erupting from his chest. "Sorry to disappoint you, but she won't be back for quite a while. I've been watching and waiting," the earl said, advancing purposefully toward her. He stopped a foot away. "Did you think you could outwit me forever?"

When she finally found her voice, she asked, "What are you doing here?"

"What kind of greeting is that for your betrothed?"

Penny continued gawking, unable to think of anything to say.

Another sickening chuckle rolled from his mouth.

Since he thrived on her fear, she schooled her face to show nothing of the terror this encounter produced. Though Parker wouldn't be back for hours and she wasn't sure of Catherine's whereabouts, this wasn't England and she would no longer play his sick games.

"As for what I'm doing here? I should think it's obvious. I'm here to take you back to England. I have a ship waiting out on the bay for my signal. We're to be married, you know."

"I'm afraid you're too late, Lord Knightsbridge." She shrugged. "I'm already married." Glaring at him, she held her head high, no longer frightened.

This time he laughed outright, the ominous sound grating on Penny's nerves and sending another signal of alarm throughout her system. When his laughter died, he eyed her, his gaze traveling from the top of her head to her feet and back up again. As quick as lightning striking, his expression changed from amusement to rage.

Backhanding her, he sneered viciously, "I thought I told you long ago to use my given name."

Not expecting the blow, Penny's head and person snapped back with force, and for a moment she saw stars.

"Now, I'd like to hear it spoken with respect from your lips," Gerald said patiently after seizing her chin roughly, forcing her head up.

Subduing pure fear, she waited for the remnants of pain to subside. Eyeing him cautiously and letting her expression go blank, she gave him what he wanted, saying in a steady voice, "Gerald. I can't marry you because I'm already married."

"Yes. I'm well aware of that fact." He leaned closer and spoke in a deceptively soft voice. "Imagine my surprise when I stopped in town looking for your maid, Melinda Bowers, and heard the latest gossip. About the fairy tale wedding." He sighed and shook his head, moving toward her. Penny took a step back. "Just my luck that bit of news led me to you."

He gripped her arm. The force of his fingernails bit into her flesh. When he glanced at something on the front of her muslin shirt, she looked down and noticed her locket had worked its way out from the blow and now hung loose around her neck. He quickly snatched it off, breaking the fragile links.

Penny resisted the urge to grab her treasure from his hands, knowing he'd somehow use its importance against her.

Fingering it, he eyed her speculatively. "Of course, I'm not happy about your marriage." His lip curled in a harsh smile. He threw the locket on the ground, his claw-like grip on her upper arm tightening.

"It will simply have to be annulled. I've come to take you home, but I've learned from my mistake. This time you'll have no way to escape." He shoved her in front of him so hard she almost lost her balance. Grabbing her arm with another cruel yank, he steadied her. His focus landed on the wedding ring on her finger. He held up her hand and wrenched the gold piece off with another cruel twist. He tossed the ring with the locket and waved his gun. "Get moving. He had no right to marry you." When she turned around to contradict him, his voice lost any semblance of control and his wild eyes flashed the fact brighter than a flare at midnight. "Understand this. You are my betrothed—mine—and you will honor your parents' agreement."

"You're too late," Penny said bravely, eyeing the gun and licking her lips nervously. "I'm carrying his babe, so an annulment is out of the question."

"Move," he barked, giving her a push in front of him.

"A child does change things. Probably for the better."

They'd been walking for quite a while and Penny thought the earl had forgotten about her claim about the child she carried. His taunt proved her wrong.

"How? It's too late." She didn't know how she sounded so calm when her insides quaked. She stopped and turned, scrutinizing his face for more meaning.

"It's simple, my dear. Now I'll have to kill him."

How Penny kept the panic raging through her from showing in her expression, she didn't know. Glancing around before starting forward again, she noted they headed toward Parker's bluff. How long before Catherine would come looking for her? Could she stall him somehow?

When they neared the same large rock she and Parker had sat talking too many times, he reached for her arm, jerking her to a stop.

"That's far enough. You might as well sit. You'll not escape me a second time, but you won't like the repercussions if you test my patience and try."

ଔ

TEMPTATION

Parker rode at a fast clip, urging his stallion faster, unable to subdue the nagging doubt now setting in his gut. Though he truly didn't think his wife was in danger, he did have an intense desire to ensure Penny's absolute safety. Too many times he'd felt this same intuition, and his reactions to such warnings had saved his life just as many times to disregard the feelings now.

When he'd finally arrived at Catherine's favored hunting ground, he dismounted. Squinting, he circled, examining the land for any signs of disturbance. When he caught a flash of something shiny, he walked over to the spot, carefully eyeing the ground. The moment he spied the locket and the ring lying next to it, his heart slammed into his throat. Squatting and picking up the pieces, his alert gaze moved even slower over the terrain, now noticing the bent branches and trodden path through dried leaves, signs his sister would never leave behind.

It took only seconds of scouting to find a definite trail. Parker tucked the locket and ring inside his coat pocket, then mounted his stallion, eager to follow. He hadn't gone far before he realized where the trail led. Dismounting once again, he tied the horse to a low-hanging branch to graze.

A heartbeat later he stepped swiftly into the brush, almost running. Like a ghost, concealed and silent, he traveled through the woods. At the edge of the clearing on the other side of the trail leading to his bluff, he halted. The blood pumping through his body turned to ice as he settled unseen to observe the scene in front of him.

Penny sat on his rock as an unknown man standing menacingly over her reached into his coat pocket, took out a piece of mirrored glass, and signaled someone on the water.

⊗

The earl swung around to face her, his expression filling with rage. "Did you think you could avoid marriage with me?" He raised an arm and struck her again.

Though she'd prepared for the blow with a flinch and a defensive hand, the force of it knocked her off the rock. His harsh laugh still held the vicious quality when he bent to help her up and his voice, as he continued speaking, sent a bitter chill over Penny.

"I planned for too long to allow some cloddish colonial steal you,

277

my dear. What were you thinking? Bloody hell! The man's common and has to die," he stated, waving his gun. "His demise won't be hard to plan and deal with. After all, I managed with your stupid parents."

"What do you mean? They were in an accident," she said, fighting to ignore his boast. She bit her lip to keep her tears from forming. She knew firsthand how he liked to instill fear and she would die rather than let him know how much the news affected her.

"They tried to renege on their agreement. Said I wasn't worthy. Only I wasn't about to let that happen. Of course, I didn't anticipate Wyndham's interference. Otherwise I would have come up with some other plan," he said. His expression hardened and he looked at her, growling, "You've gone and messed with perfect plans. No matter. You'll be punished. While I'll take pleasure in meting it out, unfortunately, it won't be pleasurable for you. You have caused me a great deal of time and money, so it's only fair."

Penny cast her gaze at the ground, thinking the entire time of how she could escape the madman, unwilling to let panic overwhelm her.

"Aren't you even curious as to your punishment, my dear?"

"No. I'm sure it can't be any more heinous than tying me down so you can torment me."

"Yes, but now I don't have to stop." He emitted a gleeful cackle, all but crowing, giving Penny the impression of a bantam rooster pleased with himself for his part in laying the egg. Then all pleasure dissipated as rage gripped his features. He knocked her hat away and grabbed her bun, yanking her head back, bringing her attention to him. His breath, inches from hers, smelled foul and dank, just like the man. Eyeing her with a glazed look in his eyes, he hissed like the snake he was, "That bastard kept you from me. Don't worry. I'll take care of him along with your husband. He won't get away with interfering with my plans."

Ignoring the pain bursting through her scalp, Penny blinked back tears. "You'll never get the chance because my husband won't let you. He's a US marshal." Though she tried to sound confident, the thought of this madman somehow managing to kill Parker had her very worried, especially after learning he'd been responsible for her parents' deaths.

TEMPTATION

"That certainly represents a challenge, now doesn't it?" Gerald still held her hair and he moved his lips to her ears, stroking the side of her face with his knuckles. He gave a soft chuckle and whispered, "You'll eventually learn to take pleasure in my touch. But if I'm to be honest, I'd have to say I don't really want you to. I truly enjoy your fear. You're so tempting, my dear. It's too bad I have to wait." Then he stood and moved away, his agitation growing. The earl turned back to her and said in a louder, more vicious tone, "That man took what was mine. It should be my babe in your stomach, not his. You'll pay for that, too."

Something caught Lord Knightsbridge's attention in the brush. Pushing Penny away, he spun around. Waving his gun, he said, "Come out or I'll put a bullet in the lady's kneecap. The shot won't kill her, but it will cripple her. I care not whether she can walk again."

When silence enveloped them, the earl yelled, pointing his gun at Penny's leg, "Now."

Slowly, Parker walked out of his hiding spot with hands raised. "Take it easy. I'm unarmed," he said, flashing an engaging grin.

Penny lunged to warn him. "Parker, run! He's going to kill you." At the same time the earl raised his arm, aiming for Parker's heart, and fired.

In stunned horror, she watched the man she loved fall to the ground. The scene unfolded in slow motion, yet she couldn't deny the brutality of what had just happened, forcing her to act. She was now totally on her own and would rather be shot in the back than surrender to the earl's control. The rage surging through her gave her strength. Penny shoved the earl with all her might, catching him off guard. Then, pushing away the heart-searing pain at seeing Parker lying prone and lifeless, Penny darted through the brush, running at a good clip, and thanking God she was wearing her boys' boots and trousers as they allowed her more agility. Using her head start, as well as her advantage of knowing the terrain, she quickly found a spot in which to hide. She covered her mouth, trying not to breathe too loudly, and waited.

Within moments, the earl thrashed through the woods and into view. He brushed past her, without discovering she crouched hidden not feet from where he'd stepped. She stayed put until she could tell he was a good distance away. Then she ran in the opposite direction.

"Penny, come out."

Lord Knightsbridge's yelling spurred her faster. She ignored the burning pain in her lungs. "You will not cry," she told herself. "Don't think of Parker lying dead. Just keep running and don't stop."

"You won't get far, my lady."

His voice got louder and stronger. She increased her pace, heading in the direction of Catherine's cave. If she could make it, she stood a chance of saving herself.

"Just give up and I'll go easy on your punishment," he yelled. "Penny? Where are you? Come, my dear. Surely you see you have no other choice. If you don't come out, I'll kill them all. Do you hear me? I'll find your maid and make sure she suffers."

When his voice became more distant, Penny halted every now and then to listen. Fear kept her heartache at bay, enabling her to keep a steady pace, while disappearing farther into the woods, gaining more distance from the madman chasing her.

Once she reached the two tall rocks covering the cave's entrance, her fears eased, and thoughts of Parker lying dead on the ground invaded her mind. She couldn't stop her tears. Soon they were flowing freely, blurring her vision and impeding her progress through the large cavern.

Somehow, she made it to their clothes. She grabbed one of Catherine's rifles. After loading it, and finally losing her fight with the tears, Penny sat with her back against the wall. Holding the rifle on her lap, she silently wept, unable to block the pain. The image of the monster shooting Parker in cold blood wouldn't dissipate.

How long she sat there crying, she wasn't sure. Eventually, she regained some semblance of control, and through sheer determination, she shoved the pain away. She'd be damned if she'd let him win. Not now. Not when she had part of Parker growing inside her. With that final thought rushing into her consciousness, she took a deep, steadying breath and wiped her tears with the back of her sleeve. Slowly, she advanced toward the cave's entrance with a renewed purpose, her rifle at the ready.

Chapter 28

"Penny? Where are you?" Catherine shouted, looking around once she'd returned to the spot she'd left Penny. She crouched, fingering some disturbances in the leaves and brush, and quickly began following the obvious trail, eventually finding Parker's horse tied to a branch.

After reaching the stallion, she stroked his head.

"So that's where you've gone," she said, letting out a relieved breath. "Humph. Couldn't even wait till I got back."

When a shot rang out, disturbing the stillness of the afternoon, all color left Catherine's face. She waited, listening, before hurriedly mounting the stallion in one jump, turning the horse in the direction of the noise and urging him forward. The minute she rounded the bend in the road, her attention moved to the prone man on the ground.

"Parker!" Her alarm increased. She dismounted and rushed to her brother. Catherine kneeled beside him, looking for a wound. Seeing none, she placed her fingers under his neck, checking for some sign of life.

When he moaned, she breathed a sigh of relief and gently patted his face. "Parker? What happened? Where's Penny?"

ᛦ

Slowly, Parker opened his eyes. The first thing he noticed was the burning ache in his chest. Placing his hand over the spot, he looked at Catherine and asked dazedly, "You didn't see them?"

Catherine shook her head. "Who?"

Parker tried to shake off the throbbing pain and sat up, grunting at how much more it hurt once he was in a sitting position. He could feel the bullet hole through his jacket. Digging into his jacket pocket he pulled out the locket, which was now a flattened, misshapen piece of metal with a slug jutting out from the gold center.

"Seems I've been shot. I think I cracked a rib," he said

incredulously, turning to Catherine and holding out the twisted piece of metal. The thought of Penny with the madman who'd shot him entered his brain just then and a fear he never known before streaked through him. "Hurts like the dickens, but I've got to get Penny. She's in danger. That bastard has her," he said with a strained voice as he tried to stand up. The pain was even more intense now and he had to sit back down, biting back the urge to vomit.

"You're in no condition to move. In fact, you're one lucky man," Catherine said, nodding toward the small hole in his woolen jacket. "That locket saved your life."

Parker closed his eyes, willing the pain away, and unsuccessfully tried to stand again. "I've got to find where he's taken her. He means her harm. Damn, why didn't I listen to Sterling and at least come armed?"

"What happened? Who has Penny?" Catherine asked, confusion moving over her facial features. "You're not making any sense. And I'm armed. Just tell me what happened and I'll track them."

"No," he yelled, fighting off another wave of nausea. When he could finally speak again, his voice was more labored. "The man's too dangerous. You're staying right here. Give me a minute and I'll be fine."

"Don't go all male on me, Parker. You can barely move. You're in no shape to track," Catherine said impatiently, rolling her eyes and shaking her head. She eyed her brother and added confidently, "I can travel faster than you and I have both my rifle and my Remington revolver. You know I'm capable. Just tell me what I'm looking for."

Parker met his sister's steady gaze, hating the fact that she had a point. Penny was in danger and it was taking every bit of his strength just to sit upright. When he looked to the heavens to send up a silent prayer, ensuring his beloved's safety, it hit him. Penny was his life and he couldn't lose her. Not now. Not when he finally realized what his brave angel meant to him. In an instant, remorse filled him. Why had he never told her how he felt? Why had he let his past feelings of others' actions keep him silent about how much she meant to him? "Please, Lord," he whispered, voicing his prayer. "Keep her safe and I'll make it up to her. Don't let her die without knowing how much I love her."

He managed to move into a kneeling position, but the effort cost him. He nodded to Catherine and said in a louder voice, "You're right. I'm unable to move as fast. Give me your gun and go. I'll follow as fast as I can. The man you're tracking is the earl she was supposed to marry. He's armed and dangerous. You take your shot if you get one. You got it? He's no better than an animal. I have no doubts that he'll kill you or Penny if he gets the chance, so be careful."

"Don't worry. I can handle him. I know how much you love her," Catherine said, nodding solemnly and handing him her gun. "I think she does too, so don't go doing anything to hurt yourself further. She'll need you when this is all over." She slung her rifle over her shoulder and started off in the direction Parker was sure her quarry had gone.

After a few minutes, Parker finally was able to stand and in a few more he could slowly walk. Following his sister's trail, he picked up more speed as he went. Still, he could only travel so fast, having to stop many times for air as his breathing was severely impaired, hampering his progress through the brush.

CƷ

Using what Catherine had taught her, Penny slowly began to track the monster. It didn't take her long to determine which direction to head because he was noisily looking for her, not bothering to cover up his movements.

In a matter of moments, she spotted him storming through the terrain. Again, using her newfound skill, she waited, becoming invisible in the brush, for the right moment to spring a surprise attack. The fact that he assiduously looked for her while she stood not more than fifty feet away amused her and filled her with a sense of security at the same time.

He'd pay for killing her love, but she didn't want him to die easily.

No. Penny wanted him to suffer.

When the time was right, she stepped from her hiding spot. "Looking for me?" she asked, leveling her rifle at Lord Knightsbridge.

He stopped and pivoted at the sound of her voice. His expression turned triumphant. When he noticed the rifle pointed at him, he grinned. "You know as well as I do you won't pull the trigger."

"Don't be too sure." Penny fired and knocked his gun out of his hand with the shot. The rifle recoiled, sending pain into her shoulder. She ignored it, oblivious to everything but the man in front of her.

His look of shock was comical.

"Go on. Pick it up," Penny said after he hesitated. "I still have another round in the chamber and I want to make it fair when I kill you. But know this. It will be a painful death and by the time I'm done, you'll be begging me to end your miserable life."

The earl stood, eyeing Penny while clearly contemplating her actions and words. Finally a menacing smile lifted the corners of his mouth. "You won't kill me," he said, his voice becoming more confident. "You're too soft."

"Then you have nothing to be afraid of and everything to gain by picking up your gun," Penny taunted, praying he'd go for the gun so she could shoot him again. He was right about one thing. She was too soft to shoot him in cold blood, giving him a better chance than he'd given Parker.

◌

Like Catherine, Parker had heard the exchange of gunfire, causing him to increase his efforts to close the gap between his sister and him. Eventually he was able to tolerate the pain. His concentration, centered on finding Penny and killing the earl, had been enough to keep him moving. In minutes, he'd come up behind Catherine, hidden in the brush watching the exchange between Penny and the earl. She nodded to him, touched her finger to her lips, and pointed to her left. Parker nodded and eased into position, training his weapon on the earl.

Together they waited to take their shot.

Neither Parker nor Catherine could miss the determined look on Penny's face or the flicker of fear in the earl's demeanor as he moved purposely to pick up the gun. Then in a flash, Gerald Knightsbridge rolled and while prone on the ground, he aimed. But he never got a chance to fire because three bullets, all fired at the same time, ripped into him.

Once it was over, Penny slowly sank to the ground and wept in despair, unaware that Parker sprang toward her with speed and agility that belied his wounded ribs.

"Penny. My God. Are you all right?" he said, dropping to sit beside her. Pulling her into his arms, he whispered, "Shush, love. It's all right. Don't cry. You know I hate it when you cry."

She glanced at him through blurry, tear-filled eyes and reached out to touch him. "Parker? You're alive? But how? I saw him kill you," she said, running her hands over his body as if to reassure herself that he wasn't a dream.

"Easy, love. That hurts." When she stilled her movements, he placed his hand over hers, taking it to his lips. He kissed it. "Cracked rib, I think. Hurts like the dickens, but I'll survive." He smiled warmly and reached into his jacket pocket, pulling her locket out. He held it out to her in the palm of his hand. "In my eyes, it's a miracle straight from heaven. They were watching over you, angel. They kept me from dying so that I could take care of you." He planted a kiss on her forehead. "I'm such a fool. Can you ever forgive me?"

Penny started to shake her head and he stopped her, putting his hand underneath her chin, lifting it so that their eyes could meet.

"I should've told you sooner. I love you and probably have since that first night I kissed you. From the moment I saw you, you've been a temptation I couldn't resist. I don't know why I even bothered." Then he tilted her chin, guiding her lips to his, letting her feel from the kiss what was in his heart. His heart beat faster when Penny's lips answered, imparting his same message.

She broke the kiss and smiled. "I love you too. I thought my life had ended when I saw the earl fire the shot."

Epilogue

Nine months later—

Rocking her two-month-old infant in the same nursery she was rocked twenty-five years before, Penny contentedly hummed a lullaby, gazing into her son's perfect face. She glanced up at a noise and smiled.

"My turn," Elizabeth declared, walking into the room and up to the rocker. "You know I can't resist my first grandchild."

Penny's grin widened and she stood, placing the sleeping infant in Elizabeth's open arms.

Elizabeth sat down in the rocker Penny vacated, keeping her eyes on her grandchild for a moment. She glanced back at Penny. "You've been a godsend, sweet Penny. You know that, don't you?"

"Oh? How so?" she asked, picking up on the warmth in the older woman's voice.

"Seeing Parker happy eases my soul. It's been too long since this family has celebrated life."

Parker strode through the door just then, catching the last of his mother's words. He stopped at her feet, bending down and giving his infant a kiss before placing one on his mother's forehead.

"We've certainly got enough life to celebrate now that both Sarah and Rebecca are expecting," he said, chuckling and moving to take Penny into his arms, nuzzling her neck. "And judging by how happy I am with my angel, little Robert Benjamin will have a brother or sister in no time," he whispered to Penny with a teasing quality to his voice, sending a rush of heat over her face. Noticing her blush, Parker flashed a disarming grin. "That blush could fell a saint," he said before bestowing a quick kiss on her lips.

Elizabeth watched Parker's affectionate display with an approving smile. "I wish I could stay in Northumberland longer, but I can't miss my other grandchildren's appearance in this world," she said wistfully. Moving her gaze back to the babe in her arms, she added, "Guess I'll have to wait to see you until your mother and father make their way home again."

"Seems we have two homes now," Parker said, releasing Penny. He walked over to the window.

"Are you disappointed to have to spend so much time in England, my love?" Penny came to stand behind him and gazed out at the expansive countryside.

"No." His followed hers.

Early summer wildflowers dotted the landscape amid the lush green landscape that hadn't given way to the dryer weather and contrasted sharply with the deep blue of the sky and the white of the billowy clouds.

"While I've never had a fondness for London, the scenery reminds me of my farm in Maryland and I feel comfortable here." He was quiet before asking, "And what about you? Are you disappointed we never made it to San Francisco?"

"I have to admit, I was looking forward to the adventure, but I have all the adventure I need right here." Penny wrapped her arms around his waist. "Since we're talking about disappointments, what about little Ben? I know it was a shock to learn your son is the new Earl of Lytherton."

Being a vain man, the first Earl of Lytherton wanted to ensure only his blood would inherit all of his worldly goods. After having five daughters, he petitioned the king and was granted a codicil granting his title to pass through the first daughter, if the present earl had no male heirs. Her first male child would then inherit the title. Fortunately for him, his wife gave him two sons, both surprises, later in life. In all the years since, there had always been a direct male Lytton to inherit, until Penny.

Parker's expression took on a serious look. "I'm only glad to finally realize that just because someone has money and power, it doesn't make them less human." Then he chuckled and his eyes danced with amusement as he added. "God has a sense of humor, it seems. It's my penance for giving in to temptation and seducing one of his angels." He leaned toward her, bestowing on her another kiss. "But I thank God I did."

ABOUT THE AUTHOR

Sandy Loyd is a Western girl through and through. Born and raised in Salt Lake City, she's worked and lived in some fabulous places in the US, including South Florida. She now resides in Kentucky and writes full time. As much as she loves her current hometown, she misses the mountains and has to go back to her roots to get her mountain and skiing fix at least once a year.

As a sales rep for a major manufacturer, she's traveled extensively throughout the US, so she has a million stored memories to draw from for her stories. She spent her single years in San Francisco and considers that city one of America's treasures, comparable to no other city in the world. Her California Series, starting out with Winter Interlude, are all set in the Bay Area.

Sandy is now an empty nester. The Timeless Series, beginning with Time Will Tell is a series connecting a time travel with historical romances as well as a couple of contemporary romances. To date, she has published eight books besides Timeless Series—four contemporary romances and four romantic mystery/suspense /thrillers. She strives to come up with fun characters—people you would love to call friends. And we all know friends have their baggage and when we discover what makes them tick, we come to love them even more. She doesn't skimp on the romance. And because she loves puzzles, she doesn't skimp on intrigue, either. Yet whether romantic suspense or contemporary romance, she always tries to weave a warm love story into her work, while providing enough twists and turns to entertain any reader.

Markham & Catherine's story in the series is due out in the fall of 2013.

Email her at sandyloyd@twc.com to be put on a mailing list for notification of her new releases. Visit her website at www.sandyloyd.com or like her on Facebook to keep apprised of her releases – www.facebook.com/sloydwrites. Follow her on www.twitter.com/sloydwrites.